the Cheetah Girls

the Cheetah Girls

Supa-Dupa Sparkle

Volumes 5–8

Deborah Gregory

JUMP AT THE SUN

HYPERION PAPERBACKS FOR CHILDREN
NEW YORK

Printed in the United States of America
First Compiled edition, 2003
5 7 9 10 8 6 4
This book is set in 12-point Palatino.
ISBN: 0-7868-1790-9
Library of Congress Catalog Card Number on file

Visit www.cheetahgirls.com

Acknowledgments

I have to give it up to the Jump at the Sun peeps here—Andrea Pinkney, Lisa Holton, and Ken Geist—for letting the Cheetah Girls run wild. Also, Anath Garber, the one person who helped me find my Cheetah Girl powers. And, Lita Richardson, the one person who now has my back in the jiggy jungle. Primo thanks to the cover girl Cheetahs: Arike, Brandi, Imani, Jeni, and Mia. And to all the Cheetah Girls around the globe: Get diggity with the growl power, baby!

Contents

The Cheetah Girls Credo

To earn my spots and rightful place in the world, I solemnly swear to honor and uphold the Cheetah Girls oath:

- Cheetah Girls don't litter, they glitter. I will help my family, friends, and other Cheetah Girls whenever they need my love, support, or a *really* big hug.

- All Cheetah Girls are created equal, but we are not alike. We come in different sizes, shapes, and colors, and hail from different cultures. I will not judge others by the color of their spots, but by their character.

- A true Cheetah Girl doesn't spend more time doing her hair than her homework. Hair extensions may be career extensions, but talent and skills will pay my bills.
- True Cheetah Girls *can* achieve without a weave—or a wiggle, jiggle, or a giggle. I promise to rely (mostly) on my brains, heart, and courage to reach my cheetah-licious potential!
- A brave Cheetah Girl isn't afraid to admit when she's scared. I promise to get on my knees and summon the growl power of the Cheetah Girls who came before me—including my mom, grandmoms, and the Supremes—and ask them to help me be strong.
- All Cheetah Girls make mistakes. I promise to admit when I'm wrong and will work to make it right. I'll also say I'm sorry, even when I don't want to.
- Grown-ups are not always right, but they are bigger, older, and louder. I will treat my teachers, parents, and people of authority with respect—and expect them to do the same!

- True Cheetah Girls don't run with wolves or hang with hyenas. True Cheetahs pick much better friends. I will not try to get other people's approval by acting like a copycat.
- To become the Cheetah Girl that only *I* can be, I promise not to follow anyone else's dreams but my own. No matter how much I quiver, shake, shiver, and quake!
- Cheetah Girls were born for adventure. I promise to learn a language other than my own and travel around the world to meet my fellow Cheetah Girls.

Woof, There It Is

For my friend Laura,
whom I adora,
And her pooch Pongo,
who plays the bongo!

Chapter 1

Thank gooseness, we have *finally* reached cruising altitude, after kadoodling for almost the whole night on the ground because of a tropical rainstorm named "Furious Flo."

That's right, Kats and Kittys: the Cheetah Girls are flying the friendly skies together, for our first time as crew! Our destination: Hollywood, California, where we're scheduled to give the most cheetah-licious performance of our very young lives, at the world-famous Tinkerbell Lounge on Sunset Boulevard.

There are going to be record-industry types in attendance, and their job is to determine if we've got the flava that they savor. We've *got* to sing our little hearts out, in order to pounce on an "op" that may not knock twice, if you know what I'm saying.

The more I think about going to Cali, the tighter I clutch the plane ticket I've been holding in my grubby little paw. This showcase could be the beginning of a dream come true, or it could turn out to be a "Nightmare on Sunset Boulevard"!

Speaking of clutching my ticket—next thing I know, I'm clutching for my lunch tray, which is bouncing up and down along with the rest of the plane!

"Is everything okay, ladies?" the flight attendant asks me and my mom. Mom's in the seat next to me, looking over the bills and receipts for her business, Toto in New York . . . Fun in Diva Sizes. Now she looks the flight attendant up and down.

I look at her, too. The attendant is wearing a big black velvet bow on top of her ponytail. She's really pretty.

"Yes, everything is okay," I say with a big smile. "I like your bow!"

"Thank you," the attendant says, like she really means it. Her pretty green eyes are sparkling as she gives me a little wave and heads on down the aisle.

Mom puts down the bills she's been looking at and says in an exasperated tone, "Galleria, honey, would you *please* put the plane ticket away so you don't lose it?"

I stare one last time at my name—Galleria Garibaldi—on the well-pawed plane ticket before I slide it into the flap pocket of my cheetah carry-on bag. Then I shove the bag under the seat. *I still can't believe the Cheetah Girls are going to Hollywoood!*

Of course, it was Mom who hooked it up. Well, not the *whole* thing, but here's the Hollywood wheel-a-deala:

Mom gets her wigs styled by Pepto B., who also does Kahlua Alexander's hair. (Yes, *that* Kahlua.) While Kahlua was getting her hair done for her latest movie project, *Platinum Pussycats*, we, the Cheetah Girls, showed up at Pepto B.'s salon, and rocked it to the doggy bone! "The Platinum Pussycat" was so taken with our cheetah-licious ways that *she* in turn arranged for the Cheetah Girls to perform in a "New Talent Showcase" sponsored by her record label, Def Duck Records.

But, believe me, we've already paid the pied

piper in full. On the night we're supposed to fly, Furious Flo blows into the Big Apple, causing most airline flights to be canceled. Not only did we have to spend six hours in John F. Kennedy Airport, but we also had to sit in the plane, on the runway, for two more hours before takeoff! By the time we took off, we were so kaflempt, we were ready to jump out of the plane window, rent a hot-air balloon, and head to Oz instead!

But like I said before, at last we're finally out of the Twilight Zone now, and safely on our way. They just served us some "lunch," even though it's about sunrise. I guess they got all messed up in their meal schedule when the plane got delayed.

I'm now happily lost in unwrapping my meal, 'cuz I'm supa-dupa hungry-poo. My mom isn't even touching her food. She's just staring at her receipts, shaking her head and frowning.

I can see she's worried. I know things have gotten kaflooeyed at the boutique—ever since Mom started working full-time as the Cheetah Girls' manager. She *had* to hire someone else to manage the store for her, but she almost ended up hitting him with her cheetah purse! The business is Mom's brainchild, even though my dad runs the factory and gives his heart and soul. *But Mom has to control everything.*

I sure hope we get a record deal out of performing in the showcase. If the Cheetah Girls can finally start bringing in some duckets, that would take the pressure off my mom and dad. All I've done lately is take duckets out of the bucket.

Suddenly, there's a pinging sound, and the pilot's voice comes on over the speakers. "Ladies and gentlemen, we're going to be experiencing some turbulence. Please buckle your seat belts and remain seated until further notice."

Uh-oh. Turbulence. I know what that means. It means we still haven't outrun Furious Flo! I buckle myself in, but while I'm doing it, the plane starts bucking like a wild horse. Before I can grab it, my "lunch" is in my *lap*!

"Yaaaa!!!!" I scream. There goes my new cheetah blouse!

The flight attendant rushes over to help. I don't know how she can walk so easy like that, with the plane doing push-ups and swinging left and right.

"Here," she says, offering me a wet towel. Then she gets down and starts scooping up all the food that spilled. Luckily, most of it is still in the plastic container. Unluckily, the part that isn't has spoiled the booti-ful cheetah blouse my mom made me. I *know* this brown gravy stain is not coming out, and I can see the worry lines in my mom's forehead getting deeper every second.

Leaning forward in my seat, I do a quickie check on my crew, to see how they're weathering the storm. It doesn't seem to be bothering Chuchie one bit. She is bopping her head, listening to her Walkman, like nothing is happening. That's Chanel Simmons for you. She's done a lot of flying with her mom to different places, so I guess she's used to this kind of thing.

I am, too—*usually*. I pull a blanket over my blouse, so Chanel won't see my gravy train.

At least I never get *sick* on airplanes. I guess you could say I was born to travel. See, Mom traveled all over the world when she was a runway model. And every summer, ever since I can remember, she and Dad and I have been going to Italy, to see my "Nona in Bologna."

Nona means grandmother in Italian. See, my dad grew up in Bologna, which is in the northern part of Italy, in a region called Emilia-Romagna, stretching east to west across the top of Italy's boot. Lucky for me, he came to America and met my mom. The rest, as they say, is history—or *my*story, to be exact. *My* story.

Next to Chuchie, Dorinda Rogers, or Do' Re Mi as we call her, has her nose in a book—just like she's at home, and at the library—one of her favorite hanging spots. The plane is doing the Macarena or something, and Dorinda, who has never flown in her life, is acting like she's just chillin'!

I don't know why, but suddenly I'm starting to feel a little funny inside. It's crazy—like I said, I never get sick on planes. Maybe it's all the pressure of the showcase we've got coming up, or maybe it's feeling like if we turn stinkeroon, I'll be letting my mom down. Whatever—between that and Furious Flo whipping the plane around, I'm kinda glad I didn't get to eat my lunch. I lean back, taking a deep sigh, and let the air that has been churning in my stomach "fly away."

I take out a wad of bubble gum, and start doin' the chomp-a-roni on it—which I know Mom doesn't appreciate, but right now, it's either chomp or stomp.

Speaking of which, just as my stomach starts to calm down, *another* natural disaster strikes: Aquanette and Anginette Walker, those fabulous Walker twins from Houston, who make up a *très* important two-fifths of the Cheetah Girls equation, start barfing up their BBQ, like bowwows gone bonkers!

Leaning over the back of my seat to witness the twins' latest performance, I can't help but get on their case like mace—even though a few seconds ago, I wasn't feeling much better than they are. "That's what you get for pretending you weren't scared," I heckle them. "Now you're paying the Boogie Man in full!"

Chanel isn't having the twins' theatrics either. "*Cuatro yuks!* Jeez, pleez, give a *señorita* some notice next time, before you serve us your *lonchando*," she moans. Then she covers her face with the cheetah throw Mom lent her, to fight the big chill left by Furious Flo.

"You didn't have to eat the pig a*nd* the poke—and that's no joke!" Do' Re Mi groans.

The three of us always gang up on the twins. Three against two—what can they do, right? Of course, it's all in snap heaven, and the twins don't seem to mind. They just think we're funny—most of the time, they laugh louder than we do! And after all, I guess it isn't the twins' fault they have such weak stomachs. Angie says they get sick whenever they ride elevators above the tenth floor. And it's even worse when, like today, they've just eaten when it happens!

Cheez whiz, what a crew I've got: Do' Re Mi has never been on an airplane before, and the twins have never been out of the country. Never mind though: as soon as the Cheetah Girls get off the ground in more ways than one, we are gonna travel all over the world together, and sing to peeps on two legs and four.

Now I feel bad for embarrassing Aqua and Angie. I reach over the back of my seat and stroke Aqua's bob back into place. It's sticking up like a pinwheel because of all the static in the plane cabin, and I know the twins are very fussy about their hair looking "coiffed."

"You'd better put on that stocking cap before we land," I giggle. "Your hair looks like it's going through electric shock treatment."

Aqua doesn't say anything back, of course, because she's still putting the barf pedal to the metal, and breathing heavy into the paper bag supplied by the airline.

"Didn't you two take your Cloud Nine tablets?" Do' Re Mi asks the twins, like she's a flight attendant or something. So that's why she isn't feelin' it like I am! I'll bet Chuchie took them, too!

Angie looks up, holding the barf bag around her mouth, and shakes her head, "No, we didn't!" Her big brown eyes look puffy, like Popeye's. Aqua finally raises her head up out of the bag, and coughs right at us.

"Uuugh, check it, don't fleck it, Aqua," I moan, covering my mouth in case some alien barf specks float in my direction.

Mom looks up from doing her accounting, and hisses in an annoyed voice, "*Basta!*"

I'll show *her* "enough"—'cuz I haven't even *started* yet on Aqua and Angie. I look at Mom and start sulking. I *hate* when she embarrasses me in front of my crew! Not that Aqua or Angie understood what Mom said, but it wrecks my flow, you know what I'm saying?

Usually, Mom sleeps like a bear, and you couldn't wake her if there was a flood nipping at her heels. Then I realize—she isn't wearing those funny-looking earplugs she usually wears when we fly. That's why she can hear everything.

I grimace at Mom, who's gone back to her work. Then I look down at my hands, and notice that my nails are already chipped!

Leaning down for my carry-on bag, I take out my bottle of S.N.A.P.S. nail polish, and flip the tray down again from the back of the seat in front of me. Steadying the bottle of nail polish like an acrobat, I wield the polish brush across the surface of my nails to cover the chips.

"Miss, you can't polish your nails on the airplane. You'll have to put that away," says the flight attendant, coming up to me. "It's against the rules. Some passengers are allergic to the fumes."

Hmph! Little Miss "Bow" Peep, wrecking my flow. Now I don't like her hairdo anymore! Cheez whiz, a little bit of "*pow!*" nail polish is gonna make the plane go "kapow"?

Now Chanel peeps her head over at me,

smirking. Then she sees the big gravy stain on my blouse, and she gives me a look, like "*Ay, Dios, mamacita*, what did you do?!"

I look away from her, furious. Ooooo, that little Miss Cuchifrita! Wait till we land—I'm gonna get her back good in Hollywood!

Chapter 2

The flight to Los Angeles from New York is five hours long, but it seems like I've been snoozing forever. I see now that the flight attendants are coming around with "breakfast." Good. I'm real hungry by now, since I never did eat my "lunch." I wonder if the Walker twins will feel like eating while we're still airborne. . . .

I look at my Miss Wiggy watch. New York and Cali are in two different time zones. That is such a cool thing. Tomorrow night, L.A. time, the Cheetah Girls will be off to see the Wizard—the wonderful Wizard of Hits—at the Tinkerbell Lounge!

It's eleven o'clock in the morning in New York. That means Dad is probably drinking his fourth cup of espresso of the morning right now, and bossing everybody at the factory around. Here in Cali, however, it's only eight o'clock in the morning.

"You think they've got a pool in the hotel?" I ask Mom, smoothing one of the hairs on her wig back into place.

"I'm sure you'll find out as soon as we get there," Mom says, then yawns, twirling her cheetah eye shades in her hand. I guess she tried to sleep, but it doesn't look like she succeeded. She's pretty punchy, and I guess it's partly my fault for dragging her into this.

Not that I even asked her to be our manager. She volunteered. But if she hadn't done it, the Cheetah Girls would have been history. So it's like she did it for me. And all it's brought her so far is headaches and baggy eyes. Not one ducket in the bucket. Well, the showcase at the Cheetah-Rama doesn't really count.

"Ooh, look, the clouds are so white they look like cotton candy!" Chanel coos. "*Gracias* gooseness, Flo isn't here!"

"Girls, don't forget to set your clocks three

hours back," Mom says, perking up. "We don't want to be three hours early for *anything*."

Believe me, no matter how worried she is about her coins, Mom is excited about taking us all to L.A. She has every hour of our trip scheduled, like she's a librarian and we're books on loan—we'll be fined if we're not back on time!

Thank gooseness, the "New Talent Showcase" is not until tomorrow night. That gives us one whole day and a half of fun in the sun—or at least in the indoor pool at the hotel—and the chance to check out Hollywood—the 'Wood.

Of course, we do have to spend some time doing our homework, so we can make up for the day of school we'll be missing. Chuchie, Do', and I all go to Fashion Industries High School together. The Walker twins go to LaGuardia Performing Arts High. They've got it like that.

Of course, if Chuchie hadn't chickened out of our audition, we might've had it like that, too. Of course, if we'd gotten into LaGuardia, we wouldn't have met Do' Re Mi, and who knows if the Cheetah Girls would've ever happened.

Still, maybe one day we'll all be going to LaGuardia together. It's one of my dreams. That, and a record deal for the Cheetah Girls, of course!

After we land, we are bustling along in the *très* busy LAX airport, which is even bigger than JFK airport in New York.

"Look, yo, there's a guy with a sign with your last name!" Do' Re Mi exclaims. The man holding the sign is wearing a black suit with a black hat.

"That's the driver," Mom says, waving at him.

"Mrs. Garibaldi?" the man asks, like he isn't sure.

"Hi there, I'm Mrs. Garibaldi," Mom says, relieved. "I'm so glad you waited. Our flight was delayed for six hours because of Furious Flo. What's your name?"

"Pedro. Welcome to Los Angeles," he says with a smile. His mustache is so neat it looks like he drew it on with a pencil. "I've been hearing all about Furious Flo on the radio."

"She almost wrecked our *flow,* that's for sure," Do' Re Mi says with a sigh.

I put my arms around her. "I'm so proud of you—you didn't barf once!" But what I'm thinking is, Next time, share the Cloud Nine tablets!

Pedro waits to get our luggage off the carousel. I notice a big sign that says: *SOME LUGGAGE LOOKS ALIKE. MAKE SURE YOU READ THE TAG CAREFULLY BEFORE YOU GRAB YOURS.*

"Hmmph. *Our* luggage doesn't look like anybody else's," I chuckle to my crew, as I see Mom's cheetah suitcases coming around the bend of the carousel.

All of a sudden, Do' Re Mi's old orange plaid suitcase comes out of the chute. It hits the bottom of the carousel and pops open, dragging her clothes behind it—cheetah bloomers and all!

"No! No! I'm not having it!" Do' Re Mi groans, putting her hand up over her eyes.

Pedro comes to the rescue. "Don't worry, *señorita*, I fix for you!" he says. He starts pushing people out of the way to get Dorinda's suitcase and her floating clothes before they go around the baggage carousel once again, for the whole crowd to see.

Just our luck—at that exact moment, some

bozo wearing a Lakers cap beats Pedro to the punch. As Do' Re Mi's pooped-out suitcase goes by him, he grabs a pair of cheetah undies, and holds them high above his head. Then he yells, "Yo, who these belong to?"

I can hear some other guys laughing, and looking around to see who's gonna claim the cheetah underwear.

"Oh, so now I get it, they've got bozos out here, too," I humph. I cross my arms, just waiting to see what the pinhead in the Lakers cap is gonna do with Do' Re Mi's teeny-weeny undies.

Thank gooseness, Pedro pipes right up. "Please to give to me, sir!"

"Oh, it's like that," Pinhead responds, but you can tell he's a little disappointed that he didn't get to meet the owner of the bloomers.

Do' Re Mi looks like she just wants to do an "abracadabra" and disappear up the luggage chute.

Pedro retrieves the undies from Pinhead and grabs Do' Re Mi's suitcase. He places it on the floor and tries to snap it shut, but the latch is broken.

A nice lady walks over to Pedro and hands

him one of Do' Re Mi's undershirts. "Sir, you forgot this one. It didn't get too wrinkled, dear," she adds, looking sympathetically at Do'.

Pedro thanks the lady a thousand times and keeps trying to close the suitcase. Finally, he looks up sheepishly and says, "No fix, *señorita.* I'm sorry."

"That's okay," Do' Re Mi says, her eyes planted downward, as if she's afraid to look up at all the people watching us.

Pedro carefully places Do' Re Mi's suitcase in the luggage cart, then puts ours on top, and pushes the cart along to the lot where he's parked his car. Mom, Pedro, the twins, and Chuchie are already inside the car, a fabulous Town Car limo, when I hear someone calling us from the other side of the parking lot.

"Yo! Cheetah Girls!" I look up to see who it is, and I nearly lose my lunch right there.

"Stak Jackson!" I gasp, as he and his brother, Chedda, come loping toward us, big pointy-toothed grins on their faces. The two of them are a rap group, Stak Chedda. And they're not too cheesy, either. They actually beat us in the Apollo Theatre Amateur Hour Contest.

Yes, we, the fierce Cheetah Girls, actually lost the Apollo Theatre Amateur Contest to these two bozos, who are carrying duffel bags bigger than they are. And now I feel like I'm seeing a mirage. They're even wearing the same yellow satin baseball jackets and caps they had on at the Apollo. Somebody better yell for "*wardrobe!*"

"What are y'all doin' in L.A.?" I ask, thinking that this can't be a "coinky-dinky," a coincidence.

"We wuz just gonna ask y'all the same thing!" Chedda says.

"Um, we're . . ."

Words fail me, as I realize I can't tell the truth. If these two bozos hear about the Def Duck Records showcase, they'll wind up worming their way into it—and we don't want them movin' in on our groove—you know what I'm saying?

"Um . . . we're here to make a music video," I say, wincing. I know it's a fib-eroni, but it's all I can think of at the moment.

"Music video?" Aqua pipes up, oblivious. "Wha— OWW!" she says, as Do' Re Mi gives her a little kick in the shin.

"Um, what are *y'all* doin' out here?" I ask, changing the subject.

"Us? Um, we're . . ." Chedda starts, but Stak cuts him off.

"We're visiting our uncle Dudley," he says. "He's rich, and we're trying to get him to back our act."

"That's dope," I say. "Well, toodles. We gotta go. See you back in the Big Apple."

"No doubt," Stak says. "Oh, by the way," he adds, turning to Do' Re Mi. "Nice cheetah undies." He and his bozo brother crack up, and slap each other a high five.

Dorinda practically sinks into the pavement. These two must have been in the crowd by the carousel!

"Put a lid on it, bozos!" I blurt out, losing my temper. "We can't all be carrying duffel bags!"

Right away, I'm sorry I said it. I know I was only trying to represent my crew, but now I've gone and made Dorinda feel even worse—calling attention to her broken-down suitcase. I could kick myself!

"Come on, yo," I say, putting my arm around her and helping her into the Town Car. "We're out," I tell Stak and Chedda, and get into the car myself.

As I shut the door behind me, I can feel the sense of doom and gloom that has descended upon my crew. "What?" I say. "Just because we happen to run into them out here doesn't mean it's an evil omen or something. It's just a coinky-dinky!"

Silence. I know they don't believe me. All my crew are superstitious, and you know this cannot be a good sign.

"It's so dope that they provided a car for us, isn't it?" I ask, trying to lighten things up, as we pull out of the lot and onto the freeway of loot in sunny Los Angeles.

"This car is *la dopa*!" Chuchie says, beginning to get in the mood. All it takes is a little luxury, and she always perks right up.

"Dag on, look at all those fancy cars we're passin'," Aqua says. "They got some serious money in this town!"

For now, it seems, they've forgotten our little meeting with Stak Chedda. I decide to do the same. So they were on the same plane with us, and saw Do' Re Mi's underwear doing the float. So what? It doesn't mean they're gonna find out about our showcase and crash it.

I decide not to worry. Good for them if their uncle Dudley's rich, and wants to back them. They need all the help they can get in the wardrobe department. Let them think we're out here doing a music video! Ha! That was a pretty good fib-eroni, if I say so myself. Good thing Do' Re Mi stopped Aqua from opening her trap at the wrong time!

I give Do' Re Mi a big hug and start tickling her. I'm trying to get her mind off the suitcase drama, but the way she's still staring at the floor of the car, I don't think I'm succeeding.

"Anything with its wheels firmly planted on the ground is a welcome sight after that plane ride," Mom says, settling into the soft leather seat in front.

"I can't wait to take a nice bubbly bubble bath," I whisper to Chanel, as we enjoy the supa-spacious ride. "Check it, don't wreck it, 'cuz we are V.I.P., yo!"

Chanel starts yapping away to Pedro in Spanish, then tells us that he is "Chicano," which means he is Mexican-American. She says he grew up in East L.A.

"He says they have a lot of Chicanos here—like millions," Chuchie tells us, sucking on her Dolly lollipop.

"We got a lot of Mexicans in Texas, too—they're called Tejanos, right, Angie?" Aqua asks her sister, then burps. "Excuse me," she giggles.

"Yeah, but this place is definitely bigger," Angie responds. They go on to compare which city—Los Angeles or Houston—has the biggest skyscrapers. Thank gooseness the barfing twins have recovered. I don't want anything else to ruin our trip, now that we've come this far. We've had enough drama and kaflamma already!

"It's actually twice the size of New York," Pedro explains.

"Yeah, and I bet *twice* the fun," I giggle, poking Chanel, who is sitting next to me in the back.

"This is kinda like a limo, right?" she whispers back to me.

"It's a Town Car limo," Mom explains.

"I've never been in car with a bar!" Do' Re Mi exclaims, finally perking up. See, Dorinda lives with her foster mother, Mrs. Bosco, and about a million other foster kids, in this little apartment in the projects. She has never been anywhere but New York—I can tell she is supa-excited to be in Cali.

Now we are driving along the freeway into the city. "Wow, they've got trees and mountains everywhere," I exclaim. It looks a lot like the hills in Italy, as a matter of fact. Only all the buildings here are new, not hundreds of years old like over there.

"The City of Angels is definitely more scenic than the Big Apple," Mom says, nodding her head approvingly.

"What's the City of Angels?'" asks Aqua.

"That's what Los Angeles means in Spanish," Chanel coos.

"Oh, that's real nice," Aqua says, smiling like a dumb sugarplum.

"Oooh, look at the birds!" Chuchie says excitedly, looking at the formation of big black birds flying in the sky. "They must be flying south 'cuz winter is coming."

"They don't have real winter out here," I point out.

Then I notice the twins, who both have spooked looks on their faces.

"Look, Aqua," Angie says. "They're spreading their wings."

"Yeah —and?" Aqua retorts.

"Remember what High Priestess Abala

said?" Angie continues. "'Look for the Raven when she spreads her wings.'"

"Who can forget what *she* says?" Aqua humphs. "I'd like to just plain forget *her.*"

"I know," Angie says. "She gives me the creepy-creeps! I wish Daddy would stop seeing her." Then she repeats High Priestess Abala's mysterious prediction for our future in L.A.: "'Look for the Raven when she spreads her wings.'"

I look up at the black birds. "They look like sparrows or blackbirds to me. They're too small to be ravens," I say. But the twins just give each other a scared look.

Man, I hope the high priestess doesn't put the royal whammy on us. It's bad enough she's got the twins' father in a trance of romance! See, he and Mrs. Walker are divorced, and she lives back in Houston, so I guess it's okay he's got a girlfriend. But what a girlfriend!

A few minutes later, we pull up to the Royal Rooster Hotel, on world-famous Hollywood Boulevard. "The Cheetah Girls are definitely about to spread *their* wings, cock-a-doodle-do-style," I say. "That's what I'm talking about!"

Chapter 3

A man wearing a bright blue top hat, and even brighter blue satin tails, opens the big glass door of the Royal Rooster Hotel for us. "Cock-a-doodle-do! How are you this fine morning, ladies?"

We are tickled by his salutation. "We're the swelliest we can ever be, sir!" Do' Re Mi chimes back at him.

"Glad to hear that, miss, and welcome to the Royal Rooster Hotel, where dreams are hatched by the Hollywood batch!"

That sends Chuchie into a fit of giggles. As soon as we get inside, a bellhop in a bright blue suit with gold embroidery on his jacket loads our luggage onto a gold luggage cart.

When he picks up Do' Re Mi's luggage, she apologetically says, "I'm sorry, this one is busted." Then she quickly drapes her jacket over her suitcase, like she's trying to hide it from plain sight.

Walking to the elevator, Angie and Aqua are looking around in awe. "Look at the ceilings," Aqua says in hushed tones. She pokes Angie to get her to look upward, then points over at the mosaics on the wall depicting roosters laying golden eggs, and farmers running after them like they're the cat's meow.

Whether we snag the record deal or not, I think, the Cheetah Girls *definitely* have something to crow about now, because at least we've stayed at the Royal Rooster Hotel!

"Holy cannoli, that reminds me of the mosaics in Venice," I gasp.

Aqua and Angie look at me like they're impressed, which makes me feel a little embarrassed for bragging. "My father has dragged me to museums all over Italy from the time I was two," I offer, waving my hand in the air like I just don't care. "He loves Venetian glass, too," I say, pointing back to the ceiling.

"Oh," Aqua says, nodding her head like she doesn't know what to say.

"You're so lucky, Bubbles," Do' Re Mi says. "You've traveled to places. I wanna go to Italy, too."

"Yeah—wait till you see it. Don't you worry, though, we're gonna have our own Cheetah Girls gondola take us around everywhere!"

Do' Re Mi shrugs her shoulders at Aqua, like she doesn't understand what a gondola is, so I try to divert their attention. I don't want them feeling bad, just because I've lived *"la dolce vita,"* or "the good life," as they say in Italy.

"Look at the gilded columns!" Aqua gushes as we continue on down the hallway. "All that glitters *is* golden."

"Even the elevators are gilded," Mom says, pointing to the glass-walled, gold-trimmed elevators that are shooting up and down the exposed elevator shafts like golden rockets!

All of a sudden, I see fear creep into Aqua's and Angie's faces as they clutch each other's hands. Oopsy, doopsy! I should've told Mom about their fear of elevators! Wait a minute—what if our room is on a high floor? I wonder.

But I guess there's a reason why Mom is our

manager, because she looks right at the twins and asks, "What's wrong? You look like we've just stepped inside Madison 'Scare' Garden instead of the Royal Rooster Hotel."

"Ms. Dorothea, you know we don't want to be any bother at all," Aqua says, "but we don't want to stay on the tippy-top floor, or something like that—if you don't mind? Angie and I are, kinda, well, afraid of heights."

"Darling, don't worry about a thing! That's why I'm your manager. I'll take care of that."

When the front desk clerk informs Mom that our suite is on the 27th floor, she asks him to switch us into two suites on a lower floor.

"You'll have to give us a second then, ma'am, because we don't have anything available right now," the clerk responds.

Oh, swelly, I think, rolling my eyes. Now we've gotta wait for a room, lest the fabulous Walker twins get another barf attack! Pouting, I walk over to the gold brocade Victorian armchair in the lobby, remove the plump pillow, and plop myself down.

Do' Re Mi wanders over, while the rest of the crew waits by the desk with Mom. "I'm starving like Marvin, yo," she moans, then sits on the carpet.

"Cheez whiz, there are roosters everywhere," I say. "It's enough to make anybody hungry!" I hand the pillow to Do' Re Mi so she doesn't hurt her butt. I notice that the pillow is decorated with an embroidered rooster. "I hope that means we're about to lay a golden egg or something!" I say.

"Yeah. I hope so, too. Aren't you scared though—about tomorrow night?" Do' Re Mi asks me, her voice cracking.

Even though I *am* scared, I don't want to tell Do' Re Mi. I don't want her getting any more ideas about leaving the group. It's only been a few weeks since she almost took a job as backup dancer for Mo' Money Monique's national concert tour. If we don't bag a record deal from this showcase, Do' might figure she made the wrong choice. Then the next time an opportunity comes along . . .

No! She *can't* leave the group—I won't let her!

"You think the other acts got it going on more than we do?" Do' Re Mi asks timidly, swallowing my own fears.

"We're not going out like that, Do',"

I humph. "We'll probably have to deal with some more 'burnt toast' bozos, though!" I snicker.

"Like Stak Chedda?" Do' Re Mi asks me. "Those 'bozos' won the Apollo Contest over *us*."

"Word. I bet you that competition was rigged, yo," I say. Not that Stak Chedda was wack or anything. They were pretty dope, but I still think we were better.

Do' Re Mi scrunches her legs up and wraps her hands around them. "I'm so hungry, I could eat some burnt toast right about now!" she says, giggling.

I giggle, too, and we do the Cheetah Girls handshake.

"Girls! Come on, now. We're in there like swimwear!" Mom yells, motioning for us to hop to it like hares. "Seven is our lucky number, girls, and the only thing I want right now is the biggest bubbly bubble bath this town has to offer."

"Grazie," I say. "Thanks for everything, Mom." I give her a big hug, to tell her how much I appreciate all the sacrifices she's making for us.

"Thanks for getting us a room that's not so high up, Ms. Dorothea," Angie says.

"Of course, darling. We don't want the best two-fifths of our group to irritate their precious vocal cords, now, do we?" Mom snickers. Looking at Aqua and Angie, I can tell they would be turning red for sure right now, if they weren't so brown to begin with.

"I'll bet you the bathtub is big enough to dive into," I giggle.

"Well, don't think you're gonna turn into Flipper before *I* do," Mom says, opening the door to suite 777. "And remember, just because we've got adjoining suites doesn't mean I can't keep all four eyes on you, girlinas."

Opening the middle door that connects to the adjoining suite—778—she instructs Aqua, Angie, and Chuchie to put their stuff in the other room. "Dorinda, Galleria, and I are gonna share this one," she instructs us.

Chanel gives me a look like "What's the deal-io, yo?" but I just wink at her. I think Mom wants to keep a closer eye on Dorinda. She's not worried about her goddaughter Chuchie, who sure won't be getting into any trouble sharing a room with the "goody-two-shoes twins"—our latest nickname for Miz Aquanette and Anginette Walker.

"Ooo, looky cookie, we even got a gift basket!" I say, running over to a big gold basket covered in gold cellophane that's sitting on top of the bureau.

What a swelly room. It's decorated in royal blue, red, and gold, just like the lobby. "Ooo, look at the rooster lamps," I say, pointing to the two matching lamps on the nightstands as I tear into the cellophane.

Mom slaps my hand and says, "Lemme open that!" After she rips open the cellophane and pulls out the card, she reads it out loud for us. "'To the Cheetah Girls. Best of luck tomorrow night. Paul Pett, Talent Showcase Coordinator, Def Duck Records.'"

"That's nice," I respond, rubbing the copper head of the rooster lamp like it's Aladdin's lamp. When I turn on the switch, its tortoiseshell glass body glows with orange light.

"Oh, that is *la dopa*!" Chanel coos, coming into the room.

"Chanel, take some chocolate," Mom says, handing her one of the chocolate eggs wrapped in gold foil from the basket.

"Can I take the guava fruit?" Chuchie asks excitedly. Chuchie loves tropical fruits—and she knows the names of all of them. I guess that's her Dominican heritage. "Can I take the chocolate, too, *Madrina*?" she asks, giggling.

"Of course, Chanel. Now, girlinas, we have to get trussed up like turkeys, because we're going to lunch. Then we'll do a little sight-seeing, okay?" Mom says. Hanging up her cheetah coat in the closet, she adds, "Spacious closets—I'm in a better mood already, darling." She looks at me with a fake grimace. "Oh, go on, Galleria, take your bath first. And *don't* use up all the bubble bath!"

I hightail it to the bathroom. It has a pretty royal blue rug, and towels with red- and gold-embroidered roosters. I love the little bottles of stuff they always have in hotel rooms — except for those "one-star bungalows," as Mom calls the cheapie hotel rooms. Actually, we might be staying in one of those hotels right now, if the record company wasn't paying for our rooms and airfare.

The tub is not as big as I pictured it, but it has pretty copper faucets. I throw the cute rubber rooster in the tub, and watch it float as I pour the little shampoo bottles into the tub along with the bubble bath. I never use hotel shampoos on my hair—they're just for girls with *real* straight hair, not kinks like mine.

"Bring on the suds, bring on the suds! Don't be a dud, 'cuz I need a rub-a-dub-dub!" I hum aloud, as I watch the tub fill up with delicious, bona fide bubbles.

"Lemme see how big your tub is," Chuchie says, crowding into the bathroom behind me.

"The same as the one in your room," I say, exasperated.

"No it isn't, *Mamacita*!" Chuchie says, flicking the bubbles at me, like we used to do when we were little. "Bubbles for bubbles!" she coos. We used to mess up the whole bathroom and make Auntie Juanita mad.

Auntie Juanita and my mom used to be close, back when we were little and they were both models. They barely get along these days, but that's because Auntie Juanita has turned a little "tutti frutti" now that she's getting older. It seems like she spends most of her time worrying about getting wrinkles, or losing weight. Not like Mom. All *she* worries about is getting everything done, and then doing *more* things. She never stops till she drops.

"Chuchie, the rooms are *exactly* the same. There is no shame in your game!" I say to my silly half, as I take off my grimy clothes.

"Excuse me, but I have to go try on everything I own now, *está bien?*" Chuchie says, then walks out of the bathroom.

"Yo! We're just going to lunch, not the Sistarella ball!" I call after her.

"Hey," Chuchie giggles, poking her head back into the bathroom. "You never know who we're gonna meet on the Hollywood Walk of Fame."

"You have no shame, Chuchie," I mutter, sliding down into paradise. "The only thing I love more than bubbles is more bubbles!"

"Está bien, Bubblehead!" Chuchie says, making fun of my silly nickname.

Whispering loud enough for Chuchie to hear me, I add, "Just make sure the twins don't wear a corny outfit today."

"Está bien, Secret Agent Bubbles!" Chuchie giggles, then finally leaves me in peace.

Do' Re Mi is upset because her clothes are

wrinkled. "Don't worry, darling, I'll just call the valet," Mom explains.

"What's a valet?" Do' Re Mi asks, dumbfounded.

"They take care of hotel guests, and cater to their every whim," Mom explains patiently.

"Well, I don't have any whims," Do' Re Mi chuckles, kinda embarrassed. "But I can iron it myself, if they just give me an ironing board."

"No, they'll do it, darling, don't worry," Mom assures her. "You know, girls, it wouldn't hurt to dress cheetah-certified today, even though you're not performing." With that, she goes into the bathroom.

"Okeydokey," I say. "You hear that, Chuchie? Get cheetah-certified or you're fried!" I yell into the open doorway that joins our suites.

Then I step out onto the balcony to take in the view. The first thing I feel is the breeze. "It's not as hot as I thought it would be in Los Angeles. It's actually kinda chilly willy, isn't it? I guess that means we won't be wearing bikinis, huh?" I snicker to Do' Re Mi.

"Yeah. We'd better wear jackets," Do' Re Mi mutters, still trying to smooth out the wrinkles in her clothes.

"You didn't lose any undies, did you?" I whisper to her.

"Yeah," she whimpers. "I did. The bozo probably stuck one in his pocket. I'll bet he's gonna wear it on his head later!" We giggle loudly.

"Ouch! Why can't they make wax that doesn't take off your skin," Mom yells from the bathroom.

Chuchie comes wiggling into our room, still in her underwear and undershirt. "Chuchie, get dressed!" I yell.

"I just wanna help *Madrina,*" she says. "*Madrina,* you should let Princess Pamela wax your mustache."

"Mustache, Chanel? I'm not a gorilla. It's just a little hair on my upper lip," Mom says loudly from the bathroom. "And besides, the last time I let some beauty wizard wax my upper lip, it looked like I had a localized case of the chicken pox!"

"*Madrina,* I'm telling you, Princess Pamela has the magic touch," Chuchie continues.

"That's for sure, 'cuz Dodo has never seemed happier!" Mom quips, and the two of them giggle at their private joke.

I have to agree. Chanel's dad, Dodo, does seem happier now that he is with Princess Pamela instead of Auntie Juanita. But Juanita seems happier, too, now that she is with Mister Tycoon, this supa-gettin'-paid Arab businessman, who lives in Paris and wears a funny mustache and fancy suits.

"Okay, girlinas, what are we wearing? I suggest the cheetah minis, and flats, 'cuz we're gonna do a lot of walking," Mom says, taking out notes from a pink manila folder.

That's my mom. She has probably scheduled everything, like a drill sergeant in the army. Hup, two, lunch! Hup, two, shopping! Hup, two, rehearsal! Hup, two, go to sleep!

"Okeydokey," Do' Re Mi replies.

"And here are our choices for lunching in the City of Angels. We could go to Porcini, for Italian peasant food," Mom says, rifling through her papers some more. "Or we could try some *gorgeous* Cantonese live seafood at Chop, Chop! Or we could go to Bombay Cafe on Santa Monica Boulevard, for 'Yuppie Indian in West L.A.' It says here they have 'wonderful chutneys, uttapams, and masala dosas,'" Mom repeats, looking up after she has read the review from some magazine.

"What is a 'Yuppie Indian'?" Aqua asks, puzzled.

We giggle, then Mom tries to explain, but even she is stumped. "Well, I guess . . . oh, I don't know—some fabulous curry cuisine, I'm sure!"

Chanel is the first to give Mom the look that says, We're *not* taking any passage to India today, *Mamacita.*

Mom is never stumped by our facial expressions, especially Chuchie's. "Humph! Adventurous as ever, are we, Cheetah Girls?" she says. Then she sighs, because even *she* knows when she has been out-kadoodled by my crew.

"I guess you can take the Cheetah Girls out of the jiggy jungle, but you can't take away their animal instincts for, well, barbecued ribs. *Okay*. Aunt Kizzy's Back Porch it is."

We chuckle up a storm, then Do' Re Mi is the first out the door. "Bring on the BBQ!" she yells, whooping it up.

Aqua licks her juicy lips and seconds that motion. "I know that's right!" she says.

Chapter 4

The first thing you notice about "La La Land," as they call L.A., is that there is a whole lot of space. "Peeps are definitely not living like cockroaches out here, like we do in the Big Apple," I comment to Chuchie as we walk down big, beautiful Hollywood Boulevard.

The second thing you notice about La La Land is that there aren't any *people* walking on the tree-lined sidewalks—not to speak of, anyway. Still, Mom *insists* that we walk to Aunt Kizzy's Back Porch, even though we could've called a taxi.

"Look at the mansions," I exclaim, ogling all the dope estates nestled high up in the looming

Hollywood Hills above us.

"I bet you that's where Kahlua lives!" Aqua says excitedly, pointing to a bright yellow mansion with white pillars at the tippy-top of a hill. "That's real nice, ain't it?"

"Yeah," Angie says, then pokes her mouth out. "I wouldn't want to live there, though—what if they had a fire, and you had to get out in a hurry?"

"An earthquake is more like it," Mom says, shivering her shoulders. Mom has gotten a map of Los Angeles that looks more like an encyclopedia, and she is becoming very roadrunnerish about the whole get-around-town thing.

"They have earthquakes here?" Do' Re Mi asks, scrunching up her nose.

"More of them than garage sales, it seems," Mom replies.

That makes all of us *really* quiet, and I can tell Aqua and Angie are a little spooked. When we get to this biggie-wiggie intersection at Hollywood Boulevard and Vine Street, I can see the twins' teeth chattering, because it seems like it's miles to the other side of the intersection.

"We haven't seen one 'blacktress' yet," Do'

Re Mi says to break the silence. "I bet they're probably getting their nails done. Look at all the cars—*they're* the real stars here."

Even though we're afraid to cross, we finally get the nerve up (okay, Mom drags us), but we soon discover, much to our surprise, that drivers here are a *lot* nicer than in New York. This shiny olive-green car with a sparkling chrome jaguar on its front hood stops right in its tracks to let us cross.

"Can you believe that?" Aqua exclaims in sheer amazement. "He let us live!"

"Don't worry, darling, he's more concerned about us bumping into his prized Jaguar than the other way around," Mom humphs.

"Jaguar," Do' Re Mi says, savoring the name of the car like it was the best slice of corn bread she ever bit into. "It's dope. I can't wait to learn how to drive."

"If you lived out here, you would learn fast. *Everybody* out here drives—even the toddlers," Mom explains, adjusting her cheetah shades to get a better look at what she suddenly sees before her eyes.

In the window of Oh, Snaps! Bookstore, there is a big, framed poster of Josephine Baker.

Collecting memorabilia is the only passion Mom has—other than being "large and in charge," of course.

"It's boot-i-ful," Chanel coos.

In this poster, La Baker is wearing a pink sequined gown, and her arms are stretched upward, like she's on top of the world—and I guess she was. Back then, she was the richest, dopest black woman in the world. "Isn't this one *gorgeous,* darling?" Mom asks me, with a touch of sadness in her voice.

"As *gorge-y* as the fifty other ones you own," I coo back. Mom already owns every other Josephine Baker poster on the planet, including the only one signed by the famous French artiste Cous Cous Chemin, in which Josephine is posing with her pet leopard, LuLu.

The leopard is in this poster, too, sure enough—off to the side, and looking like he just ate the canary. "Ooh, *tan coolio.* His collar is even leopard!" Chuchie says, pointing to the poster.

"How do you know the leopard is a he, Chanel?" challenges Dorinda.

"Guess you'll have to go to the history books and find out," I snicker at Do' Re Mi, who is always reading books of one kind or another. Anything you ever want to know, that nosey-nose will go to the library and find out for you.

I sigh wistfully at the kazillion photos of movie stars in the store window. "One day, *our* photo is gonna be in there," I say to my crew.

"That's a cheetah-certified fact," Mom commands. "Well, let's see if you're ready for the big bargaining league, Galleria."

"I'm ready for Freddy," I quip back. See, the only thing Mom likes better than collecting memorabilia is getting it at a bargain price. It's called "the fine art of snaggled-tooth haggling," 'cuz you don't stop until you draw blood!

Flinging my cheetah pocketbook like I have more in it than a tube of S.N.A.P.S. lipstick and a disposable instant camera, I stroll into the bookstore.

There are three tricks of the bargaining trade: 1. You gotta act *très* nonchalant, like you really don't want the thing in the first place; 2. After you ask how much the thing costs, act very surprised that it's so expensive; and 3. After the salesperson tells you the price, look at other stuff, so they can stew that they lost the sale, then wait for them to quote a lower price.

"Bonjour," I say to the salesperson, a blond woman with bifocal glasses crooked on her nose. The rest of my crew stands around, ogling the movie star photos, while I do my thing.

"How much is the Josephine Baker poster in the window?" I say, stifling a yawn, then casually glance at a picture of some "creepy crawler" named Adam Ant.

"Five thousand," says the saleslady, giving me a look like I can't afford it!

Don't come for me, Missy, I want to snap, but I stay cool as a fan. "Oh," I simply respond, stifling another yawn, then continue looking at Mr. Ant's photo.

It seems like five years have gone by before the saleslady says, "You know, it's a vintage 1936 photo, but I can give it to you for four thousand."

"Oh, that's fabbie-poo, darling. Let me think about it—I'm off to an auction. Toodles!"

I have to run out of the store, because I'm about to lose it, and I can see my crew trailing fast behind me.

"Bravo, darling!" Mom says, clapping her

hands when I get outside, then the rest of my crew joins in. "That was a performance worthy of an Academy Award for Best Actress in a Bookstore!"

I curtsy and prance in front of everyone till we get to the next corner. Then I catch a glimpse of my mom, looking back toward the store, with a real sad look on her face, like she wants that poster in the worst way, but can't afford to get it. Again, I get that guilty pang in my stomach. I wish *I* could shell out the duckets myself for the poster.

"Which way to Aunt Kizzy's?" I ask, changing the subject to get her mind off her misery.

"Just follow the smell of corn bread!" Aqua heckles, darting forward to the quaint little door to Aunt Kizzy's Back Porch.

Although there are no movie stars at Aunt Kizzy's, there really is an Aunt Kizzy, and she makes "the best macaroni and cheese and candied yams outside of Texas," claims Aqua after we've finished our fabbie-poo lunch.

"Just don't barf it up!" quips Chuchie as we're leaving. Everybody waves good-bye to us, too. La La Land is *definitely* a lot friendlier than New York. It must be all the sun and fresh air.

"Y'all Cheetah Girls come back and see us real soon," Aunt Kizzy says in her booming voice, waving at us from the BBQ grill. "Good luck with the showcase, too. If y'all sing as good as you eat ribs, you'll be riding around in a Bentley in no time!"

"Yo. We're getting a Jaguar, right?" Dorinda asks, looking up at me.

"Nope. A cheetah-mobile," I quip back, grabbing a toothpick from the stand by the door. I can feel all the gunk stuck in between my braces.

"That was good food in the 'hood!" I say, smacking my lips, imitating the twins. Then I get busy poking at the shredded rib with the toothpick. "Look, Chuchie, even the toothpicks are red."

"And so is the back of your skirt, *Mamacita*!" Chuchie shrieks, grabbing my arm and pulling me aside.

"Say it ain't true, blue!" I reply without thinking, because I'm turning red. "Is it my period?"

"*Sí, Mamacita.* What else!" Chuchie says, looking at me like I'm a dodo.

Chuchie knows how much I *hate* getting my period. That's why it catches me by surprise half the time. I just wish it would *pouf* and go away, and come back another day!

I run inside to the ladies' room, to check out the disaster. Walking by the table where we ate, I can't help but look at the chair I sat in. *Omigod,* there is a little red stain on the plastic cushion!

I hightail it to the bathroom, and go inside a stall, where no one can see how embarrassed I am. I sit on the toilet seat and put my face in my hands. *How could I get my period today?*

Chuchie stands on the next toilet seat, leans over the top of the stall, and peers down at me. "You okay, Bubbles?"

"No! I'm not okay, Chuchie. Get a stupid sanitary napkin or something."

Mom always tells me to carry tampons with me, and I don't listen, because I *hate* getting my period!

This time, Chuchie hands me a sanitary napkin under the stall. "You owe me a quarter," she says, giggling.

"Chuchie, you'd better sit your *butt* down before I make change!"

"Don't be mad at me," she exclaims. "Here, you can put my sweater around your skirt. Nobody is gonna notice, *está bien?*"

"Chuchie, I'm just so embarrassed, I'm never leaving this stall!"

"*Está bien*, Bubbles. I'll stay here with you all night, but let me go tell everybody not to wait for us."

"Very funny, bunny," I tell Chuchie. Then I start giggling, too. It is mad funny, in a pathetic sort of way. "Don't you hate being a girl?" I ask her.

"No," Chuchie giggles.

"I don't know why the sight of blood never bothers you, Chuchie, when you're generally such a squeam queen."

I sigh, then get up and leave the stall. "Let's go see Hollywood," I tell Chanel.

When we go back outside, Mom is patiently waiting. "It's okay now, darling?"

"Yeah, I guess," I mumble, then sulk. I'm so glad she doesn't bother me about it.

"Ms. Dorothea, that food was really good," Aqua says, trying to deflect from my misery, no doubt. That's one thing I can say about the twins—they're always looking out.

"I'm glad you enjoyed it, 'cuz that's gonna be the last meal you eat before you 'sing for your supper!'" Mom quips.

I know she's teasing. Dorinda doesn't get it, though, and she looks at Mom like she's already hungry! I wink at Dorinda, and instant relief floods her adorable little face. That's what I love about Do'—she can always go with the flow.

"Mom, is the record company paying for *everything*?" I ask, as we walk to the next destination on our supa-packed itinerary. I feel really uncomfortable with Chuchie's sweater tied around my waist—and I *hate* wearing sanitary napkins.

"No, darling. It's not *all* paid for. They paid for our airfare, car service to and from the airport in both cities, and hotel suites. The rest comes out of your Cheetah Girl retirement fund!"

I swallow hard. That was not the answer I was hoping to get. It means Mom and Dad are paying for all our little extras—and when the Cheetah Girls get together, those little extras can add up in a hurry!

"I hope we have something to retire *from*," Chuchie says wistfully.

"I heard that," Dorinda retorts, then grabs Mom's arm. "You don't think we're gonna end up on the chitlin' circuit, or something like that, do you?"

"Not as long as I'm your manager—what you do after you fire me is your business!" Mom says, and laughs out loud.

I grab Do' Re Mi by the arm, and we start skipping down the street together. Do' Re Mi doesn't really understand that the Cheetah Girls are down for the 'do—together, forever, whatever makes us clever.

There's no reason why she should she settle for being a backup dancer—yet—but I know where she's coming from, and one day, I hope she realizes where *we're* going.

"Hey, Cheetah Girls!"

That voice again! I freeze in my tracks, waving weakly as the brothers from the Big Apple come toward us. "Hey, Stak, hey, Chedda," I say, trying to smile. But my hands go straight to Chuchie's sweater, which is wrapped around my bloody dress. If they see me like that, I'll never get over it, I swear! Why is it Stak Chedda always shows up when tragedy strikes?

"How's the video comin'?" Stak asks.

"Video?" I repeat dumbly. Then I remember my fib-eroni. "Oh, that—it's goin' with the flow," I say.

"That's dope," Chedda says.

"Hey," Stak adds, "maybe we could be in your video—you know, put in a little cameo appearance or something!"

"Yeah!" Chedda says. "We wouldn't even charge y'all!"

"Uh, no!" I say, looking at Dorinda for some help.

"Our contract says 'no other artists,'" she says, pulling one out of the air. "It's an 'exclusive.'"

"Exclusive, huh?" Stak says, looking at us suspiciously. "I never heard of that . . . are you sure y'all just don't wanna share the spotlight? Afraid we might outshine the Cheetah Girls? Tony the Tiger wouldn't mind."

"Yeah, right," I say, flossing. "That'll be the day, when y'all outshine the Cheetah Girls!"

"We did it at the Apollo," Chedda reminds us with a big grin.

"Now, now, brotha," Stak says, motioning for him to back off. "Let's be gentlemen. These ladies got a good groove. Just 'cuz we won, that don't mean they ain't got it going on."

"I hear that," Chedda says, backing off.

"How's it going with your uncle *Dudley*?" I ask, trying to turn the attention away from us. Looking down the street, I see that Mom and Chuchie, along with the Walker twins, are admiring yet another window display. Why don't they get over here and help us?!

"Uncle Dudley's just fine, ain't he, Chedda?" Stak says, poking his brother.

"Uh, yeah—yeah!" Chedda says. "He's feelin' much better."

"Was he sick?" Dorinda says.

"Yeah—didn't we tell you?" Stak says, stumbling a little. "He's okay now, though. And he's gonna back us with some serious loot."

One thing I can tell is a fib-eroni when I hear one. Trust me. There ain't no Uncle Dudley, and something is fishy in La La Land.

"Uh, we gotta go," Stak says, pulling Chedda away from us. "See y'all around, Cheetah Girls!"

Funny how they decided to hightail it out of there, right when we started talking about *them,* not *us.* But I don't have time to worry about Stak Chedda, and what they're doin' out here in the City of Angels. Right now, I'd better find out where my "Road Runner" mom is dragging us.

"Where we going next, Momsy-poo?" I ask as she and the rest of my crew catch up to us.

"First, we're going to Mann's Chinese Theater."

"What's that?" Dorinda asks curiously.

"There's where they have all those famous footprints in cement," Mom says.

"Oh. Can we go where they have all the stars on the sidewalk?" Dorinda asks.

"That would be the Hollywood Walk of Fame, which is our next stop right after Mann's," Mom answers. "Then we can shoot over to Wilshire Boulevard, and head to the La Brea Tar Pits Museum, to check out some saber-toothed tigers."

"Real ones?" Aqua asks, her eyes getting wide.

"No, darling, we're the only *real* attraction the jiggy jungle has to offer today," Mom says, chuckling. "These tigers are built around bones of the ones who fell in the tar pits millions of years ago. They're truly fierce-looking. But if you don't want to go there, we can skip right to the Grave Line Tours and see the Grim Reaper. I'm sure you'll dig that!"

"Yeah!" Aqua and Angie scream in unison. "We love you, Ms. Dorothea!"

"Well, okay, I guess Hollywood's lions, tigers, and bears won't be graced with our growl power this trip," Mom says, amused. "Besides, there's nothing like a creepy cemetery for catching some peace and quiet!"

We snicker our skulls off taking in the sights, and later, the trendy boutiques on Melrose Avenue. Melrose is like the Soho section of Manny-hanny—also known as Manhattan, to the tons of tourists who swarm there *every* minute. Do' Re Mi and I don't mention our little meeting with Stak Chedda to the rest of our crew. No sense worrying them over nothing, right?

"When do we get to go shopping?" Chuchie asks, half-jokingly. *"Estoy nervosa.* I'm getting the willies about tomorrow night. I need to shop."

Poor Chuchie. Her shopping days were nipped in the bud when she ran up Auntie

Juanita's charge card. Now she has to work part-time in Mom's store till she pays off the credit card bill. Mom says Chuchie's really good at dealing with customers, too. I'm not surprised. Chuchie is really sweet—when she isn't getting on my nerves, that is.

Right as we're passing the candy-striped awning for Canine to the Stars Pooch Parlor, we get a good glimpse of how the pampered poochy half lives in La La Land. Dogs with rhinestone collars are perched in chairs, getting their paws done.

"Ooh, look at her bou bou fon fon!" exclaims Chanel, as this lady with a bleached white bouffant strolls to the entrance of the parlor with her poodle in tow.

"Oooh, excuse me, miss, can I pet him?" I ask the lady politely.

"It's a she," the lady says snobbily.

"Oh, I'm sorry, what's her name?"

"Godzilla," the lady says with a straight face. "If you don't mind, we're in a hurry, because she's late for her paw-dicure."

"Oh, I'm sorry!" I exclaim, then watch her go inside. "Wow, did you see how tight her face was?"

"Darling, that's because she's had so many face-lifts, she'd scare a mummy out of his tomb!" Mom says.

"Word," chuckles Do' Re Mi.

I'm only half listening, because I'm too busy staring into the parlor window, looking at the dope display of poochy collars they've got there. "I'm definitely angling to get my paws on that cheetah-studded collar," I whisper to Chuchie. "Toto will love it!"

Toto is my boo-boo. He's also like my brother. *Mom's* baby. She named the store after him: Toto in New York. And of course, she named *him* after Toto in *The Wizard of Oz.*

Mom gives us a look like, "Oh, go on inside."

That's all the permission we need. The five of us hightail it into the store, to ogle the pets and stuff.

"That collar you like is thirty dollars!" exclaims Aqua, fingering the price tag.

"So?" I hiss, forking over the exact amount to the saleslady. "I just won't eat lunch at school for . . . well, forever."

"Okay, Miss Galleria," Angie says, giving me a look, like "We'll see."

"My prize pooch is gonna look like a prince,"

I announce. Then I turn to Chuchie and say, "I miss Toto so much. Do you think I should get him that turkey costume for Thanksgiving?"

"No—he'll think it's a drumstick, and try to eat it," Chuchie says, fiddling with the new cheetah shades she just bought on the cheap up the block. "Ooh, look at these stick-on rhinestones. I'm gonna buy these!"

"Those are for pooches?" I ask Chuchie.

"*Yo no sé,* but I'm gonna get them."

"Do you think this is the right size collar for Toto?" I ask, holding up the cheetah collar.

"It looks kinda big," Chuchie says, shrugging. "But don't worry. If it doesn't fit him, *I'll* wear it!"

Leave it to Chuchie. "Yeah, I bet you would!"

I put the boot-i-ful cheetah collar in my cheetah purse, and swing it all the way to our next stop, which turns out to be an unplanned one.

We're passing by this building, and the sign outside says "Frederick's of Hollywood Museum." I look in the windows, and let out a little scream—it's a *bra museum!*

"We've gotta go in there!" I say, excited. I've been wearing bras since I was eleven years old (unlike Chuchie), but these in the window are really dope ones!

"Oh, great, I get to feel flat-chested," Chuchie moans, as we look at the displays of bras, some of which have cups that look like torpedos ready for takeoff.

"Oh, those are 'old school' ones," I explain to Do' Re Mi, who is fascinated with them all. She's so small, she doesn't have to wear a bra either.

Finally Mom makes us leave, and we go to a thousand more places, looking at stars' footprints in cement, stars on the pavement, and finally, real stars in the nighttime sky. Finally, we start seeing stars swimming before our eyes, because we're so tired. Still, we're happy and excited. We've had one of the best days of our lives, tooling around the incredible City of Angels.

We go back to the hotel, eat a fancy room service dinner, and spend the rest of the evening lounging around our boot-i-ful suites.

After our baths, Do' Re Mi and I flop down on the bed we're sharing. We lay there in the dark, with Mom snoring in the next bed, but neither of us is sleeping. Not yet. I know we're both thinking about tomorrow night, nervous and excited at the same time.

"This is all like a dream, isn't it?" Do' Re Mi giggles, nuzzling her head into the incredibly soft pillow.

"It sure is," I say softly. "I just hope I'm not about to wake up and find out this is another *Nightmare on Elm Street*!"

Chapter 5

Today is our "last chance, last dance" to frolic in the Royal Rooster swimming pool. At three o'clock, we have to go do a sound check at the Tinkerbell Lounge, then come back to the hotel and get dolled up and down for the 'do, which starts at seven o'clock.

A "sound check" is exactly what it sounds like. The stage manager of the venue adjusts the lights and audio to the right levels, to make sure that everything is "on the money" for the real performance.

If the microphone situation isn't right, you could get onstage and sound like a hyena singing an aria. We're all kinda nervous about it, because the other performers in the showcase will be at the sound check, too. And we know they'll be checking us out while we're checking out the competition, if you know what I'm saying.

My crew and I are hanging out at the deep end of the swimming pool, to stay away from all the noisy kids in the wading area.

Mom is lying on a beach chair, because she doesn't like to go swimming—lest her wig, she says, "does the float." Aqua and Angie are playing water volleyball, and doing flips in the water. Do' Re Mi is ferociously swimming laps, like an Olympic swimmer. Meanwhile, I'm flapping my feet like Flipper, and annoying Chuchie, who is lying nearby on a Royal Rooster inflatable float, preening behind her new cheetah sunglasses and bikini. Chuchie has an "outie" belly button, like I do, and she does look *très* cute in her bikini, because she has long legs and a flat tummy.

"Párate, Bubbles!" Chuchie moans in Spanish, putting her hands over her face to keep from getting her glasses wet. I know she doesn't like to get her braids wet, either,

because if she doesn't dry them right, they get a serious case of mildew!

"Do you think there'll be a lot of peeps at the showcase?" Chuchie asks me. I can tell she's getting nervous, but I'm just trying to chill.

"Sí, Mamacita," I say, spurting water from my mouth. "I don't think they'd fly us out here just to sit with Captain Hook and a snook!"

If fairy tales do come true, then the Tinkerbell Lounge on Sunset Boulevard is the place. We're half an hour early for the sound check, so we stand outside under the lounge's silver awning, pressing our faces against the glass window to see inside.

"Everything is silver and shiny—even the big disco balls hanging from the ceiling," Do' Re Mi reports, like she's an interior decorator or something. "Even the couches are sprinkled in stardust!"

As we wait, I start humming verses from the song I wrote, "Welcome to the Glitterdome," because it reminds me of why I have dreams, and how we got here. My crew joins in and sings along just for fun:

"Twinkle-dinkles, near or far,
stop the madness and be a star
Take your seat on the Ferris wheel,
and strap yourself in for the man of steel.

Welcome to the Glitterdome
It's any place you call home.

Give me props, I'll give you cash,
then show you where my sparkles are stashed.

Glitter, glitter. Don't be bitter!
Glitter, glitter. Don't be bitter!
Glitter, glitter. Don't be bitter!"

We're so caught up in our reverie that we don't notice someone else has arrived at the scene of the rhyme—but I would recognize *that* voice in a dark alley from the bottom of a Dumpster truck.

"Yo, Cheetah Girls—Tony the Tiger let you out the house again?" It is none other than Stak Jackson, stepping out of a black Town Car and onto the sidewalk, with his brother, Chedda, trailing right behind him.

"It's like *déjà vu*," Chuchie gasps under her breath.

"*This* isn't *déjà vu*, Chuchie," I hiss, "'cuz this nightmare already happened—and I can't believe it's happening *again*!" How could two rappers—unknown to the world as Stak Chedda—strike twice like lightning? Where is Cheetah Girl justice when you need it?

Bracing myself for a showdown, I put my hand up over my left eye as if I'm shielding myself from the sun. "Yellow satin—it's a little bright for 'Sunset' Boulevard, don't you think?"

"Not as bright as you, Cheetah Girl," Stak Jackson says, grinning from ear to ear. "You in the showcase, too?"

"Um, yeah," I say, then sigh because my last shred of hope that the bumbling bozos were here as a janitorial team has just been yanked away. "I just made that up about the music video," I admit.

"Oho!" Stak says, laughing it up. "Afraid Stak Chedda gonna come away with the cheese again?" He and Chedda high-five it, grinning from ear to ear.

"How's your uncle Dudley?" I ask, smirking, 'cuz I know there *ain't* no Uncle Dudley.

"Uh, well," Stak says sheepishly.

"I thought so!" I floss. "I guess he's resting in peace!"

Now it's the Cheetah Girls' turn to high-five it!

Luckily for all of us, just then a tall man with a lopsided buzz cut steps to the entrance of the Tinkerbell Lounge and asks, "Are you the Cheetah Girls?"

"Yes," I reply, speaking for the group like I usually do. It's one of my problems sometimes, but all in all, I'm not sorry I'm that way—a lot of times, it helps to just get it out, know what I'm sayin'?

"I'm Paul Pett, the showcase coordinator," he says, extending his hand to shake mine. I like his professional groove already.

"Hi, I'm Mrs. Garibaldi," Mom says, extending her hand now, like it's a delicate lily waiting to be sniffed for its aromatic qualities. "Remember, we spoke on the phone?"

"And we're Stak Chedda," breaks in Chedda Jackson, like someone asked him. "An A and R guy from your label peeped us at Club Twice as Nice in the Bronx, remember?"

"Ah, yes," says Mr. Pett, trying to be "twice as nice," I guess.

Aqua gives me that fabulous Walker twins puzzled expression, but Do' Re Mi steps to the plate with a piece of the puzzle. "What's an A and R guy?"

"Oh, that's the record company executive who signs an artist and is responsible for groom- their career, so to speak," Mr. Pett explains.

"Yeah. It means 'artist and repertoire,'" Chedda explains, like he's got it going on in the "knowledge department."

I want to scream, "Don't try it." But for this once, I keep my mouth shut.

"Mr. Brumble, the club manager, should be here any minute," Mr. Pett explains to us all, then turns to Mom and asks, "Did you have a good flight?"

"Yes," Mom says, telling a fib-eroni. I guess she figures there's no need to go into all the gory, snory details about the night we spent in the Twilight Zone.

"Ah, here's Mr. Brumble now," Mr. Pett says, stepping aside to let the club manager open the lounge. Mr. Brumble is wearing a black eye patch, and has two gold hoops in each ear and long wavy hair.

"Mr. Pett, how many acts will be performing

in the showcase?" Mom asks, taking off her cheetah shades as we go inside. Even though it's daytime, and bright and sunny outside, it's still kinda dark inside the Tinkerbell Lounge—making it seem even more spooky and sparkly.

Humph, I think as Stak Chedda follows us inside. What Mom should've really asked Mr. Pett is how many *animal* acts will be performing in the showcase. How else did these two bumbling bozos make it onto the same bill as *we* did?

"Let's see, we have the rap group CMG—the Cash Money Girls. Um, the male quartet—Got 2 Be Real 4 You. The Beehives—which is a hot rock group from Boston. Stak Chedda —whom we're billing as an alternative rap duo. And, let's see, the Toads—a country-western group who already have a *huge* following in their hometown, Nashville."

What does Mr. Pett mean by *alternative* rap group? I wonder. An alternative to what—death by a wack-attack?

"Mrs. Garibaldi," Mr. Pett asks Mom, smiling. "Since some of the bands aren't here yet, do you mind if your girls do their sound check first? That way, you can get on out of here and have some time to yourselves before tonight."

"It works for me," Mom says, motioning for us to go on the oval stage. Right in front of the silver tinsel strip dividers are a cool set of drums, keyboards, and bass stands. That would be so dope, if we had instruments like that! You know, just banging on some keyboards and singing songs would be off the hook!

Maybe one day. For now, Mom hands Mr. Pett the instrumental tracks we use for the songs "Wanna-be Stars in the Jiggy Jungle," "Shop in the Name of Love," and "More Pounce to the Ounce."

Mr. Brumble tells us to stand right in the center of the stage, and floods us with a glaring spotlight, then softens it to a pinkish hue, with shooting stars bouncing off the stage.

"That's dope," Do' Re Mi says, smiling.

After the lights are adjusted, the tracks are cued up, and we sing a few bars of each song to cue the audio.

At this point, I'm relieved we don't have to stay and wait for the rest of the groups. In particular, I can't wait to bounce from the Stak Chedda situation.

"Why are those hyenas grinning at us?" I whine to Chuchie as we leave the Tinkerbell Lounge and head outside. Behind us, I can feel Stak and Chedda Jackson staring at us, thinking they got us right where they want us. "We're not their next Happy Meal, okay?" The next thing I know, we're in "hyena territory," as Mom would say.

"Yo, check it, Cheetah Girls," I hear Stak Jackson yell from behind us. I turn around, and see that he's poking his head out the front door of the club. Now he pushes the door all the way open and comes over to where we're standing on the sidewalk.

"I just wanted to say, we—me and my brother—was feeling you at the Apollo. And, um, we're sorry the situation had to go down like that. Um, you know what I'm saying?" Stak says, smiling and showing his pointy fangs.

"Yeah," I pipe up, rolling my eyes to the bright blue sky. "You shouldn't have won, *we* should've!"

"Um, well, I wasn't exactly going there, you

know what I'm saying, but, yeah, you Cheetah Girls had something to say—maybe in another situation, you coulda smoked us," Stak says humbly.

"For true," I reply, not knowing quite how to handle a hyena when he's being so nice. That was the last thing I expected him to say, tell you the truth.

"That was *real* nice of you to come out here and tell us that, 'cuz you know we were heartbroken *we* didn't win," Aqua pipes up.

Who asked her? Doesn't she have a new church hymn to learn right about now?

"We'll see who's got the situation locked up later," Do' Re Mi says, egging Stak on the dis tip.

"I heard that," he chuckles, adjusting his baseball cap like the sun is in his eyes.

"Where are you from?" Chuchie asks him.

"The boogie-down Bronx. That's where we call home," Stak says, and suddenly his pointy fangs don't look so pointy. "Yo, I'd better bounce, though, 'cuz we still gotta do our sound check—so I'll catch you later, awright?"

"Whatever makes you clever!" I say, then call after him the one question I want answered. "Yo, Stak. How did you and your brother get the hookup for this New Talent Showcase?"

"One of my boys told us some peeps from Def Duck Records would be rollin' up into Twice As Nice on the Grand Concourse, on open mike night with DJ Sweet, so we signed up. And, well you know, we freaked it," Stak says, flexing his hookup.

"Freaked it, huh?" I say, trying to stop smiling. "That's how I would describe, um, what you do."

"Well, you know, that's Stak Chedda—and nobody does it better," Stak says, trying to hide his hyena fangs and flex some more by winking at me. "How'd you Cheetah Girls get the hookup, yo?"

"Kahlua Alexander told Def Duck about us, and they flew us out here," I say, flexing back hard.

"You got it like that?" Stak asks, his eyes opening wide.

"Yeah, but *we'd* better bounce now," I say. I yawn, then put on my cheetah shades. "See ya—and I wouldn't wanna be ya!"

Stak shakes his head at me, still grinning,

then goes back inside. Instantly, we all crack up laughing.

"You're so *wrong,* Bubbles!" Chuchie says, giving me a Cheetah Girls handshake as we walk a few feet to the Town Car, where Mom is already waiting for us.

"Dag on, these rap groups seem to get all the breaks," Aqua says as we settle down in the backseat. "Galleria—you don't think it's gonna turn into Nightmare on Sunset Boulevard, do you?" she asks, chuckling nervously.

The rest of my crew gives me a look like, "Oh, no, not again," but I'm not having it.

"We've already paid the Boogie Man in full," I tell them, pushing my hair from my face, 'cuz it's gotten a little stuck from the sweat. "We're here, aren't we? This time around, we'll *see* who gets to put some duckets in the bucket!"

Chapter 6

Now, it's time to do or die. Back in our adjoining suites, Mom sews some extra stitches on the tail of Do' Re Mi's cheetah costume. I've been soaking my stained cheetah blouse, and now I'm blow-drying it. The stain seems to have come out, thank gooseness!

Chuchie has had a dope idea for our hair. "We can stick the rhinestones I bought all over our hair with a little Wacky Glue!" she explains excitedly.

"I'm down," says Do' Re Mi.

"Me, too," I giggle. "After the strobe lights hit the rhinestones, and we dazzle them with our skills, we'll be the stars of this showcase, paws down!"

That's Chuchie, always hatching new hairdos. "This Wacky Glue stuff isn't gonna be hard to get out of our hair later, is it, Chuchie?" I ask. But when she doesn't answer, I figure she knows what she's doing, and I let it go.

"Lemme see yours," I ask the twins when they finish. Even on their smooth bobs, the rhinestones give mad sparkles.

"You hooked us up, Chuchie!" I yell happily.

We grab the garment bags with our costumes, and head downstairs to the lobby. "At least the Tinkerbell Lounge has a dressing room, so we can change there," I quip. "We're making a rapid climb up the food chain, Cheetah Girls!"

"I heard that," Aqua says, smiling ear to ear. "I can't believe how this all turned around! I mean, we lost the Apollo contest, and now just a couple weeks later, we're here in La La Land, performing for a record company! It's like out of a movie!"

"It sure is," Angie agrees.

"And I hope we get to see this movie again and again, *está bien?*" giggles Chuchie. She has put about fifty rhinestones into her braids, and they are shimmering all over the place, making her look like Sistarella, the fairy princess.

"All you need is a magic wand," I chide my make-believe sister. Then I give her a big, tight hug.

Without Chuchie, I could never do any of this. Actually, without the five of us, I don't even think we'd have gotten this far. Sure, Chuchie and I used to dream, but nothing ever happened until we met Dorinda, then Angie and Aqua.

When we roll up to the front of the Tinkerbell Lounge in our Town Car limo, I can't believe how beautiful the lounge looks, now that the sun has set on Sunset Boulevard. My whole body is tingling with excitement, and I can't help holding Chuchie's hand as we go inside.

"Hello, ladies. You're in the showcase, right?" says a hostess wearing a silver sparkly jumpsuit with a silver mesh net tutu.

"Yes, darling, they are," Mom says, pointing to us.

"Come right this way," the hostess says, showing off a sparkly smile.

I just love the peeps in La La Land. They're so *friendly,* and it seems like everybody here wants to be a shining star.

"You can put your stuff in your available dressing room," says the hostess, "and make yourselves at home. As talent, you're entitled to complimentary beverages and entrées of your choice. We've got a spread laid out downstairs in the club, but you can eat right in your dressing rooms. Just give your order to Raven—she's the waitress responsible for talent—and she'll bring your order to the dressing room when it's ready."

The hostess points to a pretty girl wearing a costume with silver wings. "Mr. Pett will be in to see you soon. Have a wonderful showcase!" She leaves us, and now it's time to find our dressing room.

"What a difference from the Apollo, huh?" I say to Chuchie, as we walk past a silver tinsel curtain and into the back hallway. "Am I tripping, or did she say our dressing room?"

"*Mamacita,* for once you're not 'lipping,' 'cuz *mira,* there it is!" Chuchie excitedly points to a dressing room, which has a piece of white paper with *our* name taped on its door!

I open the door excitedly, like one of those game show contestants anxious to see if we won the grand prize or just a booby prize.

Chuchie switches on the light, and I like what I see. "Lip, lip, hooray, we are definitely in the house!" I gasp, fingering all the lipsticks, powders, and oodles of beauty products and stuff on the big vanity table, surrounded by a supa-big vanity mirror with supa-big lightbulbs!

"Miz Aquanette, we didn't forget about you, 'cuz I got something for you, girlina," I start teasing Aqua, and moving sideways so she can't see what I'm hiding behind my back.

"What is it, Miss Galleria?" Aqua asks, giving me that look, like "I'm ready for Freddy, yo."

Whipping out a big aerosol can of Aqua Net hair spray, I act like I'm gonna spritz her, cornering her against the wall and making *Pssst* noises. "Did your mom name you after this little can of hair spray?" I ask, laying on the Southern accent.

"No, Miss Galleria, I really don't think she even heard of it!" Aqua pipes up. "I know Angie got her name from our great grandmother, Anginetta."

"Anginetta, I'm gonna let her—" I sing, making up rhymes like I always do.

"Shhh!" Mom hisses, and moves to the door, because all of a sudden, there is lots of giggling and noise in the hallway. As she opens our dressing room door, we all gather around to get a whiff of the action, and quickly realize that the other acts have arrived.

The center of the commotion is none other than a posse of girls wearing chain-link mini dresses featuring dollar bills.

"I guess we know who that is," Aqua chuckles, 'cuz she favors ducket designs, too — like the dollar bill decals on her tips.

Making their way to the dressing room with their name tacked to the door—"Cash Money Girls"—one of the girls turns around and says, "Sorry, we hope we didn't disturb you."

"Not at all, darling," Mom says. "We just got here ourselves. I'm Ms. Dorothea, manager of the Cheetah Girls."

"Hi—we're CMG—the Cash Money Girls. I'm Georgia Washington," the platinum blonde says.

Then the one with the upswept braids turns and says, "I'm Benjamina Franklin."

The one with the Miss Piggy eyelashes says, "Hi, I'm Abrahamma Lincoln."

"We'll check you later," I say, smiling, as we pile back into our dressing room.

"Their dresses are too short," Mom snips, then closes the door behind us.

"I'll bet you they're from out here," I offer as an explanation. All the girls out here seem to dress more "summery," if you know what I'm sayin'—probably all year round, I guess.

"You think those were their *real* names?" Angie asks.

"Lincoln, Washington, Franklin—duh!" Do' Re Mi says, exasperated. "Angie, those are 'dead presidents'—as in duckets, m-o-n-e-y, get it?"

"I get it," Angie says, kinda embarrassed, but shrugging it off. Then she mumbles, "After all, Benjamin Franklin wasn't a *real* president."

"Look at who *finally* cracked open her history book in school," quips Do' Re Mi.

"At least they had a theme—unlike those bozos Stak Chedda," I grumble.

"We're not going to wear the masks today, right?" Do' Re Mi asks as she changes into her cheetah costume.

"No, I don't think that's the move. Right, Mom?" I turn and ask.

"No, let 'em see what they're getting. I think you should put that glitter stuff around your eyes. You know, 'Cheetah Girls don't litter, they glitter!'" Mom says, chuckling.

"I *like* that, *Madrina!*" Chuchie exclaims.

"That's dope, Mom," I exclaim, then whip out my notebook and write it down. "Cheetah Girls don't litter, they glitter."

That gives me another dope idea: "You know, if—I mean, *when*—we get a record deal," I say, correcting myself, "we should come up with our own Cheetah Girls Credo that we could put inside the CD or something."

"You mean, like the Cheetah Girls Rules we have?" Do' Re Mi asks.

"Yeah, sort of, but more like things we believe in—with some flava," I add.

"Word. That's dope," Do' Re Mi chuckles.

"'Cheetah Girls don't litter, they glitter,'" I repeat out loud, staring at the scribbled page in my spotted, furry Kitty Kat notebook, which is like my personal Bible and secret diary mixed together—and it's for my eyes only.

"Should I wear my hair down?" I ask, smoothing down the fuzz that's growing by the minute. "Maybe I shoulda gotten another weave?"

"I guess you would've, if you had weave money," Mom snips at me.

All of a sudden, I feel my eyes fill up with tears. Mom would never snip at me like that if she wasn't mad at me about somthing! I was right, I suddenly realize. It's my fault Mom and Dad have to work so hard.

"Oh, weava, don't ever leava!" Chuchie giggles, not realizing what's going on with me. "I like it wild like that, Bubbles. That's the real you."

"I like it straight," I say, frowning to hide my real feelings. "I look like a Chia Pet with all this hair."

"Bubbles, if you put it up now, you're gonna mess up the rhinestones!" Chuchie says, exasperated because, I guess, I'm freaking out. "*Párate!* Now you're making me *nervosa.*"

"Okay, girlinas, calm down. It's time to growl, not *howl,*" my mom interrupts.

We start chuckling. Mom *is* mad funny, even though she is too bossy sometimes. Besides, I've got to give it to her—she didn't say anything when I stained my skirt yesterday at lunch. Of course, that's probably because she's tired of yelling at me to carry tampons.

Which reminds me. Taking out a tampon from my cheetah backpack, I make a mad rush to the ladies' room. "Come with me, Chuchie. That's all I would need is to start *leaking* onstage!"

Chuchie giggles, and follows me out the dressing room door. Four guys in big cowboy hats and boots, and bright red plaid shirts, are rambling our way. They smile at us, and I almost wave with the hand that's holding the tampon. Luckily, Chuchie pokes me, and I pull it back in time. "Oopsy, doopsy," I giggle, then say, "Howdy."

"Howdy, ladies. Those costumes are mighty pretty!" the tallest guy says.

Cheez whiz, they have a drawl even bigger than Aqua and Angie's!

"Who are you?" asks nosy Chuchie.

"The Toads," says the tall guy wearing the hundred-gallon cowboy hat. "And y'all?"

"We're the Cheetah Girls!" I say, recovering from my tampon embarrassment.

"We're y'all from?"

"Manny-hanny!" Chuchie says, then giggles. "And you?"

"Nashville, Tennessee—and believe me, we're *real* glad to be here!"

In the bathroom, I can't stop giggling about our little encounter with the lonesome cowboys. Then, I suddenly get another idea, "Maybe we should get cheetah cowboy hats, and do a 'jig'—I mean a gig—at a rodeo!"

"Where *is* the rodeo?" Chuchie asks, standing outside my stall, holding the door because the latch is broken.

"I don't know. Down South somewhere, no? Let's ask the goody two-shoe twins!"

"*Qué hora es?* What time is it?" Chuchie asks, sounding nervous.

"Six o'clock. Time is moving so slow today," I say, feeling cold and chilly, even though the weather is so perfect in La La Land. I always get cold feet when I'm nervous.

"Feel my hands," I say to Chuchie, grabbing her hand. "I'm cold as a mummy. You are too, Chuchie."

When we get back to the dressing room, Mr. Pett is waiting for us. "Oh, we're sorry to keep you waiting!" I exclaim.

"No, that's fine. I just got here. Is everything okay, ladies?" Mr. Pett asks, like he really wants to know. Nobody asked us *anything* at the Apollo—even when we were boohooing like babies backstage after we lost. That's 'cuz they didn't give a hoot *how* we felt.

"Everything is fabulous," Mom volunteers. "Do you have our place in the lineup yet?"

"Yes, I do," Mr. Pett says, flipping a page on his clipboard. Then, smiling at us, he adds hesitantly, "We want you to go on first. Now, I know that isn't the ideal spot in a showcase, but —"

"But *nothing*!" Mom encounters, interrupting Mr. Pett with a smile. Then she blurts out, "We'd have better luck facing a *firing* squad than being forced to warm up a bunch of suits."

"I know. I know, Mrs. Garibaldi, but in order to provide diversity for the showcase, we're breaking up the talent by, um, musical genre," Mr. Pett says, stammering. He sounds like a used-car salesman trying to unload a broken-down hooptie.

"Well, let me break this down for you by, um, 'growl power' genre," Mom says, very politely, so I know she's mad. "We're *not* going on first."

"Okay, lemme see what I can do," Mr. Pett says, taking a handkerchief out of his suit pocket and wiping the sweat from his forehead.

Mom picks up the menu and starts looking at

it. I know better than to say anything, so I just throw Chuchie a look, then start fiddling with my hair and staring in the vanity mirror.

"Ms. Dorothea, what did you mean by a bunch of 'suits'?" Aqua asks Mom, breaking the silence. She *would* ask a question now.

"That's what you call record industry executives—exactly who will sitting there judging us, if we go out there howling instead of growling," Mom explains, exasperated. "Let some other poor prey be led to slaughter first!"

"I know that's right!" Aqua responds.

A few minutes later, a very nervous Mr. Pett knocks on our dressing room door, and announces the new—and improved—lineup.

"Mrs. Garibaldi, I pulled a few strings, and the Cheetah Girls will go on right after the Beehives. That'll be a nice segue from rock to, um—"

"Global groove," Mom says, to help Mr. Pett from flexing fowl and calling our music by some wack name.

"Yes, that's right, 'global groove,'" he says, breaking into a nervous smile. "Anyway. After the Cheetah Girls, we'll segue into the country-western genre with the Toads, so it'll work out perfectly after all."

"I agree with you, Mr. Pett. That sounds like a *purr-fect* lineup," Mom says, to keep Mr. Pett from "cracking face" any further. "Just give us our cue when it's time to *growl*!"

That's my mom. Sometimes, she bosses me around, it's true. But I'll tell you what—when it's time to stick up for your own, there's nobody like Ms. Dorothea.

Chapter 7

As show time at the Tinkerbell Lounge approaches, we nervously open the door to our dressing room so we can keep our ear to the action, if you know what I'm saying.

Standing in the doorway, with Do' Re Mi scrunched against me, we catch four girls with supa-powdered faces, black-lipsticked pouts, and the highest "bou bou fon fons" we've ever seen, hovering together at the far end of the hallway.

"Those must be the Beehives," Do' Re Mi whispers to me.

I nod my head, like "No kidding." One thing is for sure, the Beehives must be causing quite a buzz in Boston with *that* look.

It seems a lot of girl groups have four girls — just like Karma's Children in Houston, where the twins are from, or the Honeydews. I'm glad the Cheetah Girls are "representin'" with five strong, you know what I'm saying?

All of a sudden, the audience starts clapping, which usually means that an announcer has stepped onto the stage. Sure enough, the announcer's voice booms into the microphone, trying to hype the crowd.

Do' Re Mi and I tiptoe a little farther out into the hallway, just to hear what he says. Thank gooseness Mom got us out of first place in the frying pan—we woulda sizzled for sure!

As we stand there, just a few feet from the stage, my heart starts to *thumpa, thumpa* up a storm, and I start getting so nervous I can't breathe. This is it, I tell myself. Tonight's the night we get a record contract, and start making beaucoup duckets, or else our faces are cracked.

That would be a total nightmare, I say to myself. My mom would probably have to quit managing us and get busy again in her shop. Dorinda would probably go off and dance with Mo' Money Monique and leave the group. It would be the beginning of the end for the Cheetah Girls!

No! I can't let it happen! It's all up to me, I think. I've got to come through this time!

"What's he saying?" Do' Re Mi asks quietly.

"I can't hear," I respond, but that's probably because my heart is pounding so *loud.*

The Beehive girls start shuffling closer to the tinsel curtain divider. Then, on cue, they rush out onto the stage.

We scurry back into the dressing room, because it's time to do our Cheetah Girls prayer. We do our prayer before every performance. I think it gives us good luck and, more important, reminds all five of us that we're in this together—*forever.*

After we finish doing the prayer, we take a few deep breaths. I can feel my hands tingling.

Just clear your mind and concentrate on your breathing, I tell myself. I can hear our vocal coach Drinka Champagne's voice in my mind, telling us what to do before we "hit that stage."

We all look at one another and smile. Mom looks up from eating her plate of linguine, and gives me a big smile, too.

The lyrics from the Beehives' performance

waft all the way down the hallway: "Sting me with your love/Or I'll fly away like a dove. . . ."

I look at Chuchie, and she knows what I'm thinking. "I've never heard that song before," she says, shrugging her shoulders.

Whenever we hear singers, we're always trying to figure out if they're doing "covers" or singing original songs. It seems like a lot of groups sing other artists' material. But we're not going out like that. Mom says I have a gift for writing songs. But I just feel like, why should I put duckets in someone else's bucket by singing *their* songs, when I can sing my own, you know what I'm saying?

All of a sudden, Mr. Pett appears at our door, and Mom jumps up. "It's show time!" she announces, taking the words right out of Mr. Pett's mouth.

We all hold one another's hands, and follow her lead into the hallway. Judging by the clapping, there are a lot of peeps in the house.

At this very moment, I'm not worried about anything—not about Stak Chedda, not about duckets, fame, or fortune. Right now, at this second, I don't even care if we get a record deal. I just can't *believe* the Cheetah Girls are in the house—in La La Land! Somebody throw poppy dust on me, *pleez*!

After the announcer introduces us, Mom throws us a kiss, and pushes us gently from behind the tinsel curtain. I look quickly at the crowd, and breathe a sigh of relief as we line up across the stage and wait for our audio cue.

The crowd is not so scary-looking or anything. They don't look like *our* kind of peeps, but at least they look like regular people. I mean they're not giving off any Darth Vader vibes or anything.

Mom says that the A&R peeps from Def Duck Records are definitely in the house, checking us out. That gives me the shivers again, but thank gooseness, I'm saved by the beat. The bass-heavy tracks we use to sing our song, "Wanna-be Stars in the Jiggy Jungle" crank up loud over the sound system.

Omigod, I hope that doesn't drown out our vocals! I suddenly think. I start goospitating, but there is no time left for a visit to freak city. We already did an audio check, and the engineer wouldn't have set the audio level that high if the mike level didn't match, I tell myself.

Then I start grooving on automatic, doing our dance steps, waiting for the vocal cue, counting to myself, One, two, three:

"Some people walk with a panther
or strike a buffalo stance
that makes you wanna dance

Other people flip the script
on the day of the jackal
that'll make you cackle."

By the time we get to the refrain—*"The jiggy jiggy jungle! The jiggy jiggy jungle!"*—I can tell the crowd is feeling our global groove. It's not exactly like it was on Halloween, when we performed at the Cheetah-Rama for our fellow Kats and Kittys, but this crowd is definitely *feeling* us, too.

When we do our second song, "Shop in the Name of Love," I throw Chuchie a quick little smile, and from her eyes I can tell we're on the same "weave length." I wrote the song just for her, after she got busted running up Auntie Juanita's charge card. Juanita has not been *feeling* Chanel lately, but I know Chuchie's trying real hard to make up for everything, 'cuz she let us all down.

When the intro beat pipes up, we get ready for our "fierce pose"—placing our arms over our heads—which is a fly move Do' Re Mi thought up. Then we spin around, and break into the lyrics:

"Polo or solo
Gucci or Pucci
Prada or nada
Is the way I wanna live."

By the time we take our bow, I'm so psyched, I'm not even nervous anymore—I just wish we could sing *one more song*! But that's the deal-io, yo, with showcases: you only get a teeny-weeny slice of the performing pie. I can't wait till we're serving it piping hot till our spots drop!

Because Mr. Pett told us to leave the stage quickly after we perform, we don't really get to take in all the applause. Mom is waiting for us behind the tinsel divider, and she hugs me and Do' Re Mi when we get inside the dressing room.

"Were we dope?" Do' Re Mi asks, looking up at Mom.

"Better than that," she says, smiling with pride. "One of you is fierce enough, but *five* of you? I hope the world is ready for Freddy, okay?"

"What about me, *Madrina?*" Chuchie whines, moving in to Mom for a hug, too. Mom is Chuchie's godmother, and sometimes Chanel really milks it for points.

"Prada or *nada*!" Mom sings, imitating Chuchie, and we really start giggling, because Mom's singing voice is a cross between the Tin Man's and Minnie Mouse caught in a tropical rainstorm. *Squeak, squeak, squeak!*

Finally, I can relax and eat, so I pig out on Mom's leftover linguine with white clam sauce. "Yum yum for my tum tum," I hum as I chomp away.

Raven, our waitress, knocks at the door. "Can I get you girls anything else?" she asks.

"Yeah—a record deal!" Chuchie giggles.

"Just some more soda," Mom pipes up.

"I'll be right back," Raven says, smiling. Lifting both arms over her head, she waves them, fluttering her fingers.

Aqua and Angie give each other a look. "Her name is Raven," Aqua says.

"Yeah, and she just 'spread her wings,'" Angie adds. "You think High Priestess Abala was right?"

"I sure hope so," Aqua says.

"Well, I don't know about any predictions of the future, but I do know I like her costume," Mom says after Raven leaves. "Which reminds me, girlinas—don't change from your costumes yet. Mr. Pett says that after the last act has performed in the showcase, Deejay Captain Hook will start spinning records, and we can go back into the performing area and mingle with the executives, and have complimentary cocktails."

"Complimentary cocktails, that sounds dope!" chuckles Do' Re Mi.

"Well, some sounds are deceiving, darling, because in your case, cocktails are synonymous with *Coca-Cola*!" Mom warns her.

"I know," giggles Do' Re Mi, "but you know what I'm saying."

"Yes, darling, and I'm not playing. We're just gonna go out there to sashay and parlay till it's payday!"

We all laugh at Mom's rhyme, then run back into the hallway to hear the Toads perform.

"They sound more like frogs!" Chuchie quips, after we listen for a few minutes.

"When you grow up down South, you learn to *love* country-western music," chuckles Aqua.

"Yeah, well I think it sounds too *twangy,*" I moan. "Like they should be performing in a square dance or something."

"Yeah, and those country-western acts are twanging all the way to the bank," Mom quips. "Did you know that, after rap music, country music artists sell the most records?"

I see Mom is taking her job as our manager very seriously. These days, she reads *Billboard* magazine, and she's even got bookworm Do' Re Mi reading the "trades," as she calls them.

"Well, I know there are a lot of corny people out there, so I'm not surprised that they buy corny records," Chuchie says, picking at the rhinestones on one of her braids.

"Stop that, Chuchie," I scold her, moving her hand from her hair.

"Chanel, those rhinestones were sparkling up a storm under the lights," Mom says, pleased.

"I know, *Madrina,* but I'm not so sure they come off!"

"Well, we don't have to find out right now," I scold her again, as she tries to touch her hair on the sneak-a-roni tip.

Twirling in the vanity chair, I ask wistfully, "Don't you just love getting Hollywood-ized?"

"Yeah," Chuchie says. "I can't wait till we come back out here *otra vez.*"

"I guess you will, when you have come-back-out-here money for plane tickets," Mom quips, packing some of our stuff back into her cheetah vanity case.

Man, I hope we get a record deal out of this. For Mom's sake more than mine, so she can stop working my nerves!

Do' Re Mi motions for me to come listen at the door. "They're on."

I know exactly who she's talking about. Those "dead president" divettes-in-training are finally dropping a few pennies worth of rhymes onstage. Angie comes running back into the dressing room to tell us, "Those heffas are really throwing money onstage!"

She would be impressed. "Don't worry, Angie, you *know* they aren't *real duckets*!"

"I know, but maybe *we* should do something like that," Angie says sheepishly.

"Yeah, we could throw stuffed cheetahs at the audience," I say with a smirk. "And with our luck, it would hit the vice president of the record company on the head and give him a concussion."

"You're a mess, Galleria," Angie says, chuckling sweetly.

Sometimes I can't understand why the twins are so *nice,* but they just are. "CMG's definitely got some flava," I mumble, while listening to the group's set.

Mom hates their outfits, so she doesn't even get up to hear their performance. Angie runs back by the tinsel divider, while CMG keep the flow going:

"Yeah, we rool with Lincoln,
What are you thinkin'?
But it's all about the Benjamins.
Baby, not maybe, just mighty, awrighty!"

Chuchie and I look at each other, like "all right, they got rhymes." The executives are obviously feeling CMG, too, because the Cash Money Girls get a mad round of applause.

"I'll bet you they get a record deal," Do' Re Mi says seriously. "It seems like record companies are always willing to bank on a few rhymes, yo."

"I know that's right," Aqua pipes up. "Yeah, they're good, though."

"Hey, this isn't a competition, remember," I remind my crew. "It's not like, if some other group gets a contract, we don't—it's not like the Amateur Hour at the Apollo, where only one group wins."

From the relieved looks on the faces of my crew, I know I've said the right thing. Thank gooseness!

We all hover by the door now, to wait and see CMG come back to their dressing room. When they do pass, we congratulate them

"Where are you from?" Chuchie asks the girl who calls herself Abrahamma Lincoln.

"We're from Oakland," Abrahamma says, smiling at Chuchie.

"Where's that?" Chuchie says giggling.

"It's up north," Abrahamma responds, amused.

"North *where*?" Chuchie asks again, with no shame in her game.

"Oh, y'all ain't from around here. It's up in northern California," Abrahamma says, chuckling.

"Chanel falls asleep in geography class," I offer, because I'm so embarrassed for her. Even *I* know where Oakland is!

"How old are y'all?" Abrahamma asks me, because it's obvious we're still in school. They look like they're probably twenty-two or something.

"We're freshmen in high school," I say, flossing.

"Oh, well, y'all are real cute. I love your costumes! Did you make them?" Benjamina Franklin pipes up.

"No, my—um, our manager made them," I say quietly, changing my mind about saying "my mom."

The announcer introduces Stak Chedda, so we all get quiet and listen. "How is it they *always* get to go on last?" I hiss to Chuchie.

"Oh, do you know them?" Benjamina Franklin asks me surprised.

"No," I say, because I'm definitely not telling *them* we got dis-missed at the Apollo Amateur Contest, and they won instead. "We, um, performed with them once before."

"Word. Where?" Benjamina asks me. Cheez whiz, she's like a dog with a bone, she just won't leave it alone.

"We performed with them at the Apollo Thee-ayter," Aqua volunteers. Now I'm back to hating the goody two-shoe twins *again*.

"Word. Y'all performed at the Apollo?" Abrahamma asks, like she's impressed, but not quite.

Now I *really* want to do an "abracadabra."

"We just performed in the Amateur Hour Contest," I say, my voice squeaking because I feel embarrassed now.

"Oh, yeah, that's right, we was talking to the taller one earlier—Stak Jackson—and he told us they *won* the Amateur Hour Contest," Abrahamma says, a flicker of recognition on her face.

Suddenly, the tinsel dividers fling open, and my worst nightmare starts walking *our* way, with their hands in the air like they just don't care. *"Ayiight!"* Stak Jackson says, slapping his brother, Chedda, a high five, like they definitely rocked it to the doggy bone.

I guess they did, but I'm not feeling the bumbling bozos, after the way they dissed us at the Apollo. I don't care how nice Stak's trying to be to me now.

"I'm not *feeling* him," I mumble to Chuchie, rolling my eyes to the ceiling.

"You wuz off the hook, Cheetah Girls!" Stak says on the way to his dressing room, which is at the other end of the hallway. Thank gooseness the Tinkerbell Lounge is big—just like everywhere in La La Land.

"You were, too," I hear myself saying, even as I'm gritting my teeth.

Chuchie giggles. She thinks it's so funny, 'cuz bozos always seem to like *me*.

Mom comes to the doorway. "It's show time, girlitas—*again*."

We know that means we're supposed to go back out into the performing area, and be *really really* nice to all the peeps we meet. This is real important, see—it's not enough to be talented, as my mom's been telling us—you have to go out there and "shmooze" with the "suits" if you want to nail down a record deal. And do I ever want to nail one down, right to the floor!

Deejay Captain Hook comes up to the mike. He tells us he'll be spinning on the "wheels of steel," and to sit back and dig the sounds.

"He's funny," I laugh to Do' Re Mi. "The peeps out here are kinda cooler, more laid-back than peeps in Manny-hanny. I definitely like it!"

A man in a white linen suit comes up to Mom, and extends his hand. "Hi, Mrs. Garibaldi. I'm Tom Isaaks from the A and R department at Def Duck."

Mom is really nice to him, which is surprising, because she usually gaspitates at people who wear white after Labor Day, but I guess she knows what time it is. It's definitely time to sashay and parlay!

Do' Re Mi and I back away, so Mom is free to flow. I keep an eye on her, as I accept congratulations from members of the other acts, and from people who were in the house. Everyone says they loved us, and they're wearing big, goofy smiles, so I know they either mean what they're sayin', or they're just playing.

But part of my attention is always on Mom and Mr. Isaaks, 'cuz he's the one we're after right now. There are other A and R guys here, no doubt, but this one came up to mom first thing.

As I'm standin' there, I catch Stak and Chedda Jackson high-fiving it across the floor from me, nodding their bozo heads up and down like they're all that and a bag of chips. I'm thinking I want to go over there and find out what all the hip-hoppin's about, but they beat me to the punch.

"Yo, Cheetah Girls," Stak greets me and Dorinda. "What the deal-io, yo?"

"Chillin', chillin'," I say, trying to act cool like a jewel. But what Stak says now sends a real chill up and down my spine.

"Looks like Stak Chedda got us a record deal!" Stak nods, flashing his pointy-toothed grin like he's sitting on a million duckets.

"For true?" Dorinda asks, her jaw dropping. "Man, that was fast!"

"We don't waste no time, waitin' for no dime!" Chedda gloats. "Y'all got any interest goin'?" Stak asks me.

"My mo . . . our manager's talkin' with the A and R dude right now," I say. And from the look of things, it's getting serious between Mr. Isaaks and my mom. Their smiles have vanished, and now it looks like he's explaining the ins and outs of things to her.

"Well, good luck, yo," Stak says, giving us a little hand salute. "Y'all really rocked the house. You deserve a deal, just like us." He and Chedda move off toward the cocktail bar. I guess they're old enough for cocktails, come to think of it.

Now Mom comes up to us. "Where are the other girls?" she asks. We look around for them. Chuchie is flirting with some hunky executive in a shiny suit and mirror shades. The twins are by the food spread, talking to the Beehives, their mouths full of food.

Do' Re Mi and I go round them up, and we huddle with my mom. "Well, Cheetah Girls, Mr. Isaaks is interested in signing the Cheetah Girls to a contract. . . ."

We whoop and holler for a minute, hugging one another and crying tears of joy.

My mom tries to stop the party. "Whoa, now, wait a minute, I haven't finished telling you the whole story!" We calm down, and she continues. "He says, though, that it's not all up to him. He's got to play our tape for some higher-up executives, and try to convince them he's right about signing the Cheetah Girls."

"So, what does that mean?" Chuchie asks,

the smile fading from her face.

"It means, we probably won't know anything for a while, and we're just gonna have to be patient and wait."

"How long is a while?" Dorinda asks.

"He says it could be a few weeks before he knows anything, but that we can call and check in if we start getting anxious, and he'll give us an update of his progress."

"A few weeks!" Aqua gasps. "Dag on, that's, like, forever!"

"Yeah!" Angie echoes. "How come it's got to take so long?"

"Well, apparently, not everyone was here who had to hear you girls sing," Mom explains.

"But Stak Chedda got an offer just now!" Dorinda breaks in, saying just what I was about to say.

"Well," Moms shrugs, "I don't know . . . maybe the executives from the Alternative Rap division were all here or something."

"Yeah," Chuchie says, "and maybe they're just better than us."

"Put a lid on it, Miss Cuchifrita!" I say. "If we have to wait, we'll just wait."

My crew all agrees, and we get together and

do a Cheetah Girls cheer. But inside, I feel like I'm falling apart. A few weeks! Can the Cheetah Girls even hang together that long? Without any gigs, with no duckets coming in, Dorinda might find some other paying gig performing and Auntie Juanita may yank Chuchie out of the group. And what if "a few weeks" becomes a few months? What if we don't get the deal, after all that waiting? It'll be the end for us, I just know it!

Chapter 8

If I thought the drama we had trying to get to L.A. for the Def Duck Records showcase was like being in the Twilight Zone, then I was wrong. Flying *back* from Cali on the overnight "red-eye," to go to school in the Big Apple the next day with a cold, a splitting headache, *and* a bad attitude, is *really* what it feels like to be in the Twilight Zone.

Right this minute, Chuchie and I are walking to our lockers after third period. I can't even walk fast, because it makes my head hurt more. What a roller-coaster ride our life is! "I can't believe just yesterday, we were living large in Cali, and today we're goospitating about a stupid math exam," I moan to Chuchie, who is lost in her own Telemundo channel, as usual.

I *hate* math, and would rather have someone stick my eyelashes together with Wacky Glue than have to figure out another algebra equation! "Equate this—squared times x to the fourth power equals nonsense!" I moan to Chuchie. She's even worse in math, except, of course, when it comes to adding up how much money she can spend *shopping*!

"You don't think this looks stupid, do you, Chuchie?" I ask, fingering the cheetah dog collar I'm wearing around my neck. It's a good thing the collar fit *me,* because it sure didn't fit Toto. When I got home and tried to put it around my boo-boo's neck, it was too big for him by an L.A. mile. *What was I thinking when I bought it?*

"No, *Mamacita.* It looks dope. I wish I had one," she whines wistfully. "*Pero,* I can't believe you don't know what size Toto is by now."

"I was delirious, okay, Chuchie?" I groan.

Chuchie changes the subject. "Do you think you passed the math exam?"

"I don't know, did you?" I snap back, then shove some books into my locker. "Thank gooseness it's lunchtime, 'cuz I'm fading pronto. I feel like I'm about to fall on my face."

"Well, you *are,* 'cuz here comes the Red Snapper and Mackerel," Chuchie giggles sarcastico.

Derek Ulysses Hambone, aka "DUH," is the biggest pain, but I try to be nice to him, because his mother is a very good customer at Mom's boutique. "I don't understand why all the bozos like me," I mumble under my breath.

Derek is in our face now. "Yo, Cheetah Girl. We missed you yesterday. I heard you was getting busy in Cali. That true? Kahlua Alexander hooked you up with a showcase?"

Derek is sucking on a lollipop that makes him look like a—well, like a Red Snapper. Mackerel Johnson, "his boy," is bopping around as usual, and grinning at Chuchie like he's waiting for a visit from the tooth fairy.

"Yeah, it's true," I mumble, trying to smile at Derek. He is wearing a red sweat suit, with the Johnny BeDown logo up the side of the pants and across the top in jumbo-size black letters. How tick-tacky.

"That's dope, you got it like that. Did you get a record deal yet?" Mackerel cuts in, amping up his hyper moves.

"We don't know *anything* yet," I reply, irritated 'cuz I don't wanna think about it, and I don't want them to know we've got it like that—waiting nervously like hungry cubs. "We just did it for the experience, you know what I'm saying?"

"Yeah, I hear you, Cheetah Girls. I know y'all gonna blow up one day, and I'll be like Batman—*bam*! Right there by your side when it goes down," Derek heckles, grinning at me with that awful gold tooth in front. "You should let me be your manager, yo."

"Thank gooseness, we already have a manager," I smirk back at him.

Suddenly, the Red Snapper is staring at my neck like he's a vampire, which gives me the chillies. "Yo, check that choker around your neck. That is *dope.*"

Chuchie starts giggling, and I'm really gonna whack her if she tells Derek that the choker around my neck is really a *dog* collar!

"Thanks. I bought it in Cali," I say, telling only half a fib-eroni.

"Too bad, 'cuz I'd like one of those. I'm gonna be modeling in this fashion show at my mom's church, and it would look dope with the designs I'll be wearing—cheetah stuff like you like," Derek explains, flossing.

"Well, it's not too bad, because we *make* them, too," I say, smirking at my quick comeback.

"Word? Well then *make* me one—you know I'm good for the duckets," the Red Snapper says, pulling out a wad of money from his deep-sea pockets.

"Awright, but you got to pay to play—tomorrow," I retort.

"How much? Oh—make the choker a little wider, too," Derek says, waving the hand in which he's flossing his duckets.

"For you, Derek, we'll let you slide for, um, twenty," I say, thinking off the top of my head.

"Okay, bet. Later, Cheetah Girl."

Chuchie and I hightail it outside to wait for Do' Re Mi, then walk toward Mo' Betta Burger on Eighth Avenue.

"You won't believe what Bubbles just did!" Chuchie says, grabbing Do' Re Mi's arm and filling her in on my entrepreneurial moves.

Mom would be so proud of me, I think. Instead of waiting around for a record deal to appear, I'm goin' out there and makin' things happen in the duckets department. One way or another, I'm gonna show her and my dad that I can make my own payday. I'm not some spoiled brat, like Derek Hambone!

"If Derek would just give up on the gold rush, maybe I could at least look at him without *puking,"* I mumble to Do' Re Mi.

"Word. I hear that."

Suddenly, I get a great idea. "Maybe I should send him an anonymous letter, telling him he wouldn't look like such a wack attack if he took out that gold tooth. You think that's a dope idea?" I suggest to my crew.

"Nope, 'cuz he'll know it's from you," Do' Re Mi says. She's smart, so I listen to her.

"Yeah, you're right. Too bad."

"You really gonna make him a cheetah choker?" Do' Re Mi asks, squinching up her nose as we walk inside Mo' Betta, order some burgers, and chill at a table.

"Yup," I counter. I'm getting my chomp-a-roni on with a mushroom burger, when I suddenly get another fabbie-poo idea! "I'm even gonna put my nickname for Derek on his choker, in silver letters—*scemo*!"

Chuchie almost chokes on her burger, giggling.

LaRonda, one of the girls in my math class, walks by our table. "What y'all up to?" she asks, checking out our mischief moves.

"Nothing," I reply, trying not to choke.

"The math test was hard, yo, wasn't it?" LaRonda groans, still standing by our table.

"Yeah, it sure was," I respond.

LaRonda looks at me, then gives me the same vampire look that Derek did. "That choker is dope. Where'd you get that, yo?" she asks, excited.

"Actually, I, um, I mean, we make them," I say, telling one whole fib-eroni this time. If I'm gonna sell one to the Red Snapper, I might as well sell one to LaRonda while I'm at it, you know what I'm saying? "We've got a few different styles. I, um, we could make you one like this."

"That sounds cool. How much you selling 'em for?" LaRonda asks, panting like a puppy for our product.

"Ten dollars," I say, charging LaRonda a cheaper price than the Red Snapper, since she's cool.

"Word. Can you make me one?"

"Yup. I'll bring it to school tomorrow," I tell her proudly. "But you know you got to pay to play, yo?"

"Ayiight. Don't worry, Galleria, I'll have the money. Just bring me the choker," LaRonda says, then walks away.

"LaRonda—you want me to make you one with your name on it?"

"Word—you can do that?" she turns and asks, her eyes brightening even wider.

"Yup—that's a done deal-io, yo," I say, flossing, and go back to eating my burger. LaRonda smiles, and goes to the counter to order.

All of a sudden, I notice my headache is gone, and my mind is ka-chinging like a cash register as I talk real fast to my crew. "The three of us can go after school today to the garment district, and buy the leather strips, some metal letters, snap closures, Wacky Glue, and we're in the house—in business, yo!"

Chuchie and Do' Re Mi look at me like "Bubbles is trouble." I see I'm gonna have to convince my crew to be down with the new endeavor that will make us clever.

I take a deep breath, like Drinka taught us to do, then do my wheela-deala. "Look. We can sit around here, waiting for Def Duck or some other record company to give us a record deal. And that is definitely cool, yo, but we're Cheetah Girls, and we've got the skills to pay the bills, so why not parlay and sashay?"

Chuchie starts giggling and gets excited. I can see she's finally hopping on the choo-choo train. After all, she needs money a lot worse than I do so she can pay her mother back all the money she charged on her credit card! "Maybe we should make some chokers so we can sell them at Kats and Kittys!" she suggests hopefully.

"Word, that would be dope," Do' Re Mi chimes in. I know Do' can use some duckets worse than any of us—her "family" has got no money at all, once they get done feeding all those foster kids and paying the rent. "We could even try to sell them to stores—I mean, um, little stores, anyway," Do' Re Mi adds, wincing, then shrugs her teeny-weeny shoulders.

"You think *Madrina* would sell some for us in the store?" Chuchie asks me.

"You're the one who works there part-time, so *you'd* better ask her," I chuckle. "I'm not asking Mom for any more favors. She does enough for us."

"It's not a favor, flava—it's about bizness," Do' Re Mi says, smirking and sipping on her Coke.

"Well, I think we should make up a few chokers first, then try to sell them to a boutique or something, and only then ask Mom. She'll *have* to say yes, if someone else buys them from us first, right?" I say, whipping out my Kitty Kat notebook to make some notes. "Okay, we'll make, um, eight chokers that say—what?"

"Why 'what'?" Do' Re Mi asks.

"Not *what*, silly—but what should it say?"

"Oh. How about 'Growl Power'?" Do' Re Mi says, looking at us for approval.

"Do' Re Mi, you are so *money*—that's dope!" I say, getting really excited. "Okay, we make five chokers for ourselves, so we'll wear them all the time. Kind of like a walking advertisement for our product. Then we'll make three more, which we'll try to sell. Then one more for Snapper—that says, 'Scemo'. One for LaRonda. Should we make LaRonda's name with just capital letters, or small ones, too?"

"LaRonda. I like it with capital and small letters. Maybe we should get gold and silver letters, though," Do' Re Mi suggests.

"Yeah, that's cool. Okay, after school, let's get busy, 'cuz it's time to put some duckets in the bucket!"

Chapter 9

I'm so glad the twins have finally talked their father into letting them get a cell phone. Of course, he wouldn't spring for a Miss Wiggy StarWac, like Chuchie and I have, but at least it works, even if it's a "no name" model.

"Angie, meet us at Pig in the Poke on Fortieth Street," I tell the twins, so they can get in on the choker action, too. Because Chuchie, Do' Re Mi, and I are students at Fashion Industries High, we have a special discount card that we can use at any store if we're buying stuff for school—like sewing, design, or pattern-making supplies. So our best bet is to go buy supplies for the chokers in the heart of the garment district—which is pretty much below Forty-second Street, near Times Square.

LaGuardia Peforming Arts High School is just a hop and skip down from there on the #1 train, so it only takes Aqua and Angie twenty minutes to get hooked up with us.

"That skirt is cute," Chuchie says to Aqua. The twins actually do look cute today. I mean, it's not how *we* three dress, but they're starting to get their own style groove, which is cool. They have on matching black-and-white-checked mini-skirts, with black sweaters and flats. Dressing alike is not just a cheetah thing—it's a twin thing, too.

"Did you tell High Priestess Abala about that waitress, Raven, we met?" I ask, kinda half-jokingly.

High Priestess Abala and the twins' dad are getting a little too serious too fast for Aqua and Angie's taste. Of course, it doesn't help that Abala probably goes to work on a broomstick, too! I think she's definitely part of some kooky coven, you know what I'm saying?

"Yes," Angie pipes up, "and she says that that's the sign we were looking for, and that it means the record deal is *ours*!"

"Don't you think that's going a little far, Aqua?" Do' Re Mi snips. "I mean, all Raven did was serve us some linguine and Cokes and that's no joke!" Do' Re Mi is definitely the only one in our crew with her feet planted firmly on the ground.

"You know, I could definitely use some of High Priestess Abala's Vampire Brew right about now, yo," I say, smirking. "I still cannot believe we were sitting up there in your living room that time, sipping witches' brew with a coven of psychos, just because Abala told us it would bring us good luck at the Apollo!"

"I know you're right. You remember that noise me and Angie heard in our bedroom closet before we left for Hollywooood?" Aqua says, using her drawl to do a vowel stretch.

"Yeah. Did you catch Mr. Teddy-Poodly doing the tango while eating a mango?" I riff. High Priestess Abala had given us all shoe boxes filled with teddy bear eyes and noses, poodle tails, and rabbit whiskers. She said we were supposed to put them in our closets, and not open them, if we wanted to rock the house at the Apollo. Wack advice, if you ask me.

"No, Galleria, the only thing we caught in

that closet was a mouse—that's what I'm trying to tell you!" Aqua says, bursting out laughing.

"Hold up," I say wincing. "You mean to tell us that all that shaking and baking you said was going on in the closet had nothing to do with the shoe boxes? It was a *mouse* in the house?"

"Yes, ma'am. That's right," Angie says, nodding.

We all give each other a look like we're gonna have to keep this Abala situation on the down low, 'cuz something is definitely not right.

"Were you scared?" Do' Re Mi asks.

"Well—" Aqua hems and haws.

"Stop faking that you're not quaking, Aqua!" I blurt out.

"All right, Galleria. We wuz scared to death! You happy now. I didn't sleep but forty winks, ain't that right, Angie?"

"That's right," Angie says, nodding, and eating her sandwich from a cellophane bag. "Even Porgy and Bess wuz scared!" Porgy and Bess are the twins' pet guinea pigs.

We crack up all the way to Poly and Esther

Fabrics, on Fortieth Street between Seventh and Eighth avenues—that's where Mom says they sell the cheapest cheetah suede prints this side of the jiggy jungle.

Of course, I'm in charge of bargaining and negotiations. "I'm getting really good at this," I humph, as I approach the counter. "I don't stop till the price drops!"

Well, I guess I've met my match today, because Mr. Poly isn't having any eyelash fluttering today. "Miss, you either pay the twenty-two dollars a yard, or you take your business somewhere else!"

"Okay, okay," I say, giving in, and reluctantly taking the exact sum out of my cheetah wallet. We're chipping in ten duckets each to float our Cheetah Girls choker escapades, so the rest of my crew is paying for the other accoutrements.

"Next time, I'd better negotiate with his better half—Mrs. Esther," I mumble as we leave the store, on our way to buy the silver and gold metal letters.

"Have any of your rhinestones come out of your braids yet?" I turn and ask Chuchie.

"No, *Mamacita.* Not one," Chuchie says,

touching her braids and showing me how stuck they are. "I bet you they stay in until I get my braids taken out next week."

"I can't believe you're taking your braids out, just 'cuz Kahlua did, Chuchie," I mutter. "You're such a copycat."

"What happened?" Chuchie stutters, then changes the subject, which is her favorite escape tactic. "If the Wacky Glue lasted this long on our hair, the metal letters will really stick to the suede fabric."

"You sure, Chuchie?" I ask casually.

"Sí. Estoy seguro."

"Okay, then let's roll with it," I say. In the sewing-supplies store, we get busy, grabbing a big bottle of the supa-gluey stuff, two bags of metal letters, and a bag of snap closures to secure the chokers.

"Did you get enough letter G's?" Do' Re Mi asks.

"Enough to start a Growl Power war!" I heckle back. Then I dial my Dad at the Toto in New York factory, to tell him we're on our way.

"Ciao, Daddy," I say, throwing him a kiss over the phone before I hang up. "We're lucky duckies he's gonna let us use the equipment at

the factory," I tell my crew, "'cuz I really didn't want to ask Mom to help us." I'm definitely satisfied with our escapade so far. "Mom's gonna be so psyched when she sees the chokers."

"How come she doesn't make Toto in New York accessories for the store?" Do' Re Mi asks.

"She only makes cheetah backpacks and stuff like that. She says it's easier to buy bags and jewelry than make them, 'cuz it's less manufacturing headaches," I explain. "But we're in this for more than headaches, girlitas. I have a feeling we're gonna be churning these chokers out by the baker's dozen!"

Dad supervises a staff of five at the Toto in New York . . . Fun in Diva Sizes factory, where all the clothes for Mom's store are cut and sewn, then dropped off to the *très* trendy boutique in Soho that my parents own.

"Cara, cara, and *cara!"* Dad says, kissing Do' Re Mi, Chuchie, and me on both cheeks. That's an Italian thing, you know what I'm saying? When Angie and Aqua come out of the bathroom, dad does the same thing to them. The

twins *really* like my Dad, 'cuz he's so much cooler than their stuffy pops. Cool as a fan, that's my dad.

Dad sets us up at the drafting table, where we lay out the suede fabric to cut it into strips for the chokers. *"Posso ayudarte?"* Dad asks me in Italian, our private language, but I don't want his help. I want to make these chokers with my crew.

"Dad—go do your work. We're chillin', *va bene?"* I say, mixing Italian and English together the way I always do when I'm talking to him.

"Chill then, *cara,"* Dad says, making fun of me.

He looks really tired lately, but I don't say anything about the bags under his eyes. I wish my parents didn't have to work so hard, and I can't wait till I can pay for everything, so they can just go to Stromboli, or Giglio, or any one of the cazillion beautiful island resorts in Italy that they love so much. I'm gonna buy them a house there, too, so they can retire when they're old. I'm gonna show people that I'm not so spoiled as they think.

Since Do' Re Mi is the most skilled among

us, she gets to cut the strips of suede. Angie, Aqua, Chuchie, and I use the T-square rulers to draw perfect lines for Do' Re Mi to cut along.

"How many strips did we get from a yard?" Chuchie asks after we've finished cutting up the yard of suede.

"Thirty-six strips, which we can cut in half to make seventy-two chokers," Do' Re Mi explains proudly. "We don't have to make all of them now, though."

"Awright!" I shriek. "We're in business!"

Next, we have to sew two suede strips together on Dad's industrial machine. Gracias, who has been a seamstress at the factory for ten years, sets us up at the machine, which is used for sewing leather, suede, and heavy coating fabrics like fake fur, which Mom uses a lot for fierce Toto in New York designs.

The gadget that intrigues Do' Re Mi most, though, is the machine used for applying the snap closures.

"Ouch!" I wince, as I try to clamp down on a snap I've placed over a strip of suede. Dad comes running over, and I get really annoyed at him.

"Va bene, va bene. Do it yourself," Dad says,

finally letting me have my way and leaving us alone.

The most fun we have is gluing the metal letters on the chokers.

I'm anxious to get my grubby little paws on our first "product." "It's not dry yet," protests Do' Re Mi, as I pick one up to try it on.

"Okay, okay," I say, getting impatient. Mom says that I'm too impatient, but I don't agree with her. If you want things to happen, you gotta move, you gotta groove, you know what I'm saying?

"Okay, *now* groove, Galleria," Do' Re Mi says, handing me one of the chokers.

"This is *so* dope," I exclaim, holding the cheetah choker in my hand like it's a baby or something. "Girlinas, we're ready for Freddy!"

Now I'm ready to talk to Dad, and I go running over to show him the chokers that we made all by ourselves, without his help.

"Que bella, cara!" he exclaims, and I think he really means it, even though Dad is down with whatever I do.

Dad insists that I wrap the Cheetah Girls chokers in tissue paper, then put them in a cheetah-print Toto in New York shopping bag. "You must always make a *bella* presentation when you want to sell something," he explains to me.

"Va bene, Dad," I giggle. I guess it won't kill me to accept the shopping bag and tissue papers.

We are all so amped by our first business venture that on the way home, I get another fabbie-poo idea. "Let's give our chokers a 'test run,'" I suggest to my crew. "Nobody knows us in Brooklyn, right? Why not try to sell a choker to one of the boutiques here?"

"I'm down," Do' Re Mi blurts out.

"That sounds good," Aqua seconds.

Chuchie just shrugs her shoulders and giggles as we walk down the block from Dad's factory to Fulton Street. The Toto in New York factory is only five blocks from the coolest shopping area in Brooklyn, known as Fort Greene, which is supposed to be like a black Soho or something. Kinda "boho," you know what I'm saying?

"How 'bout this one?" I turn and ask Do' Re Mi. We have stopped in front of a colorful boutique called Kumba, which has all these African caftans and safari-looking stuff in the window.

"I don't know. You think they'd go for it?"

Angie says. "It looks like the kinda stuff High Priestess Abala wears."

"For true," I say, "and she would look so much doper if she was wearing one of these!" I'm so excited by all this, I'm just dying to go in *anywhere* and see what they say.

"Está bien. Let's try it," Chuchie says, heaving a sigh.

The first thing I notice when we walk inside of Kumba is a really strong aroma. "What's that smell?" I whisper to Chuchie, who has the keenest nose for scents.

"Mija, it's just incense," Chuchie says, smiling. We stand looking around, kinda nervous, because everything looks really expensive. A dark man, wearing a turban on his head and a caftan piled with lots of beads, comes from behind a beaded divider.

"I'm Mr. Kumba. Can I help you?" he asks politely.

"Yes, sir, um, we're the Cheetah Girls, and we make chokers that we'd like to show you," I respond politely.

"Oh. Show me what you've got," Mr. Kumba says curiously. "What do you mean by 'Cheetah Girls?'"

"Oh, we're a singing group and, um, we do lots of other things," I try to explain.

"We go to Fashion Industries High School, too," Do' Re Mi says proudly. "I major in Fashion Design."

I guess she's trying to impress Mr. Kumba with the fact that we aren't just a bunch of kids, probably because everyone thinks she is so much younger than she really is.

Suddenly nervous, I pull the Cheetah Girls chokers out of the Toto in New York shopping bag, and lay them carefully on the glass display case. Glancing inside the case, I notice all sorts of African-looking beads made into necklaces, bracelets, and earrings. Aqua's right, this is the kind of stuff that High Priestess Abala would wear. Maybe after Mr. Kumba places an order, we can go bragging to her, and she'll come shopping here!

"What are these?" Mr. Kumba asks, holding up one of the chokers.

"They're, um, chokers," I explain calmly, but I can feel my face getting warm.

"They look like *dog collars,* if you ask me," Mr. Kumba retorts, then puts on his glasses to read the metal letters on the choker. 'Growl

Power'—that sounds like something for dogs. What is this—a joke? Some kind of novelty item?"

"No," I say, even though I don't know what he means by "novelty item." I'll have to ask Mom. Now I'm really starting to get ka-flooeyed, and I can hear my voice squeaking as I say, "They're chokers for *people.*"

Mr. Kumba heaves a deep sigh, then says, "Nobody is gonna wear these. Maybe a bunch of kids, but that's not my customer."

"Oh, okay," I say stuttering, then put the chokers back into the shopping bag as quick as I can, so we can do an abracadabra before I die of embarrassment.

"Thank you, for your time," Chuchie says sweetly, as we all make a mad dash for the door.

We're all real quiet on the way home. "I feel like I was just in a hot-air balloon flying over Oz, then someone let out the air," I mumble to Chuchie. We used to watch *The Wizard of Oz* together a kazillion times when we were kids.

"We're not in Oz, *para seguro,*" Chuchie moans back, resting her head on my shoulder as we head uptown on the subway. Do' Re Mi,

Aqua, and Angie get up to transfer to the West Side train.

"What do you call a mouse who eats at Mikki D's?" I yell to Aqua and Angie as they get off the train.

"I don't know, Galleria," Aqua says, looking kinda sad.

"Mikki Mouse," I say, smirking at my feeble joke. "Sleep tight, tonite."

"Thanks a lot, Galleria. We will!" Angie pipes up.

When they get off the train, I go right back to my sad face.

"What do grown-ups know, anyway?" Chuchie says, as I give her a hug good-bye.

"For true!" I agree, as she gets off at Prince Street to go home.

I ride uptown by myself. I reach into the shopping bag, and look at the Cheetah Girl chokers again. Fighting back the tears, I rub the smooth cheetah suede with my fingers.

I don't care what Mr. Bumbling Kumba says. These chokers are dope, even if I *am* at the end of my rope! After all, we can't all work that back-to-the-motherland look like he does in *his* store. But, God, please, get us a record deal before we end up homeless, selling broken-down chokers on the street!

Chapter 10

It's eight o'clock in the morning, and Dad has already left to go to work. Mom is almost ready to go to the store, because there is some drama. See, she designed all the bridal wear for L.A. rapper Tubby Rock's wedding party, but apparently the bride-to-be spent too much time at Aunt Kizzy's, eating barbecued baby back ribs!

"I can't believe Peta Rock went and gained ten pounds right before the wedding!" Mom says, sulking and spreading butter on her croissant.

I stand in the kitchen patiently, because I really need to talk to her, even though she's feeling ka-flooeyed. She was already sleeping when I got home last night. The truth is, I'm still gaspitating by what Mr. Kumba said about the Cheetah Girl chokers, and maybe he's right—who is gonna buy these things?

That's why I have to ask Mom—because I know if nothing else, she will tell me the truth. "What do you think?" I ask her with bated breath, showing off my choker.

"You look fierce," Mom says, looking up from the newspaper and glancing at me, then picking up her mochaccino latte and taking a sip.

I still don't move from the spot where I'm standing, and when Mom looks up again, I start motioning at my neck so she gets the drift.

"Darling, what am I supposed to be looking at?"

"Mom, the *choker*—I, we, made them yesterday," I insist, getting more nervous.

"What's it say? Oh, 'Growl Power'—ooh, that is too fierce," she says approvingly.

"Do you think people will wear them?" I ask her sheepishly.

"Well, I don't think grown-ups will wear them—God forbid they should get an original idea. They'd probably think it's a dog collar or something," Mom says, giggling.

She doesn't realize how crushed I am. Suddenly, I start sobbing, just like I used to do when I was little. I feel so silly willy, but I can't take any more rejection! Or maybe it's my hormones acting up.

Mom just sits there, until I tell her what happened at the Kumba boutique in Brooklyn last night. All of a sudden, she starts smiling, and asks, "Do you know why I opened the Toto in New York boutique?"

I'm not quite sure where she's going with this, but knowing Mom, she has a point to the joint. "Because you wanted to, right?" I respond.

"No—not at first. The only dream I had back then was to make diva-size clothes that would make skinny women pant with 'Gucci Envy.' So that's what I did. I designed a whole collection—and when I had about thirty designs or so, I made appointments with buyers at department stores."

Mom sips her mochaccino, her eyes sparkling. "Oh, I was so excited. I knew my clothes were fierce, and I thought the buyers would be *begging* me for orders. Do you know what happened?"

"No, Mom, what?" I ask, giggling now, because Mom sure knows how to drag out a story.

"Every single one of those buyers laughed me out of the store," Mom says, her eyes getting animated. "Not only didn't they buy *one* scraggly piece from my collection, but they told me that no 'large-size' woman would be caught *dead* in my clothes!"

"Really?" I ask, genuinely surprised. Mom never told me that happened to her!

"I was devastated beyond belief. I almost threw the clothes in the trash can after one appointment with a particularly shady buyer, I remember," she recalls, chuckling. "But I figured, I knew at least one large-size woman who *would* wear my clothes."

"Who was that?" I ask curiously.

"Me, of course," Mom says chuckling. "And if there was *one,* then there had to be *others*—they just didn't know it yet!"

"What do you mean?" I ask, puzzled.

"Well, sometimes people don't even know they want something until it's right before their eyes," Mom explains, nodding her head wisely.

Now I get her drift. It never occurred to me

that Mom's clothes were anything but fierce, and I can't believe that there were people who didn't think so back in the day!

"You gotta *make* people like your stuff, that's what you're saying?" I ask, feeling better already.

"*Exactement croissant,* darling," Mom says, speaking what she calls Poodle French. "Be prepared for a battle, though, at first. When I opened the doors of my boutique, it was so slow, I thought I was gonna lose my leopard bloomers! And believe me, there were plenty of people waiting for me to fail—talking behind my back, heckling outside the store. But eventually the divas found their way down the yellow brick road, and they've been clamoring at the door of Toto in New York ever since!"

"Thank you, Mom," I say, giving her a hug. And then I ask her what is really bothering me. "Are you gonna keep on being our manager, Mom?"

"Why, of course, Galleria—why wouldn't I?" Much to my relief, she looks surprised that I asked.

"Well, 'cuz it's causing so much drama . . .

and I know there's been trouble with the store . . ."

"Galleria," Mom stops me. "Darling, please— I always do what I want to do, don't I? Believe me, Toto in New York will survive and thrive. And someday, one day or another, I'm convinced that being the manager of the fabulous Cheetah Girls is gonna pay off—in full!"

"You really think so, Mom?"

"I know so," she says. "Def Duck may come through and quack, or it may not. But your dreams are gonna come true in the jiggy jungle, Galleria. Who knows— maybe you'll be the fashion queen of the Cheetah scene!"

I giggle with pleasure and relief. "Am I really that different from other girls, Mom?" I ask.

"I don't know, Galleria," Mom says seriously. "But I do know that you're special—if that's what you mean by different, then I guess so."

"I already got a few orders for the chokers in school," I tell her excitedly, forgetting my anxiety attack already.

"Really, darling?" Mom says smiling. "Do you need any help making them?"

"No, Mom, I *don't*!" I say, giggling, then pulling out the chokers we made last night. "We made these by ourselves. I didn't even let Dad stick his nimble fingers into our situation."

"All right, darling, don't get your bloomers in a bunch before lunch!"

Flinging my backpack on my shoulder, I kiss Mom on the forehead, then thank her for her advice. "We're gonna do what you said. We'll wear the chokers ourselves, till other peeps are panting like puppies for them!"

"Mm-hmm. I'm sure Toto will approve darling," Mom says, throwing me a kiss good-bye.

"Woof, there it is!" I giggle back, then run off to school.

On the way there, I'm thinking about my snap— that would make a dope song, I think— "Woof, There It Is!"

I whip out my Kitty Kat notebook, and start writing down a lyric. That's how I flow.

The Cheetah Girls may not have a record contract yet, and we may not have sold any chokers, either. But we're never gonna stop layin' down our global groove—not until the whole world comes pouncin' at our door! "Woof, There It Is!"

Woof, There It Is!

It takes five
To make the Cheetah Girls be,
Ah, yeah, can't you see
That they're rocking on a thing
Called the M.I.C.
The M.I.C., well that's a microphone
And when they rock it to the beat
It's rocked to the doggy bone.

Woof, there it is!
Woof, there it is!
Woof, there it is!

The Cheetah Girls Glossary

Always looking out: Representing. Watching your back.

As a matter of facto: It *really really* is true.

The bill: the lineup of performers for the evening or event.

Blacktress: Black movie star.

Boho: Black bohemian.

Bou bou fon fon: A bouffant hairstyle that's piled so high, it had to be done twice!

Cali: Los Angeles, California.

Cheetah-certified: When something is so "for true," you can take it to the bank, baby.

Cheetah-licious: Fierce, fiercer, fiercest!

The chillies: the creeps.

Coiffed: Hair that has been blow-dryed, blow-torched, and fussed-over at the beauty parlor!

Coinky-dinky: A coincidence.

Cracking face: Saying something stupid. Looking stupid.

Cruising altitude: When a plane has climbed

the distance it needs to fly the friendly skies until it reaches its destination.

Crustacean-looking slime: Something alien-like that pops out of noses or gets stuck in the corner of the mouth.

Déjà vu: A feeling that you've been somewhere before.

Exactement croissant: Poodle French for "That's right."

Fabbie-poo: beyond fabulous

Flexing fowl: Put your foot in your mouth.

Fowl like a nearsighted owl: Wack.

Flipping the script: Turning the tables, changing the subject.

Freaked it: Rocked the mic.

Fugly: Beyond ugly.

Goospitating: Shrieking inside. Getting squeamish about something.

Hooptie: a car

Kadoodling: Wasting precious time. Angling for something.

Kaflempt, Ka-flooeyed: *Really really* exasperated.

La La Land: Los Angeles, California

Let's do an abracadabra: Let's scram! Do a disappearing act.

Madrina: Godmother, but not to be confused with fairy godmother who pays for everything!

Manny-hanny: Manhattan

Milks it for points: When you act cheesy just to get attention.

Minnie-Mouse Minute: When time stands still for so long, you're ka-flooeyed to the max!

Okeydokey: A flim-flam situation.

On the dis tip: Kinda playing the dozens, or "snapping" to and fro.

On the d.l.: On the "down low," or sneak tip.

Op: Opportunity, which sometimes only knocks once!

Out-kadoodled: Out-foxed by a cheetah.

Paying the Boogie Man in full: When you're more scared than when a vampire jumps out of a coffin and runs after you with his bloody arm!

Rocked to the doggy bone: Performing to the max.

Scemo: Bozo. Pronounced like "shame-o."

Schemer: Finagler. Player.

Snaggled-tooth haggling: Bargaining someone down till you draw blood!

Stinkeroon: When something stinks.

Stop faking that you're not quaking: Stop pretending that you're not scared.

Supa-packed itinerary: Busy schedule.

Taking off points: Reading someone.

Thank gooseness: Thank goodness.

That's so radikkio: Don't try it, Miss Thingy. You know that's ridiculous!

That's the deal-io, yo: That's the way it is.

The Twilight Zone: A weird place where weird things are happening and time seems to stand still.

Venue: A location where acts will appear to perform.

A visit to freak city: Flipping out from fear.

Woof, there it is!: When you know you've rocked it to the doggy bone and you can step back and say, "How you like me now?"

Work your spots till they're dots!: Be your fiercest self until it's time to close the lid on the coffin.

It's Raining Benjamins

For my peeps John Moore
Whom I do adore
'Cuz he works the floor
Like a mad matador!
Toro, toro!

Chapter 1

Unless it's raining alley cats and Chihuahuas, everybody at Fashion Industries East High School hangs out in front of the school, blocking the whole sidewalk. It's a real mob scene most mornings before classes start. Sometimes *la gente*—peeps—can get kinda rowdy, too.

That's why *my* crew—Dorinda "Do' Re Mi" Rogers; Galleria "Bubbles" Garibaldi; and myself, of course, Chanel "Chuchie" Simmons—always meet *inside*, by the lockers.

Dorinda is already waiting there when I arrive, forty minutes before school starts. Most of us at Fashion Industries East—which is not to be confused with the *other* Fashion

Industries High, where the less *coolio* peeps go to school—come here by subway from other neighborhoods, and you have to allow for time, 'cuz the subways—well, you know how the subways can be. So if your train happens to come on time, you can get to school *real* early, *está bien?*

Dorinda is crouching with her back against a locker, happily sipping her Goofy Grape Juice. "Wazzup, *señorita?*" she yells when she sees me.

"*Nada*, that's what," I moan, swiping a sip from her pint-sized container—which I do almost every morning, and she never complains. "I wish they sold this stuff by *my* house."

"So *move*," Do' Re Mi shoots back, shrugging her shoulders. "Hey. Where's Galleria?"

"*Yo no sé*," I mumble. "I can't even get decent *café con leche* by my house. Not like the kind they sell near my Abuela Florita's."

"I remember her," Do' Re Mi says. "She's phat."

"She is not fat!" I say, misunderstanding.

"No, not fat—phat!" Do' corrects me, and we both crack up.

My Abuela (that's "grandma") Florita lives in "Dominican Land," better known as Washington Heights. It's kinda far *norte*—right before Manhattan turns into *El Bronx*.

"I'm going to be seeing my *abuela* on Saturday," I tell Dorinda. "It's Pucci's birthday."

My little brother's birthday is a very big deal around my house—mostly because it means our dad comes home to visit. I can't help being excited to see him, and neither can Pucci. He doesn't visit much, not since he left home for good five years ago.

See, he and Mom used to fight all the time—to the point where they needed a referee. They're both happier now. Mom's got her rich boyfriend, Mr. Tycoon, who lives in Paris, France.

And Dad's got his new girlfriend, Princess Pamela, who is *la dopa*, and like a second mother to me. She runs Princess Pamela's Psychic Parlor, right around the corner from my house. I go see her there, whenever I can get away without Mom knowing. Sometimes, I even see Dad there. And once in a while, I visit them at their apartment uptown. But it's *different* when Dad comes *home*. And with Abuela coming, too, it'll almost feel like we're a whole family again.

Anyway, Dad says he's gonna drive up to Abuela's early Saturday, and bring her with him to the party. Abuela doesn't take the subway by herself anymore. See, last year a guy tried to snatch her purse on the subway platform. Abuela reached in her purse for the can of mace she carries, but she spritzed the mugger with her bottle of *Santa Cría* cologne by mistake! *Gracias gooseness*, the mugger ran away anyway—probably because Abuela sounds really scary when she's cursing in Spanish!

"How old is Pucci gonna be?" Dorinda asks.

"Ten—and an even bigger pain in the pootbutt," I groan—looking straight at Kadeesha Ruffin, who has just walked up to a nearby locker and slammed it shut for no reason. Then, on top of it, she gives me a look like I'm a *hologramma*—you know, a ghost—before continuing on her way down the hall.

"She thinks she's cute. *Qué bobada*. What baloney," I mumble.

"She's just green with Gucci envy," Dorinda says, still sipping, and unfazed by the intrusion.

"Yeah, the Jolly Green Giant," I moan. Kadeesha is kinda tall—over six feet. I'm not about to start messing with her. But why's she got to mess with *me*? What did I ever do to her, *está bien?*

Most of *la gente* at Fashion Industries East are kinda cool, because they're into a lot of different things, and they even have jobs after school. My crew's claim to fame is that everybody knows we're part of a singing group—the Cheetah Girls—who are headed to the top. There are five of us—me, Do', Bubbles, and the fabulous Walker twins—Aquanette and Anginette—who were born and raised in Houston, Texas, and go to school uptown, at LaGuardia Performing Arts High.

Lately, *la gente* have been taking notice of our *adobo down* style—especially since the Cheetah Girls got flown out to Los Angeles to perform at Def Duck Records' New Talent Showcase! I still can't believe Def Duck *paid* for us to go to the City of Angels, where record company executives drive in limousines on the big, fat freeway of deals.

To tell you the truth, I was also happy to get *away* from my mom and my brother, Pucci, for a few days. They were both driving me crazy, more than usual. That week, I would have followed the Cheetah Girls anywhere, even right into the lion's den. Well, almost.

Anyway, ever since we got back, the whole school's been buzzing about us. A few people, especially Kadeesha, have shown definite signs of Cheetah envy!

Everyone wants to know if we got a record deal. It's frustrating to have to tell them we don't know yet. But it's the truth. The peeps at Def Duck said it might be a while before we heard anything. And it already seems like a *long* while, even though it's only been a few days.

"It's gonna be *tan coolio*—so cool—wearing our new Cheetah Girls chokers together," Dorinda says, ignoring Kadeesha. "That is, unless someone tries to put a leash on us!"

This whole Cheetah Girl choker thing happened faster than making Minute Rice. See, while we were out in L.A., Bubbles bought a cheetah-print suede collar for her dog, Toto. He is so cute—I wish I could have a little dog, too. But I guess I'm never gonna have one. Not if my mom has anything to say about it—which she does. She's allergic to dog hair, and even more allergic to getting dog hair off the couch and cleaning up puppy poo.

Anyway, the collar Bubbles bought Toto was *la dopa*, but it was way too big for him. So Bubbles gets the great idea to wear it herself! That's Galleria for you—when she gets an idea, she doesn't ask anybody's opinion, she just goes for it!

Bubbles wore it to school the next day, and some of the peeps here ate it up like puppies! Five or six people asked her where they could get one. That gave Galleria *another* idea—that the Cheetah Girls should make some money while we're waiting for Def Duck to call!

Well, why not? We all need duckets—especially me. I still owe my mom plenty from the time I maxed out her charge card. (What can I say? I'm a recovering shopaholic that already happened!)

Anyway, making and selling Cheetah chokers seemed like a good idea to the rest of us. We've had a couple of orders already—and we needed to make ourselves chokers, too, so we could be walking advertisements.

We went to the factory in Brooklyn where

Bubbles's dad makes all the clothes for her mom's boutique, Toto in New York . . . Fun in Diva Sizes. Bubbles's mom and dad are my godparents—my *madrino* and *madrina*—and there's nothing they won't do to help us Cheetah Girls. *Madrina*—Ms. Dorothea, as the twins call her—is even our manager!

Anyway, we made some Cheetah Girls chokers out of suede strips, then glued silver metal letters on them that say GROWL POWER, to represent our kinda flava. So now we have these *adobo down* chokers. That is, Bubbles has them. But where is she? Homeroom starts in fifteen minutes, and we've got to find our customers before that!

As you can probably tell, I'm kinda anxious about these chokers. See, two students—Derek Hambone and LaRonda Jones—have already put in orders, and we've got to deliver them first thing today, *está bien?* I mean, I'm counting on this money so I can pay back my mom and be free again!

"There's Galleria," mumbles Dorinda, catching sight of Bubbles's head of wild-and-woolly hair coming our way.

"Finally!" I say, relieved.

Galleria is so *occupada,* writing in that notebook of hers, that she almost walks smack into a guy in the hallway! Ever since seventh grade, Bubbles has been writing in her Kitty Kat notebooks. She keeps them stashed in her bedroom, the way Pucci stashes Whacky Babies stuffed animals—like they're *muy preciosas*—very precious—in the jiggy jungle!

It's not like I don't already know Bubbles's secrets. And anyway, most of the time she's just writing another song for our group—in case we ever get to make a record. Even so, Bubbles never lets anyone see the words to a new song until *she* thinks it's finished.

That doesn't stop me, of course, from trying to snatch the spotted notebook from Bubbles any way I can. I've forgotten all about the chokers, 'cuz nothing's more *la dopa* than Bubbles's songs!

"Chuchie, lemme finish!" Bubbles screams at me, giving me a whack with her notebook. "I'm trying to come up with more songs, 'cuz I know Def Duck is gonna take a dip in the players' pond and let us cut a demo, you know what I'm saying?"

"Word. I heard that," Do' Re Mi chimes in,

brushing dust off her jumper (our school is kinda falling down all over the place, and there's plaster dust all over everything, including the lockers).

Dorinda *always* agrees with Bubbles. It annoys me sometimes—'cuz *I* know that when Bubbles and I disagree, I'm right at least half the time.

I hope Bubbles is right on this one, though. She thinks we are going to get a record deal *para seguro*—for sure—because we were *la dopa* at the showcase in Los Angeles.

I'm not so sure. Performing in a showcase and getting a record deal are two different things. But like I say, I hope I'm wrong, and I guess I must be, 'cuz Galleria's mom agrees with her, and she's almost always right! *Madrina* says all we have to do now is sit back and "wait for the bait."

Bubbles is so talented—she always gets *la dopa* ideas for songs. But lately, I've been thinking that *I* probably could write songs, too, if she would just give me a chance.

"What's the new song called—or is *that* a secret, too?" I whine, still trying to get a peek at the Kitty Kat notebook. Then I start chanting a little rhyme Bubbles made up. "Kitty Kat, Kitty Kat, show me where the money's at!"

"This song is called, 'Woof, There It Is!'" Bubbles says proudly. "And you can see it when it's done!" Then she snaps her Kitty Kat notebook shut and shoves it into her backpack, without even letting us take a peek.

"Oooh, that's a cute title!" I say.

Gloating on her skills, Bubbles gets puffed up like Rice Krispies and says, "I got the idea for the song after I showed Mom the chokers. She said they looked like dog collars—and that grown-ups wouldn't wear them!"

"Where *are* the chokers?" I ask, panicking because I don't see the Toto in New York shopping bag Bubbles put the chokers in at the factory.

"Got 'em right here in this pouch," Bubbles says, patting the tummy of her cheetah backpack. She unzips it again, and pulls out a couple of the chokers. "Wait till Derek sees his." She giggles, stretching out the leather strip to reveal the silver metal letters that spell SCEMO. (It's pronounced "shay-mo.")

"*Scemo*—that means idiot in Italian, right?" Dorinda asks. But Bubbles has already told her a million times, so she knows. See, Galleria's dad is Italian—real Italian, born in Italy!—so she knows a lot of words in that language—even the bad words.

"Don't you think Derek is gonna go off when he finds out what *scemo* means in English?" I ask. "You know what I'm saying, 'cuz he may not be playing."

"He's too big a *scemo* to find out that he *is* one!" Bubbles says, then stretches her hand out for us to do the Cheetah Girls handshake with her. I don't feel good about it, but I do it anyway.

But I don't really care about Derek Hambone. I just wanna know what *Madrina* thought of the chokers. "Was *Madrina* surprised we made them without her help?" I ask. It's not that my godmother isn't really supportive of us and the things we do—except when I ran up Mom's charge card, of course—but sometimes she does *too* much for us.

"You know she ain't saying, but I think she was really proud of us," Bubbles says.

"I heard that," Do' Re Mi says, nodding her little beanie head to her own beat.

"As a matter of facto, she looked at the

chokers and said they're off the cheetah meter, *bay-beeee!*" Bubbles screeches.

"*Madrina* thinks we can sell them?" I ask.

"Yup. Forget what Mr. Kumba-bumba-baloney said." Bubbles laughs, making fun of the name of the owner of the Kumba Boutique in Brooklyn, where we went last night to try and sell our chokers.

I guess it was a stupid idea, because Mr. Kumba thought they looked like dog collars, and that nobody would wear them. I was so glad to get out of the Kumba Boutique anyway, I remember, scrunching up my nose. "*Lo odio*—that strawberry incense he was burning—yuck!" I remind my crew.

"It smelled like a psychedelic voodoo shack or something," Dorinda remembers, laughing.

I laugh, too, and scrunch up my nose again, making a funny face like I smell something bad. That's when I really *do* smell something—and it's really, *really* stinky poo.

Bubbles says I'm prissy, but I'm not. I just don't like odors. My nose is *muy sensitiva*, and I can smell things that other people can't—just like dogs do. (I think that's why I love dogs so much—because we are a lot alike.) And *speaking of dogs . . .*

"Bubbles, do you smell doggy poo?" I ask sheepishly.

"I smell it, too . . . oh, no—don't tell me!" Bubbles looks down at her shoes, and discovers the root of the problem. "I can't believe it! I'm so *over* this!"

"Woof, there it is," Dorinda says, smirking.

I crack up, and Bubbles throws me an annoyed look. "I *hate* this city," she says. "Nobody cleans up after their dog except me, and I'm the one who winds up stepping in it!"

I try to console her by saying "We didn't see one pile of doggy poo the whole time we were in Cali."

"No, we didn't," Bubbles says wistfully. "You got that right."

"It's even worse in my neighborhood than it is here," Do' Re Mi moans. Do' lives way uptown, and her neighborhood is like *el barrio*, where Abuela lives. The people there have a lot of big, mean dogs, with ferocious fangs for protection—and just for stylin'. And those kinda dogs leave some big, stinky land mines on the sidewalk.

"I'll get it off for you, Bubbles," I volunteer. (That'll show her I'm not squeamish like she says I am.) "Come on—before anybody sees it."

"You mean, *smells* it!" Dorinda corrects me. She and I crack up, but Galleria isn't laughing. She walks on her tiptoes all the way to the bathroom, holding her nose. I walk on my tiptoes, too, like I'm wearing pointshoes—my ballet slippers.

A few people walk by, heckling at Galleria. "Sashay, parlay!" they call out, imitating her walk. Bubbles sticks her tongue out at them like she doesn't care, but I know she's goospitating inside. I know I would be—*Yo sé!*

Chapter 2

The bathroom at Fashion Industries East High is right out of a prison movie—kinda dark and creepy-looking. I make Bubbles take off her Mary Jane shoes, then throw both of them in the sink and turn on the faucet.

Nothing comes out of it. "Oh, come on," I moan. The faucets at our school are broken more than half the time. At last, a little water spurts out—then suddenly, it *gushes* out, flooding the sink, and totally soaking Galleria's shoes!

"Chuchie!" Bubbles yells, running to turn off the faucet. The water is splashing everywhere now—all over the floor, and *us*.

All of a sudden, Kadeesha Ruffin flings open the bathroom door and stands there with her crew. "What's up, y'all—is it laundry day?" she asks. Her crew starts whooping it up and high-fiving each other.

I don't say anything, because Kadeesha is kinda nasty and I'm scared of her. Bubbles just ignores her while Dorinda—politely—explains the situation.

"Don't tell me y'all have never stepped in poop— So here's the scoop: back off and get out of our loop. Just leave us alone," she says. *Vaya*, go, Do' Re Mi! Her snaps are as good as Bubbles's. *Te juro*. I swear.

"Awright, shortie," Kadeesha says. She snaps her gum really loud, then marches out the bathroom without using the sink. Her crew follow behind her, still grinning, even though they're not laughing out loud anymore.

Galleria is staring at her soaked shoes, shaking her head like she's about to cry. "*Now* what do you expect me to do, Miss Cuchifrita Ballerina?" she challenges me. "Plié down the hallways all day without shoes?"

Meanwhile, I'm busy yanking brown paper towelettes from the dispenser and trying to blot her shoes dry. The truth is, I feel stupid, like a *babosa*.

Dorinda looks at the dripping shoes, and suggests hopefully, "We could put paper towels in the bottoms."

"No, *olvídate!*" I say, suddenly bursting into tears. "Just forget wearing them, okay? I'm a ding-a-ling, all right? Now just put them on the paper towels."

I can't believe I yelled at Bubbles. Suddenly I realize that it's not just the wet shoes that are bothering me. There's something else . . . something that was *annoyándome* before we went out to L.A. In all the excitement about the New Talent Showcase and the chokers, I'd forgotten all about it. Well, I *tried* to forget it, anyway, and now, that Pucci's birthday was almost here . . .

"Chuchie, what's the matter with you?" Bubbles blurts out when I can't stop crying.

"Nada," I whine. Then I take out my Yves Saint Bernard perfume spray. I spritz it in her shoes, then spritz the air for good measure. "You know how I am about stinky-poos!"

"Yeah—but what's *really* wrong?" Bubbles insists, waving away the mist of my perfume (which she hates). "You're not crying over my shoes, *girlita*, so don't lie or you'll fry." It's unbelievable how Bubbles knows me inside and out!

All of a sudden, I blurt out the truth. "Saturday is Pucci's birthday, and my mom hasn't said one thing about buying him a Chihuahua like she promised!"

"Chuchie," Bubbles says, instantly putting her arm around me. "I didn't know you were so upset about that."

"You *know* how much I want a dog. I mean for Pucci," I confess. "Remember when we were at *Madrina*'s store, and my mom said she would think about getting Pucci a Chihuahua for his birthday?"

"Yeah, I remember—but I guess *she* doesn't," Bubbles says, in that tone she gets when she's trying to push me to do something. "You'd better ask her yourself."

"I don't want to," I shoot back, wiping Bubbles's shoes furiously with the paper towels. Little wet balls of paper are now decorating her shoes.

"Oh, I get it, you're *scared* to ask her, because you haven't paid back all the money you owe her," Bubbles says.

I can't wait until I pay back all the money I owe my mother for charging up her credit cards—then I'm gonna seal Bubbles's lips closed with Wacky Glue! "So?" I hiss at her. "You'd be afraid, too."

"You know it, so don't blow it," Galleria admits. She gives me a little squeeze. "I know how much you've always wanted a dog—and you *know* that little Chihuahua would be *your* dog, 'cuz no way is Pucci gonna take care of it."

"Wait a minute," Do' Re Mi steps in. "What if you offer to pay for *part* of the Chihuahua?"

"What happened? How am I gonna pay for anything?" I ask. "I got *nada* for *nada*."

We both look at Do' Re Mi like she's cuckoo, but she continues: "We're gonna sell these Cheetah Girls chokers we've made, *ri-ight*?"

"Yeah," Galleria chimes in. "But so far, we only got orders from Derek and LaRonda. One plus one makes *two*."

"Yeah, but if the *three* of us go around all week taking orders for Cheetah Girls chokers, we can get Chanel enough money so she can go to her mom and say she'll put in thirty dollars to help buy the dog for Pucci's birthday."

Do' Re Mi looks to Bubbles for approval. "I

mean, we've got all week to sell them, *ri-ight?* And they're dope, *ri-ight?*"

Bubbles thinks hard for a minute. Then she looks at the both of us, wild-eyed, and asks, "If all three of us take orders, how many of these you think we can sell?"

"I don't know—a lot, *ri-ight?*" I offer, smiling. We all give each other the Cheetah Girls handshake, and then get busy helping Bubbles put her wet shoes back on. I feel so much better now that I've told Bubbles and Dorinda the truth about what's been on my mind. They are really my crew, *es la verdad*.

"It's our dime—and choker time," Bubbles says, handing over Cheetah Girls chokers for us to wear. Then she puts one on herself. The three of us just stand there, gazing in the dirty mirror at our cheetah-fied reflections.

"That does look so *money, ri-ight*!" Bubbles says, satisfied.

"*Sí, señorita,*" I say with a grin. "I can't wait to show Abuela Florita what we're doing. I'll bet you she'll like our chokers." I turn to Dorinda and pinch her cheeks. "Abuela would love you, too—because she just *loves* dimples."

"Well, it's time to turn some Cheetah Girl

chokers into duckets," Bubbles says, tickling our fingers as we do the Cheetah Girls handshake one more time. "Homeroom's about to jump off—we'd better get shaking if we want to sell some of these while they're still baking."

"I know what *you're* going to buy with your choker money, *mamacita,*" I tease Bubbles as we leave the bathroom and start running down the hall.

"What?"

"A new pair of shoes!"

Chapter 3

Both Bubbles and I major in fashion merchandising, while Dorinda majors in fashion design. Our homeroom classes are in Building C, on the other end of the second floor. When we get there, there are still fifteen minutes till homeroom starts. We hang in the hallway till the last minute, hoping to run into Derek Ulysses Hambone—"Mr. DUH"—and give him his choker.

"Maybe Mackerel will take the bait, too," I say excitedly. "Let's hook him on a choker!"

"Just don't get caught in his trap," giggles Bubbles.

Mackerel Johnson is Derek Hambone's best friend. He has a crush on me—*un coco* that is never gonna happen, because he doesn't know that I'm going to meet *Krusher*.

Krusher, in case you live on Mars and have never heard of him, is a *tan coolio* singer, with the brain, heart, and courage to live his wildest dreams in the jiggy jungle. It doesn't matter that *I* didn't win the 900-KRUSHER contest, which would have taken me on a trip to Miami for a date with my favorite *papi chulo*—I'll find another way to meet him, you just wait and see!

"If Mackerel didn't bounce around like a jumping bean, would you go out with him?" Bubbles asks, smirking at me. She doesn't believe that my heart belongs to Krusher, but I won't settle for less, *está bien?*

"Oh, word, I've got a dope idea," Dorinda suddenly says, then whips out a book from her cheetah backpack and hands it to me. "Check this out, Chanel," she says, her eyes twinkling. "I can't believe I didn't think of this when we were talking about it before!"

"What is it, Do'?" I ask, curious.

"I've been reading about these African pygmy hedgehogs," she says.

I flip through the book, and I can't believe what I'm seeing. These pygmy creatures look sooo cute—brownish and small, with sticky spiny things on their backs. "*Qué monos!*" I coo.

"See, I was thinking maybe you could get Pucci one of *these* for his birthday instead of a dog! They don't shed, so your mother won't have to clean its hairs off the sofa—and you don't have to walk them, like with a dog. I think they're cheaper than a Chihuahua, too—and look how cute!"

"How do I get one, Dorinda? Do I have to go to Africa?"

"No, they have special pet stores here that buy them from breeders in New Zealand," Dorinda explains. "See, I've been kinda hoping Mrs. Bosco will let me get one for my brother Topwe, because he *really* wants a pet."

I think *Dorinda*'s the one pining for a pet, 'cuz that's how it is in *my* house. It's supposed to be for Pucci, but *I'm* the one who's all upset he isn't getting a pet for his birthday.

"Why do they call them hogs?" I ask, my curiosity all worked up. "They look more like porcupines."

"I guess 'cuz they're always looking for food or something," Dorinda guesses, shrugging her shoulders.

"Always looking for food, huh?" That sounds more like Dorinda's stepbrothers and stepsisters—especially Topwe. At Dorinda's adoption party Topwe ate the whole tray of candied yams topped with baked marshmallows before I even got a *whiff* of one!

Pobrecita, Dorinda. Poor thing . . . How is her family gonna find room for a pet, with thirteen people squeezed into a tiny apartment? She's even less likely to get a pet than *I* am!

"Lemme see that book," Bubbles asks curiously. She looks over our shoulders as we flip through the pages, oohing and aahing at the cute, furry, funny creatures. Most of the pictures show the hedgehogs crouched under woodpiles—obviously looking for their next meal.

I'm thinking Dorinda might be right . . . Maybe I *can* talk Mom into letting me get one of these for Pucci's birthday. I'll bet Mom wouldn't be allergic to those spines—they'd just stick her when she gets nasty, that's all!

"Maybe you can ask your mom to buy one for Pucci," Dorinda asks.

"Yo no sé," I mumble, lapsing into Spanish unconsciously. I put my hand around my

choker, and feel the metal letters which spell GROWL POWER. I need all the growl power I can muster up to ask Mami for anything. These days, it seems like all we do is fight—*la guerra Dominicana, está bien?* Heaving a sigh, I finger the letters on my choker again, and say proudly to Bubbles, "See, I told you this Wacky Glue was the move, *está bien?* It holds the letters on real well."

"You were right—it's the move," Bubbles says, nodding absentmindedly. She is still glued to the book, and *muy fascinada* with the pygmy pets.

At last, I see Derek and Mackerel bopping down the hallway in our direction. "Red Snapper Alert," I whisper softly, nudging Bubbles's arm.

She waves at Derek from down the hall, motioning for him to come over to us. Usually, we just ignore Derek (whom we call Red Snapper behind his back), but today we're happy to see him . . . and even Mackerel.

"Mr. Hambone, here you go. You are the proud owner of a Cheetah Girls choker," Bubbles says, handing him the choker, which we made extra wide just for him.

Derek examines the merchandise with a smile on his face, and fingers the shiny silver metal letters that spell SCEMO. "Oh, *that's* how you spell that word you're always calling me. Shame on *you*, Cheetah Girl. I dig it," Derek says, flashing his gold-toothed smile. (A lot of *la gente* where Abuela lives have gold teeth. *Cuatro yuks!*)

"Do you really like it?" I ask Derek proudly.

"Oh, yeah," he says, nodding his head. "You Cheetah Girls got skills, no doubt."

"No doubt on that tip," Mackerel says, nodding along, trying to get me to look at him—but it's too early in the morning for me to look at *his* snaggletooth smile.

We stand there waiting for Derek to whip out the duckets. Finally he gets the hint.

"Word, I guess it's time to dole out the duckets," he says, laughing and reaching into his deep-sea pockets.

We wait patiently as the Red Snapper retrieves a ten-dollar bill and hands it to Bubbles.

Wait a minute—I thought Bubbles told him the chokers cost *twenty* dollars!

"Did you get amnesia or something?"

Bubbles asks Derek on the *sarcástico* tip. "We said twenty dollars, my brutha."

"Yeah, well, we heard you was charging LaRonda ten dollars, *my sista*," Derek retorts, slapping Mackerel a high five.

Derek *always* has good comeback lines. I think that's why Bubbles doesn't like him—because he can snap better than she can, and Bubbles thinks she's the best—*la mejor*.

"Can't blame a Cheetah Girl for trying to get more 'pounce for the ounce,' now can you, Derek?" Bubbles snaps back, with a smirk on her face that says she's satisfied with *her* comeback line.

"No, but I hope you don't mind that the 'Red Snapper' is always gonna be 'off the hook!'" Derek says, heckling and slapping Mackerel a high five, like he is *supa*-satisfied with *his* snap.

How'd he know we call him the Red Snapper? Uh-oh. Somebody probably told him. Fashion Industries East peeps are like *telenovelas*, it seems—there is always some "drama" to watch.

"No, we don't mind, Derek—especially if you come back and buy another choker," I throw in, giggling. Bubbles doesn't always have to get the last word. Then—even though it kills me—I blurt out, "You know, Mackerel, *you* would look *tan coolio* with a choker, too!"

"Is that right?" he says, perking up and grinning ear to ear.

Oh, no! I don't want to see his *vampira* teeth—they're so crooked and pointy, they make me cringe!

Luckily, Dorinda steps up to the snap plate and says, "You two try to roll like you're the dynamic duo, right? Well, do it, duo! Buy another choker, joker!"

"*Ayiight.* I'll take one of them, too," Mackerel says—quietly, because he's kinda shy. That's when I notice that Mackerel's eyebrows are kinda arched high—just like High Priestess Abala Shaballa Cuckoo or whatever her name is. (She is the girlfriend of Aqua and Angie's father. We went over to the twins' apartment before we flew out to Los Angeles, and we had to drink this nasty "good luck" witches' brew she cooked up.)

Maybe Mackerel is a *vampira*, too, like her. You never know how *la gente* are getting around these days—on broomsticks or the bus, *está bien?*

Mackerel gives Bubbles a five-dollar bill, then fishes around for more money out of his pocket.

"I got your back, Mack," Derek says, diving into his deep-sea pockets for more duckets. "Here you go, Cheetah Girl," he says, handing it to Galleria. Then he moves a little closer to her. "Maybe y'all wanna come to the fashion show at Times Square Tabernacle Church on Tuesday night. Tickets are ten dollars. It's for a good cause, and you'll get to see how a brutha works the runway, you know?"

"Maybe," Bubbles says, giving Dorinda and me a look, like, "We've got bigger fish to fry first." "We'll let you know, though, if we're gonna go with your flow, you know? But in the meantime, you know where to find *us*, if you need more product." She runs a finger slowly up between his choker and his neck, and Mr. DUH breaks into a goofy grin.

"Yeah, I'll look you up in the jiggy jungle!" he says, winking at Bubbles. "I gotta bounce—I've gotta go right now for a fitting. I'll check you by lunchtime, though."

"We'll save you some noodles. Toodles!" Bubbles says, waving behind her as the two of them go off, heckling like hyenas.

"He can heckle all he wants," Bubbles huffs, "'cuz we are about to get *paid*. We got *chokers*. What's *he* got to sell—*jokes*?"

"Word!" Do' Re Mi chuckles.

"What *boca grande* told Derek that we call him Red Snapper behind his back?" I ask, frowning.

"Probably that Kadeesha. They play basketball together sometimes. Can't blame her. She's probably trying to get Derek to ask her out. He's tall enough for her, right?" smirks Bubbles.

"What happened?" I chuckle, then I get my mind back on our business at hand. Turning to Dorinda, I say, "So listen. LaRonda's in my geography class. I can give her the choker and collect the duckets for us."

"Bet, *mamacita*. Better you, Do', than Miss Cuchifrita—she'd probably run off to some pygmy pet shops before we go to lunch," Bubbles says. "And you'd better check out Oakland on the map today!"

Bubbles *would* bring up the little "boo-boo" I

made in California. While we were backstage, getting ready for our showcase, I started talking to one of the other groups who were performing—CMG, the Cash Money Girls—and they said they were from Oakland. Me with my *boca grande,* I asked, "Where it that?"

How was I supposed to know Oakland is in California? I mean, I'm representing the East Coast, *está bien?*

"I bet *you* didn't know where it was either," I shoot back in protest.

"Yeah, well, I sure wouldn't have let Miss Abrahamma Lincoln in on that tip, that's all I'm saying," Bubbles says with a grin, then waves her hand in my face.

"I wonder which one of *them* writes the raps for their songs," I say, changing the subject. Bubbles has got me annoyed now, and I figure it's as good a time as any to bring up my new pet peeve. "Maybe they write them *together*?"

"Why?" Bubbles asks, smirking.

"*Porqué*—because—I don't know. Maybe *we* could write songs together," I blurt out.

There. I said it. Why *can't* I write songs for the Cheetah Girls, too? How come Bubbles is the only one who gets to write songs?

"We *who*?" Bubbles asks, like she doesn't get what I'm talking about.

"*Me* and *you, está bien?*"

"Chuchie . . . maybe you should stick with what you do best—"

"What happened? How do you know what I do best?" I ask, getting flustered.

"Chuchie, the bell's gonna ring for homeroom. And then we have to walk to first period before I can take off these wet shoes." Bubbles is showing me how exasperated she is. But I know it's just a way for her to blow me off. She doesn't want to talk about letting me write songs with her.

"One thing you did really well—taking doggy poo off my shoe," Bubbles snaps, putting me in my place. "Now I'm walking around like Flipper!" Bubbles starts walking to her desk, waddling like she's got fins on her feet. Some peeps look up like she's a little cuckoo, but I'm used to that. It's not like we're walking around unnoticed with all the cheetah-licious outfits we wear.

"So what? It's not my fault the faucets in the bathroom are older than the Dominican Day Parade!" I call after her.

"Can we stop talking about it now, please?" she says, sitting down and opening up her cheetah backpack. "By the time we sell these chokers, it'll be time for a markdown sale or something!" she mumbles, not looking at me.

"*Está bien,*" I say, giving in. I never win fights with Bubbles. She *always* has the last word. Why am I even worrying about writing songs, anyway? We don't even have a record deal! We'll be lucky if we don't end up headlining karaoke clubs and singing "Wanna-be Stars in the Jiggy Jungle" for the rest of our lives!

Chapter 4

Bubbles and I are sitting in homeroom class, turning our heads really slow, so everyone can check out our chokers—especially Keisha Jackson.

I'll never forget what Keisha did on the first day of the semester: our homeroom teacher, Mr. Drezform, asked the class if any of us spoke another language besides English. A few students raised their hands—including me and Bubbles, of course.

Keisha cut her eyes at us, like we were telling fib-eronis or something. Then, after class, she had the nerve to come up to Bubbles and ask her if she *really* spoke Italian. So now I'm not feeling Miss Keisha, *está bien?*

Luckily, a few students smile at me as I crane my neck at them. I smile back, showing off the choker. Then I turn to my right and say hi to Daisy Duarte, who is supa-chili—and also Dominican, like me.

"*Ay, qué bonita!* Your choker is so cute!" she exclaims, checking out the "product."

"My crew and I make them," I say proudly. "Support a Cheetah Girl—come on, buy one, Daisy!" I egg her on, because we're really cool like that with each other.

"How much?" Daisy asks, amused to the max.

For a second I hesitate. Then I realize, Bubbles has already gotten busted once for pricehiking—by Derek Hambone, no less. So I figure we'd better chill, and I blurt out, "Ten dollars. *Está poco,* okay?"

"*Está bien,*" Daisy says, her eyes lighting up.

I motion to Bubbles, who whips out a Cheetah Girls choker from her backpack and hands it to me. Since it's my sale, I pass the choker to Daisy.

Daisy looks as happy as my mom does at a garage sale. Her eyes are glistening, like she knows she's gotten a really good bargain, *está bien?* Daisy forks over ten dollars with pleasure, then snaps the choker onto her neck like it's a trophy.

"How does it look?" she asks me, pushing her long, wavy hair behind her shoulders to show off the choker.

"*La dopa*—and fresh as a Daisy!" I respond proudly, then hurriedly fold the crisp ten-dollar bill into my cheetah wallet. I stuff the wallet into my backpack before Mr. Drezform takes attendance.

"Talk to you later!" I whisper, pinching Bubbles under the chair. I feel so much better already!

I guess it was kinda hard, adjusting to being back in school after our dream trip to La La Land. We got to lie in a pool, perform for the bigwigs—and I even met this publicity executive from Def Duck Records at the showcase. He said that I reminded him of Kahlua Alexander, their biggest artist!

I am lost in my own *Telemundo* channel, when I hear Mr. Drezform call my name *loudly*. Bubbles pokes me really hard.

"Here!" I yell, then sit back in my chair and take out the pygmy hedgehog book. I wonder if the little hoglets only make tiny poopoos in the kitty litter box. Otherwise, you can forget it—*olvídate, está bien?* Mom is even worse about odors than I am—unless they're coming out of very expensive perfume bottles!

When attendance is over, I jump up because I have to go to the bathroom before first period. I smile at Daisy and say good-bye, then tell Bubbles I'll meet her in math class.

As soon as the bell rings, I get up to make a mad dash out the classroom door. But all of a sudden, I hear Keisha Jackson yelling at Bubbles.

"Yo, Galleria, I think you dropped something," Keisha says with a smirk, handing her—gasp—the silver letter "L" from Bubbles's Cheetah Girl choker!

Ay, Dios mío! I think I'm going to faint! Quickly, I put my hand around my neck. *Gracias gooseness*—thank goodness—I still have all my letters.

Bubbles snatches the silver letter from Keisha's hand and puts it in her pocket, like it's no biggie—but I know she is *goospitating*.

"Galleria, you know what? It doesn't look too bad without the 'L'—'Grow Power!' I like it!" Keisha says, heckling. Then she says, in a real loud voice, "I heard you and Chanel tell Daisy that *you* made the chokers?"

I am so humiliated, I wish I could do an abracadabra on the spot and disappear! "Yes, *we* made them," Bubbles whimpers. Her face has turned five shades of my favorite color—red.

"Maybe you'd better tell Daisy, before hers falls apart next period," Keisha says. Sucking her teeth, she walks off, like she's a designer herself or something. Come on—she majors in fashion merchandising, just like we do. *Qué bobada*. Phony baloney!

I stand next to Bubbles, shifting back and forth on my feet because I have to go to the bathroom really bad. But I'm not moving until Bubbles does. "I guess that Wacky Glue went wacky, Chuchie," Bubbles says, sucking her teeth.

"What happened?" I stammer. "Don't blame it on me!" We stand there frozen, contemplating whether we should say anything to Daisy. I can tell we are both thinking the same thing—*Run for the hills with the bills!*

A few of the students look at us while they're pushing their way out of class, but we don't move.

"Should I tell Daisy?" I finally ask.

"Nah. Hers is probably fine," Bubbles says. "But we'd better check with Do' Re Mi before she gives LaRonda her choker!" Dorinda's homeroom is just down the hall.

When we get outside into the hallway, I suddenly feel dizzy. I lean against the corridor wall because I feel like I'm going to faint. "Bubbles," I mumble, "what are we gonna do?"

When I hear Daisy's shrill voice calling my name, I realize the curtain is about to come down on our little *charada*. One look at Daisy's face, and I definitely know our off-Broadway production is closed for renovations until further notice!

"Um, Chanel, I think there is a problem with my choker," Daisy says apologetically, handing it to me. "The snaps popped off—I'm sorry, but I couldn't find them—I don't know where they fell. This thing just came off my neck. I didn't pull on it or anything!"

"*Está bien,* Daisy, no *te preocupas,*" I say in Spanish, because I don't want everybody to hear about our catastrophe! "Don't worry about it."

"Can you give me my ten dollars back, please?" Daisy asks me nicely.

"Oh, sure," I say, wincing. I scrounge around in my cheetah backpack for my cheetah wallet. I'm so nervous that my keys, my books, and all my other junk fall out of my backpack! The crowds going both ways through the hall start kicking my stuff all over the place!

"It's right there," Daisy says, trying to be helpful and pointing to my wallet, which is under the only notebook that hasn't fallen out of my backpack.

"Ooh, you're right," I say, giggling nervously. "Here. I'm sorry. I'll make you another one."

"Oh, that's okay," she says. She gives me a smile and shrugs. "Sorry. They're cute, though. See you later." And she turns and leaves, in a big hurry to get out of that embarrassing situation.

Daisy will probably *never* buy anything from me as long as I live. I swear, *Te juro*. It's only right, after all. And she'll probably tell everybody from here to the *barrio* that the Cheetah Girls are not ready for prime time—just broken-down cubs trying to get some grub!

I look pleadingly at Bubbles, but she gives me a look like she's gonna wring my neck.

After Daisy leaves, she hisses, "You were the one who said the Wacky Glue would be strong enough to hold the letters. Obviously it isn't."

Stammering, I point out, "Yeah, but that's not why the snap closures came undone in the back, *está bien?* It's not *all* my fault."

"Yeah, well, obviously, we didn't know how to work the snap machine either," Galleria admits, softening.

Fighting the tears welling up inside, I take a deep breath, then hightail it with Bubbles to find Do' Re Mi before she goes to her next class and gives LaRonda the soon-to-be-broken-down choker.

When I see Do' Re Mi walking toward *us,* with a look on her face like she got hit with something, I know it's too late.

"I don't know what happened," she says, shaking her head, embarrassed. "The letters came off LaRonda's choker! I had to give her back the ten dollars." Do' Re Mi hands Bubbles the choker, like it's a squashed mouse. "We couldn't find all the letters that came off, either."

"I know," I say, feeling my breath leave my body like I'm in a seance.

"How did you know?" Do' Re Mi asks, puzzled.

"Look at this one," I huff. I pull the choker I sold to Daisy out of my jacket pocket. "The snaps came off this one, *and* the letters came off Bubbles's choker!"

"Word? What are we gonna do, Galleria?" Do' Re Mi whines, rolling her eyes to the ceiling. I know exactly what she's thinking before she even says it. "If Derek's choker starts to fall apart, we are burnt toast!"

"I know—but let's just go with the flow," Bubbles says, trying to act *coolio*. "Obviously, the Wacky Glue had a wack attack."

"Don't blame it on Chanel, Galleria. It's *our* fault, too," Do' Re Mi says, hanging on to the straps of her backpack.

I stand there, stunned. This is the first time Dorinda has ever stuck up for me. One day, me and Bubbles had a big fight, right on the sidewalk outside of my house. Bubbles stormed off, and Dorinda went running after her and left me standing there on the sidewalk.

"Oh, squash it, Do', I know!" Bubbles snaps, then rolls her eyes at me.

"I'm sorry, okay?" I hiss.

"That's cool, we'll just go with the flow—like I said," Bubbles retorts.

We stand there, silent, trying to plan our next move, but I should've known we weren't getting off the hambone hook that easy. All of a sudden, we hear Derek rolling down the hallway, calling us out.

As soon as he has us in his sights, he moans, "Yo, Cheetah Girls, your product is *fowl* like a nearsighted *owl*!"

"Tell me this isn't happening!" Bubbles moans. "I wish I could use Wacky Glue on Derek's trap!"

Bubbles tries to squash the situation. "Derek, hold up—"

But Derek isn't having it. "Cheetah Girl, what you trying to do to me? You got jokes or something?" Derek asks, handing Bubbles the choker we sold him earlier.

"W-what do you mean?" Bubbles asks him, stuttering. We all stand there, pretending we don't know a tropical storm like Furious Flo is blowing our way—again.

"You *know* what I mean," Derek says, sucking on his lollipop, and posturing like he's ready to pounce—on us. "I'm on my way to

English class, where I'm supposed to be dropping knowledge, and instead I'm dropping letters from the alphabet—like I'm Daffy Duck, or Elmo on *Sesame Street*!" Derek resumes sucking on his lollipop. He's waiting for Bubbles to explain.

Cheez whiz, I'm thinking, *someone musta told Derek that we call him Daffy Duck, too!* Dorinda is the one who thought of that one.

Galleria hasn't opened her mouth, so Derek starts in again. "All I wanna say is, if this is the best joke you got, I got jokes for you, too—but you're gonna have to pay me just to hear them. In the meantime, you can gimme back my ten dollars!"

"Derek, I'm sorry. I didn't mean to sell you a wack choker. It just happened," Bubbles whimpers. She reaches into her cheetah wallet to give him back his ten dollars.

"Word, Derek, we didn't know what we were doing," Do' Re Mi offers, trying to be super-*simpático*.

"Mack, did you hear an echo or something?" Derek says, looking at Mackerel, then looking around like he can't figure out who's talking. Finally, he looks down at Do' Re Mi. "Oh, shortie! Was that you? You got something to say to me?"

"Derek, don't go there—" Bubbles tries to counter, but he cuts her off.

"No. Shame on *you*, Cheetah Girl, 'cuz I'm not the 'shay-mo' you think I am. As a matter of fact, *you* are. And you'd better go back to Finger Painting 101 before you start acting like you 'all that'—ayiight?" He throws the metal letters that fell off his choker on the ground in front of us. "'Cuz you definitely got an F on your report card for social studies."

"*Awwriight*," seconds Mackerel, handing the choker he bought back to Bubbles, too—and taking *another* ten dollars from her.

"You gotta have skills to pay the bills, Cheetah Girls—not jokes!" Derek yells all the way down the hallway, heckling with Mackerel. The two of them sound like hyenas, heading back to the hills to pounce on more innocent prey.

"Let's bounce," Bubbles mumbles, leading us toward the exit. "We're gonna have to be late for next period. We need to get outside and bounce from this situation."

* * *

"We're definitely gonna have to regroup," Do' Re Mi says, sighing, as we sit on the steps in front of the school.

"Regroup?" Bubbles retorts. "I'm *never* going back to school, *ever* again!"

The three of us sit in complete silence for what seems like hours. Then I turn to Bubbles and say, "Remember that time *Madrina* told us about the first cat suits she made?"

"No," Bubbles says quietly. "What'd she say?"

"She said she made them so small they didn't even fit an alley cat," I say, repeating what *Madrina* had told me. "She said she had a lot of problems when she started her business. She even had trouble fitting the customers, because she didn't really know what she was doing.

"I remember my mom thought it was all a big joke," I continue, "'cuz she didn't believe that *Madrina* was ever gonna be a real designer. I still remember the big fight they had about it when Bubbles and I were little," I tell Dorinda.

"I guess we're gonna have to figure out how to make the chokers so they don't fall apart," she says, trying to be helpful.

"I really do feel bad, like it's my fault," I tell my crew.

"Chuchie, just chill," Bubbles says. "We were moving too fast on the eager-beaver tip—trying to floss *and* make everybody proud of us—especially our moms. Right?"

"Right!" Dorinda and I agree.

"Well, I guess we don't have anything better to do than keep trying—at least until we hear if we got a record deal, huh?" Bubbles says. She puts her hands to her temples, like the weight of the world is on her head. "Okay, let's regroup. But I'll tell you one thing—I wish I never had to look at Derek Hambone and his gold tooth again as long as I live."

"Or Mackerel," I say with a smirk, then take a deep breath. "But I guess we have a *lot* to learn."

"And we might as well face the factos—we are definitely in the *dog pound* for now," Bubbles says.

Suddenly, I blurt out, "Woof, there it is!" Next thing you know, I'm laughing so hard, I am doubled over in pain, holding my stomach.

Dorinda and Bubbles join me in a giggle-filled chorus of "Woof, there it is! Woof, there it is!" We just keep saying it, over and over again, because we don't know any of the other words to the song.

But Bubbles soon takes care of that. Right there on the front steps of Fashion Industries East High, for all the sidewalk passersby to hear, she leads us by singing the rest of the song, and we repeat the words after her:

"It takes five
To make the Cheetah Girls be
Ah, yeah, can't you see
That they're rocking on a thing
Called the M.I.C.
The M.I.C., well that's a microphone
And when they rock it to the beat
It's rocked to the doggy bone.

Woof, there it is!
Woof, there it is!
Woof, there it is!"

By now, a small crowd of people on the street has joined us, and they're singing along! This is what I love. This is what we all love. *The beat.*

The beat is what brings us to our feet. *The beat* is why we're together—forever!

After we finish and settle down, I say, "We've *gotta* get that record deal."

Bubbles just sighs. "Yeah—a record deal, or at least a square meal. Come on, y'all—we're missing class. I guess singing is our thing, but when it comes to making chokers, we're just a bunch of jokers."

Chapter 5

By the end of the school day, Bubbles has finally calmed down. Dorinda and I spent the whole lunch period talking some sense into her. When school lets out, we hit the subway, heading for the Toto in New York factory in Brooklyn—again.

"Don't be a joker, G, let's go make some chokers," Dorinda chuckles. That's right—we've talked Galleria into trying again!

Aqua and Angie have agreed to meet us there. We paged them during lunch period, and set it all up.

The twins are getting very brave these days. Usually, we have to meet them at a subway station, and go together as a group to places—

because they don't know New York very well, and are afraid of traveling by themselves.

But since this is the second time they are going to the Toto in New York factory, they are willing to take a chance. We're hoping they won't get on the wrong train and end up back in Houston (their hometown, which has the best Cajun crawfish that side of Texas, if you let them tell it)!

The first thing *we* do when we get to the factory is "eat humble pie." After all, our mission, if we choose to accept it, is to find out what went ka-flooey with our chokers!

As usual, my *madrino* is so understanding about the whole *catástrofe* that he makes us laugh.

"Rome wasn't built in a day, my sweet *cara*." He chuckles as he greets us.

"Hi, Mr. Garibaldi," Dorinda says, smiling. You can tell she likes *Madrino* a lot, too—but then, who doesn't?

Shortly after we get situated, the fabulous Walker twins arrive—in one piece—and ready for a helping of Rosita's famous baked ziti. Rosita is the head pattern maker at the factory, and every Monday she brings a tray of baked ziti to work.

"This is goo-ood," Angie tells Rosita between mouthfuls.

"We *iz* so glad nothing happened to *our* chokers," Aqua pipes up.

"Well, that's because the two of you are just *so special,*" Bubbles hisses at them jokingly. I give the twins a wink, just to make sure they know Galleria's joking.

Rosita is especially happy to see Bubbles. She runs over to her and pinches her cheeks, then runs to the microwave to heat up some more ziti.

Madrino and his employees always cook big, fat feasts for lunch or dinner if they have to work late, and today is no exception. I feel so at home here, and I'm so used to all the different smells in the factory. First, there's always a pot of baked ziti or something bubbling in the microwave oven. Then, there's the sharp smell of cleaning fluid floating around, or the fresh heat from the clothing steamer machines. On top of that is the faint smell of sewing machine oil—because the machines are always purring softly in the background.

After we eat, Bubbles tries to be patient while her dad shows us how to use the snap contraption the *right* way.

"Oh, word," Dorinda exclaims, opening and closing the snaps on a strip of suede. She is completely fascinated with this contraption. Lucky for the rest of us, too—even after *Madrino*'s little lesson, Dorinda is the only one of us who can manage to put the snaps on the suede fabric so they don't look lumpy.

What's really bothering me is, why did the letters fall off so easily? *"Madrino,"* I ask him, "how come the letters don't stay on? I thought the Wacky Glue was strong enough to hold anything!"

"Chanel, *cara,* you cannot always believe the advertisements!" Mr. Garibaldi tries to explain.

"I think Mr. Garibaldi means 'don't believe the hype'," Dorinda says knowingly.

"Si, cara, that's right," *Madrino* says. Clasping his fingers together in order to demonstrate, he says, "In order for the fabric to hold the letters, you should sew two strips of the choker together—stitching it around here." He shows us with a strip of fabric. "Then use a glue like Duco to put the letters on. That Wacky Glue stuff is for amateurs."

Wow. This whole choker thing is gonna take a lot more work than we thought!

"Don't worry, Bubbles. Maybe by next year, we'll be able to make the chokers by ourselves!" Angie jokingly tells Bubbles. But I don't think Bubbles finds it funny, because she has her mouth stuck out. The rest of us just keep quiet while *Madrino* continues with his demonstration.

Maybe next semester I should sign up for Accessories Workshop. . . . I think that's what Derek was really trying to say—that we should really learn how to do something before we jump into the "players' pond," as Bubbles calls it. Derek sure made his point when he threw the metal letters on the floor! I'll never forget Bubbles's face when he did that!

"Okay, now we've got six chokers to sell," Bubbles says as we head back to Manhattan on the subway together. "But we'd better come back another time and make some more chokers—just to be on the safe side."

"Tutti frutti wit' me," jokes Aqua, as she gives us all a big hug. The twins are off to have dinner with their father and his girlfriend, High Priestess Abala Shaballa Cuckoo for Cocoa Puffs, or whatever her name is.

Abala claims she is a high priestess from some faraway place in Hexagonia, where cuckoos come from. I guess she must be telling the truth, because she is as cuckoo as they come—and I am used to *brujería, santería, oju,* and any other kind of witchcraft you can think of, because I'm Dominican, *está bien?* And we've got it all down there!

Anyway, the twins, their dad, and the High Priestess are all going to Mr. Walker's new boss's house, so they have to get home on time. Mr. Walker just started this big new job in marketing. He is working on some new roach spray campaign—or maybe it's fleas . . . I can't remember.

"What you up to this afternoon, Miss Chanel?" Angie asks me. "You working at Toto?"

I work at *Madrina*'s store three afternoons a week, until I can pay Mom back for the money I "borrowed" on her card. But Monday afternoons I'm free. Still, that doesn't mean I'm hanging around the house all day and night. I've got other things going—with me, it's always something.

"I'm running in the Junior Gobbler Race next

week, and I've gotta train for it," I explain. Of course, I know everybody is gonna start laughing at me as soon as they get wind of this, but that's okay—*está bien*. Let them laugh.

"What on earth is the Junior Gobbler Race?" Angie wants to know. She's holding on to a pole with one hand as the subway car rocks back and forth. With her free hand, she's cleaning her teeth with a toothpick.

"It's a race for kids in Central Park," I explain. "You're gonna stab yourself with that toothpick. Cut it out—you're making me crazy!"

"How old you gotta be to run in the race?" Angie asks, putting away the toothpick, *gracias gooseness*.

"They have two divisions for kids," I explain. "The race for the little kids is five blocks. For kids ten to fourteen years old, it's about one mile." I'm hoping the twins will run the race with me. But no—the only thing they like about turkey is eating it.

"We would love to come running with you—but tonight is very important for our daddy," Aqua explains. "You know he got that new marketing job, and he is working real hard coming up with a new bug spray campaign."

"I hope his boss ain't got no roaches in his house!" Angie adds.

"Not everybody has got roaches here, Aqua and Angie!" Dorinda exclaims, offended. I guess Dorinda is embarrassed because the Boscos' apartment *does* have roaches. We never told Dorinda, but when we were at her house, Aqua got real upset when she saw all the roaches in her kitchen. "Who invited *them* to the party," I remember her saying.

"Dorinda, do *you* want to come running with me today?" I ask, putting my arm around her shoulders. She is kinda athletic, like me, and she is the best dancer in the group—even though she never studied ballet, like I did.

"What do you get if you win?" Dorinda asks.

"A ten-pound turkey!" I say, giggling. Dorinda *loves* to eat, and *Dios* knows her family could use a big, fat turkey, to feed all those hungry foster kids.

I wonder if Mrs. Bosco cooks a big meal for Thanksgiving, like we do? Maybe we should invite Dorinda to spend Thanksgiving with us . . . Me and Mom usually go over to Bubbles's house to eat. *Madrina* cooks enough food to feed Cuba. I guess there'd be enough for Mrs. Bosco and her whole houseful!

"Okay," Dorinda says shrugging her shoulders. "We have to run anyway, for our exercise program, right? I might as well try to win the turkey."

"Yep," I say, looking at Bubbles to see how she reacts. See, *Madrina* has us all on a program. For one thing, we have to run—three times a week, to build endurance. This will also help keep our vocal cords in shape, she tells us. It's like a stamina thing, so when we perform we don't get tired, *entiendes?* And so we have enough breath power to hit all the high notes. Mom usually runs with us since she loves to exercise.

Bubbles doesn't care, though. She hates running. I remember when Mom went away to Paris with Mr. Tycoon, Bubbles convinced all of us Cheetah Girls to slack off from our running training. When Mom got back, she was pretty annoyed at all of us!

When Dorinda and I get off the subway at my stop, Bubbles throws me a kiss good-bye, winks, and says, "Gobble, gobble, Miss Cuchifrita!"

* * *

As usual, Pucci is home watching television. Since his birthday is on Saturday, I'm trying to be nice to him, but that sure takes a lot of patience. When he comes out of his room, I ask him, "Pucci, you wanna train with me for the Junior Gobbler race?"

"No, stupid, I'm a Cuckoo Cougar!" He snipes at me, shooting an imaginary machine gun, then plops down at the kitchen table with a chocolate chip cookie and a glass of milk. In two seconds, there's a huge stain on his fighter-pilot T-shirt.

"Wipe your shirt, you *bugaboo*," I hiss at him. Pucci is right about one thing—he's cuckoo, all right.

"He's always watching that stupid cartoon on television," I explain to Dorinda as we change into our running shoes. "Now he's even talking about starting a Cougar Club in school!"

At least he looks cuter now that he's starting to let his hair grow back. "Bubbles used to call Pucci 'Eight ball,'" I tell Dorinda, "because he looked so funny with a bald head."

"Where's your mom?" Dorinda asks, kinda motioning me to get up the nerve and pop the Pucci question to her.

"Probably in the den," I say, making a comical grimace in response. "I'll go see. I'd better talk to her while I still have the nerve to ask her about Pucci's pet." I mouth the last two words silently, motioning to the other room where my poot-butt brother is. He has ears like an elephant, he's so nosy.

To help support my case with Mom, I unzip my cheetah backpack and take out the book on African pygmy hedgehogs.

"*Oink, oink,*" I say, giggling, to Dorinda. "Wait here."

Bending around the corner of our loft apartment, I pad quietly to the den, and see Mom seated in front of the computer. I haven't seen her working at the computer for quite some time. Not since her book about the history of black models—*They Shoot Models, Don't They?*—was published this fall . . . and flopped. Well, it didn't exactly "flop," but Mom wasn't happy with the reviews she got, if you catch my meaning. As she puts it, "What do critics know about models, anyway?"

"*Qué tú haces, Mamí?*" I ask her curiously. "What'cha doin'?"

"Oh, I'm trying to get my thoughts together

for this new book idea I have, about the rise and fall of oil tycoons and their girlfriends. It's called, *It's Raining Tycoons,*" Mom says, running her fingers through her ponytail.

"'*It's Raining Tycoons,*'" I repeat, amused, wondering where she would get the inspiration for something like *that*! (That's a joke—*una broma, está bien?*) "I like that, *Mamí*. Are *you* gonna write it?"

Mom looks at me, really annoyed. I feel like a *babosa*. I'm supposed to be nice to her so she'll let me pick out a pet for Pucci—not get on her nerves! See, I'm not supposed to know *Mamí* used a ghost writer—not that kind of ghost but someone who helps with writing a book. I have such a *boca grande*! What a big mouth!

"I'm looking at several writers, actually," she says, sniffing. "But who knows? I may actually do more work on this one. You know what they say—if you want something done right, do it yourself."

"*Está bien!*" I say, smiling. "Um, *Mamí* . . . 'member what you said about getting Pucci a Chihuahua for his birthday?"

"Yes, I remember that—and *you* can *forget* it!" Mom says curtly.

Now I can feel my cheeks turning five shades of red. I start stammering, "*Pero*—"

"But, *nada,*" Mom says, finishing my sentence for me. "End of discussion!"

As a last resort, I shove the book into Mom's hand. I know she can't resist something as cute as these little creatures, any more than anybody else can. I just know it. "Aren't they cute?" I say, kinda casual.

"*Qué es esto?*" Mom asks, but she doesn't seem amused. "What are these things?"

"They're hedgehogs?" I answer, like I'm asking a question.

"And what is *that?*" Mom asks in a softer tone. I take the bait, because I figure maybe she'll listen to me now.

"They're animals you can have, like, um, a little pet," I explain. "Much easier than a dog!"

"They look like porcupines," Mom retorts.

"No, *Mamí,* they're not porcupines. Their closest relatives are moonrats. Um, they're members of a group of animals known as *insectivora,*" I respond, trying to sound smart, like Dorinda.

"Hmmm. They're very cute," Mom says, then hands me back the book.

"They *are*, right?" I ask, my eyes brightening, because now I know I've got a fighting chance! "Maybe we could get one for Pucci for his, um, birthday?"

"No!" she says, annoyed. "Didn't you hear me the first time? After you get tired of playing with this whatever-it-is, the only person who is gonna end up taking care of it is *me.*"

I am so mad at her, I could shake her! NO!—that's all she ever says to anything I want!

"*Está bien,*" I moan, feeling completely defeated. "I'm going running with Dorinda."

Storming out of the den, I realize that I didn't even ask her what she *is* getting Pucci for his birthday. I don't even care anymore! Whatever it is, she's not telling, and I'm not going to ask her. And I guess I'm supposed to be getting him *nada*—since all I have is *nada* money.

Dorinda takes one look at my face, and she knows what time it is. Time to run and run and *run.* . . .

"Don't be mad at your mom, Chanel," Dorinda says, trying to console me, as we cross the intersection of Forty-second Street and First Avenue.

I look over at the United Nations building, with all the hundreds of countries' flags blowing in the wind. They look so pretty . . . . I look for the flags of the Dominican Republic and Cuba—Abuela's and Daddy's countries.

Then I turn away, and think about what I'm going to get Pucci for his birthday. "I can't think of anything else to get him," I moan to Dorinda. "No more of those stupid Whacky Babies, that's for sure. If he gets one more of those things, I'm throwing them all out of the window!"

"You're buggin'," Dorinda says, smiling because she understands. I don't know how she puts up with all those foster brothers and sisters of hers. I would go *cuckoo* for Cocoa Puffs. I guess having just one brother isn't so bad—even if that brother is as big a pain as Pucci!

Chapter 6

After Dorinda goes home, all the way "uptown, baby," I shower and change into some clean clothes, but I'm still fuming about Mom and her selfishness. She was just trying to show off in front of *Madrina* and my crew that day in the store. Why else would she have said she was gonna let us get a Chihuahua if she didn't really mean it?

I put on my favorite red wool skirt with the big gold safety pin, a red turtleneck, and tights. I pick up the receiver of the red princess phone in my bedroom and call my dad's girlfriend, Princess Pamela, to let her know I'm on my way to her Psychic Palace.

She's taking the braids out of my hair tonight, even though my mother doesn't know it. By the time I hang up the receiver, I'm giggling my head off, because Princess Pamela always makes me laugh. She's so sweet to me.

That's when I decide to wear the Tiffany diamond earring studs Princess Pamela gave me as a present. Mom almost cracked her facial mask the first time she saw them sparkling in my earlobes. She made me swear that I would *never* take any more presents from Princess Pamela.

Well, maybe I will, and maybe I won't. I mean, Mom doesn't keep her word, so why should I, *está bien?* She promised to get me—I mean Pucci—a Chihuahua, and now she won't even get him a pygmy hedgehog!

I go to my musical jewelry box, and take out the little blue box I keep hidden in the bottom. Inside the little box are the tiny diamond studs. I hold them up to the light, admiring them—the most beautiful things I own—then I stick them in my ears.

Just because *Mom* doesn't want a pet, why shouldn't *Pucci* have one? Mom uses the excuse that she's "allergic to animals," and that she'll have to take care of it all by herself—but I don't believe her about either one. She's just being selfish. I'll bet if Mr. Tycoon bought her a poodle or something as a present, she would be cooing like a coconut, all the way from here to Paree—aka Paris, France!

I go into the kitchen to get some orange juice. I don't even care if Mom sees that I'm wearing the diamond studs.

Pucci bounces into the kitchen. "You'd better not drink my Burpy Soda," he says, flinging open the refrigerator and grabbing a can.

"I don't even want your stupid soda, *burphead*," I grumble. Mom lets Pucci order Burpy Soda off the Internet, but what he really needs is a muzzle. I hope she gets him one for his birthday!

"Daddy's coming on Saturday for my birthday," Pucci brags, then starts dancing around.

"Aren't *you* lucky?" I say, grimacing. What I wish is that Princess Pamela could come over here with Daddy and Abuela—but that's never gonna happen, because Mom would get so upset her face would crack, and she'd have to get a face-lift!

"I wonder what *Papí* got me for my birthday,"

Pucci says, raising his eyebrows like *el diablo* and making faces.

"I'm sure it's something *muy preciosa,* Pucci," I say, putting away the orange juice before I pour it over his head. "Bye, *Mamí,* wherever you are," I yell, as I head out the door, and over to Princess Pamela's Psychic Palace, which happens to be just around the corner. (That's how Dad met her—he went over there for a haircut and a palm reading one day when he was sick and tired of fighting with Mom.)

Now I feel like a *babosa.* Why was I feeling guilty about going to Princess Pamela's to get my braids taken out?

Well . . . that's not exactly why I'm going, actually. I'm going to Princess Pamela's because I love her, and because she makes me feel happy about everything that I'm trying to do with the Cheetah Girls.

"Chanel!" Princess Pamela coos when I come in the door. That is what I love about my dad's girlfriend—she always makes me feel like she has won the lottery when she sees my face.

"Come, sit. I *brought* just for you the best caviar I can find," Princess Pamela coos in her syrupy, heavy Romanian accent, which I love.

She shoves a little silver spoon filled with little black alien eggs at my face. "Come, try, *pleez.*"

I put the teeny-weeny alien goofballs on my tongue. Caviar tastes really different, kinda like cold *bacalao*—salted Spanish codfish—but not *exactly.*

"*Dahling,* you like?" Princess Pamela asks, her big brown eyes opening wide.

"Yeah," I say, giggling. "Salty."

"Pleez, eat some *polenta*, too," she commands me. "What I could get for this food on the Romanian black market, I cannot tell you! But, ah, those were the days."

"What do you mean?" I ask curiously, sopping up some of the Romanian potato bread, which Princess Pamela says she makes just like her mother. I love when Princess Pamela tells me stories about "the old country," which in her case is Transylvania, Romania—home of Count Dracula.

"When my country was Communist, we had such a black market—you could make a *k-e-e-l-i-n-g* if you had the right items to sell. Now, we have no Communism, no democracy, and everyone is *very* confused. Ah, *beeneh,* very well," Princess Pamela says wistfully.

I sit in the beauty parlor chair, and listen to the Romanian gypsy music wafting in the background. I try to relax, even though I feel really tense.

"What is troubling you, my booti-ful Chanel?" Princess Pamela asks me, as she takes out my braids with her nimble fingers.

I tell her the whole pygmy hedgehog story, hoping that she will have a solution for me. After all, Princess Pamela *is* a psychic, and she knows how to tell if your dreams will come true.

"I don't see the furry creature with the—how do you say—" she says, scrunching up her face so I can understand what she's trying to say.

"Whiskers?" I ask, giggling.

"Riight, *beeneh,* good. I don't see the furry creature with the whiskers coming under your pillow while you sleep—but, ah, thiz is good, becuz, some of the furrrry creee-tures make you frightened, no?"

She smiles at me, and I try to smile back—even though I'm crushed that she doesn't see any cute little pygmy hedgehogs in my future.

"*Beeneh*, good, but, something better is coming for you. You don't have to worry, Chanel,"

Princess Pamela says, her eyes twinkling the way they always do when she knows a secret.

I remember she told me once to watch out for the animals—and sure enough, Mr. "Jackal" Johnson, our so-called manager at the time, turned out to be a predator in a pinstriped suit, *está bien?*

"How is your mother, anyway?" Princess Pamela asks, while she twists my hair in sections.

"Well, I guess it's raining tycoons," I giggle.

"It's raining tycoons—what does that mean, Chanel?" Princess Pamela asks, amused.

"I don't know—I guess everything is okay with Mr. Tycoon, alrighty, alrooty."

"Ah, *beeneh,* I see," Princess Pamela says. Then she starts humming to the music.

"I hope you're right, though, Princess Pamela. I hope something good is coming, because we haven't heard anything yet from the record company," I say with a sigh.

Then I look in the mirror at my new hairdo. My hair is all wavy and loose now—it kinda looks like Bubbles's, but not as wild. "I like it," I coo to Princess Pamela, then hug her good-bye.

"La revedere, cara," she says. "You will hear something verrry soon, I promise."

If Princess Pamela's predictions are anywhere near as good as her hairdos, then I won't be searching "somewhere over the rainbow" much longer. I practically float all the way home, daydreaming about us, the Cheetah girls, singing—and furry creatures with little whiskers.

When I lie down on my pillow that night, I drift into a dream. I see lots of money falling, falling from the sky. Bubbles is in the dream, too. She has an umbrella, and we are trying to grab all the money that is falling from the sky.

Then we start fighting over the money. Bubbles is trying to grab it from me, because, she screams, "You don't deserve it!"

Suddenly it starts raining, and we're both crying because we're getting all wet. The money is getting wet, too—and Bubbles starts screaming that our dreams are ruined, and how it's all my fault!

It starts raining so hard that we both give up grabbing for the falling money. We struggle to get under the same umbrella, to keep from getting wet. All of a sudden, the umbrella starts lifting us up off the ground, and we're flying through the air! I start getting scared, but Bubbles says, "Just hang on real tight, and we won't have anything to be afraid of anymore."

Then there is this beeping noise . . . and it won't stop beeping. . . .

I sit up in bed, and I realize that the beeping sound is coming from my beeper on the nightstand. I reach over and flash the light on the beeper screen. I see the 411 code after Bubbles's number. That's our secret signal. It means that Bubbles has something to tell me.

Sometimes Bubbles does that just to bother me. I mean, I'll get on the Internet to talk to her in the Phat Planet chat room, and she'll start talking about things that are *muy idiota*! You never know with Bubbles.

I look over at my clock, and I see that it is midnight. Quietly, I get up and go to my computer, and log on to the chat room to see what Bubbles wants.

I shake my head and rub my eyes. *Qué fantasía*. What a dream that was! Maybe I'd better carry an umbrella to school tomorrow, because after a dream like that, I know it's going to rain.

"We're in the house with the Mouse!" Bubbles types on the screen.

"Shouldn't Mickey be sleeping with Toto?" I type back. I'm going to get Bubbles good for this. Getting me out of bed for another one of her little jokes, *qué bromacita!* I'll bet you she's trying to tell me that the twins found another mouse in their closet—or maybe it's something to do with Abala Shaballa, that troublemaking witch.

"Not unless Toto is going to cut a *demo* with us, baby!!!" Bubbles types on the screen in response.

What is Bubbles talking about? I'm not in the mood for jokes. "Toto needs to be checking to see if you aren't going cuckoo," I type back, yawning.

"*Mouse Almighty* is the name of the producer Def Duck Records is hooking us up with—to cut a demo!" Bubbles types back.

Suddenly I'm wide awake. "What happened?" I type excitedly.

"That's right, *mamacita*. They're gonna let us cut a few songs for a possible demo tape!"

"*Ay, Dios mío*—my goodness—Bubbles, why didn't you just say so?!" I type, gasping now for air. "Does that mean we got a record deal?"

"No, but it means they're willing to spend

some development money to put us in the studio, and see what kind of chops we've got! We have to meet Mouse Almighty and Freddy Fudge—the A & R executive from Def Duck—at the record label office on Friday at four o'clock. What do you think about *that, mamacita*?!"

"I can't believe this is true!" I type on the screen. Then I tell Bubbles all about Princess Pamela's prediction—and about the dream I had.

"It's definitely gonna start raining Benjamins now, *mamacita!*" Bubbles replies.

"'It's Raining Benjamins.' That would make a great song title, no, Bubbles?" I type excitedly.

"That is so dope, Chuchie! I'm gonna start writing it right now! Powder to the People!"

I sign off, too, and drop back down on the bed, smiling happily. And then I start thinking. . . .

"Why does *Bubbles* always have to write the songs?" I ask myself. "How come she never lets *me* help write them? *I* wanna write the song 'It's Raining Benjamins.' After all, it was *my* idea. I'm going to tell Bubbles, that's what I'm gonna do."

I start getting so nervous about talking to

Bubbles—because I already know that we are going to fight. Tomorrow night, we're all going to the Times Square Tabernacle Church to see Derek in the "Mad Millennium" Fashion Show. (Bubbles agreed to go, to make up for what happened with the chokers. And then she made us all promise to come with her for support!)

I'll tell her then, I promise myself. On the other hand, maybe I *shouldn't* tell her. . . . Well, I'm sure not gonna tell her at school.

I toss and turn, praying that I have another dream, and float away on a magical umbrella. But nothing like that happens. Why did I have to come up with that song idea, anyway? Now I can't even be happy about the demo, because I'm so busy being upset—me with my *boca grande!*

Chapter 7

The next day at six o'clock, the five of us meet at Times Square Tabernacle Church on West Forty-third Street, to go see Derek Ulysses Hambone in the "Mad Millennium" Fashion Show.

Madrina gave us the money to pay for our tickets because she feels so bad about our "boo-boo" chokers venture. Once again, we're wearing our Cheetah Girls chokers—but, as Bubbles jokes, "Let's pray we don't drop alphabets in the good house of the Lord!"

We're all in a good mood, because of the great news about Def Duck Records. Even me. I'm still kinda nervous about talking to Bubbles about writing a new song with her. But I made a promise to myself last night, when I was lying awake in bed, that I am not going to do *el pollito,* and chicken out. I swear I'm going to pounce at the right moment!

I haven't even spoken to Dorinda about this, since she just automatically sides with Bubbles when it comes to things about the group. That's because she thinks Bubbles knows everything—which she doesn't!

Tonight, the twins especially are in seventh heaven about the news. But for a moment at least, when I first see them, my new hairdo distracts them.

"Hey, Miss Chanel," Aqua exclaims. "Your hair looks *real* nice! Can I touch it? Ain't her hair pretty, Angie?"

"It sure is. It's so *looong,* Chanel!" Angie says, surprised.

"What did you think, I was wearing a weave under my braids or something?" I tease the twins.

"No, but I guess we didn't realize how *looooong* your hair really is."

As soon as she's through checking out my new 'do, Aqua tries to milk Bubbles for every *poco* detail about the phone call between Def

Duck Records and *Madrina*. "What did they say about us?"

"They said we wuz off the hook, Snook!" Bubbles says. (She loves being the one to tell us everything.) Aqua waits for more details, but Bubbles just looks at her and says, "That's it, really. They thought the showcase went really well, and now they want to put us in the studio to cut a demo—with a producer named Mouse Almighty. They said we should record three to five songs. Then they'll decide if they want to give us a record deal."

"Who is this Mouse Almighty?" Angie asks.

"They told Mom he's worked with a few other girl groups, so that's why they picked him to work with us. Let's see . . . he's worked with Karma's Children, the Lollipops, the Honey Dews, and In the Dark."

"In the Dark—who's that?" Dorinda wonders.

"You know—that little girl with the rhinestone-studded black eye patch, and the three other girls who prance around on stage with those monkey-head walking sticks, like they're all that," Aqua blurts out. "They went on tour once with Jiggie Jim and the Moonpies. Um, what's that song—oh . . . oh . . . 'Struck with Your Love and Now I See!' That's it!"

"Oh, them. I don't like them," Angie says, making a face.

"Well, the other groups he's worked with are dope, right?" Dorinda points out. "*And* he's got his own recording studio. That means he's got mad skills."

"Are we going to be able to record *your* songs?" I ask Bubbles.

"I don't know, Chuchie," Bubbles says, kinda humble. Then she breaks out a fresh wad of bubble gum. "He's the producer, so I guess we've gotta do whatever he tells us—'cuz Def Duck Records is paying for everything."

"Oh," I say. I can't get the nerve up to say anything about writing with Bubbles. Besides, I guess this isn't the right time. I don't want to talk about it in front of everybody.

"I'm telling y'all, this is the one," Aqua says, looking all satisfied with herself. "This is what we've been waiting for! I'm telling you, I know—because me and Angie have prayed enough about it!"

We go inside the church. Well, it's not exactly a church. It's more of an auditorium where they hold services. But I guess the twins are really happy just to be in *any* kind of church. They *love* going to church, and singing in the junior choir and everything.

Lady ushers with white gloves are standing at the entrance of the auditorium. "Good evening, sisters," Aqua and Angie greet them, all bubbly with excitement.

The ushers take our tickets and tear them in half. "Just go on inside and take a seat wherever you like, girls," they tell us.

"I hope the money is going to a good cause," heckles Bubbles as we go inside.

Dorinda has been reading the program intensively. Now she blurts out, "It says here, all the proceeds are going to the New York City Chapter for Homeless Women."

"That's good. That's real good," Aqua says, nodding her head in approval. (Their dad was the one who forked over the twenty dollars to pay for their two tickets, and I guess they feel better knowing it's all for a good cause.) Still, some things are more important than others, especially to the twins. "I hope they have good food here," Angie says, looking around.

"Amen to that," Aqua agrees. The only thing

the twins love more than going to church or singing is *eating*.

"They do have food—*afterward*," Bubbles tells them, rolling her eyes at the twins' incredible appetite.

A look of relief washes over Angie's face. "I've never been to a church service in an auditorium. What kind of church is this?" she asks us.

"I believe it's a 'nondenominational' church, but you know how they roll in New York. We can't have big, fancy churches like they have down South," Bubbles says, shrugging her shoulders.

(I'll bet church services in Houston must be in big, beautiful churches, *está bien?*)

"Look—it says here that the clothes are designed by students at Fashion Institute of Technology," Dorinda says, pointing to the program again.

"Oh, I get it. 'Up-and-coming' designers," Aqua volunteers.

"Yeah, let's just hope they have somewhere to '*go*' if their clothes are wack," Dorinda says with a chuckle.

"I wonder if Derek is here yet?" Bubbles asks, looking around for him.

Well, looky, cooky. Now that Derek is acting so mean to Bubbles, I think she kinda *likes* him. I'm not kidding. I know "goo-goo" eyes when I see them!

We take our seats, and wait for the fashion show to begin. Bubbles whips out her Kitty Kat notebook, and gets busy doing more work on her latest song, "Woof, There It Is!"

I try not to look, and luckily, the fashion show commentator comes on the stage. It's none other than Miss Clucky, the famous gossip columnist from television!

"Good evening, everyone. I'm Miss Clucky, and feeling lucky to be here with all of you! We're here to raise some money, and have some *fun*!"

Looking around at the audience, she lets out a big sigh. "Mmmm. Mmmm. I see we have some *fine*-looking young things in the audience tonight! You look *gooood*, y'all," she moans. Then she starts prancing back and forth in her red sequined gown, twirling to show off the draping cape thing attached to it. "*I* look *gooood*, too—don't I, y'all? Don't be shy, you can tell me!"

"*Yeah!*" the audience shouts in unison.

Personally, I think she looks like one of the ladies on the Goya float in the Dominican Day Parade—like she's full of beans!

"Hallelujah!" somebody shouts out.

Suddenly, *la luz grande*—the big lightbulb—goes off in my head. That's it! *Hallelujah!* I can put it in the chorus of my first song—"It's raining Benjamins . . . *Hallelujah*! It's raining Benjamins . . . *Hallelujah!*"

I get so excited that I almost reach over to tell Bubbles, but Miss Clucky is still talking, so I keep my *boca* shut.

"Well, let's give some praise to fashion tonight, y'all!" Miss Clucky says, then puts on some funny-looking spectacles and begins to read from the index cards she has in her hands.

The show begins, and the models start coming out onstage to the beat of the music. Miss Clucky describes all the clothes they're wearing—some of which are definitely wack, but a few of which are definitely *la dopa*!

When Derek comes out on the stage modeling clothes, I poke Bubbles. "He looks gooood!" I whisper, imitating Miss Clucky.

We're sitting too far in the back of the auditorium for Derek to see us, but we wave anyway, giggling our heads off. Derek is wearing this zebra-looking, long, flowing caftan, that kinda looks like the clothes *Madrina* designs for Toto in New York.

"That woulda looked more dope with one of our chokers," Bubbles whispers to me. I can see she feels bad, like we missed out on something.

After the fashion show, we head downstairs to eat the buffet dinner. Dorinda is really excited about all the clothes we saw, and she starts babbling about the outfits she's gonna design for our shows when we go on tour to promote our first album.

Bubbles stops her with a sharp comment. "If you ask me, those designers tonight could definitely have used some Cheetah Girl flava."

Dorinda eyes the spread, and smirks. "Now, that's what I'm talking about!"

We crowd around the buffet table, and put heaps of potato salad, corn on the cob, fried chicken, and baked beans on our plates. The church ladies serving us say chirpily, "Aren't y'all the cutest girls!"

"We're the Cheetah Girls," Dorinda says proudly.

"Mabel, look at those necklaces they got around their necks."

"Oh, these are our Cheetah Girl chokers," Bubbles pipes up, taking over the conversation. I'm surprised she doesn't tell them that we're selling them, so I turn to her and whisper, "Are we still selling the chokers?"

"To anybody with a ducket in a bucket!"

Right then, Derek Hambone comes over with his boy, Mackerel Johnson, and another tall, skinny guy we don't know. Now that the fashion show is over, Derek is back in his "street uniform"—a navy blue and red windbreaker with matching sweatpants.

He likes clothes from this designer, Johnny BeDown—a lot of the kids in our school wear his stuff, but *we* think it's tick-tacky because it has too many letters on it. Like Bubbles says, "Why should we wear clothes with anybody else's name on it but our own?"

"Hey, Cheetah Girls! Glad to see you in the house," Derek says. Then he reaches over and kisses Bubbles on the cheek! I can't believe she let him do that!

"We figured out how to make the chokers," Bubbles blurts out, fingering the one around her neck. "We've already taken orders for five more."

"That's cool," Derek says, kinda laughing. "It's all good in the 'hood."

What does Bubbles mean, she's taken orders for five more chokers? She didn't tell *me* anything! *Nada*. *Vampira*-tooth Mackerel winks at me. I guess I'd better be *super-simpática* too to make up for what happened. "What program are you in?" I ask Mackerel, even though it kills me. I feel my face turning *rosa*.

"Design," he mumbles. His voice is so soft, I can hardly hear it.

"Did you like the clothes in the show?" I ask, trying to seem like I'm interested in talking with him. I guess it's okay—as long as he doesn't start biting my neck!

"They *awwriight,* but I'm trying to flow with the street vibe," he continues—like he's flossing about his design skills.

"Whose clothes do you like?"

"I dig Trace Gear, you know what I'm saying?"

"Oh, I like that, too," I say, telling a *poco* fiberoni. I hate their clothes, because they're too baggy—but I'm not going to tell *him* that, *está bien?*

"You know what? I'll buy another choker from you, if you're still selling them," Mackerel says. Then he *winks* at me. *Cuatro yuks*—he's *flirting* with me!

If he would just keep his "trap" shut, so I wouldn't have to look at his teeth, maybe I wouldn't mind. Those teeth of his give me "the spookies." He ought to get them fixed, you know?

"Okay, *está bien*," I say to Mackerel. Then I pull on Bubbles's sleeve and ask her what to do.

"That's cool—we've got enough chokers. We can handle it," Bubbles says confidently. "That is, if it's okay with you, Derek?"

Bubbles is trying to be sooo charming to Derek—and he is eating it up like, well, a Red Snapper!

"It's cool with Mr. DUH—you know what I'm saying?"

Bubbles blushes deep purple. See, Derek has the initials of his first, middle, and last name shaved on the back of his head. That's how they roll in Detroit, where he comes from—but we think that look is so played. Besides, with initials like his, he shouldn't be broadcasting them, *está bien*? That's why we always make fun of him. But *la gente* at school obviously told him about *that* nickname, too.

"You know . . . I'm sorry about what happened," Bubbles says, and she seems like she means it for a change!

"Yeah, I know, Cheetah Girl," Derek says, grinning and showing off his gold front tooth. "Does that mean you'll go out with me, yo?"

I want to scream. *Ay, caramba!* Bubbles, *please* say *no!*

"All right. We can move, we can groove," Bubbles responds.

I think I'm going to faint! Dorinda's mouth is hanging open, too. I look over my shoulder, and see that the twins are busy talking to Derek's friend, whom we don't know.

"Bubbles, we have to go," I blurt out.

"Hold up, Miss *Señorita*, I'm trying to make things happen, you know what I'm saying?" Derek says, interrupting me.

"*Sí,*" I say nastily, like, "DUH! I can see that."

"I'll check you tomorrow," Derek says to Bubbles. "Make me another choker, too. *Ayiight?*"

"Bet," Bubbles says, as Derek and Mackerel move off to work the room.

Galleria, Dorinda, and I make our way to one of the banquet tables, and sit down with our food.

"Bubbles, are you really going to go out with Derek?" Dorinda asks amused.

"No, silly-willy! I'm just trying to make up for what happened," Bubbles says, exasperated. "And you'll notice I got our choker enterprise back in business, too—we've got new orders from both Derek and Mackerel. By the way, who was that guy they were with? Does he look familiar?"

"*Tales from the Crypt*, maybe?" I retort. Now I wanna ask Bubbles about those orders for five chokers she told Derek we had. "How come you didn't tell me we got orders for five chokers?" I ask defensively.

"'Cuz we *don't* have orders for five chokers, Chuchie. Use that *cabeza* of yours for a change and some coins," Bubbles huffs, knocking on my head with her knuckles. "I just said that to Derek, the *gnocco*, to drum up some business."

"What's a *gnocco*?" I ask, annoyed.

"A blockhead," Bubbles says mischievously. Here she just got in trouble for calling Derek names, and already she has a new one for him? That's Bubbles—always in trouble.

As for me, I don't care what she says—I *do* use my *cabeza*—because I'm not the one getting all cuckoo over some *blockhead* with a gold mine in his mouth!

The twins stop talking with Derek's friend and come over to join us at our table. "One of the ushers asked me if she could buy two of our chokers for her daughters—they're twins, like us," Aqua says excitedly, then pulls out a piece of paper with a name and phone number on it.

"We could sell two to her *right now*—because we have the five that we remade," Bubbles points out.

"I'll be right back with the cash," Aqua says, grabbing the chokers from Bubbles and jumping up to find the usher.

We sit there, not saying a word. As for me, I'm still fuming at Galleria for knocking on my head with her knuckles.

Then Angie pipes up. "His name is Spider, by the way—and he is a member of this church."

"Who?" Dorinda asks, puzzled.

"Derek's friend. He goes to DeWitt Clinton High School in the Bronx."

"Look at Angie, trying to make moves!" Bubbles says proudly. "Houston's in the house!"

"Well, I was just trying to be nice, since Derek is the one who invited y'all," Angie says, kinda embarrassed. (The twins never talk about boys.) "You know our daddy would ship us back to Granddaddy Walker's Funeral Home in little pieces if he ever even *thought* we were going out with boys!"

"How gruesome," Bubbles chuckles.

"I'm saving myself for Krusher," I coo.

"You couldn't even win a contest for a date with him, Chuchie. How are you gonna go out with him?" Bubbles asks, rolling her eyes at me.

I'm going to kill Bubbles! Luckily at that moment, Aqua runs back to the table, holding twenty dollars in her hand.

Then she sees that Bubbles is frowning. "We *are* selling them for ten dollars each, right?" Aqua asks puzzled.

"Yeah," Bubbles says absentmindedly. She is obviously thinking about something else entirely. "Oh, yeah . . . I'll hang on to the money till we split it up."

That's *it*! I'm so mad at her, I'm not even

scared anymore to ask her about the song. "Bubbles, can I write 'It's Raining Benjamins' with you?"

"What?" Bubbles looks like she's been hit by a truck.

Dorinda looks at me, smiling nervously. She knows exactly what's going to happen—Bubbles and I are about to have a big fight!

Even Aqua stops babbling for a change.

Poking her mouth out, Bubbles says in a really annoyed tone, "Chuchie, you couldn't even figure out how to glue letters on the Cheetah Girl chokers. Now you're gonna try to write songs, too? *Please*—don't make me sneeze."

"Here's a Kleenex," I say nastily, whipping a package of tissues out of my backpack. "I'll bet you I can write songs just as well as you can!"

"You two need to *stop*!" Dorinda says, jumping in before Bubbles and I start pulling each other's hair out. She has seen us fight before, so she knows. *Ella sabe, está bien?*

"Chuchie, I just don't think it's a good idea for you to write the songs with me," Bubbles says, like she is Judge Jonas on television and she's got a gavel to pound.

"Then I'm *leaving*!" I shout, wincing because leaving the Cheetah Girls is the last thing I want to do.

"Don't do that, Chanel!" Dorinda says, trying to reason with me.

"No, I'm sick of Bubbles trying to run everything!" I say. I can feel the tears welling up in my eyes, but I'm not gonna let her see me cry. I turn to go.

"Come on, y'all, let's *all* go," Aqua says, pushing her plate aside and getting to her feet.

We all walk outside in silence, and head to the subway station. I'm the only one going downtown, so I take the train by myself.

Dorinda runs after me on the platform and gives me a hug. "Don't worry, Chanel. I'm gonna talk to Galleria. This isn't right, that the two of you are always fighting."

"Whatever," I say quietly, then hug Dorinda back. Bubbles doesn't even say good-bye to me, and I act like I don't care. If she wants to control everything so badly, then let her! She can run the whole jiggy jungle by herself, for all I care!

Chapter 8

The next morning before school, Bubbles calls me on my bedroom phone.

"Look, Chuchie. If you want to *try* to write a song with me, then we can do it at your house before we have rehearsal later."

"Okay," I say like I don't care. "Whatever." Maybe Bubbles is pulling one of her tricks.

"Chuchie, I *said* we'll try to write a song together. What more do you want me to say?"

"*Nada. Pero* you could apologize for embarrassing me in front of *everybody*." I realize I am screaming into the receiver; that I'm being "emotional"—just like Mom.

"Okay, calm down, *Señorita*. I'm sorry,

okay?" Bubbles huffs. "Take a chill pill, *pleez."*

Now I feel so embarrassed for acting cuckoo that I just say, "Okay, I'll see you later." I quickly hang up the receiver, then stick my tongue out at it. That's what Bubbles does—cause trouble—just because she always wants everybody to do what *she* wants!

We should be happy that Def Duck Records is letting us record some songs for a demo tape, but instead, all I feel is worried that Bubbles is going to try to boss us around!

By the time I meet up with Dorinda and Bubbles at school, I see we're back in the Cheetah Girls choker business.

"Look! I already got the twenty dollars from Derek and Mackerel," Bubbles says, jumping up and down. "We've got forty dollars now—and counting. Here, you two try to sell two each," Bubbles commands me and Dorinda, handing us each a pair of chokers.

"Bet," says Dorinda. She gives me a hug and smiles. I realize that Bubbles probably already told her that we talked on the phone this morning. Sometimes, Dorinda and I talk on the phone, too—without Bubbles—because I think of Dorinda as a sister now. But *not* a sister that I sometimes *hate*—like Bubbles!

"You know, we should figure out how much exactly it costs us to make the chokers, so we make sure to charge enough," Dorinda says, all businesslike.

Bubbles is right. Dorinda does have her eye on the ka-*ching*—the cash register. It's really true!

Bubbles gives Dorinda a look, like, "Hold up—*I'm* running this choker show," which makes Dorinda squirm a little.

"I mean, we should write down all the money we spend for materials, um, just to make sure," Do' Re Mi says sheepishly.

"Yeah—you're right, we'll do that later," Galleria says, brushing her off. "For now, let's just roll with the duckets coming in the bucket!" Bubbles has taken command again.

We do the Cheetah Girls handshake together—but inside, I don't feel okay about everything. I don't think Bubbles is serious about letting me write a song with her after school today. She just said that to get off the hook.

"Just a reminder, we have to meet Mouse

Almighty and Freddy Fudge at the Def Duck Record Company office on Friday at four." Bubbles is talking like *she's* our manager now.

"Are we gonna record?" Dorinda asks.

"Not this time," Galleria tells her. "We're just meeting with the producer, so he can get to know us, and check out our vibe. The way the record company executive explained it, we're just going there for a 'meet and greet.' After Mouse gets a feel for our flavor, he goes out and shops around for songs he thinks are right for us. Then he puts us in a studio to record them, and cut a mini demo tape."

"Word!" Dorinda says, squinting her eyes. You can tell she's really interested in how everything works.

"Where do we have to go?" I ask.

"They have a New York office at Thirty Rock."

"*Where?*" I ask again, annoyed. I mean, we're not going mountain climbing, *está bien?*

"Thirty Rockefeller Plaza, Chuchie—right by the ice skating rink where we used to go, back in the junior high school days."

"Okay, Bubbles—I didn't understand what you were saying," I hiss at her.

Dorinda looks at us like, "Don't you two start again!"

Today, my last class of the day is Italian, which I don't really like at all. See, it's kinda hard, and I'm not that good with languages—except for Spanish and English. Two is enough, *está bien?* I'm only taking Italian because Bubbles made me do it. I wanted to take Spanish, but she got really upset with me.

"Chuchie, you *are* Spanish," she protested—which made me feel guilty, because it is *la verdad*. But why shouldn't I take a class that's easy for a change—*para un cambio?* It's not like Bubbles is helping me with my homework—even though I haven't asked her. But then again, why *should* I have to ask? She should *know* I need help!

I'm not listening to my teacher, Mr. Lepidotteri, because I'm too busy trying to write the words to "It's Raining Benjamins." It makes me feel so cool—*tan coolio*—that I am writing a song. Okay—*trying* to write a song.

Now I'm frustrated, though. I wanted to have the whole song written by lunchtime, so I could show Bubbles that I really can do it. Instead, I have simply scribbled, "*Ayúdame*!—

help me!"—all over the margins, with unsmiley faces all around the border.

Luiza Santiago, my classmate, glances over and sees my doodles. When the class is over, I make a big deal of sighing—like I'm so relieved, and have better things to do with my time, *está bien?* Luiza leans over and studies my scribbles, then asks curiously, "What does '*ayúdame*' mean?"

Luiza is "Spanglish," like me—mostly Nuyorican, which means she is Puerto Rican born in Nueva York—and part Chilean.

Unlike me, Luiza doesn't speak a word of Spanish.

"It means 'help me,'" I say, giggling. "I'm trying to write this song 'It's Raining Benjamins' for my group—but I guess the only thing I've figured out is where the doodles go!"

I can tell that Luiza is impressed, because she keeps staring at the doodled page, and tries to decipher more of my scribbles. "It must be kinda hard, writing a song."

"Yeah. I mean I've got the general idea, but it just takes a lot of time to get it down on paper. You know how I am—I can't sit still," I say apologetically.

Luiza tries to figure out some of the words on the page, and reads them aloud. "'There's precipatation in the nation . . . and not the kind you think—'"

Interrupting Luiza, I blurt out, "I think I've misspelled 'precipatation.'"

"I think it's p-r-e-c-i-p-i-t-a-t-i-o-n," Luiza says slowly. "I think that's right. Yeah, that's right."

I hurriedly cross out the "a," and replace it with an "i." That's all I need, is for Bubbles to see that I misspell words. She'll be like, "See, I told you, Chuchie, you can't write a song!"

So what if I'm not as good at spelling as Bubbles? When we were in grade school, she always won the spelling bees. In the sixth grade, she even made it to the nationals of the spelling bee contests. Me, I'm lucky if I can spell my own name. But that doesn't mean I can't write songs, does it?

As *la gente* start leaving the classroom, I suddenly realize that I didn't hear the homework assignment.

"Luiza!" I yell after her. "What's the homework?"

She just shakes her head at me, and opens

her notebook. "Idioms that go with the verb *avere.*"

Idioms? I feel like an *idiota*, because I don't know what that means. "What's an idiom?" I ask.

Now Luiza is getting a little annoyed. "Here," she says, thrusting the notebook in my hand, and letting me read the homework assignment for myself.

"Oh, I get it," I say, feeling like a *babosa*.

After I leave class, I take a deep breath and get ready for Freddy. The twins taught us this expression, and I don't know exactly what it means. I think in this case, it means "I'm ready for bigmouthed Bubbles!"

Bubbles comes over to my house an hour earlier than the rest of the Cheetah Girls, so that we can write the song together. Dorinda has gone to the library to study, so she won't have to go all the way home, then all the way back downtown again for rehearsal.

"Hey, Pucci, wazzup?" Bubbles exclaims.

Pucci *loves* Bubbles, and is always trying to show her his latest trading cards, stuffed animals, or whatever new computer gadget he's got in his room. Sometimes he tells her jokes, too.

"Bubbles, what did the elephant say to the alligator after he swallowed him?" Pucci says, grinning at her like she's the cat's meow.

"Um, lemme see—'Don't chomp on my intestines, 'cuz that's my lunch, you scaly toad'?"

"No!" Pucci says, almost giggling himself to death before he gets the joke out. "He said, 'Poop you later, alligator'! Heeheeheeheehee!!!"

"That's disgusting, Pucci!" I sneer, growling so Pucci knows I don't think his jokes are *funny*.

Bubbles, of course, giggles at Pucci's joke, like he's Dr. Doolittle or something.

"Bubbles, you coming to my birthday on Saturday?" Pucci asks her wistfully.

"Um, of course, Pucci. You're the man!" I notice her looking at me when she says it, like it doesn't matter if I want her there, because now Pucci invited her.

"Come on, let's go in the living room." I motion to Bubbles. Having Pucci around is cramping my style.

Galleria plops her Kitty Kat notebook down on the table, then whispers, "What are you gonna do about getting him a pet for his birthday?"

"*Nada,*" I whine.

"What are you gonna get him?"

"*Nada,*" I repeat.

"You have to get him *something*, Chuchie," Bubbles snaps.

"No, I don't."

"I'm not fighting with you about it," Bubbles says. Then she whips open her notebook, and starts acting like she's a *real* songwriter. "Chuchie, you're gonna see. It's not so easy to write a song, 'cuz the inspiration has to hit you. Then it just kinda comes out."

"I know that," I reply.

"Well, lemme see what you got so far."

As I take out my school notebook from my backpack and put it on the table, I sheepishly tell her the truth. "I don't really have much. I, um, just thought it would be fun if we did it together."

"I know, Chuchie—but you must have written down something!" Bubbles says, kinda annoyed.

"Yeah," I say, hesitating. I open the Italian section of my notebook, and shove the page in her face.

"W-what is *this?*" she asks, stammering. "Doodle hour?"

"No, look! What about this?" I say, pointing to the one line I wrote on the page.

Bubbles reads it aloud. "'There's precipitation in the nation, and not the kind you think—stop blinking, and don't pass me those shades . . . .' That's good . . . we could definitely work with that. . . ."

Bubbles takes a deep breath, like she's going to give me a lecture, then taps her pencil on the table. "Chuchie, first you have to write *verses* for the song, okay?"

What's a verse? I wonder. But I say, "Yeah, I know that, Bubbles."

"So. Let's work on the first verse," she says, flipping to a page in her Kitty Kat notebook. The page is filled with lots of scribbling. Obviously, she has already been working a lot on the song.

"Look at this," Bubbles says, pointing to a line on the page.

I read aloud what Bubbles has written, "'Dollar bills sure give me thrills, but it's nothing like the Benjamins, baby. Don't maybe, awrighty, they're mighty.'"

Without thinking, I blurt out my reaction. "It

kinda sounds like the song those girls, CMG, were singing in the New Talent Showcase."

"Yeah? So?" Bubbles retorts. "It's not *exactly* the same. You can't say that I'm *copying* them, 'cuz here's *their* song."

Bubbles turns to another page in her notebook, and reads aloud. "'Yeah, we roll with Lincoln/What are you thinkin'?'" Bubbles frowns. "That's kinda like what *you* wrote, Chuchie," she points out. "So don't go accusing *me* of copying!"

"Well, I don't know. We *both* wrote things that kinda sound like theirs," I volunteer. "'Thinking. Awrighty. Mighty.' It sounds the same, right?"

"Okay, scratch that," Bubbles humphs, kinda annoyed. "Let's start again."

"Oh! Oh!" I say, getting all excited. "I thought of something to put at the end!"

"What?" Bubbles asks, like she's not sure she wants to hear it.

"'It's raining Benjamins . . . Hallelujah! It's raining Benjamins . . . . Hallelujah!'"

I can tell Bubbles is pleased, even before she says, "I *like* that!"

"I got that idea when we were at the 'Mad Millennium' Fashion Show," I tell her.

"Okay—now that part's called the chorus," Bubbles says. "That's where the group sings the same thing together."

"Chorus," I repeat. "Okay."

Bubbles's wheels are spinning a mile a minute. "I like that . . . *Hallelujah*—that'll work . . . ." All of a sudden, she is deep in thought, scribbling madly.

I don't want to disturb her. I've seen her do this a million times, and the songs always come out *la dopa*.

"How about we start it with—'For the first time in *her*-story/There's a weather forecast that looks like cash . . .'"

"I like that!" I say, getting into the groove. "Then, how about something like, 'Put on your shoes and spread the news'?"

"Yeah!" Bubbles says. "That'll work!" Writing some more, she says, "Okay—'So tie your shoes to spread the news/And come around the bend at half past ten!'"

For the next hour, Bubbles and I go back and forth like this, until we have two verses and the chorus. Bubbles starts humming a melody to go with the words.

"You really are better at that than I am," I

admit to her. "How do you come up with the beat?"

"I don't know, Chuchie. It just comes to me, I guess," Bubbles says, shrugging her shoulders and smiling sweetly. "Sometimes I start hearing the melody of a song before I even think of the words."

"Oh!" I say with surprise. "Well, I guess I'm not really a songwriter—but I do want to help sometimes, okay?"

"Well . . ." Bubbles says, hesitating, "I guess so—but I don't feel right giving you equal credit."

"Credit?" I ask in surprise, because I'm not sure what she's talking about.

"You know—*songwriting* credit, in case the song ever gets published or something." Bubbles is acting like she knows everything about the music business, *está bien?*

I can't believe her. She can be so selfish about some things! *Yo no entiendo*—I don't understand why she does that. I love her, and would do anything for her—and she *knows* that. *Why doesn't she do the same thing for me?*

Then, all of a sudden, the strength of all the *brujas* who traveled the earth on broomsticks gives me the courage to speak up for myself. I blurt out, "Bubbles, if you don't give me song-writing credit, I'm never gonna speak to you again!"

"Okay, you *gnocca*!" Bubbles blurts back at me, beaten for once in her life. Then a sly grin spreads over her face, as she gets her usual last word in. "But only if it gets published, you understand?"

"Yo entiendo perfectamente, I understand perfectly, you *babosa,"* I hiss at her—which sends Bubbles into a fit of giggles.

By the time the twins and then Dorinda arrive, Bubbles and I are still giggling about our first songwriting experience. I start dancing around the living room, singing "'It's raining Benjamins . . . Hallelujah! It's raining Benjamins . . . Hallelujah. It's r-a-i-n-i-n-g . . . Amen!'"

Chapter 9

If I thought staying at the Royal Rooster Hotel on Hollywood Boulevard was something to cluck about, the Def Duck Records office in Rockefeller Plaza has definitely laid the golden egg!

"How tall do you think that thing is?" I mumble to Dorinda, as we both gaze in awe at the gold duck statue in the lobby.

"About fifty feet," Dorinda says, eyeing the duck statue like it's gonna start quacking. "They musta had a lot of artists with gold records to lay this thing!"

"Elevator is that way, ladies," says the security guard in the lobby, pointing to the back.

"Look, *that* elevator goes to the ninety-second

floor!" Bubbles whispers to me, because she doesn't want the twins to hear her. They are bigger scaredy-cats than the scarecrow in the *Wizard of Oz* when it comes to riding elevators.

Madrina pushes the button for the forty-ninth floor, and I'm just hoping the twins don't have a barf attack in front of the record company executives!

"I guess we can't ask the record company to move their offices to a lower floor *yet,*" *Madrina* says, putting her arm around Aquanette. "Not until they give us a deal, huh?"

"No, ma'am," Aqua says. She always gets very formal when she's scared.

Gracias, gooseness, I think, as we step into the reception area. The twins held on to their lunch.

The reception area is really quiet. I thought there would be music playing everywhere. Mr. Freddy Fudge comes to get us. He's a tall, skinny guy with blond, short, fuzzy hair, and a chocolate-brown complexion like the twins. He looks *tan coolio,* too, in his black-and-white-checked blazer with a red handkerchief in the pocket. I almost blurt out that red is one of my favorite colors, but I'm too nervous to even speak!

"We met an A & R gentlemen, Mr. Tom Isaaks, at the New Talent Showcase in Los Angeles," *Madrina* tells Freddie Fudge as we walk down the hallway.

"Yes, he's on the West Coast." Mr. Fudge then goes on to explain that he too is an A&R development executive—*for R&B artists.*

We're not R&B artists! I think to myself—but I'm not saying anything. Bubbles looks at me and raises her eyebrows.

Luckily, *Madrina* says something before Bubbles does. "Mr. Fudge—"

"Call me Freddy," he says, as we walk down a long, skinny hallway past a whole lot of cubicles and offices. Everybody seems really busy here.

"Freddy—you know, the Cheetah Girls aren't really an R & B group."

"Oh, I know, Mrs. Garibaldi," Freddy says apologetically. "It's just a catchphrase in the music business, for, um, 'urban music.'"

"Oh. Okay," *Madrina* says, smiling. "The girls like to think of their music as 'global groove.'"

"Excellent. There's a hook we can really work with—that is, if everything works out,"

Freddy says cautiously. He opens the door to a conference room, and motions for us to step inside.

"Thank you—" I say, then stop myself from saying his name, because I'm not sure if it's okay for *us* to call him Freddy, or if we're supposed to call him Mr. Fudge. I'll ask *Madrina* later.

Mr. Fudge introduces us to the three other people sitting in the room. "This is my assistant, Haruko Yamahaki. Mouse Almighty, the producer you'll be working with for the next few months—and hopefully longer than that, if everything goes well—and Mr. Chunky Carter, one of our new talent coordinators."

After sitting down at the conference table, *Madrina* pipes up. "Freddy, you mentioned something about a test single—"

"Yes, Mrs. Garibaldi. Let me explain. Mouse is going to be responsible for selecting songs from various songwriters that he feels would really showcase the Cheetah Girls," Freddy says, his hands propped up on the table, folded in a tent position.

"If we feel that the songs are *strong* enough, the Cheetah Girls will be given a record deal option with Def Duck, for the release of one 'test single.' If that single tests well in the marketplace, the girls will then be given a full record deal, and you'll go back in the studio and cut an album."

"I see," Mrs. Garibaldi says.

"I know it's a long process," Mr. Fudge continues. "But these days, we only add a certain number of artists to our roster each year. That way, we can spend the proper time, energy, and money on artist development, marketing, and promotion. I hope you understand that."

"Yes, we do—although you'll soon see that these girls have *already* been groomed to take over the world!" *Madrina* says with a knowing chuckle.

Everybody in the conference room laughs along with her, including Haruko, who has a *funny* laugh. All of a sudden, I start to feel more relaxed. Looking around, I see that my crew is feeling the same way.

"Would you girls like a soda?" Haruko asks, her dark eyes twinkling. "Take one, please."

I can't stop staring at Haruko's lips. Her red lipstick looks really *la dopa* with her long black straight hair. I *love* red lipstick—even though I don't wear it yet, because I'm afraid I'll mess it up. I wonder how she gets it to look so *perfect.*

"We would love a soda," Aqua pipes up, which for some crazy reason gets us all giggling again.

Now Chunky starts talking, telling us that he will be working with us to coordinate our studio sessions with Mouse, and handling everything else that needs to be done.

"Why don't you girls tell us a little about yourselves?" Mouse suggests, then leans back into his chair like a Big Willy. He doesn't look like a Mouse at all. I wonder how he got his name. . . .

"Well," Bubbles says, speaking up for us. "We're wanna-be stars in the jiggy jungle, I guess."

Haruko does that laugh again, which makes me laugh, too. Bubbles looks at me, but I'm sorry—I can't help it.

"How did you girls hook up?" Chunky asks, curious.

"Chuchie, I mean, Chanel and I have been friends since we were born. See, our mothers used to be models together, and then my mom became Chanel's godmother and everything."

"Chanel and Galleria and I all go to the same high school—Fashion Industries East," Dorinda says, smiling and showing off her cute little dimples.

"And we met *them* at the Kats and Kittys Klub!" Aqua explains enthusiastically. "We wuz singing by the barbecue grill, and they just *loved* us!"

Now Bubbles and I start laughing loudly—because that's not exactly true. Aqua is telling a fib-eroni. Bubbles *hated* her and Angie at first, because she thought they were show-offs.

Actually, I think Bubbles was just kinda jealous, because we'd never been asked to sing at a Kats and Kittys party, and we're from New York. Then here come Angie and Aqua, straight out of Houston, and they just kinda take over, *está bien?*

After we blab some more about our music, Mr. Freddy Fudge is back down to business. "What I will need is for you and the girls to sign an agreement. It states that Def Duck is providing the financial arrangements for a demo tape, but we're under no obligation to give you a record deal until such time as we deem it viable to enter into such an agreement."

"I'll have my lawyer look it over, and get back to you," *Madrina* says, like a real manager.

"Okay," Mr. Fudge says, rising from the table and reaching over to shake *Madrina*'s hand.

We say good-bye to everyone fifty times. As we're leaving, Dorinda turns to Haruko and says, "Thank you for the soda. Um, I like your name."

Haruko laughs that funny laugh of hers again, and replies, "I like yours, too."

"What does yours mean?" Dorinda asks curiously, looking around at us to make sure she's not holding up anything.

"It means 'child born in the spring' in Japanese," Haruko says, beaming like she's really happy someone asked her something about herself. "What does yours mean, Dorinda?"

"'God's gift,'" Dorinda says, smiling back.

Madrina puts her arms around Dorinda and says, "Come on, 'God's gift.' Let's go eat a well-deserved early dinner."

We all wave good-bye to each other fifty more times, before we finally head back down to the lobby, where Mr. Golden Duck Statue is still standing.

Bubbles waves good-bye to the statue. "Good-bye, Mr. Ducky, you made us feel lucky!" she says.

"Hey! That's a song!" I exclaim, feeling like I'm sitting on top of the world.

"That's *not* a song, Chuchie," Bubbles says, giggling. But she's really nice about it, and puts her arm around me.

I guess she's right—that would be a stupid song. Still, I'm so excited about the fact that Bubbles and I wrote a song together that I tell *Madrina* all about it as we walk down the street.

"I like it!" *Madrina* says, when I tell her the words to the refrain. "God knows we could use a cash money shower right about now—even if it's only a shower of George Washingtons!"

Chapter 10

"You know," *Madrina* says as we stand on the corner, waiting for the light to change, "if this all works out, I'm going to talk to the record company executives about recording some of *your* songs."

"That's a done deal-io!" Bubbles says excitedly.

"You know, at the end of the day in this business, it's all about publishing rights," *Madrina* says, getting serious. "That's where the real money falls from the sky."

"Publishing rights—what are they?" Dorinda asks.

"Well," *Madrina* explains, "the person who *writes* the song collects publishing royalties for as long as the song sells, is played on the radio, gets used for motion picture sound tracks or television commercials—you name it, there's a way to claim publishing payments."

"Word? That's dope!" Dorinda says. And now I can see that the songwriting wheels are turning in *her* head, too.

"Well, we've got to try to get every ducket in the bucket," Bubbles says emphatically. Then she turns to me. "Chuchie, we're gonna have to work on our song some more, you know?"

"*Yo sé, mamacita!*" I say enthusiastically.

"What time do we have to be at your house on Saturday?" she asks me.

"Noon, I guess," I say wistfully, because it suddenly hits me that I still don't have a present for Pucci. And now that the day is almost here, I realize that I can't just get him *nada*, like I said.

"*Madrina*, do you think I could have my paycheck today instead of Saturday?" I ask, in my sweetest voice.

For working three afternoons at Toto in New York . . . Fun in Diva Sizes, I get forty dollars a week—half of which I have to give to Mom to pay back the charges I sneaked on her credit card like a *babosa*.

"I think we can arrange something," *Madrina* says. "You're buying Pucci a birthday present?" she asks excitedly.

"Well, I guess," I say, kinda puzzled.

"Chuchie, here," Bubbles says, taking some money out of her cheetah wallet and stuffing it into my hand.

I must be dreaming, because Bubbles wouldn't give me money if the sky was falling.

"*Qué es esto?*" I ask Bubbles, my voice squeaking. "What's this?"

"It's the money from the chokers. You can have it, all right?" Bubbles turns to the twins and Dorinda for their approval.

"That's fine with us," Aqua pipes up. "I mean, come on, Chanel, you gotta give your brother more than a birthday card for his birthday! Ain't that right, Angie?"

"Yes, ma'am, that's right," Angie replies.

"Don't worry. We're gonna keep track of all the money, the way Mom does for the store," Bubbles says, pulling out a cheetah notebook out of a paper bag. "You can pay us back our share later—after you get done paying back your mother." She turns to Dorinda. "Do' Re Mi, why don't you keep the book on it?"

Dorinda's face lights up like a Christmas tree. "Word! I'll keep track of everything!"

"Good—'cuz quiet as it's kept, you're the brains behind the Cheetah Girls operation," Bubbles says proudly.

I can't believe how humble Galleria's being. That's not *like* her. *Es la verdad*—it's the truth!

"I'll go with you to buy Pucci a pet," Bubbles volunteers.

"What pet is that, darling?" *Madrina* asks, because she knows Mom does not like pets—unless it's a Chia Pet that just has to be watered!

"Chuchie's gonna buy Pucci a hog!" Bubbles says mischievously.

"Now, I *know* that must be some Cheetah Girls joke, because Juanita will ground Chanel for the rest of her life if it isn't!" *Madrina* says sternly.

"Bubbles doesn't mean a real hog, *Madrina*—it's an African pygmy hedgehog," I try to explain.

"Chanel, *that* sounds even worse—like some kind of animal used for a voodoo ritual or something!" *Madrina* says, looking alarmed. "Listen, Chanel, you two work this out over dinner, because I'm getting so hungry I may just eat a pygmy whatever-it-is!"

We all eat like we're starving for Marvin. After, *Madrina* says, "I'm heading home. I've got work to do. Galleria, I'll see you later. And don't bring back a pet with more growl power than you girls have." With a wave, she heads off toward the subway station.

"We'll come with y'all to the pet store if you want," Aqua volunteers.

I guess we're all in such a good mood because of the meeting—and the *lonchando*—that we don't want to leave each other just yet. After all, there'll be plenty of time for homework and headaches later.

"I can come, too," Do' Re Mi chimes in. And that settles it. We all take off down the street, singing "Shop in the Name of Love"—one of Galleria's tunes—at the top of our lungs.

The Exotica Pet Store on Tenth Avenue looks like a jungle paradise. Still, the snakes in the big glass case don't look like they're exactly having a ball. They seem like they're kinda cramped—and not too happy about it either.

"Too bad they don't have any dogs here," I

moan, looking around at all the exotic pets. I see a sign that says, WE'VE GOT REPTILES—NOT POODLES—SO DON'T ASK!

"Chuchie, Mom is right," Bubbles says firmly. "We'll be lucky if we can pull off this charade—giving Pucci a pet that fits in the palm of his hand."

"I'll tell you one thing," I shoot back. "We'd never get away with a dog!"

"Oooh, what kind of fish is that?" Dorinda asks, pressing her nose against the fish tank to ogle a bright-yellow fish with blue lips.

"Miss, don't lean on the fish tanks!" snaps a snarly salesman with wild curly red hair and big black glasses.

"Okay, Mr. Magoo," Dorinda mumbles under her breath, then, more loudly, asks again, "I just wanted to know what kind of fish this is—that's *all*."

"That's a blue-lipped angelfish, okay?"

Now I'm getting nervous, because Mr. Magoo is kinda mean.

"Bubbles, *you* ask him," I whisper. She's not afraid to stand up to grown-ups who are nasty and *antipático.*

"We want to see an African pygmy hedgehog, please," Bubbles says with authority.

Dorinda pulls my sleeve and says, "We gotta make sure it's a baby, though—because they only live to be six years old."

"Okay."

Meanwhile, Mr. Magoo is standing there, waiting for us to finish whispering. "You ready, or what?"

"Yes, sir. We want a baby one, okay?"

"Yeah, yeah. Everybody wants a baby. I don't know what I'm supposed to do with these animals when they're more than a day old," Mr. Magoo huffs, throwing us a dirty look. "They're over there in the cage by the wall. Next to the guinea pigs."

"Oh, that's good!" Aqua says, getting excited. The twins have two guinea pigs for pets—Porgy and Bess—and they're really cute.

"He is so mean, I don't know if we should buy a pet here. Maybe he abuses the animals," I say as we hightail it to the back of the store.

"Don't worry, the animals probably just ignore him and eat their carrots in peace," Bubbles replies. "It's not like they're dogs or cats, Chuchie."

"Ooh, *mira*, look!" I exclaim, when I see a

bunch of little brown creatures sitting in their cage, just staring up at us.

Mr. Magoo is right behind us and snarls, "Lemme open the cage, all right?" Next thing I know, he puts a hedgehog in my hand, warning, "The spines are very sharp—so don't go scaring him."

"Can we have a girl one?" Dorinda asks.

"No, Do'—it's for Pucci, not us," Bubbles reminds her.

"Oooh, look at how he's scratching my hand!" I coo. I love him already!

"What do they eat?" Angie asks.

"They like insects, frogs, mice," Mr. Magoo says in a huffy tone, like we're stupid or something.

"How much is it?" I ask nervously.

"Forty-two bucks."

I look at Bubbles, and my eyes are saying *ayúdame!* "I only have forty dollars."

"I'll put in the rest," Bubbles volunteers.

"Is that it?" Mr. Magoo asks.

"Yes, sir!" I say excitedly.

Wait till Mom sees Mr. Pygmy! If I was buying the hoglet for me, I would be worried, but she is not gonna say no to Pucci. Not on his birthday—not in front of Abuela Florita—and definitely not in front of Dad!

"Ain't you gonna get a cage, Chanel?" Aqua asks, concerned.

"Oh! I forgot about that," I say nervously. "Sir, do they poop in the cage?" Dorinda snickers.

"You can train them to use a litter box if you want," Mr. Magoo says.

Bubbles whips out her Miss Wiggy StarWac cell phone. "I'm calling Mom," she informs us. "Mom, can I borrow—wait a minute. Sir, how much is the cage?"

"Twenty-seven fifty," Mr. Magoo says.

"Mom, can I borrow twenty-seven fifty? We're still at the pet store, and we've gotta get Pucci a cage for the, um, hoggy. . . . Okay, *okay*."

Bubbles hands the phone to Mr. Magoo. "My mom is charging the cage." Then she turns to me, and says proudly, "The cage is on me. After all, I've gotta get Pucci something, too—since he did invite me to his party."

"How are you gonna pay for it?" I ask softly. Now I feel so guilty for fighting with Bubbles!

"Mom is holding the money I have left from our first gig, at the Kats and Kittys Club. Now I have nothing left."

I feel like crying, but I stammer, "I-I can't believe you had money left and you didn't tell me!"

"Why, Chuchie? So you could spend it?" Bubbles asks, laughing. Then she gives me a hug.

"Thank you, Bubbles. Pucci is gonna be so happy—because we are both his sisters."

We put Pucci's pet in his new cage. Then I hand Mr. Magoo the money for the hoglet. "I wonder if Mr. Pygmy can make noises, like 'Oink, oink!'" I say. I smile at Mr. Magoo, but he doesn't smile back at me.

"No, I don't think he can squeal like that," Bubbles says. Then she looks Mr. Magoo right in the face, and points her finger at him. "But I bet *this* one can!"

We hightail it out of that store, screaming with laughter, before Mr. Magoo fries *us* like *bacon*!

Chapter 11

It's a good thing I let Bubbles take Mr. Pygmy to her house, because the first "thing" I see when I open the door is nosy Pucci. The television is blaring from his bedroom, so I don't understand what my sneaky brother is doing in the foyer.

"Why are you out here?" I ask him.

"None of your business," he snips. Then he says, "I wonder what Daddy got me for my birthday," and runs back to his room, before I even have a chance to answer him.

I shake my head and laugh, because I realize that Pucci is probably so excited about his birthday tomorrow that he's already running to see who's at the door! I may have a sense of smell as keen as a dog's, but my brother has ears like a cat—he hears *everything*!

I debate whether I should tell Mom about the meeting at the record company, because I can hear that she is on the phone—probably talking to her boyfriend, Mr. Tycoon. He's probably in Paris, France—or anyway, in one of those places he lives.

Mom says he lives in Saudi Arabia, Paris, *and* Geneva, Switzerland. Places I've never been—but will get to see one day, now that I'm a Cheetah Girl. Bubbles says the Cheetah Girls are going to travel all over the world, until we're ready for the old cheetahs' retirement home.

I tiptoe into my bedroom and fall right into bed, hoping that I'll dream once again about the Benjamins falling from the sky. Or about all the fun the Cheetah Girls are going to have, recording songs with Mouse Almighty. . . .

The next morning, I'm s-o-o nice and helpful to Mom while we get everything ready for Pucci's birthday celebration. Humming along, I open the refrigerator and touch the bottles of *cerveza*—that's beer—to see if they're cold enough. My dad likes his *cerveza muy frío*—and we made sure to get his favorite, Wild Willy beer. I take out a few of the big brown bottles, and plunk them down on the banquet table.

"You seem very chirpy today, Chanel," Mom says, as she puts the big bowl of *fufu*—mashed yams—on the table.

"I'm happy it's Pucci's birthday," I say, all bubbly.

"Remember—don't say anything to your *abuela* about my boyfriend," Mom reminds me. "The last thing I need is for her blood pressure to go up because I'm not dating a Latin man."

"Okay, *Mamí*," I say, amused. I don't think Abuela *would* like Mom's boyfriend at all. He's *antipático*, if you ask me—not really friendly. But I guess I should just be grateful that any man would put up with Mom—because she can be a pain, *está bien?*

All of a sudden, I feel the "spookies" churning around in my stomach as a new thought occurs to me. *What if my father doesn't show up?*

No, he *has* to show up, I reassure myself. I hope Bubbles and *Madrina* don't get stuck in traffic either. I'd feel better if Bubbles was here.

Mom hands me the Dominican-style *arroz*

con pollo, and tells me to put it on the table. She puts the *sancocho* stew on the table herself, and tops it with slices of avocado. *Yum yum*!

"Pucci, you look cute!" I exclaim as he walks into the living room. He is wearing a red sweater and pants, his face is clean, and the curls on top of his head have been combed into place. I can tell he's really excited. Pucci sneaks over to the coffee table and starts rustling the wrapping paper on the big box that's sitting there.

"Cut it out, Pucci!" Mom yells from the kitchen. Pucci must get his keen sense of hearing from Mom, because she is the only person I know who has bigger ears than he does—*or* is more nosy!

When the doorbell rings, both Pucci and I run to answer it.

"I got it!" he hisses, so I stop short and let him open the door. It's his birthday.

"Hi, Pucci, darling!" *Madrina* says excitedly with outstretched arms. She grabs Pucci and gives him a big bear hug. Bubbles is right behind her, and she is holding a big cardboard box. I should have known these two would have a hideaway plan!

"What's that? Is it my present?" Pucci asks excitedly.

"Never mind, Mr. Cuckoo Cougar," Bubbles says jokingly, then puts down the box where it will be safely out of the way until it's time to open it.

"Bubbles, I have a joke for you!" Pucci says excitedly.

"Oh, I don't know, Pucci—your jokes aren't even fit for the ears of the wildest animals in the jiggy jungle," *Madrina* says hesitantly.

"Pucci!" Mom yells out.

"No, Auntie Dottie, this is a *good* one," Pucci says with a mischievous grin. Pucci calls *Madrina* "Auntie Dottie," even though she isn't really his aunt. (*Madrina* wanted to be Pucci's godmother as well as mine, but Dad let his sister, Aunt Lulu, be Pucci's godmother instead. Aunt Lulu lives in Miami, with three Chihuahuas—so of course, Mom never likes to visit her.)

"Okay, Pucci, let's hear the joke," Bubbles says, amused. I think she's trying to distract him from the box, 'cuz his eyes keep straying over in that direction.

"Okay. Why is it so hard to hide a cheetah like you?" he says.

"I don't know, Pucci . . . because I have a big mouth?" Bubbles responds.

"No! Because you're always *spotted*!" Pucci says proudly.

"Whew, that was a good one, Pucci, I must say," *Madrina* says, relieved. She sits down on the couch, takes off her big leopard hat, and hands it to me. *Madrina* hates it when her hat gets crushed, so I always put it in the closet until she leaves. That way, no one sits on it by mistake.

The doorbell rings again—but now I'm not worried about Pucci seeing his present, so I let him answer it.

"Papí!"

Gracias gooseness, my father is here! I close my eyes for a second, and ask God not to let my mom and dad fight today. Then I take a really deep breath and run to the door.

"Hi, Abuela!" I say loudly—because Abuela is hard-of-hearing. Abuela reaches up, with her walking cane in her hand, and gives me a hug.

I look up at my father and smile. He isn't really that tall, but next to my tiny *abuela*, he looks like a giant. Obviously, I take after Abuela, because I'm short, too.

Daddy hands Pucci a present, and I can tell Pucci is already sizing it up. My eyes are just as good as his, and from the shape of the present, I'd say it looks like a book.

I can't wait to tell my dad all about the Cheetah Girls' trip to Los Angeles, and big meeting with Def Duck Records! When we sit down, my dad's eyes are twinkling as I tell him *every* detail. Pucci squeezes in between him and Bubbles on the couch, and just looks on happily, listening.

"Who was that guy you were talking to after the showcase at the Tinkerbell Lounge, Chuchie?" Bubbles asks me, amused.

Why would Bubbles bring that up now—in front of my parents, no less?

"What guy?" I ask, playing innocent.

"The guy in the shiny suit and shades," Bubbles quips. "You remember . . ."

"Oh, that guy! He was a vice president for Def Duck—I think he said in the publicity department or something. I can't remember, Bubbles, *está bien?*"

"Well, I'll bet he remembers you, Miss

Chanel. As a matter of fact, everybody will, because they sure were giving you all the attention," Bubbles says, giggling.

Oh, I get it. Bubbles is trying to make me look important in front of Daddy!

"I don't think so, Bubbles—they were paying attention to *all* of us," I reply.

"What's this I hear about you flirting with some man, Chanel?" Mom yells from the dining room. "I hope you didn't go to Los Angeles and lose your mind!"

"No, *Mamí*, I didn't," I say sheepishly.

Abuela is sitting across from me, and she just smiles. I don't think she really heard anything we said. *Gracias gooseness!*

"Juanita, you *knew* we were *all* working it," *Madrina* says, coming to my defense. "He *was* a tasty-looking morsel though, right, Chanel?"

What did *Madrina* have to say *that* for?!

All of a sudden, Mom snaps at *Madrina*, "If you're *that* hungry, Dottie, maybe you'd better eat something."

You can hear the *silencio*. Why does Mom have to pick on *Madrina* now? And why did *Madrina* have to start with her?

See, Mom and *Madrina* used to be models and

everything, and they were both really skinny. Mom is still skinny, because she never eats anything and exercises all the time. She is always picking on *Madrina* for getting, you know, *más grande*.

"Juanita, this isn't a restaurant, so rest assured I *will* serve myself—when everyone else eats," *Madrina* snips back at Mom, giving her that scary look that makes men run away on the street. *Por favor, Díos,* please—don't let *Madrina* hit Mom with her cheetah pocketbook!

Luckily, Dad comes to the rescue. "So—they gave you girls a record deal?"

"No, *Papí,* not exactly—well, I mean, no," I explain, stammering.

"Uncle Dodo, what Chanel means is, they're paying for us to record a few songs for a demo tape, then they'll see if they like the songs enough to give us a test single," Bubbles explains proudly. "And if *that* goes over well, *then* we get a record deal."

"Oh. I see."

Abuela beams at me, so I jump up and I run over to hug her. "Cristalle," she says, her eyes twinkling. Since last year, Abuela calls me by my confirmation name—which I like. *Me gusta Cristalle!*

"Let's eat!" I exclaim, jumping up to get everyone plates and stuff.

"Is there chicken in the *sancocho?"* Abuela asks Mom, while she spoons some onto her plate. The two of them are rival cooks—and the truth is, Abuela *does* cook better than Mom!

"No, I made it with just beef and pork this time," Mom says hesitantly.

"Está bueno," Abuela says. Whew! Now we can all breathe easier. If Abuela is happy with the food, then we're *all* happy!

I want to tell Dad that I saw Princess Pamela, but I realize he probably already knows that. Besides, Pucci is keeping him busy—he's so happy Dad is here.

After dinner, Mom goes to the kitchen, and motions for me to follow. That means it's time for Pucci's cake! We light the ten candles on top, and Mom brings it into the living room. I'm right behind her, singing, "Happy Birthday to you. Happy Birthday to you. Happy Birthday, dear Pucci . . . how old are you?"

We all join in and sing along, and Pucci finally blows out his candles. Now comes Pucci's favorite part: opening the presents! I'm glad, too, because I'm getting a new pet! Well,

Pucci's getting it—but I know who's gonna be taking care of it, and it's not gonna be Mom!

Pucci excitedly tears the wrapping paper off the box by the coffee table, opening his birthday present from Mom. "A new computer game—aren't you lucky!" I exclaim.

It's a great present, true—but I still can't believe she didn't get him a dog, after she promised she would. That's Mom for you.

"Mom, this is really cool!" Pucci says, giving her a big hug.

Mom looks at me over Pucci's shoulder, and I can tell she's thinking, "See? I didn't give him a dog and he's still happy, you troublemaker!"

Next, Pucci opens Abuela's present. It's a beautiful yellow and black sweater. She proudly tells him she knitted it herself, just for him.

"Thank you, Abuela," Pucci says, running over and hugging her.

Abuela urges Pucci to try it on, to make sure it fits. "My eyes aren't so reliable anymore, and you grow so fast," she says, smiling.

Pucci takes off his red sweater, and puts on his new one. "It fits!" he says proudly, warming Abuela's heart.

It's obvious that Pucci is saving Dad's present for last, because he opens *Madrina*'s next. *Madrina* has made Pucci a beautiful burgundy velvet suit.

"Oooh, Pucci, you are definitely the man!" Bubbles says excitedly.

"Thank you, Auntie Dottie," Pucci says, hugging *Madrina.*

"Make sure you wear that suit when you take your girlfriend out to a fancy restaurant." *Madrina* is always joking with Pucci about having a girlfriend. Pucci goes along with it, even though I know he *hates* girls—especially *me.*

"I will," he says, smiling and winking. He's so cute sometimes—even if he is a pain the rest of the time.

Bubbles goes and gets the cardboard carton, then sets it down in the middle of the floor. "Pucci," she says, "this present is from me and Chanel."

Pucci looks over at me and gives me a smile, even though I know he doesn't want to. Bubbles tries to help him open the box, but he insists on doing it himself.

"Oh, wow, what is it?" he exclaims excitedly, even though he doesn't know what kind of animal he's looking at. He pulls the cage out of the box carefully, and stares at Mr. Pygmy, completely transfixed.

"He's an African pygmy hedgehog," I say proudly, then look over at Mom to see if I should start packing and moving out yet.

She doesn't say a word, though.

"Wow, it looks like a—"

"Porcupine?" Bubbles asks, interrupting him.

"Yeah!"

Bubbles tells me with her eyes to take over.

"It's not a porcupine, because porcupines are rodents, Pucci. It's, um, related to moonrats," I explain.

"Wow, that's cool!" Pucci says, completely fascinated. He opens the cage door gingerly, and attempts to take Mr. Pygmy into his hands.

"Be careful," I warn. "He'll roll up into a ball and expose his spines when he's frightened."

"Oh, okay," Pucci says—but he doesn't seem to be afraid of Mr. Pygmy at all.

"He won't shed hair or anything so, um, you can't be allergic to them or anything," I say, looking at Mom with pleading eyes.

"Well, I hope you're gonna help him take

care of it—because I'm not going to," Mom huffs. Making a face, she gets up to get a Coke. That means she's upset, because she only drinks soda when she's upset. She would be afraid of the calories otherwise. As she pours the drink, she cuts her eyes sharply at me.

"What are you gonna name him, Pucci?" Bubbles asks.

"Cuckoo Cougar!" Pucci blurts out.

Cuckoo Cougar?! What a *stupid* name!!

"Oh, that's a nice name," Bubbles says, but I know she doesn't mean it. "We'll call him Cuckoo for short, okay?"

"Okay," Pucci says, smiling, as he puts Mr. Pygmy back in his cage.

Cuckoo. That's what *I'm* gonna call him anyway. Him *and* Pucci. Cuckoo one and cuckoo two!

At last, Pucci picks up the present Dad gave him, and rips off the paper. It *is* a book—and from the look on Pucci's face, I realize it's a book that *he* doesn't *like*.

Pucci holds the book in his hand and stares at the cover, then throws it on the floor! "I don't want this!" he says, pouting.

I can't believe Pucci! I run over and pick up the book, and look at the cover. It says, *Harry Henpecker's Guide to Geography.*

What was Dad thinking? This is the kind of *boring* book they always make us read in school!

Pucci runs over to Abuela and puts his head on her shoulder. He really is a big crybaby. *How could he hurt Dad's feelings like that?*

But I already know the answer. Pucci is very angry at Dad for leaving us. Poor Pucci—he doesn't realize that it has nothing to do with him. He doesn't care that Dad and Mom don't love each other anymore—he just wants Dad to live with us again.

I get up from the floor and go to sit by Dad. He doesn't say anything for a long time. Then, very calmly, he says, "You said that Pucci doesn't read anything, and I was just trying to help."

"I understand, Dodo," Mom says, looking embarrassed. I can tell she wants to yell at Pucci, but she feels bad for him because it's his birthday.

"Pucci," Mom says sternly, looking at my brother. "*Papí* is going to get you another birthday present, okay?"

"Don't tell him that!" Dad blurts out. I can tell he is getting *caliente* mad, because his eyes are getting red, and he's breathing fire.

"Okay, I'm sorry," Mom says. "But it wouldn't hurt you to get him something else."

I can't believe how nice she's being! I'm so glad it's Pucci's birthday—otherwise, they'd be throwing pots and pans at each other by now!

"If he weren't so spoiled, he would appreciate any present that he got. I didn't get any presents at all when I was a child," Dad says sternly. See, he and Auntie Lulu were secretly smuggled out of Cuba when they were kids. After that, they never saw their father again. I can tell it still hurts Dad.

He gets up very slowly, and tells Abuela that it's time to go. Mom doesn't say a word while they get their coats.

"I love you, *Papí,"* I whisper in his ear, then kiss him good-bye. He hugs me tight. I hug Abuela tight, too—she's so very precious to me.

"Gracias Dios," Mom says when Dad and Abuela are gone. Shaking her head, she gets up and goes into the den.

Mom *never* talks in Spanish, so I know she

must be very upset. She probably is going to call Mr. Tycoon now, and talk for hours and hours.

Pucci wipes away his tears, then goes over to the cage and picks up Mr. Pygmy. "Chanel, I like your and Bubbles's present the best." Then, quickly, he turns to *Madrina* and adds, "Yours, too, Auntie Dottie!"

"I know, darling—don't think I feel bad," *Madrina* says, picking up her glass of soda. "I can't blame you, Pucci. Nobody wants to read schoolbooks on their birthday! You'd think we could just forget about that drama for at least one day!"

I smile at Bubbles. She turns to Pucci and says, "Next time someone gives you a present you don't like, you shouldn't hurt their feelings, Pucci."

"Okay," Pucci says. I guess he feels bad now for acting like a spoiled brat.

"Just pretend you like it. Then, later, you can toss it in the giveaway pile in the closet and recycle it!" *Madrina* says.

Bubbles and I look at each other and laugh—because once, *Madrina* forgot that Mom gave her a navy blue scarf for Christmas, and she gave it back to Mom the next year. Her "recycling rodeo" backfired!

I hug Pucci. I know how much it hurts to be disappointed—especially now that I'm part of the Cheetah Girls, and our lives have turned into a roller-coaster ride. One day, we're up and flying high, the next day we're screaming our heads off as we descend to the bottom.

"You're not such a bad sister after all," Pucci says, cracking a smile for the first time since Dad left.

"You wanna come and see my room?" I ask him. I *neve*r let Pucci come into my room, because he is so nosy.

"Okay," he says, and I can tell he's happy I asked him.

Bubbles follows us. "I'm gonna stay over," she says, hugging me.

"Great!" Pucci says, because he really does love Bubbles—I think even more than he loves me.

Pucci, Mr. Pygmy, Bubbles, and I all lie on the bed together.

"Are you really gonna make songs together?" Pucci asks me. Mr. Pygmy's little body is cupped in his right hand, and Pucci is tickling him.

"Yeah, Pucci, we *are* gonna make songs together," I say, without looking up at him. "Bubbles, can you believe we're getting a chance to record songs for a real record label?"

There is silence for a second; then Bubbles blurts out, "Yeah, I can't believe it! I just pray to God that they don't have us recording songs like the ones Pumpmaster Pooch made us do."

I wince at the memory of the producer we worked with for a Minute Rice moment. Mr. Jackal Johnson, our former manager, teamed us with Pumpmaster Pooch and put us in a studio. We recorded songs that made us sound like a pack of gangsta hyenas!

"*Gracias gooseness, Madrina* got us out of that one," I say, sighing. "What was the name of that song we recorded for them? It was *horrible*."

"'I Got a Thing for Thugs,'" Bubbles says, without missing a beat. "If Def Duck Records makes us record songs as wack as that, Chuchie, the Cheetah Girls are gonna rent a hot-air balloon—and head off to OZ!"

Giggling, I lay my head on Bubbles's shoulder and say, "You always said we were gonna follow the yellow brick road, no matter where it leads."

All of a sudden, I remember the dream I had—the one with me and Bubbles flying with an umbrella. And I also remember Princess Pamela's prediction—that good things were gonna start happening. "I don't think we're gonna need that hot-air balloon, Bubbles," I tell her.

"Why?" Bubbles asks.

"'Cuz I just heard a weather report in my head—*it's gonna be raining Benjamins*!"

It's Raining Benjamins

For the first time in her-*story*
there's a weather forecast
that looks like the mighty cash.
So tie up your shoes and
put away your blues
'cuz we're going around the bend
at half past ten
to the only place in town
where everything is coming up green
you know what I mean:

It's raining Benjamins
Hallelujah
It's raining Benjamins
Hallelujah

Now maybe you're wondering
what's all the thundering—
but we've got the root of all the loot
that got past Santa's chute
without collecting soot.

So put on your galoshes
and bring your noshes
to the only place in town
where money is falling on the ground.
That's right, y'all:

It's raining Benjamins
Hallelujah
It's raining Benjamins
Hallelujah
It's raining . . . Amen!

So here's the rest of the her-*story*
Now that there's no longer a mystery.
There's precipitation in the nation
and it's causing a sensation
in the only way that dollar bills
can give you thrills.
Yeah, that's what I mean:

It's raining Benjamins
Hallelujah
It's raining Benjamins
Hallelujah
It's R-A-I-N-I-N-G . . . AMEN!
(Say it, again!)

The Cheetah Girls Glossary

Adobo down: Mad flava.
Antipático: Dodo. Lame. Pain in the poot-butt.
Babosa: Stupid.
Bacalao: Spanish codfish.
Beeneh: Romanian for "good."
Benjamins: Bucks, dollars.
Bobada: Baloney.
Bugaboo: Pain in the butt.
Cerveza: Beer.
El pollito: Acting like a chicken.
Está bien: Okay, get it?
Gnocco: Italian for "blockhead."
Goospitating: Nervous.
Gracias gooseness: Thank goodness!
I'm so over this: Fed up to the max.
La dopa: Dope-licious.
La gente: Peeps, people.
Lonchando: Spanglish for lunch.
Madrina: Godmother.
Madrino: Godfather.

Montagna: Mountain—or a diamond ring as big as one!

Off the cheetah meter: Beyond cheetah-licious. Off the hook. Supa-dupa chili.

Pata de puerco: Idiot. Leg of a pig.

Poot-butt: Someone who is a pain or has a funny-looking booty.

Que puzza!: Italian for "what a stinky-poo."

The spookies: A nightmare. The willies.

Un coco: A crush.

Vampira: A vampire.

Wait for the bait: Wait for the right moment to pounce on an "op"—an opportunity.

Dorinda's Secret

For Abiola, who runs for her breakfast
before she says *"Hola!"*
to the mouse in the house
who peeps her granola!

Chapter 1

When I see my foster mother, Mrs. Bosco, sprawled out on the bed in her teeny cubbyhole of a bedroom, I know right away that something is up. I immediately get this squiggly spasm in my stomach. She never lies down in there before bedtime unless she's upset or sick. Either way, it's bad news.

I know she had to go down to the agency today—the Administration of Children's Services in Brooklyn—which is supposedly responsible for the lives of thousands of foster kids like me in the Big Apple. This can only mean one thing, I figure—we've lost custody of Corky!

"Please don't tell me they are going to take

Corky away!" I pray. "If anybody has to go, let it be Kenya."

Now I know that's a terrible thing to say, but you've got to understand—my foster sister Kenya is spastic-on-the-elastic tip. She's only six, and I don't want to be around when she's old enough to *really* start ad-lipping—running her mouth off the cuff, if you know what I'm saying.

Before you think we've got it on easy street or something, let me tell you about the other foster kids living here with Mr. and Mrs. Bosco. Besides myself—Dorinda Rogers (or Do' Re Mi, as my crew, the Cheetah Girls, call me)—there are five other girls. Kenya shares a room with five-year-old Arba (from Albania—she's the newest member of our foster family) and my favorite sister, Twinkie. I share my bedroom with Chantelle (who hogs *my* computer) and Monie the Meanie (who spends most of her time with her boyfriend these days).

But wait—I'm not done yet! There are also five boys! There's Corky, who I've already mentioned. Then there's Khalil, Nestor, precious Topwe (his mother is from Africa!), and last but not least, Shawn the Fawn.

So, as you can see, Mr. and Mrs. Bosco really have their hands full. The Boscos aren't getting any younger, either—they're old enough to be grandparents—and Mrs. Bosco's been sick on and off, the past couple of years. So the last thing they need is trouble with Family Court.

Which brings me back to Corky. He has lived with us since he was crawling around in diapers and eating lint off the floor. Four years later, his father comes out of the blue, trying to win back custody. Where was "Daddykins" back then, huh?

Now Mrs. Bosco has to bring Corky all the way to Brooklyn for monthly visits with "Mister Good-for-Nothing"—that's what she calls Corky's father, Mr. Dorgle. Mrs. Bosco even has to go to Family Court for the custody proceedings.

"I wish a judge would just hit that fool over the head with a gavel and be done with it. Case closed," Mrs. Bosco says, turning on her other side to face me.

"I know that's right," I humph nervously, because I just dread what's coming. I feel stupid hovering in the doorway, but Mrs. Bosco's bedroom is really tiny, so I never go in there unless she says I can.

"Come on and sit on the bed, Dorinda," Mrs. Bosco says, chuckling and wheezing at the same time. I sit on the edge of the bed, trying not to take up any space.

"I spent the whole day fighting with those people," Mrs. Bosco says, putting her hand on her forehead like it hurts.

"Those people" are what she calls the caseworkers, who "push a lot of paper around doing nothing."

"I swear they got on my last nerve today," she continues, her Southern drawl more pronounced than usual because she's upset. She raises herself up from the bed, then puts on her glasses and squints at me. "Dorinda, how come your eyes are red?"

"I guess I was rubbing them because I'm tired," I say, yawning. "You know I had dance class tonight at the Y."

"Oh, yeah, how is that Truly child?" Mrs. Bosco asks, chuckling softly.

"Still teaching us more combinations than Bugga Bear Jones does in the ring," I chuckle back. Bugga Bear Jones is Mr. Bosco's favorite boxer. Mr. Bosco watches boxing on the television at his night job as a security guard. "That Truly child" would be my dance teacher, Darlene Truly, who is, well, "truly" dope.

Mrs. Bosco calls everybody "child," because sometimes she can't remember their names. I can tell by the way she chuckles that she likes Ms. Truly, though. After all, Ms. Truly did hook me up with an audition as a backup dancer for one of the dopest dope singers on the planet—Mo' Money Monique. I got the job, too, but in the end I didn't take it—partly because of Mrs. Bosco, and partly because of my crew, the Cheetah Girls.

Yeah, the Cheetah Girls are in the house. Besides me, that would be Galleria "Bubbles" Garibaldi; Chanel "Chuchie" Simmons; and the hot-sauce twins from Houston, Texas, Aquanette and Anginette Walker. (Every week we have new nicknames for the twins—but to their faces, we call them Aqua and Angie for short.)

We're not just a crew, either. We're a supa-chili singing group. I'm not just flossin'—we're waiting to hear from Def Duck records, 'cuz they're talkin' about us making a demo, and then maybe even a record deal!

That was after I turned down the Mo' Money Monique job, though. I didn't turn it down because I knew the Cheetah Girls were about to hit it big—I did it because I love my crew. I love my foster family, too—even Kenya. I was just riffing about her before 'cuz she gets on my nerves. Nope—no way was I gonna leave my crew or my foster family—because they're really all I have.

"Do you know that fool had the nerve not to show up today?" Mrs. Bosco says, shaking her head. "He should just leave this child alone and hide back under whatever rock he crawled out of." I can tell Mrs. Bosco is just getting started. "Where I come from, he woulda never seen the inside of no courtroom. We woulda just chased him out of town with a shotgun nipping at his heels, and dared that fool to look back!"

Mrs. Bosco was "born and raised in good ole Henderson, NC," as she likes to say. NC—that's North Carolina. She is very old, and she comes from a long line of tobacco sharecroppers. She had to work in the fields when she was only eight years old, and she never went to school. That's why Mrs. Bosco is illiterate—even though we're not supposed to know that, and certainly the social workers aren't! They wouldn't let us live here if they knew, and then where would all of us be?

You know, Mrs. Bosco's being illiterate really cost me, too. She wanted to adopt me, but she didn't understand the procedure, so the adoption never went through. She and Mr. Bosco threw me a big party before we found out. She says she's still going to adopt me, but I don't ask her about it anymore.

"I'm tired of them fooling with Corky's mind," she goes on. "How can they even consider putting him with Mr. Good-for-Nothing is beyond me, but that's typical, you know."

I breathe a sigh of relief, now that I know it's just another round in the custody battle, and nothing final has been decided.

"Even after him not showing up, they are still gonna continue with this mess," Mrs. Bosco adds, taking off her glasses and lying back down on her bed. "Oh, by the way, Dorinda—*your* caseworker is coming by here tomorrow to see y'all. What's her name again?"

"Mrs. Tattle," I say, reminding her. "I'll come

straight home after vocal class. How come she's coming on a Saturday?"

"She said she had to see you—that probably just means she's leaving for her vacation and needs to finish up her paperwork," Mrs. Bosco says with a sigh.

Mrs. Bosco is probably right. I've had more caseworkers than I can count—sometimes I can't even remember their names, because they come and go so fast. Some of them look kinda sad—like they wish they were someplace else, doing something different.

I know what that's like. Before I started school at Fashion Industries East High—where I met my crew and became a Cheetah Girl—I didn't have many *real* friends, and I wasn't sure what I was going to do with my life. Now I know: I'm going to sing, dance, make costumes—and make people happy, too.

Kenya lets out a scream loud enough to chase my daydreams away. I look back at Mrs. Bosco, but she is nodding off again, so I whisper, "I'll see you later." She does that all the time. She can be talking one minute, then sleeping the next. Like a cat, I guess.

Walking toward the kitchen, I call out, "What

are y'all doing in there?" As usual, *someone* is trying to get at some food in the kitchen cupboard. "You know you're not supposed to be climbing on the counter, Kenya. How many times does Mrs. Bosco have to tell you that?" I shake my head. Kenya never listens to anybody.

"I want some popcorn!" she yells.

"I'll get it," I tell her, then pull up a chair and stand on it to reach the big bag of Brand Ann popcorn. Like I said before, Kenya is always whining about something and never shares anything with the rest of us. I know she steals candy and stuff from stores, because sometimes I find the wrappers under her bed or they fall out of her backpack and pockets. When I do, she just gives me this blank look, like she doesn't know how they got there.

When I first came to live at Mrs. Bosco's, I was really angry—I guess because my mother abandoned me, and then my first foster mother gave me up. I used to steal candy, too, but I stopped doing it after a while, when I wasn't so mad anymore. Maybe Kenya will settle down someday, too. I sure hope so.

Peering into the oven, I see my plate of food,

covered in tinfoil. The kids have all eaten dinner, and as usual, Mrs. Bosco has left me something for when I get home from class—but I'm too tired to look and see what it is. I just take the bag of popcorn into the living room and plop down in front of the television.

I give Corky the first handful, even though that makes Kenya mad. "Thank you," he says, his pretty greenish-gray eyes sparkling at me. He is so cute—I can't understand why anyone would give him away, even though I know everything is not so simple as that. Grown-ups have lots of problems, and sometimes they just can't deal with them.

I pass around handfuls of popcorn to Khalil, Arba, Twinkie, Topwe, and Shawn, who are all sitting around waiting for their favorite show to come on TV.

Corky puts his hand out for more. "I'm gonna call you Porky instead of Corky," I chuckle, watching his mischievous grin get bigger. Corky's mother was put away in a "mental health facility." I know this because I help with the paperwork and bills, so I can't help reading some of the files and reports we get.

I'll bet you if Corky's mother could see how

cute he is now, it would make her mental illness go away. Sometimes people aren't really crazy, Mrs. Bosco says—they're just tired and confused. Maybe Corky's mother is like that.

"Stop pushing me!" Kenya screams at Nestor, who is trying to get a better seat in front of the television. Nestor just ignores Kenya. He is eight, and kinda quiet. Sometimes he sits at the table and eats so fast he never even looks up at anybody. That's how he got his nickname, "Nestlé's Quik." As usual, he has already gobbled his handful of popcorn—earning his nickname to the max.

Zoning out in front of the television, I just munch away, staring at the stupid commercials.

"Gimme more!" my brother Topwe moans. I just hand him the bag of popcorn, because I'm so tired of him trying to take it on the sneak tip. Brand Ann tastes like a whole bunch of air anyway—it's not the good stuff, like Piggly Wiggly Chedda Puffs, which sticks to your fingers and has a supa-cheesy flow.

"You ate it *olle*, Dori-i-n-da!" Topwe says, peering up at me and baring the mile-wide gap between his two front teeth. Topwe cracks me up, because he speaks English with his own African groove. Topwe was born HIV-positive because his mother was a crack addict. Sometimes he comes down with nasty colds, but basically he's okay—and he eats "like a hungry hog." That's what the twins, Aqua and Angie, said after they saw Topwe in action at my "adoption" party.

Aqua and Angie made the bomb spread of yum-yums for everyone to eat, but Topwe ate the whole tray of candied yams before anybody else got a whiff of it. His name means vegetable in some African dialect, so I guess the yams were a good choice, you know what I'm saying? Now Topwe keeps asking me when the twins are coming back over with some more "kaandied yoms."

"*I* want some more!" Kenya moans, poking out her mouth in a pout.

"Mom, can we open the other bag of popcorn?" I call out to Mrs. Bosco. Ever since I almost got adopted, she said it was okay to call her "Mom," so I do. I mean, I've lived here seven years, so I don't think she's gonna give me away.

"Just make sure the kids don't leave kernels

all over the floor," Mrs. Bosco yells back.

"Okay—um," I say, holding back on calling her Mom again. I don't want to overdo it or anything.

"When is this over?" Kenya asks when the news brief comes on after the commercial.

"Soon, just watch," I reply. I'm so tired I would watch anything. Of course, they're all waiting for their favorite show to come on—*She's All That and a Pussy Cat*.

"Oh, it's the news," whines Khalil. "I hate the news. It always makes me sad."

The news announcer says, "Now, more on Paulo Rivera's Fib-ulous Ride." A picture of a cute boy flashes on the television screen. The reporter continues, "A thirteen-year-old boy's tall tale of his solo odyssey from the Dominican Republic to New York in search of his only living relative turns out to be a journey in his imagination."

Now my eyes are glued to the television screen. Even Kenya stops fidgeting as the reporter talks about this boy, Paulo Rivera, who ran away from home and took a bus from New Jersey to the Big Apple. Apparently he told everyone that he had run away from Santo

Domingo in the Dominican Republic and traveled 2,000 miles on his own—all the way to New York!

"Paulo claimed he was searching for his father," says the reporter. "But the father, it turns out, died of AIDS a year ago. 'Paulo attended the funeral, but still refuses to believe it,' says the boy's tearful aunt, with whom Paulo lived in New Jersey. The aunt reported him missing when he didn't come home from school.

"It's not clear what will happen to Paulo Rivera, who is now under the care of the Administration for Children's Services. ACS officials could not be reached for comment," the reporter says, finishing the news report.

Suddenly, I feel sorry for Paulo. All that trouble he went through, just to end up in foster care. It doesn't seem fair.

"That's cold he got caught," says Khalil, who is glued to the television screen. He has only lived at Mrs. Bosco's for a few months and has been in a lot of foster homes. He kinda keeps to himself, even though he's cool. "If that had been me, I would have been Audi 5000—they would have never found me, yo."

"How come?" I ask—because I'm really curious how an eleven-year-old kid thinks he could disappear and live by himself.

"'Cuz when I ran away from my last foster home, they didn't find me. I came back by myself," Khalil says, like *he's* bragging or something.

"How many foster homes wuz you in?" Nestor asks.

"Four," Khalil says, like he's talking about trophies.

"I was in three," Nestor says, like *he's* bragging.

"I almost got adopted," Chantelle blurts out.

Hmmm. I've never heard this one before. Maybe Chantelle is fibbing, just to get attention.

"No you didn't," Nestor says nastily.

"Yes I did, but I didn't want to stay," Chantelle says.

Twinkie nuzzles up to me and puts her head on my shoulder, her fuzzy hair flouncing all the over the place. "I bet you that boy *wuz* looking for *somebody*."

Twinkie is so smart. "Yeah. I bet you he was," I reply, then hold her tight while we watch the show.

"I wanna find my father," Khalil announces.

It's the first time he's ever said anything like that. I notice that Nestor is pretending he's not listening.

"How do you know you've got a father?" Chantelle asks, with an attitude.

"'Cuz I do. My mother told me," Khalil says matter-of-factly.

"You have a mother?" I ask, surprised.

"Of course I have a mother, stupid," Khalil says, getting annoyed now.

"Well, *I* don't," I say, just to show him I'm not stupid.

"Yes you do," Khalil says. "Everybody has a mother."

"Well, I never *saw* her!" I exclaim, embarrassed.

"Don't you ever want to find your mother?" Nestor asks, ganging up on me too.

"I don't know," I say, determined not to let them win. I'm not going to tell them about my sister at Mrs. Parkay's—she was my first foster mother, the one who gave me away. I try not to think about her anymore, because Mrs. Parkay probably doesn't want to see me anymore—and I sure don't want to see her.

"I'll bet you *my* mother has long hair like an

angel," Twinkie says, smiling. "I know she's gonna come and get me one day."

I can't believe Twinkie said that! When I was younger, I used to think the same thing. Of course, I don't anymore. I don't know where my mom is, or whether she's alive or dead—I'd like to at least find out someday, but I guess I never will.

Now Arba climbs up onto my lap. Poor Arba. Her mother came to America from Albania looking for a better life, but died of pneumonia. At least one day she will know where *her* mother is. When she's older, I'll make *sure* she knows.

"I know what Khalil's daddy looks like," Nestor says, hitting Khalil on the head.

"Yeah—how do you know?" Khalil riffs back.

"He's got a big coconut head—like you!"

"Yeah—well, we know your father probably has a big mouth, Nestlé's Quik," I tell Nestor.

Corky and Twinkie start giggling. Arba has fallen asleep on my lap, so I take her into her bedroom and put her in bed. I kiss her on the cheeks, and she whispers, "Good night, Doreedy."

Chapter 2

As I lie on my pillow, I can't stop thinking about that runaway boy, Paulo Rivera. Why did he tell all those lies? I wonder if he was just trying to pull an okeydokey and get money out of people by making them feel sorry for him. Who wouldn't feel sorry for a kid hiking, biking, and sailing 2,000 miles just to find his father, right?

When they found him, the reporter said, he had $150 in his pockets. Tossing in my bed, I decide I would *never* go looking for my family, you know what I'm saying? I don't care where my mother and father are. They obviously don't love me, or I wouldn't be here.

I can feel myself starting to cry, but I get mad

instead. I'm tired of crying about stupid people who don't care about me. All of a sudden, I start crying anyway—but I think it's because I'm crying for Paulo. They shouldn't put him in a foster home—he must feel so scared right now. Why don't they just let him go back home to his aunt?

She doesn't want him anymore—that's probably why. That thought makes me angry, and I peek out from behind the pillow to see if Monie sees me crying.

She's just gotten home from her boyfriend Hector's house. Now she's sitting at the dresser, writing something—probably a stupid love letter to Hector, because I know she *never* does her homework. She's already been left back once, and she hates me because I got skipped twice. (I'm only twelve, but my crew doesn't know I'm so young—they think I'm fourteen like them, and I'm too afraid to tell them the truth. They'd probably never want to speak with me again, let alone chill with me!)

I cover my face with the pillow again, because the light from the lamp is bothering me. Then, all of a sudden, I find myself blurting out, "Do you ever think about your mother?"

Monie looks at me like I've lost my mind. "No," she says, getting an attitude, "and I don't know why you're lying there thinking about something so *stupid*."

Chantelle doesn't say anything; she just keeps popping her gum. What was I thinking about, talking to Monie? Her brain is on permanent vacation, you know? She doesn't understand anything. Neither does Chantelle. And my other foster sisters are too young. I wish I had a *real* sister like the twins. They have each other.

Well, actually, I do have a real sister. We were together in my first foster home. But she got to stay there, and I didn't, and that's the last I ever saw or heard from her.

Thank goodness for the Cheetah Girls. Having my crew—especially Chanel—is as close to having sisters as I'll ever get. Even so, it's not the same as having a real one. . . .

I'm in an apartment, and this pretty brown lady is showing me all her beautiful clothes. "You can come live with me and pick out all the clothes you want to wear," she says.

It's a really big apartment, and there are lots and lots of beautiful clothes everywhere. I start trying on some of the clothes, but they're all too big for me.

"Don't worry, when you grow up, you can wear these clothes, because I'll give them all to you," the pretty lady says. I ask her why. She tells me, "I'm your mother, that's why."

I start crying, and I hug her. She is so tall, and her skin is smooth chocolate. When she smiles, she looks like a movie star with really white teeth.

I don't even feel mad at her anymore. . . .

The noise from a car alarm wakes me up from my dream. I look at the clock and see that it's seven in the morning—time for me to get up and go to my Saturday morning vocal and dance lessons at Drinka Champagne Conservatory.

I walk to the bathroom, but somebody is in it. "Hurry up!" I yell, tapping my knuckles on the door.

I wonder who the lady in the dream was. She didn't look like anybody I know.

Maybe it *was* my mother. Maybe I'm psychic or something, like Chanel, and her father's girlfriend, Princess Pamela, who has a fortune-telling parlor.

Leaning against the bathroom door in a trance, I daydream about what my mother looks like. I guess I *would* like to know. She's probably pretty, and brown-skinned—and too busy to take care of me.

Suddenly I realize that I forgot to do my biology homework! I never space out like that. What was I supposed to be reading? That's right—the chapter on DNA—the stuff to do with genetics.

I'm in such a trance that when Twinkie opens up the bathroom door, I fall inside the doorway. She giggles and covers her head to keep me from falling on her. "Big cheetah bobo, you going to dance class now?" she asks, peering up at me.

"Yeah."

"I wish I could go. I wanna be a Cheetah Girl too," Twinkie says, pleadingly.

She always makes me feel so guilty about being in the Cheetah Girls. It's true I spend less time with her these days. And now she wants to be a part of what I'm doing.

"You know how you like to draw all those beautiful butterflies?" I say as I wash my face and hands.

"Yeah," Twinkie says.

"Well, dancing is what *I* like to do—and now, I'm singing too." I know she doesn't get it.

"Yeah, but I wanna dance and sing, too—if you'll let me!"

"You can dance and sing, Twinkie—if you want to do something badly enough, there's nobody in the world can stop you, least of all me. I'll tell you what—we're gonna find out if you can do something at school—"

"I wanna do it with *you!*" Twinkie insists, giggling and whining at the same time, like she always does.

"You can't."

"Okay, you big Cheetah bunny—I'm gonna flush you down the toilet!"

I tickle Twinkie, then run out of there and back into the bedroom to get dressed. I love going to Drinka Champagne Conservatory for vocal and dance classes—it's the bomb, and we always have a lotta fun, too. We are the Cheetah Girls, of course, and that means all five of us meet there—unlike during the week, when we go to separate schools. Aqua and Angie just got transferred to the Performing Arts League, which is an annex of LaGuardia

Performing Arts School—they're right next door to each other near Lincoln Center, and both of them are dope performing arts schools. As for me, Galleria, and Chanel, we all go to Fashion Industries East together.

As I'm running out the door, I feel around my neck, and realize I forgot to put on my Cheetah Girls choker, so I run back inside my room to get it. We made the Cheetah Girl chokers ourselves. We bought cheetah-printed strips of suede, then glued metal letters on them to spell the words GROWL POWER. The chokers are really dope looking, and they hold together fine—*now.*

At first, when we were trying to sell them, a lot of the lettering fell off. It was totally embarrassing, and I don't even want to talk about it. It's over, thank goodness. Now I actually *enjoy* wearing my choker. It tells the world who and what I am—"Do' Re Mi" Rogers, a Cheetah Girl with Ferocious Flava!

"Can we make a butterfly dress later?" Twinkie asks me, following me into the room.

"Yeah, later."

See, for Thanksgiving, the kids in Twinkie's school are making costumes, and Twinkie wants to be a butterfly instead of a turkey—even though her teacher says she has to stay with the theme of Thanksgiving.

That's Twinkie for you. I told her to tell him that she's one of the butterflies who came with the first settlers to Plymouth Rock or something. She liked that idea.

"Twinkie, I need you to do something for me."

"Okay."

"Mrs. Tattle, our caseworker, is coming over at two o'clock—so I won't be back here in time to get everybody ready. I want you to wear your pink sweater with the pom-poms. Would you do that for me?"

"Okay. Bye, pom-pom poot-butt!"

"I'm gonna get you later for that, Twinkie," I chuckle as I put the Cheetah Girl choker around my neck. Twinkie is still standing next to me, staring.

"Twink—do you think these chokers are big enough?"

"Yeah—you look like a big Cheetah Gorilla!"

"No, seriously—is the band wide enough?"

She shakes her head, then blurts out, "How come I can't have one?"

That makes me feel really bad. How come I was only thinking about myself?

I touch the metal letters on the choker again. I can feel the letters spelling GROWL POWER. We must have it, all right, or Def Duck Records wouldn't be interested in putting us in the studio with big cheese producer Mouse Almighty to cut some tracks. I wonder when it's gonna happen. Every day we hope to hear something, but so far, *nada*.

I yell good-bye to Mrs. Bosco, who is sitting at the kitchen table with Corky, then give Arba a big hug. Twinkie is right at my heels.

"I'm counting on you, Cheetah Rita Butterfly," I whisper to her. Rita is Twinkie's real name, but I think it's her nickname—not Twinkie, but the one I gave her, Butterfly—that really makes her spread her wings.

Chapter 3

Miss Winnie, the receptionist at Drinka Champagne's Conservatory, gives me a big smile when she sees me. "Dorinda, how you doin'?" she asks, like she really wants to know.

I can't believe how nice everybody is to me here at the Conservatory—and I haven't even paid one ducket for anything! That's because Drinka (who founded this conservatory for divettes-in-training like the Cheetah Girls) gave me a full one-year scholarship. Miss Winnie even put me in Vocal 201, instead of 101, so I could be with my crew.

See, Galleria and Chanel have been coming to Drinka's for two years now, and Angie and

Aqua could sing like (almost) divas even before we met them. I'm a good dancer, but I'm still learning to sing. More important, next to the rest of the Cheetah Girls, I still feel like a wanna-be star in the jiggy jungle, just like the words in the song Bubbles wrote.

"I'm just fine, Miss Winnie. Are the rest of the Cheetah Girls here yet?"

"Yes. And you girls better take a look at the bulletin board, too. There's something you may be interested in," Miss Winnie adds, winking at me.

That must mean there's something dope, like an audition or something. See, sometimes casting directors who are looking for young talent contact Drinka's Conservatory, so the school puts up notices on the bulletin board. Drinka was the queen of disco back in the day, and she still has mad "connects" all over the place.

I wonder what's jumping down. But I don't get a chance to check it out right away, because it's time for class to begin!

"Dorinda—*qué linda*!" exclaims Chanel when I walk into the studio. The Cheetah Girls are all so hyped these days, ever since we had our big meeting with Def Duck Records. Like I said, they're gonna put us in a studio with big cheese producer, Mouse Almighty, to cut a few songs for a possible demo. We don't know *when* it's going to go down, but we are definitely "in the house with Mouse," as Bubbles puts it.

I hug Chanel first. Even though I'm down with all the Cheetah Girls, I definitely feel the closest with Chanel. We have a lot in common. I mean, her pops is gone, and she and her mom don't exactly seem to be watching the same *Telemundo* television show, if you know what I'm saying. Her mom doesn't want Chanel to just be herself. I mean, Chanel may not be good at math or spelling, but she is really sweet. She knows how to make people feel like she cares about them, and how to make you laugh—and that counts for a lot —especially in our crew.

"Guess who's here? It's Do' Re Mi—so now we can flip it like posse!" Bubbles chants, giving me a Cheetah Girls handshake. She has on a hot-pink sweater and pink lipstick, which makes her look kinda like her nickname—a juicy piece of bubble gum!

"Galleria, you heard anything else from the Def Duck peeps?" I ask. All this waiting just to hear when we can kick it in the studio makes me so anxious. I just want us to move and groove already, ayiight?

"*Nada*," Galleria says, shaking her head. I can tell she's on the anxious tip, too. "I can't wait till we can get into a studio. I mean *enuf* with the powder puff!"

"I heard that," I groan.

"Daddy doesn't understand why they just don't give us a record deal," Aquanette says, her eyes popping wide. "I told him the music business is not like the pest control business—you can't just expect a roach to crawl up into a roach motel and be done with it!"

I chuckle at Aqua's joke. The twins have definitely gotten more live, if you know what I'm saying.

After our class, Drinka pulls all five of us aside. "Now listen, Cheetah Girls, there's a notice upstairs I want you to look at—the 'Battle of the Divettes' competition."

Chanel jumps up and down like a Mexican jumping bean.

"Now, a lot of the students are gonna try out for it, but I think this one has your name written all over it—'divettes.' Drinka's red lip gloss is shining like a neon sign as she breaks into a big smile, showing off the biggest, whitest teeth I've ever seen. "Send in your tape and see if you get an audition for it."

"What kind of tape?" Bubbles asks, looking at us.

"Don't tell me you haven't made a videotape of yourselves performing yet?" Drinka asks, like she can't believe it. Suddenly, I feel like a wanna-be all over again.

"Dag on, I guess we haven't," Aqua pipes up, looking sullen.

"Well, run out and make one," Drinka commands us. "*Au revoir, mes chéries*." Drinka lays on the thick French accent, the way Chanel's mom, Juanita, does.

"*Au revoir*," Chanel coos.

"*Croissant*," giggles Bubbles, and kisses Drinka on the cheek.

Drinka was right. The "Battle of the Divettes" competition does seem like it has our names written on it. The headline on the posting reads: *If you think you're fierce, call and submit your tape. (Photo and bio optional.)*

"Oh, lawdy, lawd," Angie says, grabbing her sister Aqua's hand and continuing to read the listing. "Unsigned talent who make 'The Grade' will compete on air. MTV will finance and air a professionally produced video of the grand-prize winner!"

"Remember those girls—'In the Dark'?" Aqua asks. "You know—the leader of the group wears a fake eye patch, and the other girls have got those monkey-head canes?"

"Yeah," Angie says, scrunching up her nose. "I told you I don't like them. She's trying to look like Zorro, with that black eye patch covered with rhinestones." I think they're too flashy for the twins, if you know what I'm saying.

"Yes, we know what you think, Miz Anginette, but you know how she got to floss that eye patch in the first place? By winning the grand prize on *The Grade*," Bubbles says exasperated. "Now those girls have it made in the shade."

"Is that right?" Angie responds sheepishly.

"If *they* can get a deal by thumping around with those wack-a-doodle-do monkey canes and that fake eye patch action, then imagine what a bunch of cheetah-fied divettes could get?" Galleria continues. "We should pounce right to first place just by licking our paws on the air, you know what I'm saying?"

"Okay, Miss Galleria, we know what you're saying," Aqua says, cracking a smile now that she gets Galleria's point.

"I'd enter the 'Battle of the Divettes' contest even if they were just giving away Goofy Grape sodas for first prize!" I say, chuckling. The whole idea sounds good to me—as long as we're not actually signed by Def Duck, we're still eligible.

"I know that's right," Aqua pipes up, confirming what I was thinking without blinking.

We continue reading the listing, and find out that the Battle of the Divettes competition is being held at the Apollo Theatre uptown. We look at each other, and I know we're all thinking the same thing. *Oh, no, say it ain't so. Not another Nightmare on 125th Street!*

See, the Cheetah Girls performed in the Apollo Amateur Hour contest and we *lost*, to a pair of wanna-be rappers called Stak Chedda—and believe me, they weren't "betta." I think we're still hurting from that disaster.

As usual, though, Galleria is hyping us up. "You know what they say—lightning never strikes twice in the same place."

"Yeah, that's true—but it don't say nothing about *losing*!" Aqua blurts out.

"Don't be radikkio. It's a new day and a new situation, so let's just go with the flow and act like we know," Galleria says, whipping out her Kitty Kat notebook and scribbling down all the information.

"But, *mamacita*, the contest is next Saturday!" Chanel says. "How are we gonna get a videotape made in time to send it in and meet the deadline—by calling 1-800-ALADDIN?" She twirls her hair anxiously. Chanel always twirls her hair when she gets nervous.

"No, Chuchie, we're gonna ask Mom to help us," Galleria says, whipping out her Miss Wiggy StarWac cell phone. I wish I had a cell phone—it's so cool to be able to flex and floss on the move, you know what I'm saying?

"I'm hungry—what time is it?" Aqua asks, licking her juicy lips.

Looking at my watch, I almost shriek—"It's one-thirty!"

"Do' Re Mi, *qué pasa, mamacita*?" Chanel asks, concerned.

"I've gotta be home," I say, getting

embarrassed. Why should I tell them I have to go home because a stupid caseworker is coming over to my house? *I hate that.* All of a sudden, I feel like Cinderella or something.

Chanel gives me a look with her big, goo-goo brown eyes, like, "why won't you tell me?"

"Um, my caseworker, Mrs. Tattle, is coming over today," I say, feeling my face get warm. I keep on talking, because I'm getting more and more embarrassed. "I don't know why she's coming over on a Saturday, but I've got to be there."

Chanel puts her arm around me. "I hope Mrs. Tattle's got a *boca grande*. With that name, she'd better be talking and sticking up for you, *está bien?"*

"I guess so," I say, looking over at Galleria; but I'm relieved when I see that she isn't really listening to us, because she's on the phone, sorta fighting with her mom, Ms. Dorothea. At least I feel off the hook. . . .

"I hope Mrs. Tattle doesn't stay long, you know what I'm saying?" I confide to my crew.

"I know that's right," Aqua says, looking at me with real concern. The twins come from a close family—and I understand that they watch each other's back. They probably think my situation is so strange.

Little do they know about the ways of the Big Apple. There are a *lot* of foster kids here—something like forty thousand—so I'm not alone, you know what I'm saying? Sometimes they have articles in the newspaper about foster kids like me.

"Can't the caseworkers leave you alone, now that Mrs. Bosco adopted you?" Aqua asks, hesitating. Suddenly, I realize that I haven't told my crew about the adoption mix-up yet. Omigod, what should I do? Now I feel like Chanel—always opening my *boca grande* for *nada*—for nothing!

I take a deep breath, and fiddle with the straps on my cheetah backpack. Even though it's emptier than usual, all of a sudden my backpack feels like a "magilla gorilla" on my back.

I'm so tired of all the fib-eronis I've been telling my crew. I know it's gonna catch up to me one day—and I guess today is the day, okay?

"Mrs. Bosco thought the adoption went

through, but it didn't," I say, hemming and hawing. I'm *not* going to tell them that she can't read or write. No way, José.

"Really?" Chanel asks me, like I'm joking, her big brown eyes opening wide like she doesn't believe me.

"Really, Chanel. I wouldn't joke about something like that," I say, trying to figure out how I can explain Mrs. Bosco's mistake to them. It wasn't *all* her fault. "They couldn't find my mother to get her to sign over her parental rights, or something like that. I don't know!"

Now Aqua hugs me. Galleria is off the phone, and she catches a whiff of my so-called adoption drama. "So you're *not* legally adopted?" she asks, surprised.

"No, I'm not adopted, okay?" I huff, but Galleria is like a dog with a bone—she just won't leave it alone.

"But Mrs. Bosco is not gonna give you up or anything, is she?"

I don't even want to *think* about that. She said she wouldn't, but what do I know? "I don't know, Galleria."

They get really quiet, which makes me mad

uncomfortable, so I change the subject. "So what did your mom say?"

"Um, she wanted to know why we were just finding out about the contest," Galleria says slowly. "I told her that's how this whole show-biz thing flows, you know? It moves on a dime and our time."

"It does say a 'home-made video,' though," Angie says, trying to be helpful.

"Yeah, that's what I told her—so we've just gotta hook up the lights-camera-action situation on the Q.T.," Galleria says, like she's not stressing it. "Mom thinks my dad may have a video camera. He's over at one of the contractors' right now." Galleria's parents own a clothing factory and boutique called Toto in New York . . . Fun in Diva Sizes. I guess the contractors are their suppliers or something.

"See, I know Granddaddy Walker has a video camera," Aqua says, thinking out loud. Granddaddy Walker owns a funeral parlor in Houston.

"He's not videotaping those dead people in the coffins, is he, *mamacita*?" Chanel asks, getting the spookies.

"Yes, Chanel—he especially *loves* the part

after he puts the embalming fluid in the body, and the dead corpse jumps up on the table when the rigor mortis sets in!"

I start chuckling, because I feel so much better that we aren't talking about my home situation.

"That's what really happens!" Aqua claims, bugging her eyes.

"It's true—we saw it one time when we were little," Angie adds, giggling. No wonder the twins love horror movies so much!

We all are in a good mood now. "Well, let's get rolling on 'Operation Videotape!'" Bubbles commands. "We're on a roll now, *girlitas*!"

Chapter 4

Mrs. Tattle is waiting in my living room when I get home. She looks kinda tired, and her clothes are all wrinkled. She even has a run in her stocking, and a spot on her pink blouse (it looks like tomato sauce), but I guess I'd better not say anything. She is pretty nice as caseworkers go, and I don't want to embarrass her. Besides, caseworkers write up recommendations about whether you get to stay in your foster home or not—so they have a lot of power over kids like me, and the last thing you want to do is make a bad impression.

"Sit down, Dorinda—take a load off," Mrs. Bosco says, stroking the hair on her wig in the front. I'm so glad she is wearing her special wig. See, Princess Pamela (the girlfriend of Chanel's dad) styled Mrs. Bosco's wig for my so-called adoption party. Princess Pamela is a dope hairdresser, and a psychic, too! Now, Mrs. Bosco keeps the wig in a net in her wig drawer, and only takes it out for special occasions. I wish she would wear it all the time, because the other ones look, well, kinda fake, if you know what I'm saying.

"Can I get you something to drink?" Mrs. Bosco asks Mrs. Tattle, but I know she will probably say, "No, thank you." She always does. Mrs. Tattle is usually in a hurry. Mrs. Bosco says the caseworkers who work for the city—as opposed to private foster care agencies—always have too big a caseload, and they don't get paid enough to deal with all the headaches that come with the territory. Mrs. Bosco must be right, 'cuz Mrs. Tattle has bags under her eyes that look more like suitcases!

"How are you today, Dorinda?" Mrs. Tattle asks me, reaching over to open her briefcase, which is right next to her on the floor.

I'm trying not to stare at the railroad run in her panty hose. I wonder how high up her leg it goes? When I'm older, I'm going to carry a briefcase like Mrs. Tattle, so I can look important, too.

Mrs. Tattle seems kinda uptight. The way she is sitting so straight on the couch, you'd think she was in the Oval Office in the White House or something. The couch in our living room is covered with faded yellow-flowered tapestry, and the seat cushions are well worn. I think more people have sat on our couch than in the Oval Office, if you know what I'm saying.

"I'm fine," I say, smiling and showing off my dimples, so Mrs. Tattle will feel more comfortable. I want her to think everything is "hunky chunky." I'm also anxious to find out why she's visiting us on a Saturday.

"Mrs. Bosco told me the good news about your record deal," Mrs. Tattle says, trying to sound cheerful.

"Well, it's not exactly a record deal, but we're going to get to cut a few songs for a demo tape for the record company," I explain carefully. I'm always trying to be honest about the Cheetah Girls situation—like I said earlier, we may have "growl power," but so far, we are still a bunch of wanna-be stars in the jiggy jungle.

"Well, it must have been exciting for you to

go to Los Angeles," Mrs. Tattle says, trying to make everything seem really hunky chunky, too.

"It was the dopest dope experience I ever had in my life!" I say, because I don't want to let Mrs. Tattle down. It *was* pretty dope—but there were ups and downs, if you want to know the honest truth.

"Well, now that's more like the Dorinda I know!" she says, her voice screeching because she is talking too high. (Now that I'm taking vocal lessons, I notice *everything* about people's voices. It's really kinda strange.)

Mrs. Tattle keeps smiling at me and Mrs. Bosco. Twinkie is smiling at Mrs. Tattle, and sitting in the armchair with her hand under her chin. "And how are you, Rita?" Mrs. Tattle asks, her face brightening up. Twinkie makes everybody smile.

"I'm okay," Twinkie responds, without moving her hand from her chin. Kenya just sits on the couch looking down at her shoes. I'm proud of Twinkie, because at least she got Kenya to wear matching socks. Topwe, Chantelle, Khalil, and Nestor look nice, too.

"Dorinda, can you sing something for me?"

Mrs. Tattle asks, catching me off guard.

"Not right now," I say, getting embarrassed. None of the other caseworkers have ever asked me to sing for them before.

Kenya throws me a look, like, "Why don't you just do what Mrs. Tattle wants?" For someone who whines so much, Kenya gets awfully quiet when the caseworker visits.

I guess it wouldn't hurt me to sing for Mrs. Tattle. Maybe she thinks I'm just making the whole thing up about being in a singing group called the Cheetah Girls. I'm sure she must have put that in her reports. She's always writing things down when she visits.

"Um, okay, lemme see," I say, trying to be nice to Mrs. Tattle. "I'll sing you the song that Bubbles wrote."

"Bubbles?" Mrs. Tattle asks, like she's kinda curious.

"Oh, she's the leader of our group—that's her nickname. Her real name is Galleria Garibaldi."

"Oh," Mrs. Tattle says, nodding her head. "That's an interesting name."

"Um, yeah, her mother is a fashion designer, and she named Bubbles, um, Galleria, after the mall in Houston," I say. I start giggling, warming up to Mrs. Tattle because I see her eyes sparkling a little. "Her father is Italian—from Italy—so that's where she got her last name."

"Yes—Garibaldi was a popular hero in Italy," Mrs. Tattle says.

I just keep smiling, because I'm not sure about Italian history. I'd better ask Bubbles before I go blabbing my mouth, so I decide I'd better sing and get it over with. "Um, okay, here's the song that Bubbles wrote. It's called, 'Wanna-be Stars in the Jiggy Jungle.'"

"Oh, that's cute!" Mrs. Tattle says, scribbing stuff down in a folder—which I know is my case file.

I smile at Twinkie. She loves to join in on the chorus of this song. I clear my throat and start singing the first verse:

"Some people walk with a panther
or strike a buffalo stance
that makes you wanna dance.

Other people flip the script
on the day of the jackal
that'll make you cackle.

But peeps like me
got the Cheetah Girl groove
that makes your body move
like wanna-be stars in the jiggy jungle.

The jiggy jiggy jungle!
The jiggy jiggy jungle!"

Sure enough, Twinkie and Topwe join in for the chorus and the B verse, making a whole lot of noise—but at least it's fun:

"So don't make me bungle
my chance to rise for the prize
and show you who we are
in the jiggy jiggy jungle!
The jiggy jiggy jungle!"

Mrs. Tattle starts clapping enthusiastically. I'm so glad that I made her feel better. That's what I love most about singing—seeing how happy it makes people.

"Where *is* the jiggy jungle?" Mrs. Tattle asks me. I can tell she really is interested now.

"Bubbles says it's this magical, cheetah-licious place inside of every dangerous, scary, crowded city, where dreams come true—oh, and where every cheetah has its day." I get embarrassed, because I suddenly realize maybe Mrs. Tattle thinks the whole thing is kinda cuckoo.

But instead, she looks at me with tiny tears forming in her eyes. "I'm so glad you found a friend like Bubbles," Mrs. Tattle says softly. Then she adds hesitantly, "I remember reading in the reports that you had trouble connecting with other kids."

That makes me embarrassed. I didn't know one of the caseworkers put that in their report! They are so *nosy*!

Out of the corner of my eye, I see Mrs. Bosco nodding her head. "Yes, that's right. Dorinda has really changed a lot, now that she is in this group with the Cheetah Girls."

"This is really great, Dorinda," Mrs. Tattle exclaims.

I guess it's true. I never did have a lot of friends before, except when I was younger and I used to skateboard with Sugar Bear. Otherwise I kept to myself, hiding in my books or helping with the other kids at home.

Mrs. Tattle shifts her body on the couch. "Um, Dorinda, I came here today especially to see you. I wanted to talk to you about something before I go on vacation."

I notice Mrs. Tattle looking over at Mrs. Bosco like they've already talked about something.

"Um, Mrs. Bosco—would it be okay if you and I and Dorinda talked in private?"

"Of course," Mrs. Bosco says, smiling. "Y'all can go to your rooms," she tells the other kids. "Rita, baby, can you take Arba into the bedroom and show her how to draw those butterflies?"

"Did you draw some new ones, Rita?" Mrs. Tattle asks Twinkie.

"Yup—big, fat butterflies with purple eyes!" Twinkie says proudly.

"Would you show them to me later?" Mrs. Tattle asks Twinkie.

"Uh-huh."

Now I feel nervous again. Singing made me forget about everything for a while. Mrs. Tattle shuffles some papers, then looks at me.

"Um, Dorinda, did you know that you have a sister?" Mrs. Tattle asks me hesitantly.

"Um, yeah—Jazmine. She lives with my first foster mother, Mrs. Parkay," I respond.

I wonder why Mrs. Tattle looks so puzzled. She rifles through some of her papers again. Mrs. Bosco and I just sit quietly, waiting for her to finish.

"Oh, I see. Yes. Jazmine Jones. She was a foster child in the first home you were in," Mrs. Tattle says, reading from a paper. Then, she looks up at me, and her voice gets very quiet. "But actually . . . she wasn't, um, your biological sister," she says.

"I didn't know that!" I gasp. What a stupid thing to say, but it's all I can think of. I mean, all this time, I thought Jazmine was my *real* sister—and that mean Mrs. Parkay gave me away and kept Jazmine, separating us forever.

Obviously, I know more about the other kids' records than my own. I wonder what else is in that file Mrs. Tattle is holding. . . .

"How come she, um, Jazmine, got to stay with Mrs. Parkay?" I ask, my cheeks burning.

"Um, I don't know, Dorinda," Mrs. Tattle says. Embarrassed, she starts shuffling her papers some more. "Perhaps because Jazmine was younger than you . . . or maybe Mrs.

Parkay only wanted one child. I'll have to look it up in the files and get back to you on that. But at any rate, you and Jazmine are not biological sisters."

I can tell Mrs. Tattle is trying not to hurt my feelings. She probably knows why Mrs. Parkay gave me away, but she isn't saying anything. "Oh, that's okay. I was just asking," I say, getting defensive. "It's not important or anything."

I guess Mrs. Parkay just didn't love me enough—same as with my birth mother. Mr. and Mrs. Bosco are the only ones who *really* love me. That's why, in my heart, they're my *real* parents—whether I ever get adopted by them or not.

But now I'm really curious as to why Mrs. Tattle's here.

"Dorinda," she says, clearing her throat. "Um, Dorinda, what I started to say before was, you *do* have a biological sister. Well—*half* sister, actually. According to the records, you and Tiffany were born to the same mother, but you have different fathers."

Tiffany. I sit there, hearing the sound of it repeat and repeat inside my head. I have a half sister—a real one—and her name is Tiffany.

I look at Mrs. Bosco. I wonder if she knew about this before now—but I can't tell by the look on her face if she did or not.

"Her name's Tiffany?"

"Yes, Tiffany Twitty. She was adopted by the Twittys when she was a baby, and they changed her name."

"What was her name before that?" I ask curiously, and I'm thinking any name's gotta be better than one that sounds like a cuckoo bird.

"Oh, I'll have to look that up," Mrs. Tattle says, and now she sounds like a caseworker, instead of nice like before.

"How old is she?" I ask.

"Eleven. One year younger than you," Mrs. Tattle says with a blank face. "Well, Dorinda . . ." She clears her throat again, and I know there's more to come. "The reason why I'm telling you all this is—because Tiffany wants to meet you."

I feel a cold chill ripple down my body. All of a sudden, I feel sad and scared. Just a few weeks ago, I thought I was getting adopted—that I'd finally have a real family for the first time in my life. Now I find out Jazmine wasn't my real sister—and that I have a half sister named Tiffany Twitty, who's already been adopted!

It's all too much information trying to squeeze into my head at the same time. Suddenly I'm not sure I want to know any more about Tiffany—not yet, anyway.

And then, a familiar daydream comes to me—my mother is smiling at me in the clouds, while I'm dancing for her. I know it sounds stupid, but for some reason, the image keeps coming to me.

"Dorinda?" Mrs. Tattle says, trying to get my attention. "If you need to think about this—"

"I'm sorry—I was just thinking about things," I tell her. "I don't know what to do. . . ."

"Dorinda, you don't have to decide now," Mrs. Tattle says, being nice again.

I look up at Mrs. Bosco. She is nodding her head and smiling at me, like "Go ahead, don't be scared. I'm here for you."

"No, I *want* to meet her," I tell Mrs. Tattle.

She seems relieved. "Well, it would be better if I introduce the two of you—just to make sure everything, um, goes okay," she says very officiously, like a caseworker again. "Let's see," she says, looking in the files again. "You both seem to like skating. . . ."

"Skate*boarding*?" I say, correcting Mrs. Tattle.

"Well, I mean, you like skateboarding, and Tiffany likes Rollerblading. We could go to Central Park, perhaps—"

"Okay," I say with a shrug. "Whatever." Like I don't care how we meet, or how it goes.

But I do care. What if we don't like each other? What if she's mean, or something? What if she hates me? It's a good thing Mrs. Bosco puts her hand on my shoulder at that moment. She must sense that I'm about to back right out of this whole thing.

This is all such a trip—the sister I thought was my sister is not—but now I find out someone else is my *real* sister. . . .

Chapter 5

I can't believe all the stuff that is going down today! Before I go meet Tiffany and Mrs. Tattle at noon, right by the fountain in Central Park, I have to go meet the Cheetah Girls at Ms. Dorothea's store, Toto in New York . . . Fun in Diva Sizes.

Today's the day we're going to make the videotape to send in to the "Battle of the Divettes" competition. It turns out Bubbles's dad, Mr. Garibaldi, has a professional-quality video camera he keeps in storage!

"He wanted to be a filmmaker when he was younger," Bubbles tells me proudly. We're in the back of the boutique, changing into our Cheetah Girls costumes.

Ms. Dorothea plops down a platter of sandwiches on the shelves where hats are displayed. The sandwiches look really fancy, and I'm afraid to touch them.

"Darling, go on—take one. It's Black Forest ham and brie, laced with honey mustard."

I don't know what Black Forest ham is, but it sounds exotic, so I dig in—and it is *mm-mm* good! I'm munching away, and I look at Ms. Dorothea with a nervous smile.

Why am I nervous? Well, partly, it's the videotaping. But mostly, it's because I'm meeting Tiffany right afterward—and I haven't said a word to anybody! Not even Chanel—and I tell Chanel *everything*.

I'm wondering if I should tell Ms. Dorothea about Tiffany. I *know* Ms. Dorothea would understand how confused I feel about everything. At my "adoption" party, she was crying, and she told me everything about her missing mother.

No . . . I think it's better if I don't say anything—not yet, anyway. Not till I know what's the deal-io.

Bubbles's dog Toto (they named the store for him) is lying with his nose pressed to the floor.

Toto is the dopest dog in the jiggy jungle. Right now, he looks like a fluffy pancake.

"Hi, Toto," I coo, and he immediately cocks his head and patters over, rubbing his body against my knees. He is wearing the cutest outfit. He's gonna be featured in our video, but that's not why he's all dressed up. See, Galleria and her mom love to make outfits for him anytime there's leftover fabric. That dog has more costumes than *we* do—well, so far, anyway. This one's a yellow-net tutu, with cheetah ribbons streaming all over the place.

"Ooh, I've got a dope idea," Chanel says, fondling the cheetah ribbons on Toto's tutu. "I could put these on one of *my* tutus." Chanel used to take ballet lessons. She stopped her ballet training because Galleria didn't want to do it anymore—and those two are the dynamic duo: whatever one does, the other has to do. They're "thicker than forty thieves," as the rap song "Don't Bite the Flavor that You Savor," says. Anyway, I can tell Chanel still loves ballet, even though she pretends she doesn't.

Toto rolls over on his back and puts his front paws in the air. "He really likes getting his stomach rubbed," I chuckle.

"Yeah, and he'd be happy if you alternated it with fanning his fur and feeding him some grapes!" Ms. Dorothea humphs. "All Toto needs now is a harem." She leads us to the front of the store, where she poses us against the cheetah-wallpapered wall.

"What's a harem?" Angie asks.

"It's lots of pretty girls who run around with veils, and with their belly buttons sticking out, pampering the whims of horribly rich princes," Ms. Dorothea explains.

Chanel lets out a giggle, then starts wiggling her middle and pretending to fan Toto with her scarf. See, Chanel's mom, Juanita, takes belly-dancing lessons all the time now. Her boyfriend is this rich businessman who lives in Paris, France. Chanel calls him Mr. Tycoon. I think Chanel's mom is trying to be his one-woman harem, 'cuz she sure is working hard at those belly-dancing lessons.

"Chanel, you'd better feed him something, or he's gonna bite you," Ms. Dorothea chuckles.

"*Madrina,* I'm not giving him my sandwich, *está bien?*" Chanel says, picking up her sandwich and gobbling it down.

Mr. Garibaldi is videotaping everything we

do. He seems excited—kind of like a kid with a new toy.

"I always wanted to be like Fellini," Mr. Garibaldi tells us.

"Who is Fellini?" I ask curiously.

"Ah, Dor-i-n-d-a, *bella,* Federico Fellini was the greatest Italian movie director that *ever* lived. *É vero, cara.* It's true."

"Darling, he made a fabulous movie called *La Dolce Vita,*" Ms. Dorothea pipes in, looking over at Mr. Garibaldi with stars in her eyes. "The first time I saw it was with my Franco, and I've been living it ever since."

Franco is part of Mr. Garibaldi's first name—Francobollo, which means "stamp" in Italian. I'm not sure what *la dolce vita* means. As if reading my mind, Galleria looks at me and says, amused, "It means, 'the sweet life.'"

"Word," I say, chuckling. Mr. and Mrs. Garibaldi sure look like they have *la dolce vita*! They are so cute together—even if she is a head taller than he is.

"Okay, Cheetah Girls, stop eating, and let's get to work," Mr. Garibaldi commands us.

The five of us are wearing the cheetah jumpsuits Ms. Dorothea made for us when we gave our very first performance—last Halloween night at the Cheetah-Rama Club.

Ms. Dorothea seems to be having fun playing makeup artist and hairdresser. She keeps *pouf-ing* us with powder, and fussing with our hair.

"Everything okay?" Ms. Dorothea asks, looking at me amused.

"Tutti frutti!" I heckle back. Galleria is so lucky to have Ms. Dorothea for a mother—but then, I guess I'm lucky too, having her as a manager.

"Then let's do it!" Chanel says.

The five of us strike a pose that satisfies both Mr. and Mrs. Garibaldi, and we begin singing "Wanna-be Stars in the Jiggy Jungle."

After we finish, Mr. Garibaldi yells, "Cut," just like a real movie director.

Galleria goes over and hugs him. "Thank you, Daddy. You're even better than Fellini. Now where's the linguine?"

Ms. Dorothea runs to the back to bring out the food. We dig into the linguine with clam sauce while Mr. Garibaldi puts his coat on. He's rushing over to the processing lab, then mailing off our videotape to Looking Good

Productions, so we don't miss the deadline for the "Battle of the Divettes" competition.

"Let's go to Manhattan Mall!" Chuchie says excitedly.

Suddenly, I get nervous. I didn't count on going anywhere with my crew after we made a tape. I haven't even told them about Tiffany—let alone that I'm going to meet her this afternoon.

"I have to go meet my, um, caseworker, at twelve o'clock," I say, embarrassed.

"I thought you met her yesterday," Galleria says, puzzled.

"Yeah, well, she's, um, going on vacation for a long time, so I have to see her again," I say, stammering.

Galleria puts her arm around me. I guess she feels sorry for me or something. I feel so stupid, but I'm just not ready to tell them about the sister situation. Maybe after I meet Tiffany—if everything goes well, that is.

I kiss everybody good-bye and anchor my skateboard under my arm.

"How come you have your skateboard with you?" Chanel asks, curious.

"I'm meeting Mrs. Tattle in Central Park

with, um, some other kids," I explain, feeling my face getting flushed.

"Maybe I could come with you and just hang out," Chanel says, her eyes looking hopeful. Now I really feel bad. Chanel has been wanting me to teach her skateboarding ever since we met. Luckily, Galleria and the twins aren't having it.

"Chuchie, that's all you need is to go kadoodling around on a skateboard, and you won't be a wanna-be star anymore—you'll just be seeing stars, 'cuz you'll hurt yourself!"

"*I* sure wouldn't want to try it," Aqua pipes up. "It looks *real* dangerous."

"Well, I guess I shouldn't come today, anyway, since you're meeting with your caseworker and all," Chanel says. "We'll go skateboarding soon, though, right? When it's just us two, and you can give me a lesson, *está bien?*"

"Word, *mamacita,*" I say, chuckling.

Chanel's not quite over the disappointment yet, though. She touches the grip tape on my skateboard and follows the deck with her fingers. I can see Chanel is fascinated. That's one of the many things we have in common—she likes to move and groove with the wind as much as I do. She's athletic like me, too—I mean, she did all those years of ballet—and she could probably learn to skateboard pretty fast if I found the time to teach her.

"The kicktail on mine only has a slight angle," I explain. "It's the same in the front and back. This is the kind you get when you're into freestyle."

"Do you have to wear high-top sneakers?" Chanel asks, looking down at my sneaks.

"Yeah—with reinforcement on the side. You can really mess up regular sneakers when you do ollies or fakies—this way, you can keep your ankles tweaked." I know Chanel understands how important it is to protect your ankles because of her ballet training.

"Good, golly, what's an ollie?" Aqua asks, still munching on the linguine. When there's good food around, you practically have to pry the twins away from it with a crowbar, you know what I'm saying?

Chuckling, I put the skateboard down for a second to show them an ollie. "You hit the kick-tail with your back foot, then you kinda jump."

"Whoa, Miss Dorinda, I don't want you to

take the mannequins in the window with you," Ms. Dorothea warns me. "Shouldn't you be wearing knee pads or something?"

"I usually do—but I lent my brother Khalil my board, and he lost all my safety equipment. So till I can afford some more . . . Anyway, it's only street boarding. I don't go very fast, or try to do any really fancy tricks."

"Okay, well just be careful. Those 'In the Dark' girls may be hobbling on canes for fun—but I don't want you needing one for real."

"I'll be careful," I reassure everyone. "Bye, y'all."

I leave the store, and set off for the subway station, on my way to meet the half sister I never knew I had.

Something tells me this is going to be the ride of a lifetime.

Chapter 6

When I get off the subway at Sixty-sixth Street and Broadway, I put my skateboard down on the sidewalk and skate into Central Park. I can't believe I'm going to meet my sister—my *real* sister, you know what I'm saying? I don't know whether I'm more thrilled or more scared!

"Coming through!" I yell politely, so this guy coming at me on a ten-speeder can leave me some room on the sidewalk. He's zooming past me, like he's a werewolf and his paws are on fire or something. Bicycle peeps are outta control in the Big Apple.

Once he passes, I jump-start my stride with a few back kicks, and start cruising along the path that leads into the park.

A ferocious breeze blows my way, so I zip up my jacket, pick up my skateboard, and walk down the steep steps toward the famous fountain in Central Park. I wonder if Tiffany is tiny like me? That's how I'll know if she is *really* my sister, I think to myself, chuckling inside.

But I can't shake how badly I feel for not telling my crew about this whole drama. Now I'm quaking for faking, and I wish I could just turn back and hang with them at the Manhattan Mall, just like any other Sunday. But it's too late for that.

I see Mrs. Tattle standing by herself over by the pond area. I wave hello, then glance away, pretending that I'm looking at the ducks floating by on the dirty pond water.

I always feel self-conscious when I'm walking toward someone who's standing still. I feel like I'm gonna trip, or do something stupid, and then they won't like me anymore. Now I glance over at the people sitting in rowboats—aren't they cold? I wonder.

"Hi, Dorinda," Mrs. Tattle beams at me. "I see you brought your skateboard."

"Yeah, I boarded over from the subway

station," I say nervously, looking around. Next to me, a barefoot boy is sticking his toe in the brook. His mother glances at me, then turns back to her son and smiles. I can tell she is kinda poor, because her clothes look dirty. But at least *she* didn't give her son away. Suddenly, I feel sad about my situation. Why couldn't I have stayed with my mother from the beginning?

And where is Tiffany? I wonder. Maybe she didn't show up, after all.

As if reading my mind, Mrs. Tattle points to the hot dog vendor on the other side of the fountain, and says, "Tiffany is right over there, buying a hot dog. Would you like one?"

"No, thank you," I tell her. "Ms. Dorothea—Galleria's mom—made lunch for us," I respond. But the main reason is, I want to get a look at Tiffany before she sees me. That will give me a minute to check her out. Then, when she sees me, I can watch how she reacts to seeing me for the first time. I wonder if we look alike. . . .

In biology class in school, we're studying genetics—DNA and genes, and stuff like that. According to what our teacher says, you get half your genes from each parent. Half of who you are. So Tiffany and I will be half alike!

This is kinda exciting, after all. Scared as I am, I'm busy looking at the hot dog stand to see if I can pick out Tiffany. But I don't see anybody that looks remotely like she could be my sister.

What is Mrs. Tattle talking about? I look at her, just to make sure she hasn't gone cuckoo. I know she's supa busy with her caseload. Maybe she just goofed up; you know what I'm saying? Or maybe Tiffany went somewhere else in the park besides the hot dog stand.

Mrs. Tattle smiles at me nervously, then puts down her briefcase on the ground and folds her arms across her chest. I guess it must be kinda tiring, to carry a heavy briefcase around town all the time.

I wonder if Mrs. Tattle ever gets to have any fun, or what her husband is like. But I never ask caseworkers questions about their lives, because Mrs. Bosco says it's rude. She says, "They're just here to do their job, not to have us all up in their business."

"Here comes Tiffany," Mrs. Tattle says enthusiastically, as if she's announcing the arrival of a beauty contestant or something.

I look at the hot dog stand, to see who is walking in our direction. There's an older man with an overcoat full of holes and a feather in his hat, shuffling along like he's in a hurry. There is a group of little kids, running around in circles. And there's an old homeless lady, who is mumbling loudly to a group of pigeons while she scatters bread crumbs. Mrs. Tattle might really be cuckoo like that lady, I think, and start panicking.

Then I see a cute, chubby girl with long, straight blond hair. She is wearing white shorts, kneepads, and Rollerblades. This girl is chomping down on a hot dog, and skating at the same time. *She must be freezing*, I say to myself. I mean, I'm shivering myself!

Now the blond girl is zooming closer to us, and smiling at Mrs. Tattle. Maybe she was talking to Mrs. Tattle before or something.

"Hi," the girl says to me, smiling. She wipes the onions from the corner of her mouth with a napkin. "It's great to meet you." She sticks out her hand to shake—and drops her hot dog with everything on it, right on my skateboard!

"Oh, no!" the girl gasps.

"Don't worry, Tiffany, I'll get it," Mrs. Tattle

says, bending down and trying to clean up the mess.

Hold up, I think, suddenly stiffening. I just thought I heard Mrs. Tattle call this girl Tiffany. That's my *sister's* name. But this girl is *white*!

Maybe Mrs. Tattle meant Tiffany is *going* to be my sister or something. No, that can't be. Let me try to remember . . . she said Tiffany was my half sister, but she got adopted by some people, the Twittys or something like that.

My mind goes blank. I'm so confused, I don't even take her hand and shake it.

"Sorry about that," she says, and gives me a sweet smile and a little giggle. "I get clumsy when I'm nervous."

She has a nice smile—I like it. It shows off her chubby red cheeks and big blue eyes. She looks like the kids you see in toothpaste commercials, smiling like they're really happy to be brushing their teeth fifty times a day. But she sure doesn't look anything like me!

"Your name is Dorinda?" Tiffany asks me, her eyes getting even wider.

"Yeah."

"I'm Tiffany."

"Hi," I reply, not knowing what else to say.

"This is so weird, huh?" Tiffany says. I can tell she's excited. And it doesn't seem to bother her at all that I'm black.

Mrs. Tattle must have told her about me. But when she told me about Tiffany, she never mentioned the fact that she's white.

Why not? I wonder. Is it because she thought I'd be prejudiced and wouldn't like her?

That's ridiculous, I think. I'm not prejudiced—I've never been prejudiced. I mean, I live with a bunch of kids that are white, black, red, and brown, and I love them all just the same. But how can my natural half sister be white? It just doesn't make any sense!

I'm waiting for Mrs. Tattle to explain, but she doesn't say boo—and Tiffany just keeps smiling at me, kinda like a friendly puppy, expecting me to say something more.

Finally, Mrs. Tattle gets up. She motions for us to walk with her. "Aren't you cold, Tiffany?"

"No, I'm all right."

I think Tiffany's shorts are too short, and maybe that's why her cheeks are so red. If Ms. Dorothea saw her in those white shorts after Labor Day, she'd get sent to Cheetah Girls detention for the rest of her life! White after

Labor Day is a fashion no-no! No way is she meeting my crew in *that* outfit!

"Dorinda, are you sure you don't want something to eat?" Mrs. Tattle asks me, like she wishes I would say yes.

"No, I'm fine." What I really want to say is, what in the world is going on here!

"Well, I know you two girls have a lot to talk about, so why don't we go sit on the bench?" Mrs. Tattle suggests. Then she quickly adds, "Or would you rather go skating first?"

"Skating," Tiffany says right away. She starts skating along, and I push off on my skateboard, keeping alongside of her. Tiffany looks over at me, like she's really happy to meet me. Obviously, she couldn't care less that I'm black.

She's really nice, I think. And just then, because she's not looking where she's going, she trips over a piece of garbage, starts wobbling, and falls flat on her butt!

Dang, she is clumsy! That is not at *all* like me!

"You okay, Tiffany?" Mrs. Tattle asks, helping her up.

I just stand there, too spaced out to realize I ought to help, too. I feel stupid about it, and guilty, too. I mean my reflexes are kinda in slow motion, and my brain feels like a big blob of cotton candy. Tiffany said she gets clumsy when she's nervous. Maybe we aren't so different after all—just a different kind of clumsy.

"That's why I wear kneepads," Tiffany says apologetically. Then she sees my knees, which don't have pads on them, and I realize she knows why I don't have any safety equipment. "Oh. Sorry. That was a stupid thing to say."

"It's only cause my little brother lost them," I explain. *And because we're too poor to afford new equipment right away,* I add silently. "I usually wear all that stuff."

"I have an extra set of equipment at home," Tiffany says. "I'll bring it for you next time. You can keep it—I don't use it anymore."

Suddenly I feel bad, because I wasn't nice to Tiffany when Mrs. Tattle first introduced us. She sure is being nice to me.

"Your skates are dope," I say, warming up to her. I can tell they cost a lot of duckets; that's for sure. Her adoptive parents must be doing all right.

"Thanks," she giggles back. "How'd you learn how to skateboard?"

"When I was eight, I used to have this friend

named Sugar Bear. He taught me how to skate on his board 'cuz I used to help him with his homework. Then I got my own skateboard, last year."

"What happened to you and Sugar Bear—did you have a big fight or something? How come you're not still friends?"

"One night two years ago, his mother didn't come home. That's what my neighbor Ms. Keisha told me. Ms. Keisha knows everybody's business in Cornwall Projects. She knew I was tight with Sugar Bear. She told me he got sent down South to live with his grandmother."

I can feel my throat tighten up, remembering it. "He didn't even get to say good-bye to me."

"I'm sorry," Tiffany says. She means it, too, I can tell. Her eyes have tears in them, just as if it happened to her.

"I wanna learn how to ride a skateboard," Tiffany says, her eyes opening wide and getting twinkly. "Will you teach me sometime?"

"Okay," I say. "If you promise you won't skateboard right into a tree."

Tiffany laughs. "You must think I'm the clumsiest person on the whole planet," she says.

"You're all right," I say, and I mean it, too. It

doesn't matter to me that she's white. But I still can't believe we're sisters!

We stop in front of an old-looking park bench, and Mrs. Tattle catches up to us. "Let's sit right here," she says, motioning to Tiffany. Both of us sit down like robots, on either side of her. I can tell we're both more comfortable with each other when Mrs. Tattle isn't around.

"Tiffany, why don't you tell Dorinda a little about yourself?" Mrs. Tattle prods gently.

"You mean, about finding the records and stuff?" Tiffany asks, with a sly little smile on her face.

"Well, that's not *exactly* what I mean, but whatever you'd like to tell Dorinda would be fine," Mrs. Tattle counters, sounding like a principal.

"Oh, okay," Tiffany says. She giggles, then moves her feet in parallel motion, so her Rollerblades screech on the ground. I guess she's nervous.

"Well, I was looking through my parents' drawers—I was trying to find—I guess I had no business doing it, but I'm the curious type—nosy, you know? And sometimes I just can't help myself.

"Anyway, I came across this box, so I opened it. There was all sorts of baby stuff inside," Tiffany says, looking at me. "Baby booties, a little spoon, and some baby pictures. On the back of them it said, 'Karina, eleven months.'"

Her smile is gone now, as she remembers the moment she found the pictures. I can see the tears welling up in her eyes; and now I'm getting emotional, too—feeling it along with her.

"Then I found the adoption papers . . . and I saw the name Karina again, Karina Farber. It was next to *my* name—Tiffany Twitty. That's when I realized—*I* must be Karina Farber—the baby in the picture!"

"You mean, you didn't know you were adopted?" I blurt out.

"No!" Tiffany says, getting all emphatic like she's trying to avoid static. "I swear I didn't!"

"Don't swear, Tiffany," Mrs. Tattle says, flexing again on the principal tip. "Dorinda was just asking you a question. Some adoptive parents inform the adopted child when they're old enough to understand. Some choose not to."

"Well, my parents never told me *anything*," Tiffany says with an attitude. Then she gets quiet.

"Now, go on, Tiffany," Mrs. Tattle says, prodding her.

"So anyway, I started reading all the papers. There was a lot of stuff in there—like my real mother's and father's names—Eugene and Frances Farber!"

My mother's name was Frances Rogers. I've known that for years and years. I guess she took the name Farber when she hooked up with Tiffany's birth father.

I roll my foot on my skateboard, which is flat on the ground. I'm waiting to hear how she came to know about me.

"Then it said that my birth mother had a child from a previous marriage," Tiffany says. "It said she gave that child up, too. Just like she gave me up." She looks up at me and smiles. "So that's how I knew I had a sister."

Tiffany gets quiet again. Maybe my attitude is making her uncomfortable. I smile at her, to let her know it's okay with me that she's white.

Tiffany smiles back at me, and says, "By the way, your name was the same in the records—it's always been Dorinda. I guess that's because you weren't adopted or anything."

"Dorinda," Mrs. Tattle takes over. "Your

mother surrendered custody of both her children at the same time. You were eighteen months old, and Tiffany was seven months. You were placed in a foster home, and Tiffany was placed with adoptive parents."

"You're trying to tell me that Tiffany got adopted because she's white, and I didn't, because I'm black?"

Mrs. Tattle clears her throat. I can see this is difficult for her. "I'm sorry, Dorinda," she says. "The agencies tried to place both of you, but we were only able to place Tiffany. The caseworkers did the best they could."

Now I'm crying buckets. "That's so unfair!" I say through my tears.

Tiffany hugs me. She's crying, too. "I wish we could have stayed together," she says. "I've always missed having a sister."

I push her away, angry that no one wanted me. I'm sure it was because I'm black and Tiffany's white. Not that it's Tiffany's fault, but why can't people see that a black child is just as sweet and good as a white one?

"I still don't understand how Tiffany could be my sister," I blurt out. "She doesn't look half black. Is she?"

Mrs. Tattle gasps, surprised. "Dorinda," she says hesitantly, "you *do* know that your mother is *white*, don't you?"

"No!"

I can hear the words leave my mouth, but my mind sorta goes numb. I stare down at my sneakers, because I'm too embarrassed to look either Mrs. Tattle or Tiffany in the face. I feel stupid. "Nobody ever told me!" I moan.

I can't believe this! Here I am, wondering how Tiffany could possibly be my sister if she's not part black—and all the time, I'm half white!

Well, so what? I say to myself. Galleria's half white. Chanel's all kinds of things mixed up in one cute *cuchifrita*. I guess it's okay that I am what I am. I just can't believe I've lived all these years and never known! How could they not have told me any of this? It makes me so furious, I could scream!

Mrs. Tattle heaves a sigh, then talks quickly, like someone who is trying to cover her booty. "Dorinda, you have to understand—so many things get lost in translation when a child is placed in foster care. A caseworker enters a new situation, and there isn't always enough time to explain everything."

Yeah, well, I understand, all right. Nobody cares enough about me to tell me anything but lies—not even Mrs. Bosco! And how unfair is it that Tiffany got adopted when she was only a little baby, and I'm still in a foster home at twelve years old?

I sit there, crying and crying, and Mrs. Tattle gets really uncomfortable. I still can't look at her, but I feel her shifting her weight on the bench.

"So what happened to our mother?" I finally manage to ask through my stream of tears.

Tiffany looks at Mrs. Tattle with bated breath. She probably doesn't know where our mother is either. I guess *that* wasn't in the files—or Tiffany would have already told me the whole story.

"Well," Mrs. Tattle says, "according to the records, she went to California, and became involved in, um, some sort of social organization. But that was several years ago, and we've lost track of her since that time."

I secretly wonder if Mrs. Tattle is telling a fiberoni. Maybe she doesn't *want* to tell me—I mean us,—the truth. Tiffany looks at me as if she's thinking the same thing. What kind of organization is Mrs. Tattle talking about? Why doesn't she just come out and say it?

Instead of asking Mrs. Tattle, I turn to Tiffany. "How did you find me?"

"I told my parents I found the records," Tiffany says proudly. "Then I told them I wanted to meet my sister."

"You didn't get in trouble?" I ask, surprised.

"No way—they felt bad for not telling me everything in the first place," Tiffany explains, cracking that mischievous grin again.

I find myself smiling back. Tiffany is kinda funny. And she's got some serious mojo, too, to stand up to her parents like that!

"They know I'm here, and everything," she tells me. "They even wanted to come and meet you, but I told them, 'No way!'"

Now Mrs. Tattle is smiling too. "Tiffany's parents contacted us, and told us that Tiffany wanted to meet her sister. Then we contacted Mrs. Bosco. She gave her consent, as long as it was okay with you."

Now I feel bad that I got mad at Mrs. Bosco. She probably thought all this would be good for me. And I guess it *is*—except now I can feel this stabbing pain in my chest. It's this achy feeling, like my heart is broken. Somebody isn't telling the truth about something—*that's* what I'm talking about.

"Would you girls like to go skating together while I sit here?" Mrs. Tattle asks, concerned.

"Okay," I mumble, then get up and start dragging my back foot on the deck of my skateboard. Tiffany skates alongside me. "You don't look the way I imagined," she says smiling.

"Yeah, I guess not," I chuckle. I bet she didn't know I was black.

"No, I mean I thought you'd be chubby like me," Tiffany says, giggling.

"I'm getting skinnier, though," she goes on. "I've been on a diet. I already lost five pounds! Of course, I'll probably never be as thin as you."

That makes me chuckle. I can't imagine Tiffany without her cute, chubby cheeks. They kinda fit her. "It must be your dad's genes," I say.

"My dad's what?"

"Genes. You'll learn all about it in biology when you get to high school," I tell her.

Wait till Tiffany meets Ms. Dorothea, I say to myself with a smile. Then she won't worry about dieting anymore.

Suddenly, I shriek inside. Tiffany can't meet Ms. Dorothea—she can't meet my crew! No way, José—not yet, anyway! They wouldn't understand about me having a white sister. I had a hard enough time understanding it myself!

I look over at Tiffany, who is happily and clumsily skating along. "Did you just learn how to skate?" I ask.

"No. I've been skating for a long time," Tiffany says proudly.

I'm surprised. Maybe she doesn't have good coordination or something. Secretly, I can't help thinking, I don't believe she's my sister. We don't look alike, and she isn't anything like me.

Then the big bulb from above goes off in my head. Tomorrow I have biology. I'm gonna ask my teacher, Mr. Roundworm, about it. Maybe he can tell me if this whole thing is a hoax-arama.

"Where do you live?" Tiffany asks me.

"Harlem," I shoot back. "One hundred sixteenth Street."

"Oh," Tiffany says, kinda embarrassed.

"Where do you live?"

"Eighty-second Street and Park Avenue," she

says, then scrunches up her nose. "I hate it—I liked California better."

"You lived in California?" I ask curiously.

"Yeah, till I was seven."

"I can't believe you really found your adoption records like that!" I tell her.

"Actually, I found the locked security box, and then I searched all over the house until I found the key," Tiffany says proudly. "It took me two Saturday afternoons!"

I laugh out loud. It seems Tiffany's a whole lot better at sleuthing than skating.

"Where do you go to school?" I ask her.

"St. Agatha's of the Peril," Tiffany says, like she's disgusted. "I hate it. They're so strict there. Yesterday I had to go to detention, just because I was wearing nail polish. They made me take it off, too." She scrunches up her nose to show me she's unhappy. "Where do you go?"

"Fashion Industries East High," I say proudly.

"Wow, that is so cool!" Tiffany responds. "I love clothes but I'm tired of my mom picking out everything."

The way she looks at me, all impressed like

that, it makes me feel proud and excited about everything that I'm trying to do. So I tell her some more about myself.

"I design some stuff, too—and I'm in this singing group, the Cheetah Girls," I tell her.

"Yeah, Mrs. Tattle told me. I'm really into music. Maybe I could come hear you sing some time."

"Uh, yeah," I say, because I don't want to hurt her feelings. But inside, I'm saying, *I don't think so*. I can just see the looks on my crew's faces.

"I can tell Mrs. Tattle's really proud of you," Tiffany says.

I guess I never thought about it—but if it's true, I'm glad. "You don't have a caseworker, right?" I ask.

"No," Tiffany responds.

"Yeah, I guess not."

All of a sudden, Tiffany bumps into a garbage can and stumbles. We both start laughing. When she regains her balance, she moans, "I'm tired of skating—you?"

Even though I'm not, I say, "Let's go eat some hot dogs."

Tiffany smiles, and her eyes light up. She and

the twins would get along hunky chunky—the way they cook, Tiffany would probably never leave their house!

Whoa! There I go again, I think, and stop myself. The twins would not understand about Tiffany. And neither would the others.

"I wanna be a singer, too," Tiffany tells me, like it's a big secret.

As we skate back toward Mrs. Tattle, I tell Tiffany about everything that's happened so far with the Cheetah Girls. She seems really fascinated.

"I'm trying to get my parents to let me go to performing arts school," she says. "They want me to go to Catholic school," Tiffany informs me sadly. "We fight about it all the time." Then her big blue eyes light up. "You know, I just got a keyboard for my birthday!"

"That's dope," I exclaim. "I don't know how to play any instruments, even though I've always wanted to play the piano. See, Mrs. Bosco didn't have any money to get me lessons."

"Maybe you could come over my house and we could learn keyboard together!" Tiffany offers, getting excited.

I wonder why she's being so nice to me. She

doesn't even *know* me—and who says we're *really* sisters, huh? I'm still not totally convinced this isn't all some big mistake.

"Okay," I say, because I don't want to hurt Tiffany's feelings.

"My parents wanted to pick me up from the park," Tiffany says, grimacing. "They want to go with me *everywhere.*"

I can tell something is wrong at home, but I don't say anything. Maybe Tiffany is just spoiled or something.

We finally get back to where Mrs. Tattle is sitting. She looks at Tiffany, then at me—so I smile to let her know everything is "hunky chunky."

"Well, I guess I'd better get you girls back home safely," Mrs. Tattle volunteers.

Tiffany turns to me. "Can I have your phone number?" she asks.

I hear myself saying "Okay," like I've been doing all afternoon. I scribble my phone number on a piece of paper and hand it to Tiffany.

"Can I have a hug?" she asks me, pushing away a blond curl that has fallen in her face. She really does remind me of Chanel. Too bad I can't introduce them. . . .

"Sure," I say, extending my arms and giving

her a hug. I feel her hair on the side of my face—it's really soft. She sorta feels like a little teddy bear. I can smell the soft scent of baby powder.

"I'm so glad I met you," Tiffany says, like she's just taken a trip to Treasure Island.

Suddenly, I feel myself fighting back tears again. I haven't cried this much since my almost-adoption party!

Chapter 7

Seeing my crew on Monday morning in school is like being in the Twilight Zone. I can't shake this whole thing about Tiffany, but I'm not talking about it with my crew—not yet. I know I'm kinda secretive, but that's me.

"Do' Re Mi, what you thinking without blinking?" Bubbles coos at me after first period.

"Nothing. I've just gotta roll into this biology class, and I haven't quite gotten this DNA thing down yet," I say, mustering up a pretty good half-true fib-eroni on the Q.T.—on the quick tip.

"Well, don't feel bad. I haven't done my Spanish homework either—*Yo no sé*, okay?"

That sends Chanel into the chuckles. "If you

would ask me, I would help you, Bubbles."

"I'll bet—then you'd be asking me to borrow duckets all the time, too. No way, José," Bubbles says, half-joking—but I know she means it.

Then she turns to me again. "So who did you meet yesterday, Do' Re Mi?"

"Oh, that didn't even come through," I lie, proud once again of my Q.T. handiwork. "Mrs. Tattle—my caseworker—just wanted to hang with me and some other kids, because she's going on vacation."

"What were they like?" Chanel asks curiously.

"Who?"

"The other kids."

"Oh, I don't know, Chanel—I don't want to talk about it," I sigh, because I can't tell one more fib-eroni. I guess I've filled my quota for one day, you know what I'm saying?

"Any word yet from the 'Battle of the Divettes' peeps?" I ask, changing the subject.

"Not yet," Bubbles says, heaving a sigh. "But my mom knows she'd better let us know the Minute Rice second she hears—she swore she'd call me on my cell phone!"

"See ya at lunch," I say, hugging both of them.

I feel relieved when I'm by myself again. I wish I never knew anything about foster care, or adoption, or any of this drama!

Sliding into my seat in biology class, I am on gene alert. I can feel my ears perk up when Mr. Roundworm mentions DNA.

"One of the most fascinating aspects of genetics is that an organism's DNA is more than a program for telling its cell how to operate. It is also an archive of the individual's evolutionary history." Mr. Roundworm taps a piece of chalk on the blackboard, next to the diagram he has drawn of a strand of DNA. It looks like pieces of ribbons wrapped together.

"If it were possible to align all the DNA strands of a baby in a single line, it would be long enough to make, on average, fifteen round-trips from the sun to Pluto, the farthest planet in the solar system."

A trip around the world. That's it! I'd completely forgotten what my first foster mother, Mrs. Parkay, told me about my mom when I was little. She said my mother was on a trip around the world. Well, my mother must've had fifteen round-trips from the sun to Pluto, too, because she has never come back!

When biology class is over, I can't wait to run up to Mr. Roundworm; but somebody else has beaten me to it. As usual, Albert Casserola has a question about our biology homework. Mr. Roundworm could repeat it fifty times, and Albert still wouldn't understand it.

Finally, Albert and his foggy glasses are out of my way. "Mr. Roundworm, can I talk to you for a second?" I ask politely.

"Yes, Dorinda," Mr. Roundworm responds, then waits for me to talk.

I look around to see who's listening, and Mr. Roundworm gets my drift.

"Let's go outside. We can talk while I'm walking to my office," he says, sticking a pen into the pocket of his lab coat.

"Um, I was wondering about this whole gene thing," I begin, struggling to find the right words. I mean, I still don't know how to ask my question without sounding stupid. "If a lady has a child with one man, then has a child with another man, can the two children look like they aren't related? I mean *really* not related?"

"Absolutely," Mr. Roundworm says, adjusting his thick-rimmed glasses.

I still don't feel satisfied with Mr. Roundworm's response, so I cut to the chase. "What I mean is, Mr. Roundworm, my mother was white—so is it possible for me to have a white sister—with blue eyes and blond hair?"

"Okay, I see what your question is. This lady—your mother—has a child with an African American, and that child is you."

"Right," I respond.

"Then she has a child with a Caucasian male. What you're asking me is would this other child look Caucasian?"

"Yes," I say, feeling stupid now for real. I hate that term—"African American." It makes me uncomfortable, and it sounds like I don't really belong here or something.

"Yes, she would—and I can tell you something even more interesting," Mr. Roundworm says, smiling at me in an understanding way. "Since you have a white mother, *you* may have recessive genes for blond hair and blue eyes. That means if you had a child with a man who has blond hair and blue eyes, *you* could give birth to a child with blond hair and blue eyes."

"Word?" I say, ruminating on the situation.

"Genes are amazing things—and they have a mind of their own," Mr. Roundworm says, beaming at me.

"Yeah, I guess so," I respond, trying to appear as enthusiastic as Mr. Roundworm. He is definitely a cool teacher—at least I never fall asleep in his class.

"Good-bye, Dorinda. I hope I've helped you," Mr. Roundworm says, looking concerned.

"Good-bye, Mr. Roundworm."

After he leaves, I walk along the hallway in a daze. I feel like I'm in the Twilight Zone again. I'm so lost in my own world, I walk right into someone.

"Excuse me," I say apologetically.

The girl just smiles, nasty-like, and walks away. Sometimes I think I have a case of fleas, please, the way some peeps catch an attitude for no reason.

I still can't believe Tiffany is really my sister. If my mom was here, she could tell me. Feeling the tears well up in my eyes, I make myself snap out of it. I have to go to draping class now, and I don't want to start thinking about my mother, or I'll start crying all over the stupid muslin!

Draping class winds up being the best therapy I could have had. I get busy working on ideas for Cheetah Girls costumes, and by the time class is over, I've forgotten all about Tiffany and my mother.

I meet my crew for lunch, and that's when Galleria pounces.

"Yo, Do' Re Mi, weeza in the house, pleeza, weeza!" she exclaims, hugging me and jumping up and down. I wait for Galleria to stop, so she can tell me why she's so amped. Only this morning, she looked like she needed fifty cups of mochaccino (her favorite Italian coffee) to get her flow going—you know what I'm saying?

"We got into the competition!" she yells, and then starts taking deep breaths to calm down.

"Word!" I say, bugging my eyes, 'cuz now I'm getting amped, too!

Chanel comes outside to meet us, and Galleria puts on the same cheetah-certified show. "*Hola*, granola! Weeza in the house, weeza in the house!"

Chuchie starts jumping up and down, screaming. She doesn't even ask what Galleria is talking about. Sometimes the two of them communicate without saying a word, you know what I'm saying?

Even though I'm happy, I feel that stabbing pain in my chest again—you know, kinda like my heart is cracked in pieces. Those two are bound till death, the dynamic duo, yo. They're just letting me be part of *their* crew. They're more like sisters than any sister I'll ever have, I bet.

All of a sudden, Chanel starts hugging me too. Whew. That makes me feel a little better, like I'm part of our crew after all. I take a deep breath, and wait for Galleria to give us the details about next Saturday.

"It's a good thing we just performed in the New Talent Showcase," Galleria says excitedly, "'cuz we are definitely ready to battle with Freddy—"

"Or any divette with a microphone—'cuz when we 'rock it to the beat, it's rocked to the doggy bone,'" Chanel joins in, singing the lyrics from Galleria's song "Woof, There It Is." I join in for a chorus, as we walk to Mo' Betta Burger on Eighth Avenue to get our grub on.

When we get there, Galleria fills us in on the "Divette" scoop. "We have a microphone check at three o'clock Saturday and the doors open at seven P.M."

"Are the divettes representing from other places?" I ask, curious. See, when we performed in Def Duck Records' New Talent Showcase in Los Angeles, they had groups from all over the country.

"No doubt about the East Coast clout," Galleria says, nodding her head. "This is a regional contest, but the competition finals are gonna be held in the Big Apple, too, you know what I'm saying? Because they're not playing—they know the winner is probably gonna come from the East Coast."

Galleria bops along with a satisfied smirk. She is so sure that we are gonna blow up our spots. "We have to be there at six sharp for the performance."

"We'll be there or be T-square," I say, bopping along, too.

"What are we gonna sing?" Chuchie asks.

Oh, no, I think. Here we go again, with the drama over who gets to write our songs.

"Why, Chuchie?" Bubbles asks. "Have you written one we should memorize overnight and perform on Saturday, *so we can lose the competition*?" Like I said, these two are like sisters, Galleria can tell when Chanel has a few hedgehog tricks up her sleeve.

"What happened?" Chanel exclaims, like she always does when she gets flustered. "No, I haven't written any songs, *babosa,* but I thought maybe we could sing the one we wrote together—'It's Raining Benjamins.'"

Actually, Galleria told me that Chanel only wrote one line in the whole song, but I can't blame Chanel for trying. She just wants to feel like she has "Big Willy" skills too.

"Chuchie, we *are* going to perform 'It's Raining Benjamins'—but not on Saturday. We need more time to practice it and work out a routine or something." Galleria crosses her arms in front of her, like that's the end of the conversation.

The big bulb from above goes off in my head again. "Yo, check it, remember what Aqua said? Maybe we should throw money on the stage for 'It's Raining Benjamins'—like the Cash Money Girls did at the New Talent Showcase," I suggest. "We could come up with some dope choreography and everything, right?"

"Do' Re Mi has a point. That sounds like the joint," Galleria says, looking at Chanel like, "Give it up, *mamacita*."

"*Está bien*," Chanel says, twirling her hair, then breaking out in a mischievous grin. "You're right. We should wait."

That grin reminds me of Tiffany. It's the same exact look! I'm about to burst out laughing. But then, the chill comes back, and I force myself to get my mind on the game plan at hand.

Galleria hugs Chanel, and I can see they have squashed their beef jerky for now. Then Galleria lets out a rally like she's in Cali: "We're not having a 'Nightmare on 125th Street' again—this time, we're bringing the noise, 'cuz we're poised!"

Chapter 8

When I get home, Mrs. Bosco tells me that Tiffany phoned and asked for me. "Dorinda, what's the matter, baby? You didn't like her?" Mrs. Bosco asks, because she sees the troubled look on my face.

"No, she was nice," I reply. I don't want to bad-mouth Tiffany for no reason. She *is* nice, and I feel sorry for her, 'cuz she *needs* a big sister or something. I could tell that she was kinda lonely. "I just feel strange about the whole situation."

What I don't want to tell Mrs. Bosco is the truth—that I'm mad at her. I know it's not all her fault—she can't read or write, so she probably doesn't know what's in my records—but

I *feel* like it's her fault anyway.

"Mrs. Tattle says my mother is white," I blurt out.

"I guess so," Mrs. Bosco says. I try to figure out if that means she didn't know, or that she can't believe it—like me.

Mrs. Bosco starts coughing—*badly*. I get scared that she's getting sick again. She was hospitalized for acute bronchitis last summer, and she hasn't really recovered from it. I don't want to get her upset now or anything.

She sits down on the couch in the living room, keeping the tissue held up to her mouth. "You know, it wouldn't hurt you to spend some time with that child," she says, talking through the tissue.

"Okay," I say. "But I can't this week. I have rehearsals every day for the competition on Saturday."

"You got another show?" she asks, her eyes getting brighter.

"Yes," I say, smiling because I'm so excited about it. At least the Cheetah Girls are still in the running, in more ways than one, you know what I'm saying? "It's called 'Battle of the Divettes' competition," I explain.

That makes Mrs. Bosco chuckle, and that makes her start coughing again. I decide to shut up, but she keeps egging me on. "Where's it gonna be?" she asks.

"It's at the Apollo Theatre," I say, and then wait for her response. Mrs. Bosco felt so bad for me when the Cheetah Girls lost the Amateur Hour contest.

"Never mind what happened last time," she says, reading my mind again. "Remember what I told you then—one monkey don't stop no show."

I smile, because I know how she loves me. I just hope she doesn't get sick. If I ever lost Mrs. Bosco, I don't know what I would do—not to mention all the other foster kids in our house.

"They ain't gonna have that Sandman fool onstage again," Mrs. Bosco says, her eyes twinkling. The Sandman is the one who pulls groups offstage when the Amateur Hour crowd boos them.

"No, I don't think so," I tell her. "But they are gonna have a lot of judges."

"Lord, I don't know which is worse," Mrs. Bosco says, wanting to laugh but not daring to 'cuz she might start coughing again.

"The winner of the competition gets to compete in the finals, then *that* winner gets to appear on the television show *The Grade,*" I say, talking slowly so she can follow what I'm saying.

Mrs. Bosco nods her head. "They sure make you dance around like a monkey with a tin cup full of pennies before they give you anything, huh?"

Now it's my turn to laugh. "Yeah, I guess so."

"I left that child's number on a piece of paper in the kitchen," Mrs. Bosco says, looking at me like she wants me to call Tiffany.

"Okay. Um, I'll get it later," I say, to avoid talking about it anymore. "I have to go down to Chanel's house now for rehearsal." I get out of that room before she starts in on me to call Tiffany.

I'm in my bedroom, getting everything I need to go downtown with, and I'm thinking things over. I wonder why Tiffany called me. Maybe she wants to be like real sisters, calling each other all the time, getting all involved with each other's lives.

Well, that may be fine for her, but I don't

know if I'm really ready to let a new sister into my life. I've already got all these kids in the house with me who I love, and take care of. And I've got my crew—which brings me to the other thing. How are they gonna react when they hear I have a white sister? Would they accept her if she started hanging around with us?

See, Galleria's an only child, Aqua and Angie don't have any other brothers and sisters, and Chanel's only got her little brother Pucci, who just turned nine. It would be way different if Tiffany were there at our rehearsals—she's almost my age!

Which is another thing—Tiffany knows how old I really am! What if she told my crew? Would they still even want to be friends with me, let alone let me stay in The Cheetah Girls?

And what if Tiffany decides she wants to be *part* of the group? I don't think my crew is gonna be down with taking on any new members, let alone Tiffany!

So I'm standing there, fretting about all this stuff, when Twinkie runs over and hands me a cookie. "Thank you," I say, giving her a big hug.

"Can I come with you?" she pleads.

"It's just a boring old rehearsal," I say, so she won't feel bad. "Guess what—when I come home later, we are gonna do our own Cheetah Girls rehearsal! Would you like that?"

"Yeah!"

I hug Twinkie again. One day, I want her and all my brothers and sisters to come to a big stadium, sit in the front row, and watch the Cheetah Girls perform. But not yet—not while we're still divettes!

When I walk into Chanel's house, her little brother, Pucci, practically grabs my arm out of its socket. "You gotta see Mr. Cuckoo!" he exclaims.

Pucci is so cute—he's got that big gap in between his two front teeth, and the Cupid's bow on his upper lip—and that same jumping-bean energy like Chanel. You can't help smiling at him all the time.

"Come on, I'll show you," he says, dragging me into his bedroom, which is inhabited by a tribe of Whacky Babies stuffed animals, who look like they're ready to pounce off the shelves!

"*There* he is!" Pucci says, pointing to the cage in the corner of his room, where I see the African pygmy hedgehog I helped Chanel pick out at the exotic pet store for Pucci's birthday.

I bend down to check out Mr. Cuckoo. "Wow, Pucci, you hooked him up—Cuckoo is definitely chillin' in his new crib!"

Pucci grins. I see a book peeking out from under the bedspread on his bed. Dragging it on the floor, I read the title: *Harry Henpecker's Guide to Geography*. It's the book Pucci's father gave him for his birthday. I flip through the pages and look at all the places around the world I wanna see.

"You can have it if you want it," Pucci offers.

"No, that's all right," I respond. I feel bad for him. I know what it's like to get presents you don't want. When I first got to Mrs. Bosco's, Mrs. Parkay sent me a present on Christmas. It was some stupid stuffed giraffe, and I threw it in the corner behind the Christmas tree, because I didn't want anything from her. Besides, what I really wanted was a doll wearing pretty clothes.

The doorbell rings, and I hear Aqua's and

Angie's voices cackling away. "I gotta go, Pucci, we have rehearsal now."

"You gonna go to the Apollo again, right?" Pucci asks.

"Yeah."

"How come they let you back in there, if you already lost?" he asks, his eyes opening wide. I chuckle, realizing he doesn't understand.

"That was the Amateur Hour contest we lost, Pucci," I say. "Now we're gonna perform in the 'Battle of the Divettes' competition. It just happens to be at the same place, but it has nothing to do with the Apollo—you understand?"

"Oh," Pucci says, fiddling with his computer. "You gonna have Cheetah Boys now? Can I be in the group?" Pucci flashes his mischievous grin so I know he's angling for a dangle—a cheesing skill he learned from his older sister, no doubt.

That's all we need. Pucci in the group, with Tiffany, too—and throw in Twinkie for good measure. "Who knows?" I joke to Pucci. "Maybe Cuckoo will come onstage and perform with us, too—you know what I'm saying?"

"Yeah, right," Pucci says, smirking.

"I'm not playing, you know what I'm saying?"

I hear Chanel calling me, so I run to the exercise studio, where we usually rehearse.

"Hi, Aqua. Hi, Angie," I say, hugging the twins. I don't get to see them as much as I see Chanel and Galleria, since we don't go to the same school. They're all wrapped up in talking about going home to Houston for Thanksgiving. I can definitely tell they're excited about it.

"I wish Daddy was coming with us, though," Angie says, kinda sad. "We're scared to leave him here with that High Priestess girlfriend of his."

"I know that's right," I chime in. I met their father's girlfriend, High Priestess Abala Shaballa, and she does seem to be tripping in another galaxy, if you know what I'm saying.

"There's plenty of time to worry about looking good in the 'hood, Miz Aquanette," Galleria says cheerfully, tapping her foot like she's ready to get down to the business at hand. "'There's always a new day in the jiggy jungle,'" she starts singing, "'so let's not bungle our chance to rise for the prize, and show you who we are, in the jiggy jiggy jungle—'"

We all sing along, since that's what we're here for—rehearsing our act, you know what I'm saying?

I'm so tired by the time I get home from Chanel's house that I head straight to my bedroom. Today's rehearsal was exhausting—not only running through all our songs and dance routines, but having to keep my mind off everything that's happening in my personal life. I'll tell you, if I didn't have Saturday's competition to think about, I'd be going loony right about now.

Just as I flop down on my bed, I hear Mrs. Bosco calling my name from her bedroom. "I'll be right there," I yell. Getting back up, I poke my head into Mrs. Bosco's bedroom.

"Dorinda—that child called *again* while you were out."

"Tiffany?" I ask, sighing, but what I'm really thinking is, Doesn't she have anything better to do than bother me?

"Thanks, Mom," I say, hoping she'll squash this conversation, but I shoulda known better.

"We had a nice long talk, you know," Mrs.

Bosco continues. She is propped up on the bed eating a bowl of rice pudding. "I think that child needs someone to talk to."

"Yeah," I say, nodding my head.

"She says her parents want to meet you 'cuz she can't stop talking about you," Mrs. Bosco says, beaming.

Oh, swelly, just what I need. Not just a new sister, but her parents, too!

"Maybe it's something important she needs to talk to you about," Mrs. Bosco suggests. "I think you better call her."

"After we do the competition," I say quickly. What I really mean is, after I've had time to break the news to my crew. "Then I'll go see Tiffany and her family," I offer, and quickly move on, changing the subject. "We had a great rehearsal tonight."

"That's good."

"I think we could really win this competition," I say—and for a change, I really mean it. I hope Mrs. Bosco doesn't ask to come to the competition, though, because I'm not ready to perform in front of her. I don't really want any of my family around until I feel ready for the big time, know what I'm sayin'?

"Good night," I say, stifling a yawn. Mrs. Bosco doesn't like to kiss or anything—I guess she doesn't want to get too close to us, in case we get taken away someday—so I just smile and walk out of her bedroom and back to my own.

Lying on my pillow, I wonder what Mrs. Bosco and Tiffany talked about. Tiffany Twitty sure gets chatty with everybody. I mean, she really runs her mouth faster than the Road Runner clocks miles.

I wonder if she looks like our mother . . . ?

Chapter 9

No matter how many times the Cheetah Girls perform, I always get a case of the spookies beforehand. Okay, so we haven't performed that much, but I'll bet it never goes away. Today is no exception. Even Aqua and Angie are faking that they're not quaking.

"Where's the Sandman?" Aqua asks, popping her eyes as she nervously looks around for him. Not that he booted us off the stage at the Amateur Hour contest—we came in second—but still, he's a scary somebody to think about when you're about to perform at the Apollo Theatre!

We are instructed to head backstage and see the competition coordinator. On our way down the aisle, I check out the big sparkly banner that is spanning the stage: HOT 99 PRESENTS 'THE BATTLE OF THE DIVETTES' COMPETITION.

Ms. Dorothea, who as our manager goes everywhere with us, is wearing a cheetah-spotted bustier, and her chest is covered with glitter. She looks like a movie star or something. One of the stagehands is goo-gahhing and peering down at Ms. Dorothea from the top of his ladder.

"If he paid as much attention to his job as he does to me, this place wouldn't be falling apart!" she humphs as she herds us around her.

The other stagehands are busy putting up banners. It seems like there are lots of companies sponsoring the competition.

"Ooh, looky, cooky, S.N.A.P.S. Cosmetics is one of the sponsors," Galleria tells us, pointing to a banner.

A pretty girl with a Dr. Seuss–type hat and a clipboard is talking into a walkie-talkie. Then, spotting Ms. Dorothea, she calls out our group's name and walks over to us. "Well, I guess I had no trouble figuring out who you are," the Dr. Seuss lady says to Ms. Dorothea.

Ms. Dorothea beams, then says, "I'm Dorothea

Garibaldi, the manager of the Cheetah Girls."

"Omigosh, I thought you were part of the group!" the Dr. Seuss lady exclaims. "Well, you look *fabulous*—I love that bustier. Where did you get it?"

Ms. Dorothea goes on to tell the Dr. Seuss lady all about her boutique, Toto in New York . . . Fun in Diva Sizes. I can tell the Dr. Seuss lady is supa-dupa impressed.

"Oh, too bad I'm not big enough to shop there," she whines, like she really means it.

"Size is just an attitude, darling," Ms. Dorothea quips. "You're welcome to stop in any time."

"Thank you!" the lady gushes. Then she gets down to the business at hand—trying to organize the lineup of struggling divettes. "I'm Candy Kane, the Talent Panel Coordinator, and I'll tell you how everything works. Let's see . . ." she goes on, peering down at her clipboard. "The Cheetah Girls are number seven in the lineup."

"Sounds sweet to me, Miss Candy Kane," Ms. Dorothea responds. "How many groups are performing?"

"Um, let's see—seven."

"Oh, so we're last!" Ms. Dorothea says, her eyes brightening.

"Yes, I guess so," Candy Kane giggles.

"Are all the groups from New York?" Galleria asks nervously.

"I believe they are—since this is a regional contest."

"How many contests are there?" Ms. Dorothea asks.

"There are quite a few, but the finals are going to be held in New York City, you'll be happy to know."

Candy Kane winks at Galleria. I can tell she likes our groove. "Now here are the rules: You may wait in your dressing room if you like, or you may wait backstage. It's your responsibility to be backstage and standing under the green light in time for your performance."

Pointing upward to the green light, Candy continues, "You are not allowed to take pictures or use recording devices backstage. You are also not allowed to drink, eat, or smoke. After you finish your performance, you should exit the stage *quickly,* then wait back here for the announcer to give you your return cue—that is, *if* you become one of the finalists."

"Return cue—is that when the audience picks the winners?" Ms. Dorothea asks.

"No, Mrs. Garibaldi, the panel of judges seated in the first row is solely responsible for picking the finalists. The announcer will be handed three envelopes, and read the winners for the first and second runner-ups, as well as the regional winner. Only if your name is announced should you come back onstage. Do you understand everything?"

"Yes!" we say in unison.

Handing Ms. Dorothea some papers, Candy Kane explains, "Now here are the releases for you to sign. It's a standard release—stating that you're aware this event is being videotaped, and that you've not been promised any monetary compensation from Looking Good Productions for participating in the 'Battle of the Divettes' competition."

Ms. Dorothea puts on her cheetah glasses and scans the forms.

"When you're done, you can hand the forms to any of the production assistants backstage—oh, and here are your gift bag tickets. I'll give you six—one for you, too, Mrs. Garibaldi. Just give them to Gator, the guy in the blue baseball cap standing right over there."

"I see him. And thank you!" Ms. Dorothea says, spotting the guy.

"He'll give you your gift bag, girls—you're gonna love all the goodies from our sponsors. And good luck!" Candy Kane whisks off to do her supa-spiel with the next divette-in-waiting, leaving us all hyped about this whole thing.

"The peeps doing this competition are definitely more chili than the Amateur Hour people," Galleria says, impressed. Then she turns to Chanel. "You sure perked up as soon as you heard there were free goodies," Galleria chides her.

Chanel breaks out in a mischievous grin. I love her so much—she makes everybody feel better with her *señorita* energy. For the moment, I've forgotten all my troubles—even my nerves are gone!

We hightail it over to Gator to get our gift bags. "See you later, Gator," Galleria says sweetly, as he hands us our last bag.

"Ooh, it's heavy," Chanel says excitedly, as she swings her red canvas McDonald's bag back and forth.

"They wouldn't put food in this thing, would they?" Aqua asks hopefully, as she gingerly puts her hand inside.

"No, silly, willy! McDonald's is obviously just one of the sponsors," Galleria mumbles. "Oh—S.N.A.P.S.!" she exclaims, taking a free lipstick sample out of her bag.

"Ooh, what color is it?" I ask, waiting for Galleria to take the top off and swivel up the lipstick. It turns out to be a red shade.

Galleria looks at the bottom of the tube to check out the name of the color. "'Desire.'"

Chanel has taken hers out, and giggles, "Mine is 'Destiny'—but I don't like the color." I have to agree with her—it *is* a wack shade of yellow.

The twins have dug the tubes of lipstick out of their gift bags—naturally, they get the same color. "'Lust'?" Aqua moans when she reads the label. "We better not even take this home, or Daddy won't let us out of the house again!"

The twins' father, Mr. Walker, *is* kinda strict, so I decide to help them out. "I'll switch with you," I say. "I got a tube of 'Destiny,' too."

"I don't want that—our lips are big enough without looking like banana peels!" Aqua moans.

"Well, Aqua, you can either meet your 'Destiny' by getting shipped back to your Grandma's in Houston, or you can wear it," I chuckle, like a game show host. *"The choice is yours."*

"Awright," she mumbles, swiping my tube, and handing over hers. I can't believe how many goodies are stuffed in these bags! Little bottles of shampoo, pencils, an ugly paperweight, a *Sistarella* magazine, Miss Wiggy glitter lip gloss, and sheets of butterfly stickers.

"Ooo, I can give these to my sister Twinkie!" I exclaim.

"Hey, Do' Re Mi—how come you never invite your family to come see you perform?" Chanel asks me sweetly.

My breath catches in my throat. Suddenly, my nerves are all back, and I can feel my stomach jumping. "I'm just not ready," I mumble, looking away.

"Yeah, I know what you mean. I sure wish Mom wasn't coming tonight," Chanel laments. "And guess what else—she's bringing her boyfriend with her—Mr. Tycoon himself! I'm not feeling in the mood for him, *está bien?"*

I feel so relieved that none of my "family"

will be in the house, because I don't know if I'm ready for that yet. Performing is scary enough without more drama. I'm afraid that if anybody I knew was out there in the audience, I'd just freeze up totally right there onstage.

I look up, wondering if Chanel has sensed how scared I am. But no, I have nothing to worry about—her greedy little paws are already digging into her bag, looking for treasures.

A little while later, after we've finished switching our Astrology bottles of cologne (inside of my bag is a bottle of "Virgo," so I give it to the twins, since that's their astrological sign), we decide it's time to check out the talent. Galleria, Chanel, and I don't recognize any of the other girls hanging out in the backstage area with us. But the twins do.

"There's that girl JuJu from school," Angie winces to Aqua.

"Her name is JuJu 'Beans' Gonzalez," Angie explains to the rest of us, sucking her teeth. "She's a singing *and* drama major—with emphasis on the drama, you know what I'm sayin'?"

"Yeah—and her middle name describes her

exactly, 'cuz she iz 'full of beans!'" Aqua adds, poking out her juicy lips for extra measure.

By this time, JuJu "Beans" Gonzalez has gotten the drift that all eyes are on her. She looks over in our direction, then turns away as if she doesn't see us.

"I wonder how she got in this competition, 'cuz I didn't see any notice at school," Aqua ponders.

"The world of divettes is very small," Galleria offers in explanation. "Everything that's going down sure gets passed around."

"Yeah, well the world sure ain't big enough for us and JuJu!" Aqua laments, sucking on her lollipop. "She looks like one of those beauty pageant contestants back home in that outfit. Ain't that right, Angie?"

"Yes, ma'am," Angie agrees. "And we sure got a lot of girls who look like her back home."

I take in JuJu's red sequin gown, and the fake red gardenia flowers pinned in her upswept "do," and decide "I think she looks like the runner-up for Miss Botanical Gardens!"

We all giggle, which helps us forget how nervous we are.

A woman in a red sweat suit and baseball

cap is walking around introducing herself to all the contestants. Now she comes up to us.

"Hi, I'm P.J. Powers from HOT 99," she says in a bubble-licious way, extending her hand to Galleria.

We all get instantly excited because we have just met P.J. Powers—the radio deejay on "The Power Hour," which plays the most flava-fied songs in heavy rotation. After she's shaken all our hands, she moves on to greet the next group.

Ms. Dorothea, meanwhile, has signed all the papers. "I guess it's time to pounce, girls. Let's go on up to the dressing room, so you can put on your costumes." She herds us toward the back stairway, which we remember from the Amateur Hour.

"Now we gotta go climb those creaky stairs into the tower of the haunted house," jokes Aqua. "I sure hope *this* horror show has a happy ending!"

Chapter 10

We decide to wait backstage rather than in our dressing room, because it's seven o'clock—and that means, "Show time at the Apollo!" Sometimes shows don't start on time, but you never know—and half the fun of performing with competing acts is hearing them do their thing, you know what I'm saying?

"Should we leave our gift bags in the dressing room?" Aqua asks Ms. Dorothea.

"No way, darling," she replies. "Why should one of these desperate divettes get their grubby little paws on our products?" Ms. Dorothea huffs then gathers up all six of the gift bags and puts them in her big cheetah carryall. She always has a lot of papers and folders to carry, so she carries these really big bags.

All of a sudden the chatter in the audience dies down. Then they begin to clap loudly, which means the announcer has hit the stage. "How y'all doing tonight, Big Apple?!" P.J. Powers bellows into her microphone. Then she lets out a raucous chant: "Y'all are on HOT 99—so it's your dime!"

"Oh, that's *la dopa*! They're broadcasting the show *live* on the radio," Chanel says, jumping up and down.

Suddenly, I get the squigglies in my stomach again. Wow—this is really it! I grab Chanel's hand. Please don't let us lose, I pray. Not at the Apollo. Not again. Not live on the air!

"We've got prizes for you people!" P.J. Powers screams into the microphone, hyping the crowd. "So keep those ticket stubs. Because at some point during the show, we're going to be calling out winning numbers, to give back what you give me every day on HOT 99—the flava, baybee!"

The crowd is cheering wildly.

"How many of y'all want to win a trip to the Bahamas, courtesy of HOT 99? That's right, you know what they say—it's betta in the

Bahamas! So you'd better stay in your seats, or you might miss out—you know what I'm saying?—'cuz P.J. Powers ain't *playing*!"

The curtain backstage is too thick to let us get a peek at anybody in the audience. "That's just as well," Angie offers as consolation. "The less we know the better."

"I just wonder who the judges are," I whisper.

Angie is wiping her forehead with a tissue. The twins sweat when they get nervous. They are *deathly* afraid of heights, and you should see them sweat whenever they ride an elevator above the tenth floor!

The first divette to perform is called Witch Hazel. What a name! I can't see her through the curtain, but I'll bet she comes onstage with a broom or something. I hear her drop an R & B song, which was originally sung by Diamonds in the Ruf. It's called "Bewitched."

I hate when acts perform covers of other artist's songs. It's like, "Can't you write your own music?"

We just look at each other and smile, and I know what we're all thinking: Witch Hazel better be putting a spell on the audience, because the hardest spot in a showcase is the first.

"Better her than us," Angie whispers in my ear. Witch Hazel gets a nice round of applause. That makes us feel a whole lot better—knowing that the audience will probably be all warmed up by the time we perform.

The next few singers also sing R & B tunes, but they aren't that good—except for the Butta Cups. They have a nice three-part harmony.

"I think the Cheetah Girls have got this one in the bag, baby," Galleria says, crossing her fingers because it's getting closer to our turn.

P.J. Powers announces Fakie Quakie, and two short girls in black vinyl miniskirts go running onto the stage. They start singing a song that sounds sorta gospel-ish. "'Since you left me/My heart's so achy. I'm not fakin' that I'm just quakin' . . . .'"

Aqua and Angie start bouncing around, because they *love* gospel music. And I've gotta admit these Fakie Quakie girls have nice soprano range. Better than mine, that's for sure. If I go too high up, my voice gets squeaky. It's better if I stay in the middle—that's what Drinka Champagne says.

It's time to do our Cheetah Girls prayer, so we gather in a circle and join hands. At the end of each prayer, we always end with our Cheetah Girls oath:

"We're the Cheetah Girls and we number five.
What we do is more than live.
We'll stay together through the thin and the thick.
Whoever tries to leave, gets hit with a chopstick.
Whatever makes us clever—forever!!!"

P.J. Powers *finally* announces us. We take a deep breath together, and run onstage. When we get there, the cheering drowns out everything else.

I try not to look for the video camera that is taping the competition, but I can't help sneaking a peek as we wait for our taped track to kick in. I don't see the camera, though—that must mean it's far in back of the house.

I notice that the klieg lights are *really* bright this time. I liked the way they did the lighting for us at the New Talent Showcase in L.A. This is definitely way too bright. Oh, well, part of performing is just acting like everything is supa-dupa chili, so that's what I do as we dive into the song.

Is it me, or is the tape-recorded track louder than usual? There must be an echo in this place, or maybe it's haunted. I try to remember if I noticed that the last time we performed here, but I can't remember.

As we sing, I notice that it's taking us a while to really get into our flow, you know what I'm saying? Maybe it's the lights being so bright, or the track being so loud—or maybe it's just that we're goin' out live on the radio. Anyway, by the time we get to the third verse, we've got it all together, and we're rockin' the house:

"Some people move like snakes in the grass
or gorillas in the mist
who wanna get dissed.

Some people dance with the wolves
or trot with the fox
right out of the box."

When the five of us hold hands and take our bow, I feel how clammy Chanel's hand is. Or maybe it's my hand! I'm sweating a lot, and I didn't even notice it till now.

Right before we exit the stage, we cup our hands like cheetahs to make our "growl power" sign, then scrunch up our faces like we're gonna pounce. I hear a few people laughing in the audience, and the applause gets louder. Everybody loves that "growl power" thing—it's kinda cute, I guess.

Backstage, as we wait for the winners to be announced, the tension is so thick you could cut it with a knife. After all, this is it: do-or-die time. As far as I'm concerned, it's first place or nothing—I mean, who wants to be a runner-up every time, you know what I'm saying?

Chanel is clutching my hand really hard.

"All right y'all," P.J. Powers announces. "This is the moment we've all been waiting for. It's time to do *battle!* Which one of these divettes is gonna make it to the finals?" The audience whoops and shouts, calling out the names of different groups—including ours.

"Let me tell you something, I know those divettes are backstage quaking in their weaves," P.J. continues. "You know why? Well, lemme tell you in case you don't know. One *very, very* lucky and plucky divette act—that's unsigned talent, y'all, in case you don't know—is gonna make *The Grade* and compete on MTV!"

The crowd lets out another hoot.

"That's right, y'all. MTV will finance and air a professionally produced video of the grand prize winner! Now that winner could be one of these fierce divettes you just saw perform. Now what else we got?"

"What?" yells someone in the audience.

"We got *two* other hot spots—that's right, y'all, *two* other *lucky, lucky, lucky* divettes are gonna be our first and second runner-ups. Now they're not going to get to go to the finals—"

"Awwww," moans the audience.

"I know—life in the fast lane can be a pain, baby, *but* the first runner-up receives a cash prize! That's right—who doesn't like a little loot? Lemme hear ya if you would say no to a Benjamin knocking on your door! Lemme hear ya!"

There is one second of silence.

"That's what I thought," P.J. Powers continues, which wins a raucous laugh from the crowd. "The first runner-up will win a five-hundred-dollar cash prize—that's enough money for a new weave, right? Am I right, ladies?"

More laughter. Chanel is holding my hand so tight it's cutting off my circulation. I yank my hand away from her, and she giggles, then quickly covers her mouth when Galleria shoots her a look.

"The second runner-up? Well, we can't dis the second runner-up, can we? They're gonna get a guest deejay spot on my show—that's right, hanging on 'The Power Hour' with the P.J. till payday! *And,* they will receive two backstage passes to MTV's *'The Hookup,'* to hang with today's hottest groups in the green room! Now that's the way I like to eat ribs, what about y'all?"

The crowd is cheering again. Galleria shoots me a look like, "Would she shut her trap, pleez, or we're gonna sneeze!"

"Okay, by the way, y'all, have you met our illustrious panel of judges? In the house with us tonight is everybody's favorite gossip diva—Miss Clucky!"

After the round of applause, P.J. introduces eight more judges, including "Miss Lela Lopez from *Sistarella* magazine, and Destiny

Davenport, Corporate Sponsorship Executive from S.N.A.P.S. Cosmetics."

I look at my crew. I guess we know where the name of that wack lipstick "Destiny" came from!

The squigglies start in my stomach again. If the Cheetah Girls weren't already quaking in our boots, we sure are now that we know who the judges are!

"Now for the moment we've all been waiting for. Miss Clucky, the envelope, please," P.J. Powers says, her voice tingling with excitement.

All five of us grab each other's hands as a drum roll sounds.

"Our *second* runner-up is—the Butta Cups! Give them a hand, people!"

We breath a sigh of relief. At least we aren't second runners-up!

When the Butta Cups hit the stage, P.J. Powers asks the audience, "Aren't they dainty little divettes? I love those cute little gloves. Do you eat ribs with them on?"

"No," says one of them into the microphone.

"Well, you girls have to tell me all about yourselves when you come on my show—so be ready for these dainty flowers on 'The Power Hour!'" P.J. chuckles at her little joke.

"Now for the first runner-up. Ms. Davenport, may I have that envelope, please? I'm loving that new shade of lipstick—Destiny—was it named after you?"

Obviously, the S.N.A.P.S. lady must've shaken her head yes, because P.J. continues, "Y'all, run out and treat yourself to S.N.A.P.S. lipsticks—see, mine is still on, and I've been running my mouth *all* day—and you know I don't play! Oh, where was I?"

The audience chuckles again.

"That's right—I'd better open this envelope before one of those divettes backstage starts fainting. Our first runner-up is—the Cheetah Girls! Oh, they were too cute—growl power in the house tonight, y'all!"

We look at each other, and I see that Chanel has little tears in her eyes. Ms. Dorothea throws us all a look like, "Never let them see you sweat."

Running onto the stage, I feel so embarrassed. I *hate* losing, even though I know we didn't exactly *lose*. First runner-up isn't so bad, really—and a hundred dollars each is sure better than nothing, especially when you count in all the other free stuff we got—and our first time on the radio, too.

We stand next to P.J. Powers on the stage, and wait until the applause dies down. "I just wanna know, where did you girls get these cute outfits? Aren't they cute?" P.J. turns to the audience, and under the bright lights I can see she has too much makeup on. She is glowing like it's Halloween.

"Um, my mother is our designer," Galleria says proudly, and I can tell she is being more shy than usual.

"Yours even has a little tail on it—turn around so we can see that," P.J. says, pointing to me.

I'm so embarrassed, but I turn my booty to the audience—and they start laughing, then clapping. I feel like I just wanna do an abracadabra right on the spot and disappear!

"Now, people, I want y'all to know that *all* the divettes who performed in this competition are fierce—or they'd still be singing with their hairbrushes in the mirror! Am I right? That's right! So just because these girls didn't win first prize—a chance to compete in the finals—doesn't mean they aren't fierce. Honey, who knows? *They* could be the ones that go on and get the record deal!"

At least we still have a shot with Def Duck Records, I think gratefully. They're still willing to give us a chance. We are ushered off the stage, and wait with everyone else to hear who the winner is.

"Okay, y'all, I'm gonna get to it. Miss Lopez, would you hand me the envelope, please? You know I love your magazine. Where else can I read about 'How to Find a Man'? And Lord knows, I need one!"

Ms. Dorothea puts her arms around me and Galleria as we wait. "The winner is—Fakie Quakie!"

The two short girls let out a squeal like Miss Piggy, and jump up and down. I can't blame them. They must feel on top of the world.

"The battle is over!" P.J. says as the girls hit the stage. "Fakie Quakie, how do you two feel, now that you know you have a shot at appearing on MTV?"

"I'm not quaking anymore!" giggles the one who calls herself Quakie.

"Where are you girls from?"

"Mamaroneck," one of them says, and they both start giggling.

"Mamaroneck is in the house, y'all! The

Boogie-down Bronx can't get all the props—am I right?" P.J. squeals.

I can feel the stabbing pain in my chest again. Five hundred dollars—that is a dope prize, but it's not *first* prize, you know what I'm saying? Oh, well, at least my family wasn't here to see us come up short. Except now, I'm gonna have to find a way to tell them all about it. I am *not* lookin' forward to *that*.

After we change and head for the exit, Aqua says, "I'm not performing here anymore. This place is bad luck—with or without the Sandman."

"At least you girls won five hundred dollars—that's nothing to moan and groan about," Ms. Dorothea says sympathetically.

"We know, Mom," Galleria says, looking sad.

"*Madrina*, can we just leave?" Chanel asks, whining. "I don't want the people to see us crying."

"Now, if we don't find your mother outside, she will have a soap opera fit off the air, Chanel. You know that," Ms. Dorothea says, putting her arms around her. "If you girls don't want that five hundred dollars, I'll be very happy to take it and spend it for you."

What I'm thinking is, Ms. Dorothea deserves it more than we do. But I guess we don't have enough duckets in the bucket to be turning up our noses at any cash they want to give us.

"Are we gonna be on television?" Angie asks. "They were videotaping the show, weren't they?"

"The release didn't say the contest was going to air anywhere," Ms. Dorothea explains. "It's just a videotape for the production company's purposes—Looking Good Productions. They're the promoters of this competition, not MTV."

All of a sudden, I hear a squealing sound that's familiar. "Dorinda!" I look over and see—*Tiffany*! What is *she* doing here?

"Who's that?" Galleria asks curiously.

I freeze in my tracks, and don't say a word. Tiffany comes running over with this blond lady in a fur coat and a bald man wearing glasses. They must be her parents, I realize! Like a deer caught in the headlights of a car, I secretly pray I could do an *abracadabra*.

"You were dope!" Tiffany says, running up and giving me a hug.

I stand there, still frozen to the spot. "Hi," I

tell her—but my eyes are saying, "Why did you come here?"

"Hi, we're Tiffany's parents—I'm Brenda Twitty," the blond lady coos to me, "and this is my husband, Fred." Her hair is like a *bou bou fon fon*—it's piled really high and looks like it's hiding under a can of hair spray.

All of a sudden, you can feel the tension on the sidewalk. *All* of us seem really uncomfortable. Leave it to the twins to break the ice.

"Hi, I'm Aquanette Walker, and this is my twin sister, Anginette."

"I'm Tiffany—I'm Dorinda's sister," Tiffany says proudly. My crew just kinda looks at her, then at me. They've been over to my house, so they know Tiffany is not one of my foster sisters. Nobody says anything, though.

I feel so guilty and ashamed! Why did they have to come? We didn't even win the stupid competition!

"We've heard so much about you," Mrs. Twitty says warmly, putting a hand on my arm.

I guess I'm just staring at the ground, because Ms. Dorothea takes over, and chats with Tiffany and her parents about the show.

"You didn't tell us you invited your sister," Galleria says, like she's waiting for me to give her the lowdown.

"I didn't know she was coming," I say in a low voice.

Tiffany overhears us and pipes up, "Mrs. Bosco told me about the competition when I phoned—so I thought I would surprise Dorinda."

I can't believe Mrs. Bosco would do this to me! She *knows* how uncomfortable I am about people seeing me perform. I haven't even invited *her* yet!

"I hope you don't mind—I just wanted to surprise you," Tiffany says, her blue eyes twinkling. Then she turns to Chanel and says, "I wanna be a singer, too."

"Oh," Chanel says. "Do you sing?"

"Well, um, not like you all do—but I *want* to." The next thing I know, Chanel and Tiffany are deep in conversation—talking about which groups they like and who they think is cute! It's like they're already friends!

"Blanco from the Nastee Boys is really hot," Tiffany says, giggling.

"I have *un coco* on Krusher!" Chanel says,

breaking into a fit of hysterics. "I'm saving my first kiss for him!"

Galleria puts her arm around me and says, "Don't worry about it, Do'—just go with the flow."

I look at Galleria, and I just want to cry. She sees the tears in my eyes. I know I have a lot of explaining to do to my crew. But the main thing is, they've accepted Tiffany as my sister—just like that! Not one of them blinked twice at the fact that she was white.

What was I thinking? That my crew would be prejudiced? I see now how crazy that was—I mean, Galleria's half white herself, Ms. Dorothea married an Italian man, and Chuchie's got all kinds of mixed-up genes in her. They do look kind of surprised, of course—and I can tell I'm gonna have a lot of explaining to do later on. But the worst is over. Suddenly, I'm glad Tiffany showed up. It saved me having to break the news to my crew.

After what seems like forever, Tiffany and the Twittys say good night. "You wanna go to the park again?" Tiffany asks me, really sweetly.

"Okay," I say, and this time I really mean it.

"It's gonna be nice to have a real sister—someone who's got some of the same genes as me."

"And you're gonna tell me about genes, too—promise?" Tiffany begs.

I laugh, and put my arm around her shoulder. "I promise," I say. "I'll call you tomorrow, and we'll make a time to meet." We give each other a little kiss and a hug, and then I shake hands with her parents, promising to come over for dinner sometime.

When we get into Mr. Garibaldi's van, Galleria says, "Chanel is sneaky deaky, but Do' Re Mi, I've got to give it up to you—you sure do keep a lot of secrets!"

"I know," I admit. "But I only found out about Tiffany a week ago—and I didn't know how you'd all take it about her being white—and about me being half white."

Galleria smiles. "Just like me!" she says, giving me five. "Hey, it's a rainbow nation, *girlita!*"

All of a sudden, Galleria starts humming, "'Do' Re Mi on the Q.T./Do' Re Mi on the D.D.L./ That ain't swell./ Do' Re Mi on the Q.T./ Do' Re Mi on the D.D.L./ Why won't you tell?'"

"Hey! Now that's a song," coos Chanel.

"For once, Chuchie, you are right," Bubbles

says with a giggle. "Once more, I have come up with a master jammy whammy!"

I burst out laughing, 'cuz everything just seems so crazy! "Well—at least we got a song outta this situation!" I say. "And some money, too."

"And you got a new sister, too, looks like," Angie says.

"I like her," Chanel says, nodding slowly. "When you gonna bring her around sometime?"

"Pretty soon," I promise. "I thought you two might hit it off."

The car pulls into traffic. Aqua looks out the window and yells, "Good-bye Apollo—and the next time we come back, you're gonna have to *pay* us!"

I put my head on Chanel's shoulder and start us harmonizing on Galleria's new song: "'Do' Re Mi on the Q.T. Do' Re Mi on the D.D.L.'" I can't stop nodding to the beat. "It's definitely a whammy jammy," I tell Galleria.

The rest of the way home, I'm quiet. What a night! But I have to admit, the best part of it was Tiffany showing up like that—like she really cares about me.

I can't believe it—*I have a real sister!*

Do' Re Mi on the Q.T.

This is Galleria and this is Chanel
We are coming to you live
From Cheetah Girls Central
Where we process the data that matters
And even mad chatter
But today we're here to tell you
About our friend, Do' Re Mi
(That's Miss Dorinda to you)
Kats and Kittys, the drama
Has gotten so radikkio
Just when we thought we knew our crew
Bam! The scandal was told!

There's a new girl in town
That's Miss Dorinda to you,
She bounced into our lives
But now she's part of our crew

Do' Re Mi on the Q.T.
Do' Re Mi on the D.D.L.
(That ain't swell)
Do' Re Mi on the Q.T.

Do' Re Mi on the D.D.L.
(Why won't you tell?)

Dorinda's got a secret
And it's cutting off her flow
(Is that right, girlita*?)*
According to our sources,
She thought we didn't know
(Kats and Kittys, you'd better take notes)
Today for the first time (the very first time)
Do' Re Mi found out she's not alone
(What are you saying?)
She found out she got a sister
And it's making her moan and groan!

There's a new girl in town
That's Miss Dorinda to you,
She bounced into our lives
But now she's part of our crew

Do' Re Mi on the Q.T.
Do' Re Mi on the D.D.L.
(That ain't swell)
Do' Re Mi on the Q.T.
Do' Re Mi on the D.D.L.
(Why won't you tell?)

But we peeped you!
And now we beeped you!
So what you know about that, huh?

Let's tell Miss Dorinda
That she's got all the flavor
And when she keeps things to herself
It's Do' Re Mi that we savor
Don't turn quiet on us
Like you got nothing to say
We found out you got a sister
So why can't she come out and play?

Do' Re Mi on the Q.T.
Do' Re Mi on the D.D.L.
(That ain't swell)
Do' Re Mi on the Q.T.
Do' Re Mi on the D.D.L.
(Why won't you tell, tell, tell!)
We said Do' Re Mi's on the Q.T.
(That's the sneak tip)
Do' Re Mi on the D.D.L.
(That's the down, down low)
Do' Re Mi on the Q.T.
Do' Re Mi on the D.D.L.

Do' Re Mi on the Q.T.
Who you trying to be?
Do' Re Mi on the D.D.L.
That's right, you know that's fowl
like a nearsighted owl
Do' Re Mi on the Q.T.
Why you got secrets
that make us growl?
Do' Re Mi on the D.D.L.
(Is that really true her sister is—Ahhhh!
Yes, mamacita *. . .)*

(Fade with growl sounds)

The Cheetah Girls Glossary

Ad-lipping: Talking nonsense. Blabbing with an attitude.

Amped: Excited. As in, "What are you so amped about?"

Angle for a dangle: Cheesing or manipulating a situation so you can get a chomp on the carrot dangling in your face. Kinda like angling for an "op," but more cheesing is involved.

Audi 5000: Gone like the Road Runner. To do a *fast* getaway.

Beaucoup swelly: Supa cool.

Beef jerky: Static. When you have a beef with someone.

Big Willy: Someone who is really important. Something that is really dope.

Blab your trap: Talk too much.

Blow up: Become really really successful.

Bozo: A boy who thinks he's all that but he isn't.

Coming out of the box: All of a sudden. Out of the blue but not true blue—not for real.

D.D.L.: On the down, down low. For example: you just got your report card and you got a C in biology. When you get home, you run to your room and stay on the D.D.L. from your mom until dinnertime.

Emphatically: On the serious tip.

Enuf with the powder puff: Dress rehearsal is over. It's show time, baby.

Feels like a "Magilla Gorilla": Feels too heavy.

Fib-eronis: Teeny weeny fibs. Purple lies and alibis!

Flex and floss: Do your thing. Make things happen faster than Minute Rice.

Hoax-arama: Something that isn't true.

Hunky chunky: Cool, fine, as in: "Everything is fine" (even if it isn't).

Jammy whammy: A dope song. As in, "That's a master jammy whammy!"

Joint: Supa chili. As in, "That song is the joint."

Jumpstreet: The place where you get to the point, as in, "You shoulda just asked me that from jumpstreet."

Muslin: Plain white fabric used for draping and making a pattern for clothes.

Piggly-wiggly giggle: An oinky-sounding laugh.

Posse: Crew. The peeps you hang with.

Put in check: Straightening out someone who is dissing you. Letting them know, it's not like that, okay?

Q.T.: On the hush, hush, sneak, sneaky or the quick tip.

Radikkio: Ridiculous. As in, "Don't be radikkio!"

Rigor mortis: Temporary stiffening of muscles in a corpse.

Spastic-on-the-elastic tip: Someone who doesn't know how to go with the flow.

The big bulb from above: The mysterious source of all Big Willy ideas.

The spookies: The "willies."

Thinking without blinking: When you really know something is true.

To hype up: Support. Represent to the max.

Toodles: Bye. See you later.

Toodly: Fine, okay. Like when someone asks you, "How are you?" You respond, "I'm toodly."

Twizzling: Twisting something into pretzel shapes or just messing around with it.

Growl Power

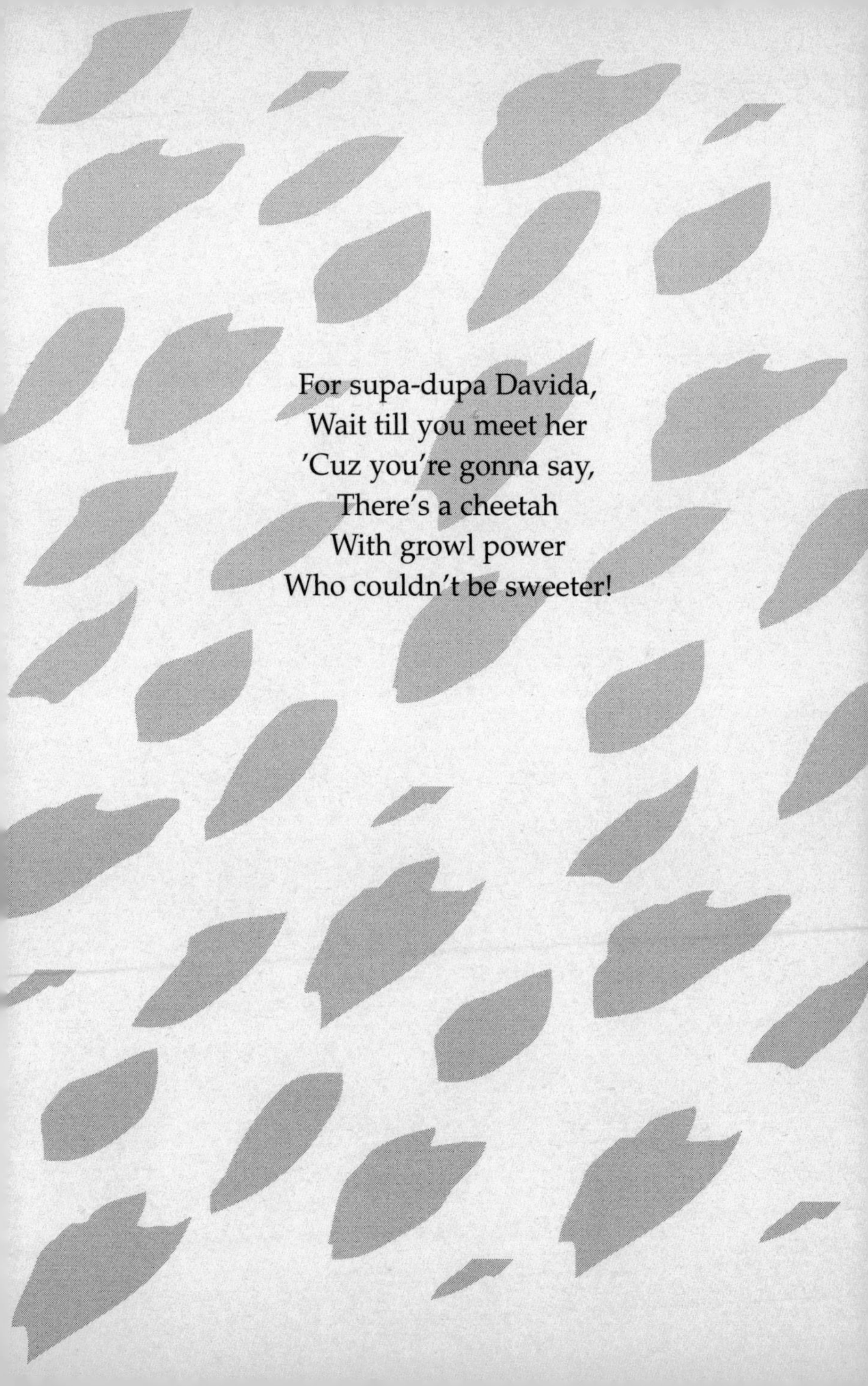

For supa-dupa Davida,
Wait till you meet her
'Cuz you're gonna say,
There's a cheetah
With growl power
Who couldn't be sweeter!

Chapter 1

Angie and I are *soooo* grateful that school is out for the Thanksgiving holidays! A whole week off this year, too—thanks to construction at our school, LaGuardia Performing Arts League. All we can think about is heading home to Houston, and telling everybody about the Big Apple till they're green with envy!

We, of course, is me, Aquanette Walker, and my twin sister Anginette—but *I'm* usually the one doing the talking, because I can't help *thinking* of the two of us as one person. (It's something you'd understand if people were always confusing *you* for your twin!)

Right now, *we* are fixing up a special dinner

in the kitchen of the big New York City apartment we share with our daddy. We've been living here since June, and already there's been more excitement than we had in all those years back in Houston!

But that doesn't mean we don't want to go back home to visit. Our ma is down there, still living in the old house we love so much. And *her* mama—our grandma, whom we all call "Big Momma," still lives in the house she and Granddaddy Selby lived in for fifty years or more. Granddaddy died seven years ago, but that don't stop Big Momma. *Nothing* stops her!

Granddaddy Walker will be waiting for us, too. Angie and I can't wait to visit the Rest in Peace Funeral Parlor again—that's where he lives! It's granddaddy's business, and he lives up top, two floors above the corpses. I guess that's why our daddy has always been such a serious person—and why Angie and I just *loooove* horror movies!

The dinner we are fixing is not for our daddy. He wouldn't eat it, so why bother? He only eats the kind of food his new girlfriend makes him—seaweed shakes and stuff like that. Daddy is looking thin and peaked, if you ask me; but he thinks he's never looked better.

I believe he's been bewitched by High Priestess Abala Shaballa Bogo Hexagone. That's his girlfriend's name, believe it or not. She claims to be a real high priestess. I don't know about that, but she sure is strange. I don't like her one bit, and neither does Angie.

Anyway, we're cooking a holiday dinner for the Cheetah Girls right now—that would be Galleria "Bubbles" Garibaldi, Dorinda "Do' Re Mi" Rogers, and Chanel "Chuchie" Simmons. The five of us are a cheetah-licious girl group, and we've got mad skills, too. Being Cheetah Girls is the best thing that ever happened to me and Angie. Not only do we have a crew of our own, but we're close as can be to getting a record contract! Can you believe it?

The first time the Cheetah Girls came over to our house, Princess Abala Shaballa was doing the cooking. She made up this good-luck brew for us out of some nasty roots and herbs. It was supposed to help us win the Apollo Theatre Amateur Hour Contest—which it didn't. We came in second.

Right now, Chanel and Dorinda are sitting at the kitchen table, watching me and Angie do the cooking. Suddenly Chanel stands up and puts her dirty, sneakered foot up on the edge of the sink to stretch it!

Angie and I look at each other like, "Yes, she really is doing that!"

"I've *gotta* stretch my legs, or I'll get rigor mortis, and they'll fall off or something," Chanel giggles. Ever since Chanel and the rest of the Cheetah Girls found out that our granddaddy owns Rest in Peace Funeral Parlor, they are always trying to take a stab at us with "corpse jokes." Ha, ha, yes, ma'am.

I would say something back, and make her get her feet off my clean sink, but I know Chanel's legs are extra tired. See, she ran in the Junior Gobbler Race in Central Park this morning. She *won*, too! They gave her a big ol' turkey, but she turned around and gave it to Dorinda's foster mother, Mrs. Bosco, so all those foster kids in their house would have turkey for Thanksgiving.

"That was real nice of you to give Dorinda your turkey, Chanel," Angie says, thinking the same thought as me, like always.

"Don't worry, *mamacita,*" Chanel says. "At least *someone's* gonna get to eat it—because *I* sure can't eat all of it by myself." Chanel is laughing at the thought of it, making a face like she just ate a whole turkey.

Angie and I are laughing with her, but then I get a look at Dorinda, and I realize she has been sitting like a frog on a log ever since she and Chanel plopped in.

"Are you tired or somethin'?" I ask her. "Did you run in that race, too?"

"I did," she says. "But I'm not tired. I'm just . . ." She heaves a big sigh and looks at Angie and me. "You two are so lucky you're going home for the holidays," she moans.

I guess we do still consider Houston our home, even though we live in the Big Apple. But sometimes it seems like something is missing—I guess it just doesn't feel right without the smell of Ma's Shalimar perfume wafting through the air.

Still, at least *I'm* going home to see *my* ma. Dorinda doesn't even *remember* her real mother. I can see she is depressed. This must be a hard time of year if you're a foster child like Do' Re Mi. She lives with ten other foster kids uptown in Harlem. She likes it there okay, but around the holiday season, I'll bet she misses having a real family—even a split-up one like ours.

"Here, Do' Re Mi, why don't you cut these up?" I say, passing her a knife and chopping board. I figure it's better to put her on onion patrol than have her sitting there looking glum.

Not that we need her help. Angie and I are cookin' this special dinner for our friends without *anybody's* help, thank you.

"I wish *I* was going somewhere for the holidays," Chanel pipes up. "You two get to have all the fun."

Our lives back in Houston may seem glamorous to Chanel, but what she doesn't realize is that Angie and I were sleeping in twin coffins before we became part of the Cheetah Girls—that's how *boring* our lives were. But, like Big Momma says, "the grass always looks greener on the other side."

"Bubbles should be here soon," Chanel says, trying to lick some cream off the spatula.

At least *Galleria* is happy about spending Thanksgiving in New York. That's mostly because her grandmother and favorite aunt—I think her name is Aunt Donie-something (it's hard for me to pronounce)—are flying in from Bologna, Italy.

Imagine that—having family in another country! Now to me, *that* is glamorous. Bubbles is late today because she had to go to the airport with her father, Mr. Garibaldi, to pick the relatives up.

"You gonna eat at Bubbles's house too, right?" I ask Chanel delicately.

"I guess so. *Mamí*'s going to Paris to see her boyfriend—"

"The sheik that makes you shriek?" Dorinda asks, scrunching up her cute little nose.

Chanel's parents are dee-vorced, just like ours, but Ms. Simmons has this strange new boyfriend who lives in Paris, Zurich, *and* Saudi Arabia.

"*Sí, mamacita*. The loony tycoon!" Chanel says, giggling at her own joke. Then she stops smiling and adds in a sad voice, "And Daddy is going to Transylvania with Princess Pamela, to see her family over there."

Princess Pamela is Chanel's father's girlfriend. She has a hair salon and a fortune-telling parlor, and she is quite mysterious—just Angie's and my cup of tea. Chanel is really crazy about her, too. But her father and Pamela didn't invite Chuchie to Romania with them.

They left her home with her *abuela*—her grandma. I know Chanel loves her *abuela*, but I also know she'd rather have gone along to Transylvania.

If you ask me, it's a good thing Galleria's family invited the two of them over. That Abuela Florita of Chanel's is getting too old to cook a big dinner all by herself. And forget about Chanel. I don't think she knows how to make anything except reservations.

"I don't know why y'all are so sad about staying in *New Yawk*," Anginette says to Chanel. "At least you'll have *fun* over at Ms. Dorothea's. Not like at home with your mother."

Chuchie doesn't respond, even though I can see Dorinda is trying to take her side. I know Chanel has problems at home, always fighting with her mom—but nobody told her to run up her mother's credit card behind her back! That isn't exactly the best way to win brownie points!

"At least we've all got some money to spend," I say, trying to cheer Chanel up. You'd think she'd be happy we won a hundred dollars each for coming in second at the Apollo

Theatre in the "Battle of the Divettes" Competition. That's right—we came in second in *that* one, too! It seems like when it comes to the Apollo, the Cheetah Girls always come out second best. Lord, keep me away from that place from now on!

Galleria, Chanel, and even Dorinda were upset that we only came in second. But not me. A hundred dollars is a hundred dollars, that's what I say. Shoot, Angie and I got over it real quick—as soon as those bills touched our palms! We were just so happy to win *anything*!

"What are you gonna do with your share?" Angie asks Chanel.

I frown at Angie. She should know better than to ask her such a nosy question. I'll bet Miss Shopaholic has already spent her share.

"I . . . I paid back my mother with the money," Chanel whispers sadly.

"Well, that's real good, Chanel," I say, genuinely surprised. I know how much she must be hurting to part with all that money. I feel terrible for thinking badly of her before, so I put my arm around her shoulder and give her a hug.

"Sí, mamacita," Chanel says, "but you're getting to go home, while we have to stay here

and freeze to death or die from boredom, whichever one happens first."

"I'm not going to lie, it'll be nice to go home," Angie sighs.

"And you get to go to the Karma's Children benefit concert, too!" Chanel laments. "I wish I could go. They're *tan coolio*!"

"Yeah, well, I don't think *we're* going—even if half of Houston is," I huff.

Karma's Children may be the biggest singing group in Houston, but I don't have to *like* them. Ever since Angie and I were little girls, singing in the church choir, it was always, "Someday they'll be as good as those Karma girls."

They are older than we are, from the same neighborhood, and definitely our nemesis—they're big time, and we aren't, 'cuz they've got a record deal—*and we don't*!

"That's all anybody is talking about back home—Karma's Children, Karma's Children—I'm so *sick* of those girls!" Angie says, trying to stick a finger in my eggnog to "test" it.

"You're just green with Gucci envy, both of you," Dorinda says, breaking into a sly little smile.

"I guess so." I have to admit it, 'cuz it's true—we *are* jealous. And we'll *stay* jealous, until Def Duck records finally calls us back and tells us the Cheetah Girls have got themselves a record deal!

The doorbell rings, and Angie goes to open the front door. Galleria is finally here with her father.

"Hi, *cara, cara*, and *cara*!" Mr. Garibaldi says, greeting us with hugs and kisses. He is such a sunny personality—he always makes us smile.

Meanwhile, Galleria waltzes into the kitchen and plunks her cheetah backpack down on the linoleum floor. She looks upset.

"*Aquanetta*—when are you going home?" Mr. Garibaldi asks, hovering in the doorway. He always puts an extra "a" at the end of my name, making it sound *soooo* beautiful.

"I'm gonna name my eggnog 'Aquanetta-does-it-betta Eggnog' in your honor, Mr. Garibaldi," I coo. Then I answer his question. "We're leaving tomorrow morning."

"*Chè pecato*. I wanted your mother to try my specialty—chocolate cannolis. I think if she takes one bite, she would fly to New York to live, no?" Mr. Garibaldi asks, grinning from ear to ear.

Then his eyes widen. "I know—tomorrow morning, I can take you to the airport and I bring the cannolis—specially made for you, no?"

I hesitate, only because I know our daddy will have a proper fit if we agree to let Mr. Garibaldi drive us to the airport.

Angie knows it too, because she pipes right up. "Our father is driving us, but that is so sweet of you, Mr. Garibaldi."

"Call me Franco, please, *cara Anginetta*. I come by in the morning anyway, and bring them for you." I open my mouth to say he doesn't have to, but Mr. Garibaldi shoos the words away.

"Won't you have some eggnog?" I say, trying to tempt him. "I've outdone myself again!"

"Okay, *va bene*. I've been charmed once again by the Cheetah Girls," Mr. Garibaldi says, sitting down.

Suddenly, Galleria blurts out what's on her mind. "You are not going to believe what happened. Nona was supposed to arrive on Flight #77, but the airlines from Italy are on strike."

Mr. Garibaldi comes to his daughter's aid real quick. "I tell you a funny story. When I was a young boy, I cut school one day so I could go to Lake Como just to see a girl I like." Mr. Garibaldi sips my eggnog. "Hmm, this is *perfecto,*" he says, and I blush with pride.

"So I go to see this boot-i-ful girl—her name, by the way is *Pianga*, which means 'to cry' in Italian—so I should have known. My mother thinks that I'm going to school, and I tell her we have soccer practice afterward, so I will be home late. No problem. Well, when I'm ready to leave Lake Como and sneak back home to Bologna, the train is on strike! *Scioporro!* I cannot believe it!" Mr. Garibaldi moves his left hand like he is shaking flour off chicken drumsticks before frying them.

"You got in trouble?" Dorinda asks.

"I cannot tell you how much trouble," Mr. Garibaldi says, shaking his head, "all because on that day the train workers decide to strike and ruin my life!"

"How did you get home?" Dorinda asks fascinated.

"I come back to Bologna the next morning—but believe me, when I saw my father's face, I wish the strike never ended!"

Galleria is unfazed by her father's story. You

can see the disappointment on her face, even though I know Mr. Garibaldi is trying to make her feel better.

"I know, *cara*, how much you wanted to see Nona and Zia Donatella," he says, giving her a hug.

"Who is Zia Donatella?" Dorinda asks, making sure to pronounce it right. She is always transfixed by family stories.

"She's my sister—Galleria's aunt," Mr. Garibaldi offers, his face beaming.

"I wanted you to meet her," Galleria says sadly. Then she looks at me and Angie and coos, "I'm gonna miss you two."

Now Dorinda slumps in *her* chair—glum as a plum.

"When are you going to perform again, Cheetah Girls?" Mr. Garibaldi asks, trying to make us all happy again.

"Your guess is as good as ours!" Dorinda quips.

"Don't you worry, the Cheetah Girls are gonna be bigger than the Spice Rack Girls—even bigger than the invention of oregano!"

We burst out laughing, then get quiet again.

"Sitting around waiting to hear from Def

Duck Records is making us a little daffy, if you know what I'm saying," Galleria moans.

"Well, *caras*, I'd better go," Mr. Garibaldi says, getting up. "I'll see you in the morning with those chocolate cannolis. And again—the eggnog was *primo—perfecto*!" He kisses Angie's and my hands, and we giggle. Then he tips his cap and leaves.

"When is *your* dad coming home?" Galleria asks us.

"Any minute now—and he's bringing the High Priestess with him," I sigh, not looking forward to her royal presence. "If you feel a strong breeze knock you off your feet, I guess that means her broomstick has landed!"

Chapter 2

A few minutes later, we hear Daddy putting his key in the door. We're glad he is finally home from work, and we give him a big hello. We know that Daddy is under a lot of pressure with his new job at the world's biggest bug spray company, S.W.A.T. They're after him to "beef up the bottom line," he says.

Walking to the kitchen to get Daddy a glass of eggnog, I chuckle to myself. Maybe some Benjamins will fall from the sky for Daddy, just like that new song Galleria and Chanel have written, called "It's Raining Benjamins."

"Daddy, wait till you taste my latest and greatest 'Aquanetta-does-it-betta Eggnog'!"

"Not for me," Daddy grumbles.

I can't believe Daddy turned down my eggnog! I know his High Priestess girlfriend must have definitely put a spell on him, 'cuz Daddy *loves* my eggnog.

Daddy plops down on his brown leather reclining chair in the living room. Chanel, Galleria, and Dorinda hightail it back to the kitchen.

Angie and I just stand there looking at each other. I know she's feeling the same thing I am—*guilty*—'cuz Daddy is spending all this money to send us back home for the Thanksgiving holidays. He even let us go to the beauty parlor yesterday to get our nails and hair done for our trip, and I know plane tickets are especially steep this time of year. All that money pressure must be the reason he's in such a bad mood. I feel like we've ruined his holidays!

Daddy shoves some tobacco into his pipe, lights it, puffs on it a second, then blurts out what's really bothering him. "I worked so hard on this damn account, and somebody over at Sticky Fingers got wind of my campaign before we put it out. How else can you explain their coming up with the *same* slogan I created for a flea spray—'*Flee, you hear me*?'"

"Yeah, it sure sounds to me like the devil is working overtime," Angie offers, nodding her head like she's listening to Reverend Butter give a sermon at church.

"Y'all cleaned my blender after you used it, right?" Daddy says, looking right at me and arching his eyebrow like he does. Dag on, he cares about that blender more than he does us! Just 'cuz High Priestess Abala gave it to him as a housewarming present.

Which reminds me, I'd better remind Angie that she'd better not breathe one word about the High Priestess on a broomstick to Ma, or our Thanksgiving vacation is gonna be *ruined*.

"I bet y'all have made a mess of that kitchen, too," Dad says absentmindedly. See, this is the first dinner we've actually been allowed to cook by ourselves. "I don't want y'all spending all night cleaning up—'cuz I know you haven't packed yet."

"No, Daddy, we haven't," I mutter. How could we pack, when it took us all afternoon just to fix dinner? We had to go to school, then come home and run to Piggly Wiggly

Supermarket and buy the food, then prepare it. How could Daddy ask us such a question—and with our friends in the other room? He can be so mean sometimes!

"Don't worry, we'll get everything done in time," I assure him.

"What did y'all make for dinner, anyway?" Daddy asks, his eyes brightening a little. I think he just needed to air all that bug-spray drama to people who care about him.

"Well, let's see," I begin, "we made some honey-glazed turkey legs, collard greens with ham hocks, macaroni and cheese—"

"Blackened catfish with swamp rice," Angie chimes in.

"And gravy!" I add.

"Well, that sounds real good, girls. Y'all go ahead and enjoy yourselves with your friends." Daddy looks down at his newspaper like we're dismissed.

I look at Angie like, "Can you believe him?" I thought for sure Daddy would at least sit down to dinner with us—seeing as how we cooked it ourselves.

Looking up and seeing us still standing there, Daddy softens. "Now, you know Abala is coming over, and we're going to drink her special shakes together. Go on—can't you see how much healthier I'm looking just from drinking her shakes?" Daddy moves his eyes down to his stomach to make his point.

Yes, he has lost some weight, I think, but what if he starts disappearing before our eyes?

Like Big Momma says, though—"One monkey don't stop the show." If she ever met the Cheetah Girls, she would really get a chuckle at how true that saying is. No sooner do we sit down at the dining room table than Dorinda dives into the food like a hungry cub who hasn't eaten in days—and so do the rest of us! Later for Daddy and Abala Shaballa! *We* are going to eat this dinner, and have ourselves a good time!

Sucking the bones out of the catfish, I warn my friends, "Y'all be careful and leave the bones alone." Suddenly, I'm stricken with holiday sadness. I wish Big Momma and Ma could meet the Cheetah Girls. Going home would be so much more fun with them there. Digging into the collard greens, I know better than to say anything. I mean, it wouldn't take much to turn this crowd into an even glummer bunch!

"Good evening, good evening, ladies!"

I turn my head to see the "Holy One" waltzing into the dining room, wearing yet another of her scary creations. I mean, the wrap on her head alone is so high, it looks like it could anchor a catfish boat!

And what is that—a whole row of *teeth* around her neck? Suddenly, I realize I'm staring. Catching my manners, I blurt out, "Hi, um, High Priestess. You look nice!"

"Why, thank you, blessed one, um . . ."

Angie breaks out in a smirk, and so do I. I guess we like seeing her squirm, because she still can't tell us apart. (Angie has a beauty mark on her left cheek and I don't—but we're not going to tell her that!)

"I'm Aquanette," I say, finally coming to Abala's rescue.

"Why, yes, of course," she says, as her whole kooky coven of friends files into the dining room area. They sort of stand around like they're uncomfortable, except for the bald-headed one carrying a wicker basket full of strange vegetables I've never seen before. I can't for the life of me remember her name . . .

"I hope you Cheetah Girls save some room

for our brew," says Abala Shaballa. "We've brought special ingredients just for you."

"Well, we're really kinda full . . ." Galleria says, looking around at all of us for backup.

"Yes, ma'am, I don't think we're gonna be able to drink any brew tonight," I say, speaking for the rest of us.

The High Priestess looks like Chicken Little when the ceiling fell on her—I mean, she really looks panicked! "I—I was really counting on you girls participating in our ritual tonight," she stutters.

"I know, but I'm sorry—this is our last night together before we have to go home to Houston," I explain, feeling kind of bad for her.

Daddy can drink all of the strange brews he wants, but we are not going to be a part of this hocus-pocus any longer!

"Could you excuse us for a minute?" Abala Shaballa says, regaining her queenlike composure. She scurries into the living room with her coven behind her, and we can hear them whispering among themselves.

"What are y'all whispering about?" we hear Daddy asking them. But we decide not to worry ourselves with Daddy and his strange new friends. After all, this is the Cheetah Girls' last night together in New York for a whole week—and we have plenty to growl about, believe me!

Chapter 3

True to his word, the next morning Mr. Garibaldi drops off a box of chocolate cannolis for us to take back home. Daddy puts the cannolis on the dining room table, and yells for us to clean our room before we go to the airport.

The way Daddy has been acting, I'm worried that Porgy and Bess, our cherished pet guinea pigs, are gonna be sliced up and put in some Priestess-Pocus magic brew, instead of being fed and loved the way they deserve. Angie and I just don't trust Abala Shaballa—especially not with our pets!

"I've got a great idea," I say, my eyes lighting up. "Why don't we just bring Porgy and Bess *with* us?"

Angie puts her hand over her mouth and starts to giggle.

"I know we could get in trouble, but I'm sorry—I cannot bear the thought of losing Porgy or Bess! Now, you've gotta distract Daddy," I tell Angie. In my mind, I'm already planning how we're gonna pull off Operation: Save Porgy and Bess.

"We should call Galleria," Angie says, chuckling, even though we've got to be downstairs in five minutes so Daddy can drive us to the airport. But Angie is right—if there is anybody who can pull off a mission impossible, it's Miss Galleria. That's what we like about her best—she's got growl power, as she calls it, and she's not a show-off. (Well, not exactly!)

"Come on, help me think of a plan, 'cuz we've gotta get this rodeo on the road," I whine.

Even though it's only nine o'clock and our flight to Houston is at noon, you have to check in at the airport two hours before departure—even for domestic flights! What that means is a whole lot of sitting around in the airport terminal for nothing.

"Why don't we hide the cage in Daddy's

bedroom, then yell for him to come help us with the luggage?" Angie says.

"Yeah—then you show Daddy your math homework or something, and ask his advice. While you keep him busy, I'll bring the cage down and stick it in the van! I'll get a towel from the bathroom, too."

"What's the towel for?"

"To cover the cage," I reply. Sometimes I have to spell things out for my sister.

I shove Porgy and Bess's cage into a corner of Daddy's bedroom. That's when I notice a few bottles on his nightstand. I know I'm not supposed to be in Daddy's room, but I walk over and pick up one of the bottles anyway.

I read the label. Fenugreek? *What on earth is this*? I feel a chill inside me. I open the lid of the jar and smell it: kinda like some of the herbs Big Momma uses for cooking. I run into our bedroom, and drag Angie back into Daddy's with me.

"I bet you he got these bottles from Abala Shaballa," Angie says.

"We *know* that—but what are they for?" I whisper.

Angie just shrugs her shoulders, and I can

tell she's getting as concerned about Daddy as I am. "He never even used to take an aspirin or anything—now he's running a spice shop in his bedroom!" I say, shaking my head.

Because Big Ben is ticking, Angie hightails it back to our bedroom and calls for Daddy to come help us with our suitcases. Once he's in there with Angie, I creep down the spiral staircase—which is really steep and narrow, so I have to be really careful carrying the cage.

After I put Porgy and Bess in the van and cover them, I run back inside to the refrigerator to pack a shopping bag of leftover food for our trip. I go back out to the van, place the big brown shopping bag in front of the cage, then check to see if it keeps the cage out of view. It seems Operation: Save Porgy and Bess is ready for Freddy!

When I go back inside, Daddy says to me, "Make sure to take along all that food you cooked."

"I already did," I say, happy I beat him to it. "I left you some, though."

"No need to," Daddy grunts. "You'd better take it all, because I'm not gonna eat it."

I feel the sting in my chest. "Daddy, are you

sure you're getting enough nutrients from those shakes in the blender?"

"Aquanette, I'm your Daddy, so I know what I'm doing, okay? I can't even believe I used to eat all that junk."

Junk? I know God made turkey legs and gravy for a reason!

"Abala gave me herbal supplements to take at bedtime—so don't you girls worry about me. I'm getting all the vitamins and minerals I need." Daddy smiles serenely at us.

"Okay, I'll just pack up the rest of the food," I say. Fine, if he wants it that way. The more bags in front of Porgy and Bess's cage, the better!

When we get into the van and drive off, I give Angie a meaningful look that says we were right to bring Porgy and Bess with us to Houston. Daddy didn't say one word about taking care of them, and didn't even notice they were missing!

To go to Houston from New York City, you have to fly out of LaGuardia Airport, as opposed to JFK, like we did when we went to Hollywood—the most fun experience of our lives, for sure. Suddenly, I think about the Cheetah Girls.

"A whole week without Galleria, Chanel, and Dorinda," I mumble to Angie, who is sitting next to me in the back of the van.

"I'm gonna miss them," Angie says, sad as she can be. "I feel bad for Dorinda and Chanel especially—'cuz they didn't seem like they wanted to spend Thanksgiving at home. I wish we could have invited them to come with us."

Daddy is lost in his own thoughts, but he hears the tail end of our conversation. "When are you girls gonna perform again?" he asks.

"We sure don't know," I groan. "It just seems like we can't get a break—sitting around waiting for some record company to tell us what to do. It just seems like *forever*."

"Well, on a happier note, we got here in record time," Dad says, smiling as we pull up to the Ready Rabbit Airlines entrance at the airport.

I am so furious. He's acting like he didn't even hear what I said! I heave a big sigh. That's just the way Daddy is, I tell myself.

I look at my watch. It's 9:30. It only took us twenty-five minutes to get here! Now we're gonna have to wait around for two and a half hours! "That was quick," I say, sure that Daddy won't notice the sarcastic tone in my voice either.

Before we get out of the Bronco, he turns to us and says, "Let me give you girls some extra money," then hands us each a twenty-dollar bill.

"Thank you, Daddy!" I exclaim, tears coming to my eyes. I suddenly feel terrible again, for thinking such bad things about a person when he doesn't deserve it. I've gotta stop doing that, and Angie too!

I realize now that we've been stupid and selfish, sneaking Porgy and Bess out of the house. Daddy is gonna be piping hot when he finds out, too.

"You sure twenty dollars is enough money?" he asks, concerned.

"We haven't spent one penny of our prize money yet," Angie says proudly. That reminds me that poor Chanel had to give her money to her mother to pay off her credit card debt. Now I feel bad for her *and* Daddy.

With him being so nice, suddenly I lose my resolve for Operation: Save Porgy and Bess.

"Daddy, we wanted to bring the guinea pigs with us to Houston. Is that okay?"

"What? Now why do you want to do that?" he asks, getting that mean tone in his voice.

"Because, um, we'd miss them." It seems I've suddenly lost my resolve to tell Daddy the truth. I know if anyone disses Abala Shaballa in front of him, he loses it completely.

"Well, they're home, right where they belong. They'll be fine," Daddy says sternly, like he has dismissed me.

Angie is as quiet as a church mouse. Dag on, she's never any help when I need her!

A Ready Rabbit porter comes over to help us with our luggage. "That's okay," Daddy says to him briskly. Daddy doesn't like anybody helping him with anything.

I feel my heart pounding. Now is as good a time as any to tell Daddy the truth. "Daddy—Porgy and Bess are in the back with our luggage."

When Daddy gets mad, he breathes more fire than Puff the Magic Dragon! Without saying a word, he takes our luggage out of the van, then grabs the two shopping bags of leftover food—almost spilling the collard greens on the ground.

"I'll get it!" Angie says, like a little scaredy-cat, running after the plastic container that is rolling away down the sidewalk.

"I'm raising two daughters without their mother's help—I can certainly take care of a pair of *guinea pigs*," Daddy says, emphasizing the words like he was talking about a bunch of rodents he had to kill with S.W.A.T. flea spray!

"I'm sorry, Daddy," I say, tears coming to my eyes. I look over and see that Angie is about to cry, too.

Daddy frowns, then sighs. "Ah, go ahead and take them with you," he says, putting the cage on the luggage cart and pushing it inside. "Let them be your headache, not mine."

Well, we're just fine with that. Fine, that is, until a Ready Rabbit Airlines representative comes up to Daddy and says, "That will be seventy-five dollars for the pets, sir."

"Oh, I won't be paying for it," Daddy says. "*They* will," he says, pointing to us.

The representative turns to Angie and me. "If you plan on bringing your pets on board, ladies, you'll have to pay an additional seventy-five dollars."

I almost start stuttering, I'm so upset. "I'll pay it," Angie says, whipping out her wallet.

I can feel Daddy's gaze on us, but I'm too

scared to look at him. I reach into my backpack and take out my bottle of air-sickness pills. I'm already feeling airsick, and we're not even off the ground yet.

I hand one to Angie, too, and she pops it into her mouth. Last month, when we flew to Hollywood with the Cheetah Girls, Angie and I were so excited we forgot to take our pills. We ended up throwing up *everything*. It was so embarrassing!

"Bye, Daddy," Angie says, after she's parted with most of *her* prize money and we've been checked in. Bye, Daddy, is right. And bye, prize money, too.

When we finally reach Porgy and Bess's storage space, which is almost at the tail of the plane, I set the cage down on its rack. "I hope you two enjoy the ride—'cuz it sure cost enough," I tell them.

"I bet *our* tickets cost a whole lot more than seventy-five dollars," Angie reminds me as we walk back to our seats in the middle of the plane. "Come on, let's forget about it. We still have some spending money left. Let's just pray that Galleria, Chanel, and Dorinda have a blessed Thanksgiving."

We sit down, buckle up, and Angie takes my hand. Like we do every time we fly, we hold hands now, and say a prayer until the plane takes off.

When we're finally airborne, and we can see the big, white fluffy clouds that look just like cotton balls, we let go of each other's hands and breathe a deep sigh of relief.

Hot sauce, Houston, and Karma's Children, here we come!

Chapter 4

I never thought I'd be so happy just to walk through a busy airport terminal—but that's exactly the exhilaration I feel when we hit George Bush Intercontinental after our six-hour journey, which included a layover in Chicago, where we caught our connecting flight to Houston.

"Hi, Ma!" Angie screeches, throwing her arms around our mother like she's been lost at sea, and Ma's a lifesaver.

Meanwhile, Ma is peeking over Angie's shoulder at Porgy and Bess in their cage.

"What on earth?" Ma mumbles, her eyes twinkling because she knows we are up to something.

"Um . . ." I hesitate when Angie looks at me.

We have to be *very* careful what we tell Ma. Angie and I have decided we are not going to tell her about Daddy's kookiness—drinking concoctions out of the blender and such—and definitely not one word about his new girlfriend Abala, not even if Ma spoon-feeds us turnips for forty straight hours to force a confession out of us!

"Um—we've never been away from Porgy and Bess for a whole week, and we don't want them getting lonely," I say.

"Your father let you bring them down here?" Ma asks, her eyes bright with disbelief.

"Well, we had to pay an extra seventy-five dollars and the flight attendant didn't even serve them lunch!" Angie moans.

"If we'd have known about that, Porgy and Bess would still be home, munching on their carrots!" I quickly add.

Laughing, Ma grabs the handle of the cage and puts it on the luggage cart. She looks smaller than I remember her. At first I think it must be because Angie and I have gotten taller. But then, looking down at her feet, I realize it's probably because she isn't wearing high heels.

I wonder why not. Ma always wears high

heels with her pantsuits, and she is wearing a pantsuit today—this one is powder blue with a pretty (fake) flower in the lapel of the jacket.

"You look nice," I tell Ma, giving her a hug, and savoring the sweet scent of her Shalimar cologne. I sure miss that smell.

"Thank you, 'Nettie One,'" Mom says, stroking some misplaced strands on my bob into place. (That's Mom's nickname for me. Angie's is "Nettie Two." I guess it's because I was born first—by five minutes.)

"I don't know where your uncle Skeeter is, but he was supposed to come to the airport with me to pick you girls up," Ma adds, a flicker of darkness passing through her warm, brown eyes.

I feel a twinge of disappointment, but I try to hide it. I love my uncle Skeeter, and I just assumed he would come with Ma to meet us. Uncle Skeeter is Ma's younger brother—and a whole lot of fun.

"How was your flight?" Ma asks, regaining her sweet composure.

"Everybody loved our corn bread!" I tell her, breaking out into a big grin.

"We made dinner all by ourselves, for our

friends the Cheetah Girls," Angie explains. "And we thought we'd bring you the leftovers. But you know how bad airline food is. Well, Angie and I ended up feeding half the passengers!"

"Angie is exaggerating, of course," I say. "We only fed about *fifty*." I chuckle as I hand Ma the last container of potato salad, which we saved just for her. "Tell us what you think—it's not as good as Big Momma's, but I think you'll like it. Our friends loved it."

"I'll bet they did," Ma says with a big smile. "Thank you, sweeties."

"Oh—here are some chocolate cannolis Mr. Garibaldi made for us," Angie says, handing Ma the box.

"Who is Mr. Gari-body?"

"He's Bubbles's father—you know, Galleria from the Cheetah Girls," Angie says, acting kinda "bubbly" herself.

"We wish you could meet our friends. You'll love the Cheetah Girls!" I add.

"Well, I love these outfits—you picked these out yourselves?" Ma asks, curious.

"No, remember we told you about Ms. Dorothea—that's Bubbles's mom, and she's now our manager, too. Well, she made them for us after we performed at the Apollo Theatre. They were supposed to be a victory gift, but you know—we lost. So she surprised us with them anyway."

"Well, they are beautiful," Ma says, but there is a tinge of something sad in her voice. Suddenly I feel guilty about being so close with Ms. Dorothea. 'Course, I know that's silly, because Ma wants the best for us, even if she can't be there to share in all the good and bad times.

We all get real quiet for a second, and that's when I notice Ma's nails. The polish on them is chipped—which is strange, because she always keeps her nails nice. I can tell Ma's still thinking—probably about Ms. Dorothea making us outfits and doing stuff for us. I can tell she feels sad about *something*.

We drive onto the Southwest Freeway to get to our house in Sugar Land, which is a suburb in southwest Houston. Mom has put on her dark Gucci sunglasses, and her permed hair is blowing like feathers fluttering in the wind.

"You just washed the car?" I ask her, admiring the spanking-clean upholstery.

"Yes, indeed," she says, taking a deep sigh. "You girls got any concerts coming up?"

Dag on, why does everybody ask us that? You'd think we were Karma's Children or something—touring around the world, and only coming back home to Houston for some corn bread and bedtime stories when we got exhausted from all that fame and fortune!

"No, we don't," I respond.

"Well, when are you gonna start recording for the record company—what's it called again, Daffy Duck?"

"No. It's called Def Duck Records, Ma—but they might as well be 'Daffy,' 'cuz we sure haven't heard anything yet," I huff. "Ms. Dorothea says we just have to sit tight."

Ma gets real quiet again. Why is it every time I mention Ms. Dorothea's name, she seems to get upset?

There *is* something different about Ma. Maybe it's just because we haven't seen her since June. That's when we moved to New York, after a whole lot of hushed phone conversations and long-distance screaming. Personally, I think CIA negotiations for hostages went smoother than our parents' dee-vorce. Oh, well—at least now that it's over, Daddy and Ma are polite and civil to each other on the phone.

"Big Momma is expecting us at her house, but I told her y'all probably wanted to hang out at home for a little while first," Ma says.

"I know Big Momma can't wait to see us, but we do need a bubble bath!" Angie chuckles.

"You know how Big Momma is. She wants to see her 'babies.' Egyptian and India are waiting for y'all too."

Egyptian and India are our cousins—Uncle Skeeter's children from his first marriage. They spend a lot of time over at Big Momma's now that their father is living there. Uncle Skeeter is a grown man, but Ma says he seems to have fallen on hard times. That's why he moved back into Big Momma's house.

"Wait till y'all see the outfit Skeeter put together for the Karma's Children benefit," Ma says, chuckling. She doesn't realize that she has just opened up an old wound for me and Angie. "He went to Born-Again Threads and bought himself some metallic purple bell-bottoms, and an even more ridiculous fedora—oh, and a red fake-fur jacket—"

"Ma!" Angie says, chiding her.

"Don't 'Ma' me—just wait till you see Mr. Disco! I told him just because it's a benefit for the homeless, doesn't mean he has to *look* homeless!"

Angie puts her hand over her mouth and giggles. She can pretend she isn't jealous of Karma's Children all she wants. I *know* she is *just* as jealous as I am.

"I don't know if we're gonna go to the benefit," I blurt out.

"Why not?" Ma asks, looking at me in the rearview mirror. "I told you, I'll pay for the tickets."

The tickets for the Karma's Children benefit concert are fifty dollars each. All the money is going to the Montgomery Homeless Shelter, which is in the worst part of Houston.

Ma is still waiting for an answer, but then she figures it out all by herself. "Don't tell me y'all are jealous of those girls, just 'cuz they're famous now. You used to *love* them. I 'member that time when nobody knew who they were, and y'all wanted to go see them at the Crabcake Lounge. You cried for two days 'cuz I wouldn't let you go!"

"We were nine years old—that was a long time ago!" I grumble. "They aren't any more talented than we are. Why should we go see *them* perform?"

"You should be happy they're doing well—that means *you* have a chance, too," Ma says, in that tone of voice she uses when she's giving us a lecture.

We all get quiet, for what seems like hours. Then Angie asks Ma, "Do you think Big Momma will mind if we bring Porgy and Bess over to her house, so they can run around in her garden?"

"I don't know—you'd better call and ask her first," Ma says hesitantly.

"Ooo, wait till they get a hold of her strawberries!" Angie says, snickering.

"Big Momma will have you in that garden on your hands and knees replanting fruits and vegetables till you're ninety, if you don't watch out," Ma warns us.

She pulls her Katmobile into our four-car garage, and it finally hits me: *We iz home!*

Once we've hauled all our things inside, I ask, "Ma, is it okay if we call Galleria and tell her we made it here?"

"Who's Galleria again?" Ma asks absentmindedly, clearing some plates off the dining room table.

I can't believe my eyes. This place is a *mess*. If we had left the house like this, she would have grounded Angie and me for the rest of our lives!

"*Galleria Garibaldi*. She's the leader of the Cheetah Girls—our singing group," I say in a sarcastic tone, since Ma obviously doesn't remember things that are important to *us*.

"Oh, I don't think you ever told me her name," Ma says.

"Her mother, Ms. Dorothea, named her after the Galleria mall here in Houston—ain't that funny?" Angie says, trying to be helpful like always, even though Ma isn't really listening. "See, Ms. Dorothea was here in Houston working—I think she was modeling for some catalog—and she was pregnant. She went shopping at the Galleria and bought her first pair of Gucci shoes, so that's why she named her daughter Galleria."

"Lucky for her she could afford Gucci shoes," Ma says firmly. "When your father and I were raising you, by the time we finished paying for everything, I was lucky to be able to get a pair of Payless pumps."

Finally, Angie gets the message. Meanwhile,

I have dialed Galleria's bedroom phone, and luckily she's there. "We're home!" I say, trying to sound chirpy.

"That's good," Galleria says, sniffling.

"What's wrong, Bubbles?" Now Angie is hovering by me, trying to hear the phone conversation.

"Nona is not coming after all! She went to Turin for a mud bath, and she slipped and broke her hip. Daddy is flying over there to be with her, but Ma's working, so we're *stuck* here!"

"Oh no, I can't believe it!" I say, trying to console her. "Angie and I are gonna say a prayer for you."

"We're gonna say one for you, too," Galleria says.

Ma throws me a look. "You two better start getting ready."

"Yes, ma'am," I say without thinking. I can feel tears welling up in my eyes. That's the first time Galleria has ever said anything about praying. She always used to make fun of Angie and me with our church stuff.

You know what? God really *does* work in mysterious ways. . . .

Chapter 5

If there is one thing we miss about Houston, it's taking a bite out of Big Momma's peach cobbler! Well, finally our long wait is over. Stepping out of Ma's car as we pull up in front of Big Momma's house, I notice that some of the kids hanging out down the block stop to stare at us. This one boy, with red kinky hair and freckles, starts walking toward us, waving.

"Who is that?" Angie asks.

"I don't know," I respond, watching him and thinking how much faster he could walk if he tied his sneaker laces.

"What, y'all moved up to the Big Apple and forgot about us?" the redheaded boy screeches as he approaches.

"It's Beethead!" Angie whispers.

It sure is—even though his hair is not as bushy. Major "Beethead" Knowles is the reason why I have seven stitches in my left knee and don't like wearing skirts. When I was about four years old, I was swinging real high, showing off, of course. Beethead kept throwing rocks at me, to see if he could reach my head. He did, causing me to fall off the swing and bust my knee on a jagged rock edge. Big Momma told Beethead never to come anywhere near us again. And he hasn't—until now.

"Hey, Beethead," I exclaim, and he breaks out in a grin.

"Check y'all out," he says, examining our cheetah outfits. "Y'all sure look *different*."

The other kids are still staring at us, too—like we're in a zoo or something. I guess we're gonna cause quite a stir in Houston with our new "cheetah-ness."

"I'll see y'all inside," Ma yells as she walks up to the front of Big Momma's house. Beethead waves at Ma, and she waves back, smiling.

"Y'all got tickets yet to the Karma's Children's concert?"

"No, we haven't," I reply.

"Well, you better get 'em soon, 'cuz they're almost sold out," Beethead says, trying to be helpful.

"Well—we'll see," I respond, without further explanation.

Beethead props himself against the big oak tree outside Big Momma's house. I never noticed that he had such long eyelashes before—almost like a girl's.

"What's that?" Beethead says, pointing at Porgy and Bess's cage.

"That's our guinea pigs," I reply.

Beethead heckles so loud, I almost expect him to expose hyena fangs any minute. Ugh. Now I don't think he's cute *at all*.

We say good-bye to the heckling Beethead, and go up the front steps. Angie chuckles, and says, "He sure got skinnier."

"He sure did," I say, then coo at Porgy and Bess. "That's okay if Beethead doesn't like y'all. I'll bet Big Momma's gonna *love* you."

Big Momma never did have the pleasure of meeting Porgy and Bess when we lived at home, because she never came upstairs to our bedroom. These last few years, she has slowed down quite a bit, and she uses a cane to get around.

"Look at y'all!" Big Momma says, standing still in the doorway so she can get a look at us. She peers closely at my cheek—I guess to see if there's a beauty mark.

"It's Aquanette, Big Momma," I say, helping her out.

"I know how to tell my grandchildren apart, Nettie One," she says, shooing me with her hand. "My, my, my—those are quite some get-ups y'all got on!"

"This is what we wear when we're the Cheetah Girls!" Angie exclaims, and we pose so Big Momma can admire us.

"Don't just stand there, take off your coats—the pawnshop's closed!" Big Momma says, chuckling at her own joke.

I set Porgy and Bess's cage down, and hug Big Momma real tight. Then she hugs Angie. Our cousins Egyptian and India come running into the foyer. Egyptian is ten and India is almost eight, but she is the same height as her older sister.

"We're so glad y'all finally got here—now we can eat!" India says sassily. She has big bug eyes, just like Uncle Skeeter, but her demeanor is more like her mother's—Aunt Neffie—high and mighty.

Personally, I don't think Aunt Neffie's name is really Nefertiti like she claims, even though Ma says that now she sure is a queen, "sitting alone on a throne." (She means because Aunt Neffie and Uncle Skeeter got separated.)

"Is Uncle John coming?" Egyptian asks me, even though she knows Daddy moved to New York because he and Ma got dee-vorced.

"No. Is Aunt Neffie here?" I ask, playing the same game. Aunt Neffie doesn't come to Big Momma's now that Uncle Skeeter is living back home.

"Oooo!" India says, eyeing Porgy and Bess in the cage.

Now Big Momma sees them too, and grunts, "Guess there ain't much bacon under those hides. Not worth cookin'."

"Big Momma!" I squeal, then grab her waist. She's just joking, though. Big Momma wouldn't hurt a fly.

"Can we take them out to the garden?" India asks, picking up Porgy and Bess's cage.

"That's where they belong," Big Momma says, smiling.

"Why didn't Skeeter meet me to go to the airport?" Ma asks Big Momma as she helps her put the "good" silverware on the table. (Big Momma always puts out the good stuff when company comes.)

"I don't know," Big Momma says, distracted. "I think it's time to get the corn bread out of the oven."

She hobbles over to it, and Ma runs to help her. "Sit down now—I'll take care of everything."

Egyptian cuts me a look and tries to mouth something to me, but I can't understand what she's saying. I put my finger up to my mouth and tell her to "shhh" and tell me later.

"Big Momma, how was the Quilt Festival this year?" I ask quickly, so she doesn't know we were whispering. Even though she's slowed down some, Big Momma wouldn't miss the Quilt Festival for anything.

"Junie—how many quilts did they have there this year?" Big Momma turns and asks Ma.

"I think more than nine hundred," Ma calls out.

"They sure were beautiful," Big Momma says.

Egyptian starts mouthing at me again. I shake my head at her and tell her to stop. She probably is trying to give me a blow-by-blow account of one of Aunt Neffie and Uncle Skeeter's battles.

Angie and I feel bad for Egyptian and India because they're younger than we are, and it's hard for them to understand that sometimes grown-ups are better off separating than staying together and being miserable.

"Are y'all gonna go down to Kemah's Boardwalk to audition?" Egyptian asks nonchalantly, dabbing pink lip gloss on her lips from a Glitter Gurlie tube, like she's grown.

"What audition are you talking about?" I respond, not looking up because I'm trying to get a napkin into the holder just right, so the fan shape is perfect.

"You know—they're looking for unknown groups for the Karma's Children benefit concert. Didn't Aunt Junie tell you?" Egyptian licks her lips again, then jumps up to get Ma's attention. "Aunt Junie, didn't you tell Nettie One and Two about the poster up in the Galleria?"

"What poster are you talking about?" Ma shoots back.

"Aunt Junie—you'd have to be blind to miss it. It's got their picture on it and everything," Egyptian says, exasperated.

"Whose picture?" Angie asks.

"Karma's Children!" Egyptian says, like we're all stupid.

"They've even got on outfits like y'all's," India says, grinning straight at me, even though her left eye isn't. India has a wandering eye, which is probably why she is nicer than her sister. Kids have been making fun of her eyes ever since she could talk, and I think getting made fun of makes a person more sensitive.

"No, they don't," Egyptian says, cutting off her sister. "They're polka dots, stupid!"

"Well, they look the same," India says, shrugging. She pours some of the beads and crystals out of the pinto beans can she uses to store all her arts and crafts stuff.

"Don't do that now! Big Momma will get mad!" Egyptian hisses, picking up the beads, some of which have rolled onto the floor. "Now look what you've done!"

Ma comes out of the kitchen with a serving

pan of corn bread, and puts it on the table. "What poster are you talking about, 'Gyptian?" she asks.

"They are looking for unknown groups to open for Karma's Children for the benefit concert at Kemah's," Egyptian says, like she is *so-o* tired of repeating herself.

"'Gyptian, how am I going to tell them about a poster I never saw?" Ma shoots back.

"*Everybody* is talking about it," Egyptian counters. "It's right outside the Glitter Gurlie store in the Galleria. Even people who can't sing are gonna audition for it!"

"'Gyptian, I haven't been to the Glitter Gurlie store, now have I? But it's obvious *you* have," Ma says disapprovingly, first looking at the tube of lip gloss in Egyptian's hands, then at the glittery gunk she has smeared on her lips.

Egyptian puts her head down meekly, toying with the lip gloss tube in her hand.

"Now, you know you'd better go wash that stuff off before Big Momma sees it," Ma says sternly.

"India, exactly what does the poster say?" I ask my younger cousin, since she's more levelheaded than her sister.

"They're having auditions tomorrow for unknown groups who want to sing at the Karma's Children concert," India says.

"That's what it said, huh?" I respond. The wheels in my head are turning faster than on a Bronco.

"'Help Us Sing for Their Supper,'" Egyptian adds nonchalantly. "That's what it says at the top of the poster."

"I wonder if they're paying," I mutter out loud.

"Who cares?" Ma shoots back. "It sounds like it could be the opportunity of a lifetime!"

"Well, we've sure heard *that* one before," I chuckle, and look at Angie.

"We'd better get down to the mall tomorrow morning and look at the sign," Angie says, ignoring me.

"You don't have to," India says.

"Why not?" I ask.

"'Cuz I wrote down the number for myself!" she answers proudly. Then she sees Egyptian glaring at her, so she stutters, "'Gyptian and I just want to meet Karma's Children and get an autograph."

"I didn't see you write down any number," Egyptian hisses.

"I did it when you went inside the store!" India says adamantly, pulling out a paper from her purse. "Here it is!"

I take the paper from India and run to the phone. "Let me hear!" Angie insists, as I dial the number and wait.

"It's just ringing!" I hiss back. A recorded message comes on, and I tilt the phone receiver so Angie can hear it too:

"We care about Houston. Do you? If you want to help out Houston's homeless, then make a date with stardom. Unknown groups can audition for the Karma's Children benefit concert on November 23rd, at The Crabcake Lounge, Kemah's Boardwalk in Galveston Bay. If you're a singing group in the Houston area, this may be your chance to shine. Auditions will be held on November 21st from 10 A.M. to 4 P.M. Come help Houston's hottest stars sing for their supper. Call 800-000-GET-HOME to order your tickets now!"

Angie and I look at each other. "We have to swallow our pride and go to that audition," I confess excitedly.

Ma just looks at me, and smiles. "I'm glad to see you've come to your senses, Nettie One."

"Yes, ma'am, I am too!" I tell her. Then I turn to India and give her a big hug. "I guess if it wasn't for your divette detective skills, we wouldn't be going to any audition!" I tell her.

"You know, they only want groups from here," Angie points out.

"Yes—and?" I ask.

"What about the *rest* of the Cheetah Girls?"

"Oh," I say, finally realizing what she means. I was so busy thinking about Angie and me performing that I forgot about them. "That's right—they're from New York City. So what are we gonna do?"

Big Momma has brought out the rest of the food, and overhears the end of our deep discussion. "What's wrong?" she asks.

We explain the predicament to her while shoveling food into our mouths.

"I think y'all should go—one monkey don't stop no show," Big Momma says, giving us her familiar line of advice.

"All right," I respond, looking at Angie, who nods her head like she agrees.

"Momma, where is Skeeter?" Ma asks Big

Momma again. She's been quiet all this time, and I guess she's been worrying about her brother.

I chuckle to myself. He's probably down at Slick Willie's in Bayou Place, playing pool as usual. That's one of the reasons he and Aunt Neffie used to fight—'cuz he wasn't home half the time.

"Never mind about Skeeter, Junifred." Big Momma only calls Ma by her real name when she is irritated. I wonder why that should be. . . .

I dig into my macaroni and cheese, and a thought hits me like a can of lard upside my head: *How can we go on an audition without the Cheetah Girls?*

I look over at Angie. Like always, she knows just what I'm thinking. Big Momma is right. One monkey don't stop no show. We'll just go on the audition and see what happens. Judging by what Egyptian said, probably everybody and their mother will be there. We'll be lucky if we even *get* to audition.

We go out in the garden to play. Outside, Egyptian rushes up to me and blurts out what's been on her mind the whole time. "Daddy hasn't been home for three whole days!" she says.

"Is that right?" I gasp, alarmed.

India runs outside when she hears us out there. "We don't know where he is. He hasn't called or anything. Big Momma is worried sick—and so are we!" India looks exasperated, which seems to make her wandering eye wander even farther.

I check through the window. Ma and Big Momma are still chattering away in the living room.

"You don't know where Uncle Skeeter is?" Angie asks.

Egyptian firmly shakes her head "no."

India's eyes light up, and she says, "He has a girlfriend downtown. I heard him talking on the phone with her."

"How do you know he was talking to his girlfriend?" Egyptian asks, like she doesn't believe her sister.

"'Cuz he was giggling a lot," India says, like she knows what she's talking about.

Angie and I just smile at her. I think my cousin India really does have the makings of a "divette detective," but now is not the time to make a big fuss over her. We have more important matters at hand.

I don't like this situation one bit—especially since Big Momma is trying to cover it up. "Do you have the girlfriend's phone number?" I ask India.

"No," she says, disappointed.

"What was her name?"

"I don't know, but Daddy said into the phone, 'Girl, you are just like your name—softer than a mink coat.'" Sadness flickers in India's eyes.

"We'll find out what's going on," I assure my cousins, trying to sound hopeful. They seem so scared about their daddy having disappeared for three days, and I don't blame them one bit. I'm anxious about it myself.

"Can Porgy and Bess stay here with us one more day?" India asks, not missing a beat.

"Of course they can," I say, pleased that I'm able to give my cousins something that'll make them happy.

At the end of the evening, walking back to Ma's car, Angie mutters, "We'd better call Galleria as soon as we get home."

"Yeah—I don't feel right about this whole thing."

"You mean about Uncle Skeeter?" Angie

asks, as we lean against Ma's Katmobile, waiting for her to come outside.

"No—about going on some audition without them."

"Yeah," Angie agrees.

When Ma gets in the car, I blurt out what our cousins told us about Uncle Skeeter. "Ma, he hasn't been home for three days."

Ma lets out a sigh. "Big Momma was never good at lying—I'll tell you that," she says.

Chapter 6

When we get home, I ask Ma if we can call Galleria on the phone. I *know* it would be too much to ask if we could log on to her computer, but we're dying to talk to all of the Cheetah Girls. If there was ever a time when we needed a council meeting, it's *right now*.

"Whazzup, Houston?" Galleria cackles into the phone.

It's kinda weird telling Bubbles about our predicament—an audition that popped up outta nowhere.

"Well, the three of us can't afford to come down to Houston and tiptoe through the tulips with the two of you, Miz Aquanette," Galleria says, trying to sound like it doesn't bother her.

But I *know* Bubbles—she's usually down for anything, and always up to something, as Big Momma would say. She says good-bye with a chirp in her voice, but I can hear the sadness underneath.

"We could just end up singing in a soup kitchen, for all we know," Angie says, spritzing the dining room table with Splendid cleaning spray.

"Angie, don't use that!" I hiss to my absent-minded sister. She's always pulling stuff like that when she's too lazy to do something the right way. "Go get the lemon oil and a nice soft rag."

It's nine o'clock in the morning, but Ma is still upstairs sleeping, which is very unusual in itself. On top of her not wearing her high heels with her pantsuit, and her chipped nails, things are beginning to add up, and I don't like the answer I'm getting—something is wrong with our ma.

We're creeping around downstairs trying to clean, because I can't believe how messy the house is. It's just not like her—*especially* leaving cigarette butts in the ashtrays.

"Those are Uncle Skeeter's," Angie says, picking up one of the butts and seeing the "Lucky Ducky" brand on the filter. Yes, that's Uncle Skeeter's brand, all right.

Suddenly, I feel a pang in my chest. I can just see him smoking, cackling and coughing at the same time. I wonder where he could be?

"Do you think Galleria was upset?" Angie asks, spreading a few drops of lemon oil on a corner of the table and wiping it carefully with the rag like she should.

"I think Bubbles is more upset about her grandmother than anything else," I tell Angie.

"We'd better wake Ma up," Angie says with a sigh. Ma is driving us to the audition, and we'd rather go earlier than later, just to get it over with. Like I said before, who knows what we're walking into?

Just then, right on cue, Ma walks past us and plops down at the kitchen counter.

"Good morning, Sleeping Beauty," Angie says.

"I knew something was fishy when Skeeter came over the other day," Ma says. Heaving a deep sigh, she covers her face with her hands.

"When did he come over?" I ask concerned.

"Monday—no, it was last Sunday, that's right. His eyes were glassy. I could tell he'd been drinking."

Ma screws up her face like Uncle Skeeter and imitates him. "'That uptight husband of yours, John Walker, may be my brother-in-law—but Johnnie Walker Red is my *cuzzin.*'"

Johnnie Walker Red is the brand of Scotch Uncle Skeeter likes. Even Daddy keeps it in the bar at our house in New York, but he has never made one joke about having the same name as a brand of liquor. That's Daddy for you.

I walk over and give Ma a hug. I'm so glad she has stopped pretending we are too young to understand these things. We've known since we were real little that Uncle Skeeter drinks, smokes, and doesn't go to church, and that it bothers everybody in my family. We also know that Uncle Skeeter and Daddy never got along.

"What did Skeeter say when he came over?" Angie asks.

"He said he was tired of trying to make everybody happy, and just wanted to go somewhere he could 'rest in peace,'" Ma says sadly. Then she chuckles, because Uncle Skeeter was probably making a joke off Granddaddy Walker's funeral parlor, Rest in Peace.

"But India says he has a new girlfriend?" Angie asks gingerly.

Ma doesn't seem at all bothered that we know. "Yeah. I don't remember her name—something Wilkerson. Skeeter said, 'That Wilkerson woman sure knows how to treat a man.' That's all I remember."

Hmmm. "India says she heard him on the phone with his girlfriend, saying something like, 'you sure are just like your name—softer than a mink coat!'"

Ma rubs her eyes and dismisses me. "What would India know? She's just a child." No sooner than the words are out of her mouth, Ma realizes what she's said, and who she's talking to. We chuckle along with her.

"Ma, what's wrong?" I ask, hoping that now that we've been so honest with each other, she won't try to cover up other things. "I mean, *besides* Uncle Skeeter being missing?"

All of a sudden, I see the tears well up in Ma's eyes, and she lets them roll down her cheeks without even wiping them. Angie and I sit real still at the table, waiting for Ma to talk.

"I don't know which is worse, living with your father and being miserable, or living without him and being so damn *lonely*," Ma says, her voice cracking. "All I do now is get up, go to work, pay bills, then get up and do it all over again. Not that I have anything to get up for now, with y'all gone."

Now I know what's bothering Ma. She *misses* us—all this time pretending she didn't mind if we lived with Daddy! Angie starts whimpering, and now I feel the tears well up in my eyes, too.

"We don't want to go on the audition," Angie says. "Let's just stay here together. I mean, what if it isn't for real?"

"Egyptian and India told you about it, right?" Ma stops her.

"Yeah," Angie replies, wiping tears from her cheeks.

"Well, then I suggest the two of you go, because those kids seem to be the only ones around here who *do* know what's going on." Ma laughs, then looks down at her raggedy nails. "Lord knows I need to do something with these claws."

Angie and I chuckle, but I know we both feel

guilty inside. *Our* hair and nails look nice, 'cuz Daddy pays for us to go to the beauty parlor twice a month in New York. But I don't think we deserve that, if Ma is miserable.

I look over at Ma, and she suddenly breaks out in a smile. It's the first time her smile has seemed genuine since we've been here. "I love y'all, you know that?" she says. "It's so good to have you back here—even if it's only for one week."

Galveston Bay is about thirty minutes by car from where we live. Ma puts the top down on her Katmobile, and Angie and I start singing "It's Raining Benjamins."

"For the first time in her-*story*
there's a weather forecast
that looks like the mighty cash.
So tie up your shoes and
put away your blues
'cuz we're going around the bend
at half past ten
to the only place in town
where everything is coming up green
you know what I mean:

It's raining Benjamins
for a change and some coins
It's raining Benjamins
I heard that
It's raining . . . again!!!!"

Ma is bopping along with us. "Y'all sound g-o-o-d!" she shouts over the noise of the wind.

"That's what we're gonna sing for our audition," I say triumphantly.

"We are?" Angie seems surprised, even though that's the song we were rehearsing just before we left. "I guess I'm just used to us singing 'Wanna-be Stars in the Jiggy Jungle.'"

I can tell Angie is a little nervous, but that's too bad—*I've* made up *our* mind.

"We're only going to be doing two-part harmonies instead of five—it's a better song for that, Angie," I say, just wishing she would go along, just this once, without questioning things.

"Okay," she says, shrugging her shoulders. "It doesn't matter, anyway. We'll be lucky if we even get *into* this dag-on audition."

"If nothing else, we got out of the house!" Ma says chirpily. I can definitely see she is feeling much better. "Y'all sing so different than you used to in church."

"We're not in church, Ma!" I exclaim. "We can't sing the same way."

"I know, I know. Don't worry, I like it," Ma says nicely, then asks, "Who thought up that song?"

"Well—it's a long story," I say, looking over at Angie. "See, Chanel's mom—"

"Who's Chanel?" Ma asks, smiling, like she knows I'm gonna brain her if she doesn't get all these names right.

"Chanel and Galleria are best—well, I mean, oldest—friends, because their mothers were friends—"

"And big models," Angie blurts out.

"Okay, so Chanel's mom, Mrs. Simmons, she's got this boyfriend we call Mr. Tycoon—he's a sheik or something—"

"*Real* rich!" Angie chuckles, but I poke her. She knows Ma is feeling lonely, so why does she have to rub it in?

"Anyway, Mrs. Simmons is writing this book, called *It's Raining Sheiks*, about women who have sheiks for boyfriends or something."

"But not all of them are happy," Angie adds,

like she knows what she's talking about.

"Stop interrupting me," I hiss.

"Okay, I'm sorry, I'm just trying—"

"I know." I cut her off. "So, Chanel—that's our friend from the Cheetah Girls—"

"I *know* who Chanel is now," Ma says, switching on her blinker because she is about to change lanes on the freeway.

"So Chanel had this dream about money falling from the sky, and she told Galleria. But see, Chanel doesn't like it that *Galleria* writes all our songs, so she goes ahead and writes two lines for the new song—"

"Uh-uh," Angie says, holding up her hand. "She only wrote *one* line."

"Yes, you're right—bless her heart—she wrote one little line in her notebook, Galleria said. Galleria went over to Chanel's house, and *she* wrote the rest of the song—but it's cute, right?"

"Yeah, it's cute," Ma says as we approach the exit for Kemah Boardwalk, which is right on the water.

I hum some more of the song. I wish Ma could meet the Cheetah Girls, and Ms. Dorothea, and even Mr. Garibaldi. They sure know how to have fun. Ma would love them.

I know I've been running my mouth, but I've got to tell Ma the story of how Mr. and Mrs. Garibaldi met each other. I remember when we first heard the story, Angie and I thought we had just met the kookiest people in New York. Who knew they would turn out to be the happiest people we've met there so far?

"Ma—you know how Galleria's mom and dad met?" I ask.

Now Angie throws me a look like, "Why you wanna bring that up when you know Ma and Daddy are dee-vorced!" I decide maybe I'd better not tell Ma, but she eggs me on.

"Why'd you stop talking? Tell me the story," she says, amused.

"Well, they met through the *New York* magazine personals ads."

"Really?" Ma says, and now she seems real interested.

"Yes. Mr. Garibaldi's ad said, 'Lonely oyster on the half-shell seeks rare black pearl to feel complete,'" I say, laughing out loud, and even Angie joins in. I don't care how many times I hear that, it just tickles me silly. "I *saw* the ad, Ma—they have it in the family photo album!"

Ma bursts out laughing. "That is funny. Is he Eye-talian?"

"Yes, he is—and he cooks, too! Weren't those chocolate cannolis dee-licious?" I ask.

"Yes, indeed," Ma says wistfully. "Maybe that's what I need to be doing."

"Making cannolis?" Angie asks, puzzled.

"No. Answering personal ads like Ms. Garibodi," Ma chuckles.

"Ma—her name is Ms. Gari-baldi—and you'd better not be doing anything foolish like that!" Angie exclaims.

"I don't know how foolish it is—y'all seem to like those people, so they must be nice—'cuz I know we raised you right. But do you know what the chances are of a black woman over forty finding another man?"

"What?" Angie and I ask in unison.

"Less than the chances of getting hit by a plane falling from the sky," Ma says.

We both laugh, relieved, because Ma is obviously joking.

"You laugh? One in forty thousand—that's what it said in *Sistarella* magazine," Ma says, getting out of the car and shutting the door. "Y'all want me to go inside with you?"

That's just like Ma, changing the subject when she's talking about something serious. I'm not gonna let her off the hook that easy. "Those statistics don't say anything about a beautiful woman like you, Ma," I say, giving her a hug.

"Well, I guess your Daddy didn't think I was so beautiful."

We are stunned, so we don't say anything. We are definitely not telling Ma about Daddy's new girlfriend!

"Don't think I don't know your Daddy is up to something, either," Ma says, shoving the keys into her purse and zipping it up. "He's been awfully nice these past few months."

"Well . . ." Angie begins.

"Nettie Two, don't open your mouth before you know what's coming out of it. You never were good at lying—so don't think you've suddenly improved overnight."

I was gonna get Angie back good myself, but Ma beat me to it.

"That's all right—if I was your daddy, I'd be careful of any woman fool enough to put up with him. That's all I've got to say," Ma huffs, then looks at the thousands of people descending on the Boardwalk like locusts. "Boy, they sure have a lot of tourists here for the holidays, don't they?"

"I guess so," I mutter.

As we walk closer, we see that all the people are concentrated in one area, making it impossible for us to get by. That's when we hear the man with the bullhorn, saying, "Everyone is going to get to audition. The line will go a whole lot quicker if you stay to the left of the railing."

Ma looks at us and says, "Well, I guess we should have brought our lunches—'cuz it looks like we're gonna be here all day!"

Chapter 7

We can't believe how people are pushing and shoving out here on Kemah Boardwalk. It's just like in New York!

"All this commotion for a gig that's not paying one red cent," grumbles an older man with several missing front teeth. He is standing on the out-of-control line directly in front of us, with his somewhat younger crony, who is a good-looking man wearing a red baseball cap and dark sunglasses.

"Don't get me wrong, though," the toothless man says. "It's not often old-timers like us get the opportunity to show our chops. Everybody wants to see you young folks." He grins shamelessly, then accidentally jabs Angie with his beat-up instrument case.

Ma winces and takes control of the situation. "Sir, maybe you should move that case off your shoulder," she says nicely.

"Oh, I'm sorry," Mr. Toothless says, apologizing sincerely, but turning and hitting Angie *again* with the case.

"Ouch," Angie says, making a comical grimace.

We look at his baseball-capped friend with pleading eyes, hoping he'll help his manner-impaired crony.

"Fred," the man says, "take Bertha off your arm and hold her in front of you, before you poke that poor girl's eye out!"

Bertha. Lord, don't tell me they are carrying body parts in that case! As if reading my mind, the man with the dark glasses says, "That's Fred's banjo—he calls her Bertha, 'cuz she's been with him for thirty-five years."

"That's right—longer than any other woman," the man called Fred says, chuckling at his own joke.

"Y'all in a group together?" Angie asks, folding her arms to protect herself from any more attacks from moving instruments.

"Yes, indeed, young lady," the younger one

says. "We're Fish 'N' Chips. He's Fred Fish. I'm Chips Carter." Mr. Carter adjusts his sunglasses and looks up at the bright, blue sky. "Young people don't listen to the kind of music we play—heart-thumpin' blues," he says.

"What instrument do *you* play?" Angie asks Mr. Chips Carter. It's hard to tell by the shape of his duffel bag—which he is smart enough to hold in *front* of him.

"I play the tambourine—shakin' up the blues."

"We always used to listen to blues music at our grandfather's house when we were little," I inform Fish 'N' Chips.

"Muddy Waters and B. B. King—Granddaddy loved them," Angie adds, grabbing on to Ma's arm.

We don't remember much about Grandaddy Selby Jasper—Ma's daddy—but we'll never forget his music. "Nothing like the blues," he used to say, playing it loud enough on the stereo so he could hear it sitting out on the porch, sipping his lemonade and watching us play in the backyard. Uncle Skeeter would bang out beats on a crate, while Angie and I hummed along, making up our own melodies.

"I guess we are the oldest fools out here," Mr. Fred Fish says to his partner.

Finally, we hear one of the security guards yelling into a bullhorn. "Listen up, people. Everybody is going to get to audition for the Montgomery Homeless Shelter Benefit. But it would help us a lot if you would just form one line against the left railing. We're getting a lot of complaints from the patrons on the Boardwalk!"

"Montgomery Homeless Shelter Benefit—is that the same thing y'all are here for?" Ma asks, concerned.

"Yes, ma'am," I tell her. "Karma's Children are performing, but all the proceeds from ticket sales are going to the Montgomery Homeless Shelter."

"Oh," Ma says, nodding her head. "I thought the benefit was for *all* the shelters in Houston."

"No, ma'am. Montgomery is the one with the most homeless women and children, so they need money to build another wing," Mr. Carter explains.

I nod my head in agreement. We know it's true, because the members of the Houston chapter of the Kats and Kittys Klub were talking about it. We still have Kats friends here—and we call them from New York every once in a while.

Now a bunch of girls are bumping into us from behind. We turn around, and almost shriek at their big gold earrings and freeze-dried curls.

"Twanda, there's no way they are gonna have all these people audition by six o'clock," one of the girls says to another, getting all upset.

What on earth are we doing out here? I wonder.

"Ma, I can't believe that you're being so nice and staying out here with us," Angie says.

"Excuse me," says one of the freeze-dried girls, poking me in the back. I never realized before that we had manner-impaired people down here too!

Ma sees the look on my face, so she addresses Miss Bo-bangles. (I'm sorry, but those are not earrings she is wearing on her ears. Those are bangles, and they belong on her arm!)

"Yes?" Ma asks politely.

"What's wrong with her? She can't talk?" one of the other girls mumbles out loud so I can hear, but I don't say a word.

The girl who poked me keeps talking. "We wuz wondering—do you think Karma's Children are going to be inside?"

"I don't know," Ma says politely, then folds her arms across the pale yellow sweater she's wearing.

"I don't know either," I say, finally speaking up for myself. I'm not afraid of these girls either.

Miss Bo-bangles sucks her teeth. "Shoot, Twanda—we shouldn't waste our time standing out here if they ain't gonna be inside. I want to get those pants down at the Galleria before they close, and I am not standing here all day."

Now another girl in the line turns, and asks someone else if Karma's Children are gonna be inside at the audition. What are they thinking? That Karma's Children would be sitting in the Crabcake Lounge, looking at all these people?

Angie looks at me and reads my thoughts. "I hope they at least stop by or something."

"With this crowd, I wouldn't count on it," Ma says sympathetically. "This is a mess."

We all take a deep breath. Now the security guards with bullhorns are walking around and *ordering* people to form "an orderly line."

"I don't think the line has moved at all," Angie moans.

"Twanda, I'm not playing—let's *go*," Miss Bo-bangle says to her friend. They are both wearing Gucci sunglasses like Ma's, but I think they are fakes.

"Not everybody is willing to work for their dreams like you girls are," Ma says when they leave. She hugs both Angie and me, which makes us feel a whole lot better for standing on a line like cattle waiting to be slaughtered.

"*We* could go get those leather pants at the Galleria, too," Angie says, imitating one of the Bo-bangle girls.

"How do you know they're *leather* pants, Angie?" I ask, chuckling.

"Well, just look at those girls, Aqua—they ain't running to the Galleria mall just to buy jogging outfits!"

Even though Ma is wearing her dark sunglasses, I can tell by the way her face is tilted that she's getting that faraway look in her eyes again. "Ma—where do you think Uncle Skeeter is?" I ask.

"I *really* wish I knew, 'cuz I'm worried sick about him—and so is Big Momma."

"After we finish with this audition, we're gonna help you find him," I promise.

I don't know what I'd do if my Daddy was as irresponsible as Uncle Skeeter. Still, Egyptian and India need their father, just as much as Angie and I need ours.

It *is* almost dark by the time we get anywhere near the front of the line. At this point, one of the attendants hands us a form to fill out.

"Come on, Fish 'N' Chips—you know it's your turn to sing for us," Ma chides the blues singers. Truth is, they've been entertaining us on and off for the past few hours—which otherwise would have seemed like *years*.

Almost everybody on line has been doing some singing, but I don't mind telling you *our* performance got a bit of a standing ovation. Even so, Fish 'N' Chips got the most applause by far. I think most of the young people in the line had never heard anything like their music!

"All right, Fred—let's give the young ladies—and that includes you, too—a taste of the blues," Mr. Chips says, winking at Ma.

Omigod—I think he likes her! "See, Ma, I told you those statistics were incorrect," I tease her.

"Well, what do you expect? He can't half see behind those shades," Ma jokes. "Okay, then, let's hear it," she says, turning back to Fish 'N' Chips.

"Duh-do, duh-do," Fred starts warming up, then Chips joins in, and Fish 'N' Chips start frying up another blues song:

"I went down to the store to get a root beer
But when I came back, nobody was near
Not my woman, not my banjo, and not my dear
Then one of my neighbors made it real clear
He said, son, you done lost your woman
to a bad case of the blues
The next time you go to the store
you'd better look at the news
I said, I lost my woman to a bad case of the blues
And maybe that's why she ran off with my shoes
I've got those lost-woman blues
those dirty, lowdown, lost-woman blues!"

We clap up a storm, because Fish 'N' Chips deserve it! They sure seem to make Ma happy, too. She almost seems like her old self again. "Why don't y'all come on over Tuesday night for some pre-Thanksgiving dinner?" Ma asks them both.

"Well, I reckon we could," Mr. Chips says, winking at Ma again. "What do you think, Fred, have we lost our heads?"

Fred chuckles loudly at his partner's joke.

"Well, Miss . . . uh . . ." Mr. Chips pauses, because he doesn't know what to call Ma. He probably thinks she's married.

"Call me Junifred," Ma says, her eyes twinkling.

I gasp. I haven't heard Ma call herself that in *years*!

"Well, Junifred, we would be delighted to accept that invitation!" Mr. Chips says, beside himself.

"What part of our town do y'all live in?" Ma asks them.

Fish 'N' Chips just sorta pause and look at each other. "Well, we live over by Montgomery," Mr. Chips says quietly.

"Oh, y'all live over by the shelter?" Ma asks.

"No, ma'am," Mr. Fish says, taking over for his partner, who has become speechless. "We live at the shelter."

I'm so embarrassed. We didn't know they were homeless!

"Well, that's fine," Ma says, not backing

down from her invitation. "If you need a ride to my house Tuesday night, just let me know. Otherwise, I expect to see the two of you at my dinner table around eight o'clock!"

We are so proud of Ma. Now I wish the rest of the Cheetah Girls could meet *our* mother—they would be proud of her too!

"Gentlemen, could you step inside?" says a security attendant to Fish 'N' Chips.

"Well, ladies, it looks like it's curtain time," Mr. Fred Fish says, as the two of them go inside for their audition.

We wish them good luck—and we really mean it. Fish 'N' Chips sure earned their tartar sauce tonight! I start humming a bar from their song as we wait for our turn.

After about fifteen minutes, Fish 'N' Chips reemerge in the doorway of the Crabcake Lounge. Ma seems genuinely happy to see them again. "Why don't you two wait out here with me, while the girls go inside?" she suggests to them.

Angie and I grin from ear to ear as we are ushered into the Crabcake Lounge for our audition. "I'll be waiting right here!" Ma yells after us.

The first thing I notice when we get inside is the stacks of forms. They are piled in big bins on top of a table with a checkered paper tablecloth. The place really looks a plain mess.

I can feel the disappointment in my heart when I look around and don't see Karma's Children. I knew they weren't here, because we would've seen them come in. But somehow, I guess I held out hope that they were hiding under the bar or something.

Angie and I smooth down our cheetah skirts, and stand quietly on the tiny stage until we're addressed. There are about six people sitting at the tables talking, and a few more running around, busy doing things.

"Okay," says one of the ladies, who is wearing a ten-gallon cowboy hat, a fringed jacket, and a badge that says VOLUNTEER.

"You girls are . . . ?" the lady asks, then pauses, obviously waiting for us to fill in the blank.

"Angi—" my slow sister starts in.

"The Cheetah Girls," I say, thinking quickly. That's what the lady wants to hear—the name of our group. "My sister was trying to say that she's Anginette and I'm Aquanette Walker—but we're the Cheetah Girls. The other members of our group are in New York—you know, for the holidays."

"Ah, yes," the cowboy hat lady says. "You girls are from Houston though, right?"

"Yes, ma'am, we are," I say proudly.

"Good—because 'Houston Helps Its Own' is the name of the benefit concert, as you may have heard by now," the lady continues.

"Yes, ma'am, we know." I nod again.

A man with thick glasses and a bright red tie clears his throat. He seems to be getting impatient. They are probably tired and irritated after seeing hundreds of people all day.

"Well, would you mind singing for us now?" the lady asks.

"You mean, just a capella?" I ask.

"Yes, that would be fine."

"Oh." I nod, then move toward Angie so we can begin our two-part harmony. Why didn't we rehearse a gospel song? I wonder, shrieking inside. Maybe our kinda of music isn't appropriate for a homeless benefit! No, that's ridiculous, I assure myself.

Angie is looking at me, waiting to begin. So are all the auditioners. We sing "It's Raining Benjamins," and by the time we get to the second verse, they all seem to be smiling. Some of them are even keeping time with their hands and feet. That gives us confidence, and we really lay into the chorus:

"It's raining Benjamins
For a change and some coins
It's raining Benjamins
I heard that, so let's join
It's raining Benjamins . . . again!"

The volunteer lady starts clapping, then the others join in. "Wonderful, girls. We'll let you know," she says enthusiastically. "We've got to move along now, but it was great meeting you."

"How many groups are they gonna pick?" I ask as we're leaving.

"Well, we want to give as many groups a chance as we can," the nice volunteer lady rambles on.

"Each group will get to do one song," the man in the glasses and red tie explains, getting more to the point. "We plan on having about three to five warm-up spots."

"Oh, well, thank you," I gush, even though

I'm not exactly sure what he means. Then, remembering my manners, I ask the lady her name, so I can say good night to her properly.

"Oh, I'm sorry—I'm Mrs. Fenilworth, and this is Mr. Paddlewheel."

"Good night, Mrs. Fenilworth. Good night, Mr. Paddlewheel."

Once we're outside, Angie asks, "When he said warm-up spots, that's what we were auditioning for, right?"

"I guess so. Thank goodness, we've got spots to spare!"

We see Ma standing by the railing with Fish 'N' Chips, a little way from the crowd. We are so happy to see them that we hug all three of them one after another.

Ma wants to know all about the audition, but Angie and I have only one thing on our minds right now. "Let's go eat!" we scream at Ma in unison. We're always hungry after we perform—just like real cheetahs!

Chapter 8

Big Momma calls first thing in the morning, and this time we can really hear the strain in her voice. "I'm praying for Skeeter," she says, sobbing. I can just see her wringing her good handkerchief in her hands—the one she keeps balled up in her skirt pocket and takes out for "sneezing and wheezing."

"Big Momma, don't you have any idea where he could be?" I ask, getting so anxious I can hardly contain myself.

"I've called everybody that knows that boy, and nobody has seen hide nor hair of him," Big Momma says sadly.

"What about, um, a lady friend?" I ask gingerly.

"You know he never brought her around

here—which means she ain't no Christian woman," Big Momma says gruffly.

"We're praying for him, Big Momma," I say, sniffling into the phone. "We love you."

Ma comes over to me, sits down at the table, and puts down her coffee mug. She takes the phone from my hand. "No news?" she asks, then listens. "Hang on, Momma—that's my other line beeping. Someone's trying to get through. Yes, I *have* to get it. Just hold on for a minute."

That makes Angie smile. Big Momma hates call waiting. "If the line is busy, let 'em call back!" she always insists. She refuses to get call waiting on her phone, and sometimes it takes us hours to reach her!

"This is Mrs. Walk— um, Junifred speaking," Ma says to someone on the other line. She still seems confused about what to call herself, now that she and Daddy are dee-vorced. "Could you hang on a second please?" Ma says to the person on the phone, then clicks to the other line, "Momma, a lady is calling for the girls on the other line. Hmm. Hmm. Call me as soon as you hear something. Hmm. Hmm. What? Yes, I'll tell them."

Ma clicks the line and hands us the phone, chuckling. "Big Momma says Porgy and Bess have worn out their welcome. She said it'll take her two years to replant the strawberry patch they trampled to death!"

"Yes, ma'am," I say quickly, hardly even paying attention. I grab the receiver from her and greet the person on the line. "Hello?"

"Yes, this is Mrs. Fenilworth, from the 'Houston Helps Its Own' Committee?"

"Hi, Mrs. Fenilworth! This is Aquanette Walker," I say, suddenly getting a jittery feeling in my stomach.

"Well, Miss Walker—we had a really hard time narrowing down all the candidates for the benefit concert," Mrs. Fenilworth says, very slowly.

Oh, no—we didn't get it! I let out a big sigh. Oh, well, at least she was nice enough to call and let us know.

"There were just so many wonderful performers from our fine city," Mrs. Fenilworth rambles on, "but we had to think about what would be, um, the best complement for Karma's Children—and that's how we finally decided on picking you girls."

Did she say what I thought she said? "Do you mean you picked us out of all those people?" I ask, holding my breath.

"Well, we have narrowed it down to five groups, but yes, we thought your group—the, um, Cheetah Girls—would be a nice addition. That is, if you're still interested. We understand that there is no money involved, so it could be difficult—"

I just start screaming my head off.

"Miss Walker?"

"I'm so sorry, Mrs. Fenilworth, but you have no idea what this means to the Cheetah Girls!" Then I suddenly realize—what about the rest of the Cheetah Girls? We can't perform onstage without the others—that just wouldn't be right!

Angie grabs the receiver from me. "Hi, Mrs. Fenilworth, this is Anginette Walker—did you say *all* the Cheetah Girls could come? No, they live in New York—but if you paid for their plane tickets, they'd be here tomorrow!"

I look at Angie in disbelief. Has she lost her mind? I turn to Ma, who is just sitting there, smiling and shaking her head.

"No, no. We have plenty of room for them to stay at our house. Hmm. Hmm. Okay. Bye."

"Mrs. Fenilworth is gonna let us know if they'll pay to fly the Cheetah Girls from New York to Houston!" Angie screams.

"That's real good, Angie," Ma says, delighted. "And good for you for having the courage to ask!"

"Angie, what if they change their minds about using us because of what you just did?" I ask my sister, stunned.

"If Fish 'N' Chips can stick together for thirty-five years, then so can the Cheetah Girls—all *five* of us!" Angie insists proudly.

The phone rings, and all three of us jump up. Ma is first to grab it. "Hello?" she says. "Yes, this is their mother. Oh, that's wonderful news! The girls will be so pleased! Uh-huh. Let me get a pen. Well, the girls do have a manager—I'll tell her to call you and make the travel arrangements. Uh-huh . . ." Ma continues writing furiously on a notepad.

I motion to her to give me the phone. "That's real good news, Mrs. Fenilworth!" I exclaim.

"Well, it's the least we could do, since you girls are giving your time and talent for such a good cause," Mrs. Fenilworth says.

"Um, Mrs. Fenilworth, what are some of the

other groups you've picked?"

"Let me get the list," Mrs. Fenilworth says. I can hear her shuffling some papers, then she returns. "We have Diamonds in the Ruff—they are so cute—older girls than you, I think. Um, Miggy and Mo', Moody Gardens, and—oh, that's it. Funny, I thought there were five. . . ."

"Well, Mrs. Fenilworth," I say, sounding professional, "while we were waiting to audition, we had the pleasure of hearing this amazing blues group, Fish 'N' Chips."

"Uh, yes, I remember them," Mrs. Fenilworth says, hesitating. "We thought they were very good, but perhaps . . . not appropriate as an opening act for, um, the Karma's Children audience."

"Well, Mrs. Fenilworth, we are only thirteen, and we *love* them. My generation isn't just interested in R & B, rap, and pop music—we love the blues, too!" I try not to look at Angie, who is making me laugh, hopping around with her hand over her mouth.

"Of course," Mrs. Fenilworth says, like she's trying not to say anything to offend me. She *is* nice.

"And you know Houston does help its

own—everyone is real proud of Fish 'N' Chips at the Montgomery Homeless Shelter—where they *live*, tirelessly helping the other residents and cheering them up with their music."

"They *live* at Montgomery?" Mrs. Fenilworth asks, surprised. "They never mentioned that."

"Well, they are proud, fine musicians first of all—so I'm not surprised they didn't say anything about living in a homeless shelter."

"Let me see what I can do—because your point is very well taken, young lady. If I can pull a few strings here, we'll contact the gentlemen ourselves, okay?" Mrs. Fenilworth says. "Um . . . do you have any *more* requests?"

"Oh, no, ma'am!" I reply quickly. "We, um, the Cheetah Girls look forward to seeing you at the rehearsal, Mrs. Fenilworth—and we can't thank you enough!"

"OMIGOD!!" Angie and I hug each other like two cuddly teddy bears.

"That was real nice what you did, Nettie One," Ma says to me—and now I'm beaming, because I've made her proud, too.

The phone rings *again*. "Well, pick it up. Don't look at me—I just live here," Ma says, half smiling. I think she's afraid to pick it up, to tell you the truth—'cuz it might be bad news about Uncle Skeeter.

"Hello?" I say apprehensively.

"Anginette?"

"No, it's Aquanette," I say to Big Momma, who sounds upset.

"Put Junie on the phone," she says quietly.

Ma sees the fear on my face as I pass her the phone. "What is it?" she asks, while we look on. "On Sycamore Road? Yeah, that's all we can do now, sit and wait."

Ma hangs up, and we can feel her heaviness. All the excitement about performing at Karma's Children Benefit Concert has flown out of the room like fairy dust.

"We've got to go on with our lives until we know more, Aquanette," Ma explains, calling me by my full name, which she only does when she's being real serious. "You'd better call Galleria and get this rodeo in motion." She hands me the phone to call New York.

"Yes, ma'am," I say, trying to shake the bad case of the spookies that has come over me.

"Houston is boostin,' baby!" Galleria exclaims excitedly when I tell her the good news. "Now I know that dreams do come true in the jiggy jungle, because I've been *praying* for a way to get out of Dodge for Thanksgiving!"

I try to calm my nerves down as I tell Galleria all about Fish 'N' Chips, Mrs. Fenilworth, Mr. Paddlewheel . . .

All of a sudden, Galleria interrupts, blurting out, "Miz Aquanette, what's wrong? You don't really sound like yourself. If you don't want us to come and perform with you . . . we'll understand."

I am shocked that Galleria thinks we don't want the rest of the Cheetah Girls to come down and perform with us. "Oh, no! It's not that," I reassure her. "But there is something wrong. Our uncle Skeeter hasn't come home for five days. He hasn't even called his kids—our cousins Egyptian and India. Now we found out that his car has been spotted on Sycamore Road, but we don't know anybody who lives over there."

"Don't you worry, Aqua," Galleria says confidently. "When we get there, and once we take care of our business, we're gonna put our Cheetah Girl heads together and get to the bottom of this."

Angie talks to Galleria for a few minutes, and

then we *finally* sit down to eat breakfast. I feel so overwhelmed by everything that is happening that I don't know if I should cry or laugh. I know we're only singing one song in the benefit, but it's a *big* deal. And I know Uncle Skeeter is probably okay, but that is a big deal too. Please God, help us through this.

Ma gets up from the table and puts the phone in the living room. "I don't want to hear another phone ring all day!" she says.

"Amen to that!" Angie and I say together.

Chapter 9

We're disappointed Ms. Dorothea can't come down with Galleria, Chanel, and Dorinda to Houston. Galleria, on the other hand, is tickled silly to be away from her mother.

"Free at last!" she screams, practically jumping on top of me when we meet her at the airport.

"Have you seen Karma's Children yet?" Chanel asks.

"No, we haven't," I assure her. "You'll be the first to know when they hit Kemah Boardwalk—you and everybody else!"

"Girls, I hope you don't mind, but we're

gonna have to take you right over to rehearsal first," Ma informs our friends.

"That's cool-io with us," Dorinda says.

Ma chuckles, "You girls have such a cute way of talking!"

"That's how we flow in the Big Apple!" Galleria shouts.

"Gracias pooches, for letting us come stay with you," Chanel says, making Ma chuckle some more.

"You're quite welcome. I haven't seen my girls this excited before—about *anything*!"

Angie and I start talking a mile a minute about everything that has happened so far. Dorinda is especially keen on hearing about Fish 'N' Chips.

"You actually got them on the bill with us?" she asks, surprised.

"Well, hopefully we did!" I say. "You should have seen the committee's faces when we sang 'It's Raining Benjamins.' At first, we thought we picked the wrong song—"

"Hold up," says a breathless Galleria. "You told them we're gonna sing 'It's Raining Benjamins'?"

"Why, yes," I say, flustered.

"Aqua, you can't make those kind of decisions without us!" Galleria says, getting agitated. "*I'm* the one—I mean, *we* decide *together* what numbers we're going to perform."

Everybody gets real quiet. Now I know exactly how Chanel feels when Galleria rags on her!

"Well, what's done is done," Galleria huffs, giving up for once. Thank gooseness.

"Ooh, look at all the water!" Dorinda coos as we pull up to Kemah's Boardwalk.

"This is Galveston Bay," Angie says proudly. "You should see it in the spring when all the flowers are in full bloom—it almost looks like a tropical paradise."

"Word. I *feel* like I'm in paradise," Dorinda chuckles.

"Y'all are staying for the rest of the holiday weekend, aren't you?" Ma asks, like she's not taking no for an answer.

"Yeah!!!" Galleria, Chanel, and Dorinda say in unison. Angie and I smile at each other. Who woulda thought *we* would be showing *them* the time of their lives?

"Here we are," Angie says, as we pull into the parking lot of the Crabcake Lounge.

"This is so dope," Dorinda says, marveling at everything. Walking through the parking lot, we pass a group of people wearing cowboy hats, fringed jackets, and boots. "Word, look at their outfits!"

"You know the rodeo is real big in Houston," I explain to the New York Cheetah Girls. "Everybody has at least one cowboy hat and pair of boots."

"Well, howdy doody, I'm diggin' it," Galleria says, tipping an imaginary hat to the ten-gallon cowboy hoofers, who are staring at us like we're the main attraction in the rodeo!

"Everybody is feeling our cheetah-ness!" I exclaim.

"There they are!" Angie says, spotting Fish 'N' Chips. "Look, they're playing!"

Fish 'N' Chips are holding court for the tourists walking by. Mr. Fred Fish is plucking on his banjo and Mr. Chips Carter is shaking his tambourine. Mr. Fred's banjo case is opened and lying on the ground. A few tourists throw change into it.

As soon as Fish 'N' Chips see us, they light up as bright as a Christmas tree. Then they circle around us, and start singing up a storm:

"I went down to the store to get a root beer
But when I came back, nobody was near
Not my woman, not my banjo, and not my dear
Then one of my neighbors made it real clear
He said, son, you done lost your woman
to a bad case of the blues
The next time you go to the store
you'd better look at the news
I said, I lost my woman to a bad case of the blues
And maybe that's why she ran off with my shoes
I've got those lost-woman blues
those dirty, lowdown, lost-woman blues!"

Galleria, Chanel, and Dorinda are grinning from ear to ear and clapping.

"See?" I tell Angie, "I *told* Mrs. Fenilworth we young people can groove to the blues—it's just in our blood!"

"Can you believe they picked a couple of old-timers like us, out of all them younguns?" Mr. Fish exclaims.

Angie and I grin like two foxes who've swallowed some hens. I poke her, just to make sure she doesn't say a word to Fish 'N' Chips about us pulling a few strings. I'm just grateful we had a few strings to pull!

I look at Dorinda, and see tears welling in her eyes. "Can I see that?" she asks, pointing to Mr. Fred's banjo.

"Sure thing, little lady."

Dorinda is just fascinated with Mr. Fish's instrument. We all sit on the railing and watch, while he shows her how to play.

"Now, when you pluck the banjo to play the blues, you gotta *feel* the blues—you know, slump down some, and think about all the people who done you wrong," Mr. Fish says, grinning his toothless grin.

"Word. That won't be too hard," Dorinda says, slumping her tiny little shoulders and putting a funny scowl on her face.

"Now just make up any words you want, so you can get the melody to match the plucking."

"Um, okay—um, let's see:

"I'm sitting on the porch
just minding my bizness
trying to light a torch
For my big ole' horse
But my dern little cat
keeps coming back.
I can't get no slack

for my wack attack blues!!
I said, I can't get no slack
for m-y-y-y wack-attack blluuues!"

A tourist stops to listen, and puts another dollar in Fish 'N' Chips' banjo case! We all start howling at Dorinda.

"Well now, that's interesting how you got the rap mixing up with the blues," Mr. Fred Fish says, tickled.

We are laughing so hard that we don't see Mrs. Fenilworth motioning for us to come in for rehearsal. Ma taps us on the shoulder and points to where Mrs. Fenilworth is standing quietly, waiting for us to finish.

Mr. Fred Fish seems a little embarrassed by the money in his banjo case, and he shovels it quickly into a pouch he takes out of his pocket.

Suddenly a light goes off in my head—this is probably how they make money to live—by singing on the streets!

Two little girls with pigtails and freckles come inside behind us, and sit down at one of the tables. "Hi, we're Miggy and Mo'!" the more freckly one says. I wonder if they're fraternal twins. They must be sisters, and they look really young.

"Hi, we're the Cheetah Girls," Chanel says, real friendly.

"Mr. Paddlewheel, is everybody here?" Mrs. Fenilworth asks.

"No—we're missing the Moody Gardens."

All of a sudden, three boys wearing plaid shirts and jeans barge into the Crabcake Lounge. "Uh, sorry we're late."

"Just take a seat," Mr. Paddlewheel says nicely. "Tomorrow night," he tells us all, "we are throwing a very special benefit concert, to help raise money for Houston's homeless population. The benefit, we are happy to report, is *completely* sold out, and we are expecting an estimated five thousand people to fill the Turtle Dome Arena out in back. You have been selected to sing one song each—sort of a tribute to Houston's burgeoning undiscovered talent, and the possibilities that lie ahead of all of us."

Five thousand people! I swallow hard just thinking about it. We've never performed for that many folks at once!

"What's the game plan now?" Galleria asks

excitedly, as we head back to Ma's car.

"Well, I made some crawfish and potatoes stew for dinner, if anyone is interested," Ma chuckles.

"Yes, bring on Mr. Crawdaddy!" Galleria shouts.

"Gentlemen, that invitation still holds." Ma is talking to Fish 'N' Chips, who are about to walk out of the parking lot. I'll bet you they walk all the way back to Montgomery Shelter, since they don't have a car!

"We'll be there, Ms. Junifred, don't you worry," Mr. Chips Carter says. Lifting his sunglasses, he gives her a wink. "Yes, indeed. Wouldn't miss it for the world."

"Wow, this is *la dopa*!" Chanel exclaims, "It looks like right out of a magazine."

I guess we forget how pretty Ma's house is. It's so country and flowery—the exact opposite of Daddy's apartment in New York.

"Don't mind the mess," Ma says, moving some mail off the table. As she does, she looks at one of the envelopes. "I've got to mail this census form in," she says, putting it aside.

"The ones who don't get counted are usually

the really poor people," Angie explains to Dorinda.

"So what?" Dorinda asks.

"Well, see, how much money the government gives Houston depends on how many people say they live here. So when poor people don't fill out their census forms, the government gives less money to help the poor."

"Oh," Dorinda says, and you can tell it makes her feel sad.

We sit down in the living room while Ma starts getting ready to cook dinner. Fish 'N' Chips will be coming over later, and she wants everything to be perfect, so there's a lot for her to do.

Meanwhile, Galleria wants to hear about the whole Skeeter business. I tell her about his red Cadillac being spotted on Sycamore Road.

Ma hears us talking about him, and she reminds us of his last words to her: "He said he was tired of everything, and just wanted to 'rest in peace.' That's why we are so frightened at what he might do."

"Don't forget what India said, about Uncle Skeeter's girlfriend having a name that's softer than mink," Angie adds, trying to be helpful. "And what Big Momma said about her last name being Wilkerson."

"Don't snooze on the clues!" Galleria exclaims, and we can see the lightbulb going off in her head. "Get me a phone book—you'd be surprised by who has a listed number."

Angie and I just look at Galleria like, "What on earth are you talking about?"

"Your mother says her last name is Wilkerson, right?"

"Yeah . . . so?"

"So, let's see if she's in the phone book."

"Galleria, do you know how many Wilkersons there are in the Houston phone book? That's a *typical* Southern last name!" I'm starting to get exasperated by Galleria's over-eagerness. Of course, I should have known she would have a plan.

"Yeah, but how many of those Wilkersons have a first name that's softer than mink?"

Now we all look at Galleria in awe. Why didn't *we* think of that?

"Let's look at every Wilkerson in the phone book!" Chanel says excitedly.

We huddle around, going down the names of Wilkersons carefully and reading them out loud—"Annabel, Karen, Katie, Sandy, Sable, Twanda, Toinette—"

"Wait a minute," Dorinda says. "Go back—*Sable!* Remember what India said? 'Soft as mink.' Well, sable is a kind of fur, and so is mink."

"Omigod," gasps Angie. "Look. She lives on Hummingbird—that's right around the corner from Sycamore!"

"We've gotta think of a plan," Ma muses.

"I've got an idea," Galleria says with a satisfied smirk. "We go over there, and say we're from the Census Bureau, and that we need her to fill out a form, because people aren't handing them in on time. Your Mom could be the census lady—and we'll be her kids. She can say she's working late to earn extra money or something."

"Oh, I get it—get her sympathy and wheedle our way in. Then, when Ma wins her confidence, they can do girl talk—about their boyfriends, right?" It sounds like a good plan to me.

"Yeah!" Galleria says.

"But what if she recognizes Ma?" Angie asks, concerned, even though Ma has obviously never met Sable.

"She's not going to recognize your mother," Chanel says.

"Why?" we ask in unison.

"Because we're gonna put her in a Cheetah Girl disguise, just in case, *mamacitas*!"

"I haven't had so much fun playing dress-up since I was a kid," Ma says while we fuss with her. We wrap her hair in a cheetah turban and try on a pair of cheetah sunglasses.

"Well," Ma says, looking in the mirror. "It sure doesn't look like me—I guess it's worth a shot. But I don't have too long—I've got to get dinner together, remember."

"Don't forget the form," Dorinda says, handing Ma the envelope with the census form inside.

"Oh, right—and I should take my clipboard from work, and my briefcase," she adds.

I can tell Ma is feeling much better—at least we're *doing* something about finding Uncle Skeeter, instead of sitting around thinking the worst.

"I think it's best if Dorinda and I pretend to be your ma's daughters," Galleria says. "Just in case Skeeter already told Sable that he has twin nieces."

Even though I feel disappointed, I know Bubbles is right about that. Uncle Skeeter does love bragging about us to everybody, just like Big Momma.

"Why can't *I* be one of the daughters?" Chanel asks, feeling left out, too.

"'Cuz, Chuchie, you have a Spanish accent—maybe Sable won't buy that you're Ms. Walker's daughter."

"Oh—I've got to change my name," Ma says. "I'll say my name is Mrs. Cobbler—that way I won't forget, 'cuz I was planning on making y'all a cobbler for Thanksgiving Day." Ma seems amused by her own cleverness.

"Okay, 'Mom,' let's go," Galleria says, taking Ma by the arm. Suddenly I feel jealous—but then I catch myself for being so selfish.

When we drive past Sycamore Road, we see that Uncle Skeeter's car is still parked there. I get a bad case of the spookies again, and take a deep breath. Ma keeps driving until we get to Hummingbird Road, and Sable Wilkerson's house. There, she pulls over and cuts the engine.

"Someone's home," Angie says quietly.

"Good luck," I whisper as Ma, Galleria, and Dorinda get out the car.

There are kids playing on the sidewalk, and they check out the three of them as they walk up to Sable's front porch.

Angie, Chanel, and I sit in the car on lookout. The plan is that if we see Uncle Skeeter going into the house, or sneaking out the back, we honk the horn.

It seems like hours before Ma, Galleria, and Dorinda come out. I can tell by the way they're walking that they've had no luck with their census charade.

"She's more clueless than we are," Ma says, visibly upset as she gets into the driver's seat. "She hasn't seen Skeeter in five days." Ma's hands are shaking as she tries to put the keys in the ignition. She stops, then puts her head down on the steering wheel, and starts bawling like a baby.

Galleria puts her arms around Ma's shoulders, and we just sit and wait until she pulls herself together. I bite my lower lip. I don't want to start crying too.

"What are we going to do?" Angie says, feeling as helpless as I do.

"Exactly what we were doing before—wait," Ma says, pulling herself together and taking a deep breath. She's all right for the moment, ready to concentrate on driving home.

The sadness looms over all of us. All of sudden, it doesn't matter that we are going to sing a song in front of five thousand people tomorrow night. All that matters is that we find Uncle Skeeter—and that he's all right.

Chapter 10

The next morning, the gloomy cloud is still hanging over our heads even though we had a great dinner the night before with Fish 'N' Chips. They ate everything but the tablecloth! We got ready to go see Granddaddy Walker at his funeral parlor. (He's seventy-two years old, and has never missed a day of work!) Granddaddy Walker has been chomping at the bit, because we have been four whole days in Houston and still haven't come to see him.

"Let's go wake up the dead!" Galleria says, when we tell her about his hurt feelings.

Dorinda is excited about going, too. "We might as well take a 'coffin break' before the show," she smirks.

"Now remember girls, we can't stay too long," Ma preps us.

I don't know why she says that, because we have plenty of time. We have ironed our costumes, bought the cheetah umbrellas we're gonna hold, and the play money we're going to throw onstage for our performance, and we've practiced "It's Raining Benjamins" till we could sing it backward.

But I guess Ma feels bad about the dee-vorce and all, even though Granddaddy Walker still treats her like family, and we know he loves us, well, "to death."

Rest in Peace is the biggest funeral parlor in Houston, and it's housed in the landmark district, in a beautiful building with a white marble front, and white pillars on the porch. When we get inside, Granddaddy Walker gives Ma a real long hug and doesn't let go.

"We'll get through this, Junifred. We sure will," he tells her. Obviously, Ma has already told him about Uncle Skeeter.

"Should we call the police?" Ma asks him, distraught.

"No—not yet. The Lord will tell you what to do—just wait and see," Granddaddy Walker says, laying down words of wisdom like he always does.

"Good morning," says Grandma Selma, greeting us all cheerfully. She is Granddaddy Walker's second wife, and also his secretary. He married her after Grandma Winnie passed (which raised a few eyebrows—since Selma is twenty-four years younger than he is!).

Granddaddy Walker peers over his bifocals to look at me and my friends. "How y'all doing?" he says, grinning and extending his hand to shake Galleria's.

Bubbles seems a little nervous, acting very polite and looking down at the floor. I guess Granddaddy Walker can seem a little intimidating. He is a great big man, and he always wears a black suit with a white shirt, and a red handkerchief in the jacket pocket. You can tell how important he is just by the way he looks.

"You know, that boy hasn't been himself since his daddy died," Granddaddy says, shaking his head.

All of a sudden, Galleria is looking straight at Granddaddy Walker, and watching him real closely. "Skeeter's father died?" she asks, her eyes narrowing.

"Oh, yes, seven years ago. I buried him myself. Skeeter loved his daddy something awful," Granddaddy goes on.

Galleria looks at the literature laying on the table, then mutters, "'Rest in Peace . . .' that's what Skeeter said. . . ."

"What?" I ask Galleria, confused.

"Your ma said Skeeter was acting strange the last time she saw him, and he told her, 'I'm tired of everything. I just want to rest in peace.'"

"Yeah," Ma says, wondering what Galleria is getting at.

"So Skeeter's father had a funeral service here at Rest in Peace Funeral Home," Galleria continues, talking out loud. "Where did you bury him?"

"Where I bury everybody—at the Creekmore Cemetery, about ten miles from here," Granddaddy Walker says, his big voice booming. "Of course, Selby Jasper's coffin is buried in his own mausoleum—the biggest one in the cemetery."

"I think we should go over there and take a look," Galleria says, like she's onto something.

"Go to the cemetery? Now?" Angie asks, surprised.

"I think we'd better," I say, sticking up for Galleria. I know she's like a dog with a bone. When Miss Galleria is onto something, she won't leave it alone. Let her sniff around Granddaddy Selby's grave—maybe she will come up with something.

"At this point, I'm willing to try anything that will help us find my brother," Ma blurts out. "The worst that could happen is I get to visit my Daddy's grave, and y'all get to do some sightseeing at a cemetery!"

"Take a bunch of magnolias with you," Grandma Selma says, pointing to some beautiful purple flowers in a vase on the table.

Granddaddy Walker picks up the phone and calls Willie, who drives the hearses for all the funeral processions to the cemetery. "Willie, we're gonna need a hearse—bring out the best one we have."

Then he puts his arms around Angie and me. "Willie will drive y'all to Creekmore," he says, his eyes twinkling. He knows how much Angie and I love riding in his big, black hearses, with their cushioned seats and draped windows.

"You sure about that, Granddaddy Walker?" Ma asks. Now that she and Daddy are dee-vorced,

I don't think she likes asking Granddaddy Walker for anything.

"Yes, Junifred, I'm sure," Granddaddy Walker says, his eyes twinkling. "No 'body' is in a hurry this week."

After burying half the dead people in Houston, Granddaddy Walker has quite a sense of humor about corpses. That's just one more reason why we love him. Angie smiles, then looks down, trying to be respectful.

"Wow, this is supa dupa cushy," Dorinda says as we climb into the hearse.

"This is the biggest one I've been in!" Chanel coos.

"Chuchie, you've *never* been in one," Galleria says, shaking her head.

"I know," Chanel responds, grinning sheepishly. "That's what I meant."

"Just sit back and relax, girls. Willie's gonna take good care of ya," the driver says, looking at us in the rearview mirror. Willie looks spiffy in his black uniform with matching black chauffeur's hat and white gloves. We tell him all about our singing group, as he takes the long, scenic route to Creekmore Cemetery.

"I used to play the keyboards when I was younger—with a group of my boys," Willie chuckles. "Nothing serious like you Cheetah Girls are doing. 'Cheetah Girls'—that sounds catchy, all right."

"Catch the rising stars while you can!" Galleria giggles.

"You know, Skeeter used to play the keyboards when we were kids," Ma says. "He was always beating or strumming on something. But Daddy was always telling him to get a serious job—be somebody. So Skeeter gave it up, and went to work for the sanitation department."

"I remember Uncle Skeeter always pounding out beats on cans and things," I say, "when Granddaddy was playing his blues music. Uncle Skeeter liked the blues a whole lot."

"Oh, yeah—that's his favorite music," Ma says, getting tearful again.

"You girls should keep singing—keep following your dreams, even when it seems people are trying to take them from you," Willie the driver says, like he knows what he's talking about.

I look at Chanel, who is sitting next to me,

and smile at her. I wonder if Willie's dreams have come true. I sure don't think Uncle Skeeter's dreams have . . .

Tears well in my eyes. I stare out of the window as we drive past the big wrought-iron gates into the cemetery.

Chanel grabs my hand tighter. "Look at all the tombstones—all those people who can't have fun anymore, like we do," she says wistfully.

"The most famous people in Houston are buried here. Yes, indeed," Willie says, driving real slow so he can show us some of the tombstones as we pass. "That mausoleum right there is the permanent home of the Great Abra Cadabra—one of the greatest magicians that ever lived. And there's where General Sam Houston rests. This city is named after him. And here . . . is your mausoleum." He pulls over and we get out of the hearse.

"It's so quiet here," Dorinda says, taking in the peaceful scene.

"If you listen real quietly, you can hear the souls whispering," Willie chuckles, then starts humming a gospel hymn. We all walk down the lane where Granddaddy Selby Jasper's mausoleum stands. "I'll be waiting right here for you," Willie says softly. "Take your time."

Ma sets the bunch of magnolias down in front of the mausoleum. As we walk up to the entrance, we see that the door is slightly ajar!

"I can't believe this," Ma says, freezing in her tracks. "One thing is for sure, *someone* has been here."

"Should we go inside?" I ask, quivering. Angie is holding my hand. Chanel has grabbed Galleria's, and poor Dorinda is just standing in the background, like she's ready to run if she has to. We look around, but there isn't one person in sight except us and Willie.

"I think we're out here all by ourselves," Angie says. Taking a big gulp, she folds her arms across her chest, like she's bracing herself for whatever comes popping out from behind a tombstone.

"Well, let's get to it," Ma says, pulling on the heavy mausoleum door.

The door creaks all the way open, and a few cobwebs fall on Ma's head. We peer inside behind her, but we can't really see anything, it's so dark. "Can *you* see anything, Ma?" I ask, shuddering.

"No, but—aaaah!" Ma screams, then takes a step back. "I heard something—I think it's a mouse!" We are all deathly afraid of mice, more than of any ghoul or goblin, that's for sure.

"I think we need a flashlight to go inside," Ma says, backing out.

We hear a rustling sound again. There's definitely something crawling around in there! "Hello!" Ma yells deep into the mausoleum. "Is anybody in there?"

We hear more stirring. "Ms. Walker, I don't think that's a mouse, 'cuz it moves every time you say something!" Galleria says, squinting her eyes and trying to get a peek.

"I think you're right—and I have a feeling I know exactly *who* it is," Ma says sharply. I can tell she isn't afraid anymore. "Skeeter—I know you're in there, so you can stop hiding!"

We wait for what seems like years, and then we hear a noise again—this time it sounds like a bottle rolling on the ground inside.

"Skeeter, I'm not playing. Whatever is wrong, we can work this out," Ma says, determined not to back down.

"All right . . ." we hear a man's voice grumble. "Shoot, it figures *you* would find me!"

Ma gasps, and puts her hand over her mouth. Tears well up in her eyes. "Skeeter—Omigod, I can't believe this!"

"Yeah, I can't believe it either. I'll be right out."

We back away from inside Granddaddy Selby's mausoleum and wait. And wait . . .

"Maybe he's not gonna come out,' Angie whispers.

But a moment later, like a ghost from Thanksgiving past, Uncle Skeeter emerges from the mausoleum. Believe me, he *looks* like a ghost!

We try not to let the shock show in our eyes, but we can't help it. Uncle Skeeter's eyes are bloodshot, his face is full of whiskers, and his clothes are all wrinkled. He scratches his head, like he has lice or something, and asks sheepishly, "Who are all these people?"

"These are Nettie One and Two's friends from New York," Ma says defensively, then she bursts into tears. "Why didn't you come talk to me, Skeeter?"

"I was finished talking for a while," Skeeter says, looking down at his feet. I guess the sun is hurting his eyes. "How did you find me?"

"I didn't—the girls did," Ma says, pointing to all of us.

"Yeah—you two were always the smart ones. You could be detectives," Uncle Skeeter chuckles, scratching his head some more. Maybe he really *does* have lice!

"Well?" Ma says, like she's waiting for an explanation. "Daddy would turn over in his grave if he saw what you're doing to yourself."

"Yeah . . . well, that's why I guess I decided to join him, for a little peace and quiet. I'm tired of everybody telling me what I should be doing," Uncle Skeeter says defensively.

"So, that's your solution? Give up on your life and hurt all of us, just because we care about you?" Ma screams at the top of her lungs.

Uncle Skeeter breaks down, crying like a baby. "I thought maybe Daddy could give me some *answers*, Junie. I-I-I didn't know where to look anymore," he says, barely able to talk.

"What answers do you need, Skeeter?" Ma cries back.

"What to do with myself! I *hate* my life—my job—all of it. I don't want to pick up people's garbage anymore. My wife *hates* me. I can't afford to take care of my kids . . ."

"Stop feeling sorry for yourself, Skeeter!" Ma cries out.

"I'm so ashamed that y'all have to see me like this," Uncle Skeeter says, looking at us with embarrassed eyes. "These are your friends I heard about?"

Angie and I start crying. We're too choked up to answer.

"We're from New York," Galleria pipes up.

"I can see that," Uncle Skeeter says, peering at Galleria, Chanel, and Dorinda.

"Uncle Skeeter," I cry, running up to him and hugging him tight. "Don't leave us, ever again."

Uncle Skeeter heaves a deep, long sigh. "I won't, Nettie One. I promise. Not until the Good Lord takes me."

Chapter 11

Now that Uncle Skeeter is safe and sound, all we can think about is the Karma's Children benefit concert. We have taken two hours just to get ready, and it shows in the way we "prowl" to the backstage entrance of the Turtle Dome Arena.

The pathway is lit with beautiful Chinese paper lanterns that brighten the sky. Dragonflies swirl around the globes of light, giving off twinkle-dinkle sparkles every now and then.

As we push our way through the crowd to get to the "talent entrance," people are staring at us. "Oooo, look at their outfits!" we hear them saying. We smile at them, and Chanel even raises her hand into the "growl power" sign, which causes quite a few giggles.

"Are y'all performing?" one little girl asks us, as we try to move past the hordes of ticket holders.

"Yes, ma'am," Galleria says, leading the way behind Ma.

"Wait till Mr. Chips Carter gets a whiff of what's cooking!" I tease Ma. Since her cheetah-fied escapade worked, we talked her into wearing a leopard silk scarf around her neck tonight. She looks real pretty—and she even did her nails!

"Never mind, Nettie One—you just concentrate on getting your turns down right, and not hitting anyone with that fake money," Ma says, kinda bossy.

She can say whatever she wants—I *know* there is something cookin' between her and Mr. Chips Carter. And why not? He may not have money, but he has music. Besides, he's not bad-looking. He's not too old for Ma—and at least he has all his teeth!

"Do you think Uncle Skeeter is gonna show up?" Angie asks, concerned.

"He gave us his word."

"How old do you think those two are?"

Dorinda interrupts, staring at Houston's own kiddie rappers, Miggy and Mo'.

"They must be about Egyptian and India's age, ain't that right, Angie?" I ask.

"Yup."

"Who's Egyptian and India?" Chanel asks, obviously intrigued.

"They are our cousins," I exclaim. "Uncle Skeeter's daughters. You'll meet them, and Big Momma, and everybody else at Thanksgiving dinner."

"Ain't this like a dream come true?" Angie yells over the noise of the crowd.

"I'm not sure yet—wait till we get inside," I holler back. If we don't make our way through this mob and get into the arena soon, this night could turn into a Nightmare on Kemah Boardwalk!

"All these people paid fifty dollars for concert tickets?" Galleria asks in utter disbelief.

"Yes, ma'am," I tell her, as we approach the promised land—the backstage door. There we're stopped by a ten-foot-tall Mighty Man security guard. "Can I help you?" he asks.

"We—they—are perfoming for the benefit," Ma says, pointing to us. The Mighty Man looks us over, then lets us through. Even a dodo bird can see we are performing. Why else would be parading around in cheetah outfits?

Once we're back in the talent holding room, we plop down on the couch and wait for instructions. We wave hi to Miggy and Mo'. They are still wearing pigtails, and I can tell they've put makeup on to try and cover their freckles, but you can still see them!

"Hey!" yells Mr. Fred Fish, coming over with his arms outstretched to greet us.

"You ladies are the reason we are here," Mr. Chips Carter starts in. I look at him, puzzled. I wonder if Mrs. Fenilworth told him we got them into the show—but then I realize, he's just flirting again.

"'Cuz if you ladies weren't here, me and Fred woulda went and caught some deer!" Mr. Carter says, laughing loudly at his own joke. "'Cuz I got the lost-woman blues!"

Ma is just beaming from ear to ear. Mr. Chips Carter takes her hand and kisses it, like he's found gold! "That was some fine dinner last night, Ms. Junifred."

"Why thank you," Ma says. "We'll have to do it again sometime. . . ."

"Ahem. I wonder where Karma's Children's dressing room is?" Dorinda asks, diverting our attention from the grown-ups.

"You can bet it ain't in here, lovely lady," Mr. Fred Fish says, chuckling loudly, "'cuz stars always get dressing rooms as big as the Taj Mahal!"

"I wonder if they're here," Galleria muses.

"You'll know when they're here," Mr. Fish says, "because I have a notion there will be lots of commotion in the ocean!"

"Y'all are like rappers," Dorinda says, looking up at Fish 'N' Chips, amused.

"Lovely lady, before they even invented the word rap, we were rapping," Mr. Chips Carter says. "That's what the blues is all about—speaking your mind."

"And before you had rap, we had the snap *and* the tap," Mr. Fred Fish says, snapping his fingers and tapping his foot wildly. "*Yessiree.* We always had to find the rhythm *somewhere.*"

"I never thought about it that way," Galleria says, getting excited. She whips out her Kitty Kat notebook and starts scribbling in it madly.

"Yo, Galleria—you're like the mad scientist of lyrics," Dorinda chuckles.

"He's here!!" Angie says excitedly, pointing to the door.

Now it's my turn to scream. "Uncle Skeeter!"

"Ooh, look how nice you look!" Angie says, touching Uncle Skeeter's wild flowered shirt. He's also wearing a straw hat, and his shoes are spit-polished just the way he likes them.

"Fish 'N' Chips," I say excitedly, combining their names, "this is my Uncle Skeeter. He's into the blues too!"

Uncle Skeeter starts blushing, "Well . . ."

"Let's hear what you got!" Mr. Fish says, cutting him off. He whips out his banjo, and Mr. Carter takes out his tambourine.

"What's your name?"

"Skeeter Jasper," Uncle Skeeter says, pulling a harmonica out of his pants pocket.

"Omigod, I remember that thing!" Angie says.

I'd forgotten that Uncle Skeeter used to play the harmonica. Like I said before, he was always playing *something*. Mr. Fish and Mr. Chips pull up three chairs, and Uncle Skeeter sits on the one in the middle.

"Okay, now, Skeet—I'm gonna start in, then Chips, then you follow us," Mr. Fish starts strumming, nodding his head like he's in heaven. Mr. Chips joins right in, shaking his tambourine, tapping his foot. Uncle Skeeter starts blowing on his harmonica. Then Mr. Chips starts singing, "'I woke up this morning with a bad case of the lost-woman blues . . .'"

"'I said I woke up this morning . . .'" Mr. Fred Fish cuts in.

We start clapping our hands together, and Miggy and Mo' and the guys from the Moody Gardens band come over and join in. I look over at Ma, and I can see the tears welling up in her eyes.

All of sudden, we hear screaming. Dorinda runs to the doorway to see what's going on, then she comes running back. "They're here! *Karma's Children* are here—in the room right next to us!"

Uncle Skeeter and Fish 'N' Chips keep playing, but I have to run out and see if I can catch a glimpse of Karma's Children. I crane my neck, but all I see is a crowd clogging up the hallway. "Can *you* see them?" I ask the girl standing in front of me.

"No. They went inside the dressing room, and there's a security guard blocking the doorway."

"Too bad."

I go back and listen to Uncle Skeeter and Fish 'N' Chips do their thing.

"Look at how happy Uncle Skeeter looks," Angie says, squeezing my arm.

"I know. His whole face just lights up when he plays the harmonica.

"He's good, too."

"Well, of course," Ma butts in. "He's a Jasper!"

Miggy and Mo' come over and sit by us, eating tuna sandwiches and nodding along with their heads. Uncle Skeeter and the dynamic duo, Fish 'N' Chips, finally stop playing, and we all clap *real* loud, and scream, "Woop, woop," too.

"Well, Mr. Chips," Mr. Fred Fish says, "I think tonight Fish 'N' Chips is gonna be going on 'with special guest, Skeeter Jeeter.'"

"Jasper!" Ma shouts out, proud of her maiden name.

"Well, now, that's Jasper to you, but Jeeter to us," Mr. Fish says, nodding at Uncle Skeeter and Mr. Chips, and showing off those empty spaces where his front teeth used to be. Now I wonder what Fish 'N' Chips's *real* names are . . .

"Oh, word, I get it—a stage name! That's what he means," Dorinda says, smiling.

"Well, I like it," Ma says, nodding her head in approval.

We run over and hug Uncle Skeeter. "Well, I guess this has turned out to be a family affair," Ma says, smiling. Then, looking at Dorinda, Chanel, and Galleria, she adds, "Now don't forget that y'all are family too."

"Thank you, Mrs. Walker," Dorinda says, touched by Ma's generosity.

"Call me Junifred, sweetie," Ma tells her.

Galleria hands us each a batch of fake Benjamins. "Y'all, we should each hold on to our own Benjies."

"You said *'y'all!'*" I tease Galleria.

"I reckon I did, Miz 'Aquanetta does it betta!'" Galleria shoots back.

"I could sure use some of your eggnog right about now," Dorinda says.

"Wait till you taste *mine,*" Ma says proudly. "We are going to have a good-time Thanksgiving, trust me!"

"Oh, no! We're first!" I moan, looking at the lineup for the warm-up acts. "I wish Ms. Dorothea were here. She'd set them straight! No offense to you, Ma."

"No offense taken," Ma quips back.

"We *hate* going on first," offers Miggy.

I just look at her. She's only nine or ten years old. How would she know? They've probably only been performing all of two days!

As if reading my mind, Angie asks Miggy, "How long have you two been performing?"

"Five years," Miggy says proudly. "We started when I was five and she was four."

"Oh," says Dorinda, shrinking into her chair.

"Listen, we're gonna be doing this gig at the Okie-Dokie Corral—" Mo' says.

"What's that?" Dorinda asks, squinching up her nose.

"It's the first urban rodeo," Miggy says.

"It's gonna be in Fort Bend County," Mo' volunteers.

"And they're looking for more talent—if you wanna try out for it," Miggy says, shrugging her shoulders.

"Let's do it!" Chanel says excitedly.

"Um, sorry," Ma tells them. "But these girls are headed back to New York City on Sunday."

"Ain't y'all from here?" Miggy asks.

"Originally," I say quickly, wanting to stop the conversation right there.

"Uncle Skeeter, Fish 'N' Chips—y'all should try out for it!" Angie exclaims, motioning for them to get the information.

"Well, why not? I always wanted to be a hot diggity cowboy!" Mr. Fish cackles loudly.

Now that show time is just around the bend, Galleria commands us, "Let's do the Cheetah Girls prayer!" We join hands and do our chant, which ends, "Whatever makes us clever, forever!" Then it's time to get into position backstage.

Uncle Skeeter winks at me and Angie. "Don't wear them out, Nettie One and Two. Leave some applause for us!"

We are ushered past production crew and guests standing in the hallway. I'm clutching the fake "Benjies" tightly in my hand. I feel jittery and jumpy. No matter how many times we've performed, whether it's in the church choir or at the Apollo Theatre, it's always scary.

Mrs. Fenilworth has taken the stage. "We have a long tradition of helping our own in Houston," she says, "and tonight we continue that tradition, by giving these singing groups the chance to show their talents. If there's anything we have here in Houston, it's Texas-sized talent."

The crowd roars, "Yeah, Houston! Yeah, Texas!"

"Our first guests are the Cheetah Girls, a singing group that hails from right here in Houston." (Now the rest of the Cheetah Girls know how Angie and I feel every time an M.C. says we're from New York.)

When we get onstage, I take a real good look at the crowd. I can't believe how many people there are! When the music track kicks in, Galleria opens her umbrella, Chanel and Dorinda huddle under it with her, and Angie and I stand next to them. After two beats, we begin singing "It's Raining Benjamins."

At the onset of the chorus, we throw the fake money into the audience and bounce around onstage:

"It's raining Benjamins,
for a change and some coins
It's raining Benjamins
I heard that
It's raining . . . again!"

The crowd goes wild! People are pushing each other trying to grab the fake "Benjies" that are floating through the air. After we finish the song and take our bow, we hightail it off the stage, just as we've been instructed. They're still applauding, long after we get backstage!

"I can't wait for the day when we can just stand there and go with the flow, 'cuz it's *our* show," Galleria says.

Miggy and Mo' are being ushered onstage. "Good luck!" I whisper to them. They wave back, smiling. They may be little, but they sure are pros!

"That's my girls!" Uncle Skeeter says when we get back to the holding area. He takes turns giving me and Angie hugs and "squiggles," like he used to when we were little. "I'm so proud of you two," he says, tears in his eyes.

"We're proud of you, too, Skeeter," Angie says.

"Are you gonna become part of Fish 'N' Chips?" I ask him.

"Well, why not?" Uncle Skeeter says, looking at Mr. Fish and Mr. Carter. "You know what? I finally figured out what I'm really tired of."

"What?" I ask, curious.

"I'm tired of not chasing *my* dreams," he says, wiping the sweat off his forehead. "I love the rhythm, you know—I guess it's in the Jasper blood—so I'm gonna have to 'go with that flow,' as your girl Galleria here would say."

We chuckle at how astute Uncle Skeeter is. He gets everybody's program *real* quick.

"I really dig your little group," he says, pointing to all five of us now. "When are y'all going back home?"

"Not until we get an autograph from Karma's Children—*and* a photo," Galleria huffs.

"Not until we go to the Galleria Mall and go window-shopping!" Chanel smirks.

We turn to Dorinda to see what she's gonna say, but she just shrugs her shoulders and says, "Not until you kick me out."

Bless her little heart.

"And I *know* you're not going before you eat my Thanksgiving dinner!" Ma says, getting into the mix. "You know, I never knew what Aqua and Angie meant when they told me you girls had 'growl power'—but after watching you perform in front of five thousand people, I'll tell you this—ain't nobody gonna stop the Cheetah Girls!"

It's Raining Benjamins

For the first time in her-*story*
there's a weather forecast
that looks like the mighty cash.
So tie up your shoes and
put away your blues
'cuz we're going around the bend
at half past ten
to the only place in town
where everything is coming up green
You know what I mean:

It's raining Benjamins
for a change and some coins
It's raining Benjamins
I heard that, so let's make some noise
It's raining . . . again!

Now maybe you're wondering
what's all the thundering—
But we've got the root of all the loot
that got past Santa's chute
without collecting soot.

So put on your galoshes
and bring the noshes
to the only place in town
where money is falling on the ground
That's right, y'all:

It's raining Benjamins
for a change and some coins
It's raining Benjamins
I heard that
It's raining . . . again!

So here's the rest of the her-*story*
now that there's no longer a mystery.
It's the precipitation in the nation
that's causing all the sensation
in the only way that dollar bills
can give you thrills.
Yeah, that's what I mean:

It's raining Benjamins
for a change and some coins
It's raining Benjamins
I heard that, so make some noise
It's R-A-I-N-I-N-G . . . AGAIN!
(Say it, again! Okay . . .)

The Cheetah Girls Glossary

The blues: Heart-thumpin' music from back in the day. B. B. King and Muddy Waters are the kings of "snappin,' tappin'" blues music, but the legend of the blues will live forever.

Boostin': Jammin'.

Dee-vorced: Divorced. No longer married.

Get the rodeo on the road: Bounce. Make moves.

Hush the mush: Stop whining. Stop getting mushy.

Manners-impaired: Someone who is so clumsy that they keep stepping on your foot even though a blind crocodile could see it!

Mausoleum: A big, gloomy place where dead people are buried in cemeteries.

Pawnshop: A place where you can bring your valuable stuff when you're po' up from the floor up and they lend you some duckets and give you a pawnshop ticket for your belongings.

Sanitation department: Garbage collection.

Spookies: A bad case of creepy, crawly feelings. Also known as the "willies" and the "heebie-jeebies."

Squiggle: A hug with squealing and shaking involved.